For the real
Frances L. Neagley

'Reacher has no doubts about his objective: to rid the world of the bad guys. And nobody does it better'
SUNDAY TELEGRAPH

'Reacher is today's James Bond'
KEN FOLLETT

'Reacher gets better and better'
NEW YORK TIMES

'Reacher is vengeance personified, a walking, fighting revenge fantasy… what he normally chooses to do is right wrongs and defend the weak against the forces of oppression'
SUNDAY EXPRESS

'Ridiculously addictive'
NEW STATESMAN

Lee Child is one of the world's leading thriller writers. He was born in Coventry, raised in Birmingham, and now lives in New York. It is said one of his novels featuring his hero Jack Reacher is sold somewhere in the world every nine seconds. His books consistently achieve the number one slot on bestseller lists around the world and have sold over one hundred million copies. Lee is the recipient of many awards, including Author of the Year at the 2019 British Book Awards. He was appointed CBE in the 2019 Queen's Birthday Honours.

The Jack Reacher series

For more information see www.jackreacher.com

BAD LUCK AND TROUBLE

Lee Child

PENGUIN BOOKS

TRANSWORLD PUBLISHERS
Penguin Random House, One Embassy Gardens,
8 Viaduct Gardens, London SW11 7BW
www.penguin.co.uk

Transworld is part of the Penguin Random House group of companies
whose addresses can be found at global.penguinrandomhouse.com

Penguin
Random House
UK

First published in Great Britain in 2007 by Bantam Press
an imprint of Transworld Publishers
Bantam edition published 2008
Bantam edition reissued 2011
Penguin paperback edition reissued 2023

A CIP catalogue record for this book
is available from the British Library.

ISBN
9781804991602

Typeset in Times by Kestrel Data, Exeter, Devon.
Printed and bound in Great Britain by Clays Ltd, Elcograf S.p.A.

The authorized representative in the EEA is Penguin Random House
Ireland, Morrison Chambers, 32 Nassau Street, Dublin D02 YH68.

Penguin Random House is committed to a sustainable future for
our business, our readers and our planet. This book is made from
Forest Stewardship Council® certified paper.

ONE

The man was called Calvin Franz and the helicopter was a Bell 222. Franz had two broken legs, so he had to be loaded on board strapped to a stretcher. Not a difficult manoeuvre. The Bell was a roomy aircraft, twin-engined, designed for corporate travel and police departments, with space for seven passengers. The rear doors were as big as a panel van's and they opened wide. The middle row of seats had been removed. There was plenty of room for Franz on the floor.

The helicopter was idling. Two men were carrying the stretcher. They ducked low under the rotor wash and hurried, one backward, one forward. When they reached the open door the guy who had been walking backward got one handle up on the sill and ducked away. The other guy stepped forward and shoved hard and slid the stretcher all the way inside. Franz was awake and hurting. He cried out and jerked around a little, but not much, because the straps across his chest and thighs were buckled tight. The two men climbed in after him and got in their seats behind the missing row and slammed the doors.

Then they waited.

The pilot waited.

A third man came out a grey door and walked across the concrete. He bent low under the rotor and held a hand flat on his chest to stop his necktie whipping in the wind. The gesture made him look like a guilty man proclaiming his innocence. He tracked around the Bell's long nose and got in the forward seat, next to the pilot.

'Go,' he said, and then he bent his head to concentrate on his harness buckle.

The pilot goosed the turbines and the lazy *whop-whop* of the idling blade slid up the scale to an urgent centripetal *whip-whip-whip* and then disappeared behind the treble blast of the exhaust. The Bell lifted straight off the ground, drifted left a little, rotated slightly, and then retracted its wheels and climbed a thousand feet. Then it dipped its nose and hammered north, high and fast. Below it roads and science parks and small factories and neat isolated suburban communities slid past. Brick walls and metal siding blazed red in the late sun. Tiny emerald lawns and turquoise swimming pools winked in the last of the light.

The man in the forward seat said, 'You know where we're going?'

The pilot nodded and said nothing.

The Bell clattered onward, turning east of north, climbing a little higher, heading for darkness. It crossed a highway far below, a river of white lights crawling west and red lights crawling east. A minute north of the highway the last developed acres gave way to low hills, barren and scrubby and uninhabited. They glowed orange on the slopes that faced the setting sun and showed dull tan in the valleys and the shadows. Then the low hills gave way in turn to small rounded mountains. The Bell sped on, rising and falling, following the contours below. The man in the forward seat twisted around and looked down at Franz on the floor behind him. Smiled briefly and said, 'Twenty more minutes, maybe.'

Franz didn't reply. He was in too much pain.

The Bell was rated for a 161-mph cruise, so twenty more minutes took it almost fifty-four miles, beyond the mountains, well out over the empty desert. The pilot flared the nose and slowed a little. The man in the forward seat pressed his forehead against the window and stared down into the darkness.

'Where are we?' he asked.

The pilot said, 'Where we were before.'

'Exactly?'

'Roughly.'

'What's below us now?'

'Sand.'

'Height?'

'Three thousand feet.'

'What's the air like up here?'

'Still. A few thermals, but no wind.'

'Safe?'

'Aeronautically.'

'So let's do it.'

The pilot slowed more and turned and came to a stationary hover, three thousand feet above the desert floor. The man in the forward seat twisted around again and signalled to the two guys way in back. Both unlocked their safety harnesses. One crouched forward, avoiding Franz's feet, and held his loose harness tight in one hand and unlatched the door with the other. The pilot was half turned in his own seat, watching, and he tilted the Bell a little so the door fell all the way open under its own weight. Then he brought the craft level again and put it into a slow clockwise rotation so that motion and air pressure held the door wide. The second guy from the rear crouched near Franz's head and jacked the stretcher upward to a forty-five-degree slope. The first guy jammed his shoe against the free end of the stretcher rail to stop the whole thing sliding across the floor. The second guy jerked like a weightlifter and brought the stretcher almost vertical. Franz sagged down against the straps. He was a big guy, and heavy. And determined. His legs were useless but his upper body was powerful and straining hard. His head was snapping from side to side.

The first guy took out a gravity knife and popped the blade. Used it to saw through the strap around Franz's thighs. Then he paused a beat and sliced the strap around Franz's chest. One quick motion. At the exact same time the second guy jerked the stretcher fully upright. Franz took an involuntary step forward. Onto his broken right leg. He screamed once, briefly, and then took a second instinctive step. Onto his broken left leg. His arms flailed and he collapsed forward and his upper body momentum levered him over the locked pivot of his immobile hips and took him straight out through the open door,

10

into the noisy darkness, into the gale-force rotor wash, into the night.

Three thousand feet above the desert floor.

For a moment there was silence. Even the engine noise seemed to fade. Then the pilot reversed the Bell's rotation and rocked the other way and the door slammed neatly shut. The turbines spun up again and the rotor bit the air and the nose dropped.

The two guys clambered back to their seats.

The man in front said, 'Let's go home now.'

TWO

Seventeen days later Jack Reacher was in Portland, Oregon, short of money. In Portland, because he had to be somewhere and the bus he had ridden two days previously had stopped there. Short of money, because he had met an assistant district attorney called Samantha in a cop bar, and had twice bought her dinner before twice spending the night at her place. Now she had gone to work and he was walking away from her house, nine o'clock in the morning, heading back to the downtown bus depot, hair still wet from her shower, sated, relaxed, destination as yet unclear, with a very thin wad of bills in his pocket.

The terrorist attacks of September 11th 2001 had changed Reacher's life in two practical ways. Firstly, in addition to his folding toothbrush he now carried his passport with him. Too many things in the new era required photo ID, including most forms of travel. Reacher was a drifter, not a hermit, restless, not dysfunctional, and so he had yielded gracefully.

And secondly, he had changed his banking

methods. For many years after leaving the army he had operated a system whereby he would call his bank in Virginia and ask for a Western Union wire transfer to wherever he happened to be. But new worries about terrorist financing had pretty much killed telephone banking. So Reacher had gotten an ATM card. He carried it inside his passport and used 8197 as his PIN. He considered himself a man of very few talents but some varied abilities, most of which were physical and related to his abnormal size and strength, but one of which was always knowing what time it was without looking, and another of which was some kind of a junior-idiot-savant facility with arithmetic. Hence 8197. He liked 97 because it was the largest two-digit prime number, and he loved 81 because it was absolutely the only number out of all the literally infinite possibilities whose square root was also the sum of its digits. Square root of 81 was nine, and eight and one made nine. No other non-trivial number in the cosmos had that kind of sweet symmetry. Perfect.

His arithmetic awareness and his inherent cynicism about financial institutions always compelled him to check his balance every time he withdrew cash. He always remembered to deduct the ATM fees and every quarter he remembered to add in the bank's paltry interest payment. And despite his suspicions, he had never been ripped off. Every time his balance came up exactly as he predicted. He had never been surprised or dismayed.

Until that morning in Portland, where he was surprised, but not exactly dismayed. Because his balance was more than a thousand dollars bigger than it should have been.

Exactly one thousand and thirty dollars bigger, according to Reacher's own blind calculation. A mistake, obviously. By the bank. A deposit into the wrong account. A mistake that would be rectified. He wouldn't be keeping the money. He was an optimist, but not a fool. He pressed another button and requested something called a mini-statement. A slip of thin paper came out of a slot. It had faint grey printing on it, listing the last five transactions against his account. Three of them were ATM cash withdrawals that he remembered clearly. One of them was the bank's most recent interest payment. The last was a deposit in the sum of one thousand and thirty dollars, made three days previously. So there it was. The slip of paper was too narrow to have separate staggered columns for debits and credits, so the deposit was noted inside parentheses to indicate its positive nature: (1030.00).

One thousand and thirty dollars.

1030.

Not inherently an interesting number, but Reacher stared at it for a minute. Not prime, obviously. No even number greater than two could be prime. Square root? Clearly just a hair more than 32. Cube root? A hair less than 10.1. Factors? Not many, but they included 5 and 206 along with the obvious 10 and 103 and the even more basic 2 and 515.

So, 1030.

A thousand and thirty.

A mistake.

Maybe.

Or, maybe not a mistake.

Reacher took fifty dollars from the machine and dug in his pocket for change and went in search of a pay phone.

He found a phone inside the bus depot. He dialled his bank's number from memory. Nine forty in the West, twelve forty in the East. Lunchtime in Virginia, but someone should be there.

And someone was. Not someone Reacher had ever spoken to before, but she sounded competent. Maybe a back-office manager hauled out to cover for the meal period. She gave her name, but Reacher didn't catch it. Then she went into a long rehearsed introduction designed to make him feel like a valued customer. He waited it out and told her about the deposit. She was amazed that a customer would call about a bank error in his own favour.

'Might not be an error,' Reacher said.

'Were you expecting the deposit?' she asked.

'No.'

'Do third parties frequently make deposits into your account?'

'No.'

'It's likely to be an error, then. Don't you think?'

'I need to know who made the deposit.'

'May I ask why?'

'That would take some time to explain.'

'I would need to know,' the woman said. 'There are confidentiality issues otherwise. If the bank's error exposes one customer's affairs to

15

another, we could be in breach of all kinds of rules and regulations and ethical practices.'

'It might be a message,' Reacher said.

'A message?'

'From the past.'

'I don't understand.'

'Back in the day I was a military policeman,' Reacher said. 'Military police radio transmissions are coded. If a military policeman needs urgent assistance from a colleague he calls in a ten-thirty radio code. See what I'm saying?'

'No, not really.'

Reacher said, 'I'm thinking that if I don't know the person who made the deposit, then it's a thousand and thirty bucks' worth of a mistake. But if I do know the person, it might be a call for help.'

'I still don't understand.'

'Look at how it's written. It might be a ten-thirty radio code, not a thousand and thirty dollars. Look at it on paper.'

'Wouldn't this person just have called you on the phone?'

'I don't have a phone.'

'An e-mail, then? Or a telegram. Or even a letter.'

'I don't have addresses for any of those things.'

'So how do we contact you, usually?'

'You don't.'

'A credit into your bank would be a very odd way of communicating.'

'It might be the only way.'

'A very difficult way. Someone would have to trace your account.'

'That's my point,' Reacher said. 'It would take a smart and resourceful person to do it. And if a smart and resourceful person needs to ask for help, there's big trouble somewhere.'

'It would be expensive, too. Someone would be out more than a thousand dollars.'

'Exactly. The person would have to be smart and resourceful and desperate.'

Silence on the phone. Then: 'Can't you just make a list of who it might be and try them all?'

'I worked with a lot of smart people. Most of them a very long time ago. It would take me weeks to track them all down. Then it might be too late. And I don't have a phone, anyway.'

More silence. Except for the patter of a keyboard.

Reacher said, 'You're looking, aren't you?'

The woman said, 'I really shouldn't be doing this.'

'I won't rat you out.'

The phone went quiet. The keyboard patter stopped. Reacher knew she had the name right there in front of her on a screen.

'Tell me,' he said.

'I can't just tell you. You'll have to help me out.'

'How?'

'Give me clues. So I don't have to come right out with it.'

'What kind of clues?'

She asked, 'Well, would it be a man or a woman?'

Reacher smiled, briefly. The answer was right there in the question itself. It was a woman. Had to be. A smart, resourceful woman, capable of imagination and lateral thinking. A woman who knew about his compulsion to add and subtract.

'Let me guess,' Reacher said. 'The deposit was made in Chicago.'

'Yes, by personal cheque through a Chicago bank.'

'Neagley,' Reacher said.

'That's the name we have,' the woman said. 'Frances L. Neagley.'

'Then forget we ever had this conversation,' Reacher said. 'It wasn't a bank error.'

THREE

Reacher had served thirteen years in the army, all of them in the military police. He had known Frances Neagley for ten of those years and had worked with her from time to time for seven of them. He had been an officer, a second lieutenant, then a lieutenant, a captain, a major, then a loss of rank back to captain, then a major again. Neagley had steadfastly refused promotion beyond sergeant. She wouldn't consider Officer Candidate School. Reacher didn't really know why. There was a lot he didn't know about her, despite their ten-year association.

But there was a lot he did know about her. She was smart and resourceful and thorough. And very tough. And strangely uninhibited. Not in terms of personal relationships. She avoided personal relationships. She was intensely private and resisted any kind of closeness, physical or emotional. Her lack of inhibition was professional. If she felt something was right or necessary, then she was uncompromising. Nothing stood in her way, not politics or practicality or politeness or even what a civilian might call the law. At one point Reacher had recruited her to a special investigations unit. She had been a big part of it for two crucial years. Most people put its occasional spectacular successes down to Reacher's leadership, but Reacher himself put them down to her presence. She impressed him, deeply. Sometimes even came close to scaring him.

If she was calling for urgent assistance, it wasn't because she had lost her car keys.

She worked for a private security provider in Chicago. He knew that. At least she had done four years ago, which was the last time he had come into contact with her. She had left the army a year later than he had and gone into business with someone she knew. As a partner, he guessed, not an employee.

He dug back in his pocket and came out with more quarters. Dialled long distance information. Asked for Chicago. Gave the company name, as he remembered it. The human operator disappeared and a robot voice came on the line with a number. Reacher broke the connection and redialled. A receptionist responded and Reacher asked for Frances Neagley. He was answered politely and put on hold. Altogether his impression was of a larger operation than he had imagined. He had pictured a single room, a grimy window, maybe two battered desks, bulging file cabinets. But the receptionist's measured voice and the telephone clicks and the quiet hold music spoke of a much bigger place. Maybe two floors, cool white corridors, wall art, an internal phone directory.

A man's voice came on the line: 'Frances Neagley's office.'

Reacher asked, 'Is she there?'

'May I know who's calling?'

'Jack Reacher.'

'Good. Thank you for getting in touch.'

'Who are you?'

'I'm Ms Neagley's assistant.'

'She has an assistant?'

'Indeed.'

'Is she there?'

'She's en route to Los Angeles. In the air right now, I think.'

'Is there a message for me?'

'She wants to see you as soon as possible.'

'In Chicago?'

'She'll be in LA a few days at least. I think you should go there.'

'What's this all about?'

'I don't know.'

'Not work related?'

'Can't be. She'd have started a file. Discussed it here. She wouldn't be reaching out to strangers.'

'I'm not a stranger. I've known her longer than you have.'

'I'm sorry. I wasn't aware of that.'

'Where is she staying in LA?'

'I don't know that either.'

'So how am I supposed to find her?'

'She said you'd be able to track her down.'

Reacher asked, 'What is this, some kind of a test?'

'She said if you can't find her, she doesn't want you.'

'Is she OK?'

'She's worried about something. But she didn't tell me what.'

Reacher kept the receiver at his ear and turned away from the wall. The metal phone cord wrapped around his chest. He glanced at the idling buses and the departures board. He asked, 'Who else is she reaching out to?'

The guy said, 'There's a list of names. You're the first to get back to her.'

'Will she call you when she lands?'

'Probably.'

'Tell her I'm on my way.'

FOUR

Reacher took a shuttle from the bus depot to the Portland airport and bought a one-way ticket on United to LAX. He used his passport for ID and his ATM card as a debit card. The one-way walk-up fare was outrageous. Alaska Airlines would have been cheaper, but Reacher hated Alaska Airlines. They put a scripture card on their meal trays. Ruined his appetite.

Airport security was easy for Reacher. His carry-on baggage amounted to precisely none at all. He had no belt, no keys, no cell phone, no watch. All he had to do was dump his loose change in a plastic tray and take off his shoes and walk through the X-ray hoop. Thirty seconds, beginning to end. Then he was on his way to the gate, coins back in his pocket, shoes back on his feet, Neagley on his mind.

Not work related. Therefore, private business. But as far as he was aware she had no private business. No private life. She never had. She would have everyday trivia, he guessed, and everyday problems. Like anyone. But he couldn't conceive of her needing help with any of that kind of stuff. A noisy neighbour? Any sane man would sell his stereo after one short conversation with Frances Neagley. Or give it away to charity. Drug dealers on her corner? They would end up as a line item on an inside page of the morning newspaper, corpses found in an alley, multiple knife wounds, no suspects at this time. A stalker? A groper on the L-train? Reacher shuddered. Neagley hated to be touched. He didn't really know why. But anything except brief accidental contact with her would earn a guy a broken arm. Maybe two broken arms.

So what was her problem?

The past, he guessed, which meant the army.

A list of names? Maybe chickens were coming home to roost. The army seemed like a long time ago to Reacher. A different era, a different world. Different rules. Maybe someone was applying today's standards to yesterday's situations, and complaining about something. Maybe a long-delayed internal inquiry had started up. Reacher's special investigations unit had cut a lot of corners and busted a lot of heads. Someone, maybe Neagley herself, had come up with a catchphrase: You *do not mess* with the special investigators. It had been repeated endlessly, as a promise, and a warning. Deadpan, and deadly serious.

Now maybe someone *was* messing with the special investigators. Maybe subpoenas and indictments were flying around. But in that case why would Neagley compromise him? He was as close to untraceable as a human being in America could get. Wouldn't she just play dumb and leave him be?

He shook his head and gave it up and got on the plane.

He used the flight time figuring out where in LA she would hole up. Back in the day it had been part of his job to find people, and he had been pretty good at it. Success depended on empathy. Think like them, feel like them. See what they see. Put yourself in their shoes. *Be* them.

Easier with AWOL soldiers, of course. Their aimlessness gave their decisions a special kind of purity. And they were heading away from something, not toward something. Often they would adopt a kind of unconscious geographic symbolism. If their route into a city was from the east, they would hole up on the west. They would want to put mass between themselves and their pursuers. Reacher would spend an hour with a map and a bus schedule and the Yellow Pages and often he would predict the exact block he would find them on. The exact motel.

Tougher with Neagley, because she was heading *for* something. Her private business, and he didn't know where or what it was. So, first principles. What did he know about her? What would be the determining factor? Well, she was cheap. Not because she was poor or a miser, but because she didn't see the point in spending a buck on something she didn't need. And she didn't need much. She didn't need turn-down service or a mint on the pillow. She didn't need room service or tomorrow's weather forecast. She didn't need fluffy robes and complimentary slippers heat-sealed in cellophane. All she needed was a bed and a door that locked. And crowds, and shadows, and the kind of anonymous low-rent transient neighbourhoods where bartenders and desk clerks had short memories.

So, scratch downtown. Not Beverly Hills, either.

So where? Where in the vastness of LA would she be comfortable?

There were twenty-one thousand miles of surface streets to choose from.

Reacher asked himself, Where would *I* go?

Hollywood, he answered. A little ways south and east of the good stuff. The wrong stretch of Sunset.

That's where I would go, he thought.

And that's where she'll be.

The plane landed at LAX a little late, well after lunch. There had been no meal service on board and Reacher was hungry. Samantha the Portland prosecutor had served him coffee and a bran muffin for breakfast, but that seemed like a long time ago.

He didn't stop to eat. Just headed out to the taxi line and got a Korean guy in a yellow Toyota minivan who wanted to talk about boxing. Reacher knew nothing about boxing and cared less. The sport's obvious artificiality turned him off. Padded gloves and above-the-belt rules had no place in his world. And he didn't like talking. So he just sat quiet in the back and let the guy ramble on. He watched the hot brown afternoon light through the window. Palm trees, movie billboards, light grey traffic lanes striped with endless twin tracks of rubber. And cars, rivers of cars, floods of cars. He saw a new Rolls-Royce and an old Citroën DS, both black. A blood-red MGA and a pastel blue '57 Thunderbird, both open. A yellow 1960 Corvette nose to tail with a green 2007 model. He figured if you watched LA traffic long enough you would see one of every automobile ever manufactured.

The driver took the 101 north and exited a block from Sunset. Reacher got out on the off-ramp and paid the fare. Hiked south and turned left and faced east. He knew Sunset had a dense knot of cheap places right there, both sides of the boulevard, covering about three-quarters of a mile. The air was Southern California warm and smelled of dust and gasoline fumes. He stood still. He had a potential mile-and-a-half walk ahead of him, down and back, and a dozen motel desks to canvass. An hour-long task, maybe more. He was hungry. He could see a Denny's sign ahead and on the right. A chain diner. He decided to eat first and work later.

He walked past parked cars and vacant lots boxed in by hurricane fencing. Stepped over trash and softball-sized tumbleweeds. Recrossed the 101 on a long bridge. Entered the Denny's lot by cutting across a grass shoulder and the drive-through lane. Walked past a long line of windows.

Saw Frances Neagley inside, sitting alone in a booth.

FIVE

Reacher stood for a moment in the parking lot and watched Neagley through the window. She hadn't changed much in the four years since he had last seen her. She had to be nearer forty than thirty now, but it wasn't showing. Her hair was still long and dark and shiny. Her eyes were still dark and alive. She was still slim and lithe. Still spending serious time in the gym. That was clear. She was wearing a tight white T-shirt with tiny cap sleeves and it would have taken an electron microscope to find any body fat on her arms. Or anyplace else.

She was a little tan, which looked good with her colouring. Her nails were done. Her T-shirt looked like a quality item. Overall she looked richer than he remembered her. Comfortable, at home in her world, successful, accustomed to the civilian life. For a moment he felt awkward about his own cheap clothes and his scuffed shoes and his bad barbershop haircut. Like she was making it, and he wasn't. Then the pleasure of seeing an old friend swamped the thought and he walked on through the lot to the door. Went in and stepped past the *Please Wait To Be Seated* sign and slid straight into her booth. She looked up at him across the table and smiled.

'Hello,' she said.

'To you too,' he said.

'Want lunch?'

'That was my plan.'

'So let's order, now you're finally here.'

He said, 'You sound like you were waiting for me.'

'I was. And you're about on time.'

'Am I?'

Neagley smiled again. 'You called my office guy from Portland, Oregon. He saw the caller ID. Traced it to a pay phone at the bus depot. We figured you'd head straight for the airport. Then I figured you'd take United. You must hate Alaskan. Then a cab ride here. Your ETA was easy enough to predict.'

'You knew I would come here? To this diner?'

'Like you taught me, back in the day.'

'I didn't teach you anything.'

'You did,' Neagley said. 'Remember? Think like them, *be* them. So I was being you, being me. You'd figure I'd head for Hollywood. You'd start right here on Sunset. But there's no meal on United from Portland, so I figured you'd be hungry and want to eat first. There are a couple of possible places on the block but this one has the biggest sign and you're no gourmet. So I decided to meet you here.'

'Meet me here? I thought I was tracking you.'

'You were. And I was tracking you, tracking me.'

29

'*Are* you staying here? In Hollywood?'

She shook her head. 'Beverly Hills. The Wilshire.'

'So you came out here just to scoop me up?'

'I got here ten minutes ago.'

'The Beverly Wilshire? You've changed.'

'Not really. It's the world that has changed. Cheap motels don't do it for me any more. I need e-mail and the internet and FedEx service now. Business centres and concierges.'

'You make me feel old-fashioned.'

'You're improving. You use ATMs now.'

'That was a good move. The bank balance message.'

'You taught me well.'

'I didn't teach you anything.'

'Like hell.'

'But it was an extravagant move,' Reacher said. 'Ten dollars and thirty cents would have worked just as well. Maybe even better, with the period between the ten and the thirty.'

Neagley said, 'I thought you might need the air fare.'

Reacher said nothing.

'I found your account, obviously,' Neagley said. 'Wasn't too much more trouble to hack in and take a look. You're not rich.'

'I don't want to be rich.'

'I know. But I didn't want you to have to respond to my ten-thirty on your own dime. That wouldn't have been fair.'

Reacher shrugged and let it go. Truth was, he wasn't rich. Truth was, he was almost poor. His savings had eroded to the point where he was starting to think about how to boost them back up again. Maybe a couple of months of casual labour were in his future. Or some other kind of a score. The waitress came over with menus. Neagley ordered without looking, a cheeseburger and a soda. Reacher matched her for speed, tuna melt and hot coffee. The waitress retrieved the menus and went away.

Reacher said, 'So are you going to tell me what your ten-thirty was for exactly?'

Neagley answered him by leaning down and pulling a black three-ring binder out of a tote bag on the floor. She passed it across the table. It was a copy of an autopsy report.

'Calvin Franz is dead,' she said. 'I think someone threw him out of an airplane.'

SIX

The past, which meant the army. Calvin Franz had been an MP and Reacher's exact contemporary and pretty much his equal all the way through his thirteen years of service. They had met here and there in the way that brother officers often tended to, rubbing shoulders in different parts of the world for a day or two at a time, consulting on the phone, crossing paths when two or more investigations had tangled or collided. Then they had done a serious spell together in Panama. Quality time. It had been very short but very intense, and they had seen things in each other that left them feeling more like real brothers than brother officers. After Reacher had been re-habilitated from his temporary demotion disgrace and given the special investigations operation to build, Franz's name had been near the top of his personnel wish list. They had spent the next two years together in a real unit-within-a-unit hothouse. They had become fast friends. Then as often happened in the army new orders had come in and the special operation had been disbanded and Reacher had never seen Franz again.

Until that moment, in an autopsy photograph punched into a three-ring binder laid flat on a sticky laminate table in a cheap diner.

In life Franz had been smaller than Reacher but bigger than most other people. Maybe six-three and two-ten. Powerful upper body, low waist, short legs. Primitive, in a way. Like a caveman. But overall he had been reasonably handsome. He had been calm, resolute, capable, relaxing to be around. His manner had tended to reassure people.

He looked awful in the autopsy photograph. He was laid out flat and naked on a stainless tray and the camera's flash had bleached his skin pale green.

Awful.

But then, dead people often looked pretty bad.

Reacher asked, 'How did you get this?'

Neagley said, 'I can usually get things.'

Reacher said nothing in reply to that and turned the page. Started in on the dense mass of technical information. The corpse had been measured at six feet three inches in length and weighed a hundred and ninety pounds. Cause of death was given as multiple organ failure due to massive impact trauma. Both legs were broken. Ribs were cracked. The bloodstream was flooded with free histamines. The body was severely dehydrated and the stomach held nothing but mucus. There was evidence of rapid recent weight loss and no evidence of recent food consumption. Trace evidence from the recovered clothing was unexceptional, apart from unexplained ferrous oxide powder ground into both trouser legs, low down, on the shins, below the knee and above the ankle.

Reacher asked, 'Where was he found?'

Neagley said, 'In the desert about fifty miles north and east of here. Hard sand, small rocks, a hundred yards off the shoulder of a road. No footprints coming or going.'

The waitress brought the food. Reacher paused as she unloaded her tray and then started his sandwich, left-handed, to keep his right grease-free for turning the autopsy pages.

Neagley said, 'Two deputies in a car saw buzzards circling. Went to check. Hiked out there. They said it was like he had fallen out of the sky. The pathologist agrees.'

Reacher nodded. He was reading the doctor's conclusion, which was that a free fall from maybe three thousand feet onto hard sand could have produced the right amount of impact and caused the internal injuries observed, if Franz had happened to land flat on his back, which was aerodynamically possible if he had been alive and flailing his arms during the fall. A dead weight would have fallen on its head.

Neagley said, 'They made the ID through his fingerprints.'

Reacher asked, 'How did you find out?'

'His wife called me. Three days ago. Seems he kept all our names in his book. A special page. His buddies, from back in the day. I was the only one she could find.'

'I didn't know he was married.'

'It was recent. They have a kid, four years old.'

'Was he working?'

Neagley nodded. 'He set up as a private eye. A one-man band. Originally, some strategic advice for corporations. But now mostly background checks. Database stuff. You know how thorough he was.'

'Where?'

'Here in LA.'

'Did all of you set up as private eyes?'

'Most of us, I think.'

'Except me.'

'It was the only marketable skill we had.'

'What did Franz's wife want you to do?'

'Nothing. She was just telling me.'

'She doesn't want answers?'

'The cops are on it. LA County sheriffs, actually. Where he was found is technically part of LA County. Outside of the LAPD's jurisdiction, so it's down to a couple of local deputies. They're working on the airplane thing. They figure it was maybe flying west out of Vegas. That kind of thing has happened to them before.'

Reacher said, 'It wasn't an airplane.'

Neagley said nothing.

Reacher said, 'An airplane has a stall speed of what? A hundred miles an hour? Eighty? He'd have come out the door horizontal into the slip-stream. He'd have smashed against the wing or the tail. We'd see perimortem injuries.'

'He had two broken legs.'

'How long does it take to free-fall three thousand feet?'

'Twenty seconds?'

'His blood was full of free histamines. That's a massive pain reaction. Twenty seconds between

35

injury and death wouldn't have even gotten it started.'

'So?'

'The broken legs were old. Two, three days minimum. Maybe more. You know what ferrous oxide is?'

'Rust,' Neagley said. 'On iron.'

Reacher nodded. 'Someone broke his legs with an iron bar. Probably one at a time. Probably tied him to a post. Aimed for his shins. Hard enough to break the bone and grind rust particles into the weave of his pants. Must have hurt like hell.'

Neagley said nothing.

'And they starved him,' Reacher said. 'Didn't let him drink. He was twenty pounds under-weight. He was a prisoner, two or three days. Maybe more. They were torturing him.'

Neagley said nothing.

Reacher said, 'It was a helicopter. Probably at night. Stationary hover, three thousand feet up. Out the door and straight down.' Then he closed his eyes and pictured his old friend, tumbling, twenty seconds in the dark, cartwheeling, flailing, not knowing where the ground was. Not knowing exactly when he would hit. Two shattered legs trailing painfully behind him.

'Therefore it probably wasn't coming from Vegas,' he said. He opened his eyes. 'The round trip would be out of range for most helicopters. It was probably coming north and east out of LA. The deputies are barking up the wrong tree.'

Neagley sat quiet.

'Coyote food,' Reacher said. 'The perfect dis-posal method. No tracks. The airflow during the fall strips away hairs and fibres. No forensics at all. Which is why they threw him out alive. They could have shot him first, but they didn't even want to risk ballistics evidence.'

Reacher was quiet for a long moment. Then he closed the black binder and reversed it and pushed it back across the table.

'But you know all this anyway,' he said. 'Don't you? You can read. You're testing me again. Seeing if my brain still works.'

Neagley said nothing.

Reacher said, 'You're playing me like a violin.'

Neagley said nothing.

Reacher asked, 'Why did you bring me here?'

'Like you said, the deputies are barking up the wrong tree.'

'So?'

'You have to do something.'

'I will do something. Believe it. There are dead men walking, as of right now. You don't throw my friends out of helicopters and live to tell the tale.'

Neagley said, 'No, I want you to do something else.'

'Like what?'

'I want you to put the old unit back together.'

SEVEN

The old unit. It had been a typical U.S. Army invention. About three years after the need for it had become blindingly obvious to everyone else the Pentagon had started to think about it. After another year of committees and meetings the suits and the brass had signed off on the idea. It had been dumped on someone's desk and a mad panic had started to get it going. Orders had been drawn up. Obviously no sane CO had wanted to touch it with a stick, so a new unit had been carved out of the 110th MP. Success was desirable but failure had to be deniable, so they went looking for a competent pariah to command it.

Reacher had been the obvious choice.

They thought his reward was promotion back to major again, but the real satisfaction for him was the chance to do something properly for once. His way. They had given him a free hand in personnel selection. He had enjoyed that. He had figured that a special investigations unit needed the best the army had to offer, and he had figured he knew who and where they were. He had wanted a small unit, for speed and flexibility, and no clerical support, to prevent leaks. He had figured they could do their own paperwork, or not, as they deemed necessary. In the end he had settled on eight names in addition to his own: Tony Swan, Jorge Sanchez, Calvin Franz, Frances Neagley, Stanley Lowrey, Manuel Orozco, David O'Donnell, and Karla Dixon. Dixon and Neagley were the only women and Neagley was the only NCO. The others were all officers. O'Donnell and Lowrey were captains and the rest were all majors, which was totally screwed up in terms of a coherent chain of command, but Reacher didn't care. He knew that nine people working closely would operate laterally rather than vertically, which in the event was exactly what happened. The unit had organized itself like a small-market baseball team enjoying an unlikely pennant run: talented journeymen working together, no stars, no egos, mutually supportive, and above all ruthlessly and relentlessly effective.

Reacher said, 'That was all a long time ago.'

'We have to do something,' Neagley said. 'All of us. Collectively. You *do not mess* with the special investigators. Remember that?'

'That was just a slogan.'

'No, it was true. We depended on it.'

'For morale, that was all. It was just bravado. It was whistling in the dark.'

'It was more than that. We had each other's backs.'

'Then.'

'And now and always. It's a karma thing. Someone killed Franz, and we can't just let it go.

How would you feel if it was you, and the rest of us didn't react?'

'If it was me, I wouldn't feel anything. I'd be dead.'

'You know what I mean.'

Reacher closed his eyes again and the picture came back: Calvin Franz tumbling and cartwheeling through the darkness. Maybe screaming. Or maybe not. His old friend. 'I can handle it. Or you and I together. But we can't go back to how it was. That never works.'

'We have to go back.'

Reacher opened his eyes. 'Why?'

'Because the others are entitled to participate. They earned that right over two hard years. We can't just take it away from them unilaterally. They would resent that. It would be wrong.'

'And?'

'We need them, Reacher. Because Franz was good. Very good. As good as me, as good as you. And yet someone broke his legs and threw him out of a helicopter. I think we're going to need all the help we can get with this. So we need to find the others.'

Reacher looked at her. Heard her office guy's voice in his head: *There's a list of names. You're the first to get back to her.* He said, 'The others should have been a lot easier to find than me.'

Neagley nodded.

'I can't raise any of them,' she said.

EIGHT

A list of names. Nine names. Nine people. Reacher knew where three of them were, specifically or generically. Himself and Neagley, specifically, in a Denny's on West Sunset in Hollywood. And Franz, generically, in a morgue somewhere else.

'What do you know about the other six?' he asked.

'Five,' Neagley said. 'Stan Lowrey is dead.'

'When?'

'Years ago. Car wreck in Montana. The other guy was drunk.'

'I didn't know that.'

'Shit happens.'

'That's for damn sure,' Reacher said. 'I liked Stan.'

'Me too,' Neagley said.

'So where are the others?'

'Tony Swan is assistant director of corporate security for a defence manufacturer here in Southern California somewhere.'

'Which one?'

'I'm not sure. A start-up. Something new. He's only been there about a year.'

Reacher nodded. He had liked Tony Swan, too. A short, wide man. Almost cubic in shape. Affable, good-humoured, intelligent.

Neagley said, 'Orozco and Sanchez are out in Vegas. They run a security business together, casinos and hotels, on contract.'

Reacher nodded again. He had heard that Jorge Sanchez had left the army around the same time he had, a little frustrated and embittered. He had heard that Manuel Orozco had been planning to stay in, but overall it wasn't a huge surprise to find that he had changed his mind. Both men were mavericks, lean, fast, leathery, impatient with bullshit.

Neagley said, 'Dave O'Donnell is in D.C. Plain-vanilla private detective. Plenty of work for him there.'

'I guess there would be,' Reacher said. O'Donnell had been the meticulous one. He had done the whole unit's paperwork, pretty much single-handed. He had looked like an Ivy League gentleman, but he had always carried a switch-blade in one pocket and brass knuckles in the other. A useful guy to have around.

Neagley said, 'Karla Dixon is in New York. Forensic accounting. She understands money, apparently.'

'She always understood numbers,' Reacher said. 'I remember that.' Reacher and Dixon had spent the occasional hour trying to prove or dis-prove various famous mathematical theorems. A hopeless task, given that they were both rank amateurs, but it had passed some time. Dixon was dark and very pretty and comparatively small, a happy woman who thought the worst of people, but inevitably she had been proved right nine times out of ten.

Reacher asked, 'How do you know so much about them?'

'I keep track,' Neagley said. 'I'm interested.'

'Why can't you raise them?'

'I don't know. I put calls out, but nobody's answering.'

'So is this an attack on all of us collectively?'

'Can't be,' Neagley said. 'I'm at least as visible as Dixon or O'Donnell and nobody has come after me.'

'Yet.'

'Maybe.'

'You called the others the same day you put the money in my bank?'

Neagley nodded.

'It's only been three days,' Reacher said. 'Maybe they're all busy.'

'So what do you want to do? Wait for them?'

'I want to forget all about them. You and I can stand up for Franz. Just the two of us.'

'It would be better to have the old unit back together. We were a good team. You were the best leader the army ever had.'

Reacher said nothing.

'What?' Neagley said. 'What are you thinking?'

'I'm thinking that if I wanted to rewrite history I'd start a lot farther back than that.'

Neagley folded her hands together and rested

them on the black binder. Slim fingers, brown skin, painted nails, tendons and sinew.

'One question,' she said. 'Suppose I had gotten ahold of the others. Suppose I hadn't bothered to try that thing with your bank. Suppose you found out years from now that Franz had been murdered and the six of us had just gone ahead and fixed it without you. How would you feel then?'

Reacher shrugged. Paused a beat.

'Bad, I guess,' he said. 'Cheated, maybe. Left out.'

Neagley said nothing.

Reacher said, 'OK, we'll try to find the others. But we won't wait forever.'

Neagley had a rental car in the lot. She paid the diner check and led Reacher outside. The car was a red Mustang convertible. They climbed in together and Neagley hit a button and dropped the top. She took a pair of sunglasses from the dash and put them on. Backed out of her slot and turned south off Sunset at the next light. Headed for Beverly Hills. Reacher sat quiet beside her and squinted in the afternoon sun.

Inside a tan Ford Crown Victoria thirty yards west of the restaurant a man called Thomas Brant watched them go. He used his cell phone and called his boss, a man named Curtis Mauney. Mauney didn't answer, so Brant left a voice mail.

He said, 'She just picked the first one of them up.'

*   *   *

Parked five cars behind Brant's Crown Victoria was a dark blue Chrysler sedan containing a man in a dark blue suit. He too watched the red Mustang disappear into the haze, and he too used a cell phone.

He said, 'She just picked the first one of them up. I don't know which one it is. Big guy, looks like a bum.'

Then he listened to his boss's reply, and pictured him smoothing his necktie over the front of his shirt, one-handed, while he held the phone with the other.

NINE

Like its name suggested the Beverly Wilshire hotel was on Wilshire Boulevard, in the heart of Beverly Hills, directly opposite the mouth of Rodeo Drive. It was made up of two large limestone buildings, one behind the other, one old and ornate, the other new and plain. They were separated by a valet lane that ran parallel to the boulevard. Neagley nosed the Mustang into it and stopped close to a knot of black Town Cars and Reacher said, 'I can't afford to stay here.'

'I already booked your room.'

'Booked it or paid for it?'

'It's on my card.'

'I won't be able to pay you back.'

'Get over it.'

'This place has got to be hundreds a night.'

'I'll let it slide for now. Maybe we'll take some spoils of war down the track.'

'If the bad guys are rich.'

'They are,' Neagley said. 'They have to be. How else would they afford their own heli-copter?'

She left the key in and the motor running and

opened the heavy red door and slid out. Reacher
did the same thing on his side. A guy ran up and
gave Neagley a valet stub. She took it and tracked
around the hood of the car and took the steps up
to the back of the hotel's main lobby. Reacher
followed. Watched her move. She floated, like
she was weightless. She ghosted through a
crowded dog-leg corridor and came out in a reception area the size and shape of a baronial hall.
There was a check-in desk, a bell desk, a concierge desk, all separate. There were pale velvet
armchairs with beautifully dressed guests in them.

Reacher said, 'I look like a bum in here.'

'Or like a billionaire. Nowadays you can't tell.'

She led him to the counter and checked him
in. She had reserved his room under the name
Thomas Shannon, who had been Stevie Ray
Vaughan's giant bass player back in the day, and
one of Reacher's favourites. He smiled. He liked
to avoid paper trails, whenever possible. He
always had. Pure reflex. He turned to Neagley
and nodded his thanks and asked, 'What are you
calling yourself here?'

'My real name,' she said. 'I don't do that stuff
any more. Too complicated now.'

The clerk handed over a key card and Reacher
put it in his shirt pocket. He turned away from
the desk and faced the room. Stone, dim chand-
eliers, thick carpet, flowers in huge glass vases.
Perfumed air.

'Let's make a start,' he said.

They started in Neagley's room, which was
actually a two-room suite. The living room

portion was tall and square and stately and had been done up in blues and golds. It could have been a room in Buckingham Palace. There was a desk in the window with two laptop computers on it. Next to the laptops was an empty cell phone cradle and next to that was an open spiral-bound notebook, new, letter sized, the kind of thing a high-school student might buy in September. Last in line was a thin stack of printed papers. Forms. Five of them. Five names, five addresses, five telephone numbers. The old unit, less two dead and two already present.

Reacher said, 'Tell me about Stan Lowrey.'

'Not much to tell. He quit the army, moved to Montana, got hit by a truck.'

'Life's a bitch and then you die.'

'Tell me about it.'

'What was he doing in Montana?'

'Raising sheep. Churning butter.'

'Alone?'

'There was a girlfriend.'

'She still there?'

'Probably. They had a lot of acres.'

'Why sheep? Why butter?'

'No call for private eyes in Montana. And Montana was where the girlfriend was.'

Reacher nodded. At first glance Stan Lowrey had not been an obvious candidate for a rural fantasy. He had been a big-boned black guy from some scruffy factory town in Western Pennsylvania, smart as a whip and hard as a railroad tie. Dark alleys and pool halls had seemed to be his natural habitat. But somewhere in his DNA there had been a clear link with the

48

earth. Reacher wasn't surprised he had become a farmer. He could picture him, in a raggedy old barn coat, knee-high in prairie grass, under a huge blue sky, cold but happy.

'Why can't we raise the others?' he asked.

'I don't know,' Neagley said.

'What was Franz working on?'

'Nobody seems to have that information.'

'Didn't the new wife say anything?'

'She isn't new. They were married five years.'

'She's new to me,' Reacher said.

'I couldn't interrogate her, exactly. She was on the phone, telling me her husband was dead. And maybe she doesn't know anyway.'

'We're going to have to go ask her. She's the obvious starting point here.'

'After we try the others again,' Neagley said.

Reacher picked up the five sheets of printed paper and gave three to Neagley and kept two for himself. She used her cell phone and he used a room phone on a credenza. They started dialling. His numbers were for Dixon and O'Donnell. Karla and Dave, the East Coast residents, New York and D.C. Neither one of them answered. He got their business office machines instead, and heard their long-forgotten voices. He left the same message for both of them: 'This is Jack Reacher with a ten-thirty from Frances Neagley at the Beverly Wilshire Hotel in Los Angeles, California. Get off your ass and call her back.' Then he hung up and turned to where Neagley was pacing and leaving the same kind of message for Tony Swan.

'Don't you have home numbers for them?' he asked.

'They're all unlisted. Which is only to be expected. Mine is, too. My guy in Chicago is working on it. But it's not easy these days. Phone company computers have gotten a lot more secure.'

'They must be carrying cell phones,' he said. 'Doesn't everyone now?'

'I don't have those numbers either.'

'But wherever they are they can call in and check their office voice mail remotely, can't they?'

'Easily.'

'So why haven't they? In three whole days?'

'I don't know,' Neagley said.

'Swan must have a secretary. He's an assistant director of something. He must have a whole staff.'

'All they're saying is that he's temporarily out of the office.'

'Let me try.' He took Swan's number from her and hit nine for a line. Dialled. Heard the connection go through, heard Swan's phone ringing on the other end.

And ringing, and ringing.

'No answer,' he said.

'Someone answered a minute ago,' Neagley said. 'It's his direct line.'

No answer. He held the phone at his ear and listened to the patient electronic purr. Ten times, fifteen, twenty. Thirty. He hung up. Checked the number and tried again. Same result.

'Weird,' he said. 'Where the hell is he?'

He checked the paper again. Name and number. The address line was blank.

'Where is this place?' he asked.

'I'm not sure.'

'Does it have a name?'

'New Age Defense Systems. That's how they've been answering.'

'What kind of a name is that for a weapons manufacturer? Like they kill you with kindness? They play pan pipe music until you save them the trouble and slit your wrists?' He dialled information. Information told him there was no listing for New Age Defense Systems anywhere in the United States. He hung up.

'Can corporations be unlisted too?' he asked.

Neagley said, 'I guess so. In the defence business, certainly. And they're new.'

'We have to find them. They must have a physical plant somewhere. At least an office, so Uncle Sam can send them cheques.'

'OK, we'll add that to the list. After the visit to Mrs Franz.'

'No, before,' Reacher said. 'Offices close. Widows are always around.'

So Neagley called her guy in Chicago and told him to track down a physical address for New Age Defense Systems. From the half of the conversation Reacher could hear it seemed like the best way to proceed was to hack into FedEx's computer. Or UPS's, or DHL's. Everyone received packages, and couriers needed street addresses. They couldn't use Post Office boxes. They had to hand stuff across the transom to actual people and get signatures in return.

'Get cell phone numbers too,' Reacher called. 'For the others.'

Neagley covered the phone. 'He's been on that for three days. It isn't easy.' Then she hung up and walked to the window. Looked out and down at the people parking cars.

'So now we wait,' she said.

They waited less than twenty minutes and then one of Neagley's laptops pinged to announce an e-mail incoming from Chicago.

TEN

The e-mail from Neagley's guy in Chicago contained New Age's address, courtesy of UPS. Or actually, two addresses. One in Colorado, one in East LA.

'Makes sense,' she said. 'Distributed manufacture. Safer that way. In case of attack.'

'Bullshit,' Reacher said. 'It's about two lots of senators. Two lots of pork. Republicans up there, Democrats down here, they get their snouts in the trough both ways around.'

'Swan wouldn't have gone there if that was all they were into.'

Reacher nodded. 'Maybe not.'

Neagley opened a map and they checked the East LA address. It was out past Echo Park, past Dodger Stadium, somewhere in the no man's land between South Pasadena and East LA proper.

'That's a long way,' Neagley said. 'It could take forever. Rush hour has started.'

'Already?'

'Rush hour in LA started thirty years ago. It'll finish when the oil runs out. Or the oxygen. But whatever, we won't make it over there before they close. So it might be better to save New Age for tomorrow and go see Mrs Franz today.'

'Like you said in the first place. You're playing me like a violin.'

'She's closer, is all. And important.'

'Where is she?'

'Santa Monica.'

'Franz lived in Santa Monica?'

'Not on the ocean. But still, I bet it's nice.'

It was nice. Way nicer than it could have been. It was a small bungalow on a small street trapped halfway between the 10 and the Santa Monica airport, about two miles inland. On the face of it, not a prime real estate location. But it was a beautifully presented house. Neagley drove past it twice, looking for a place to park. It was a tiny symmetrical structure. Two bay windows with the front door between them. An overhanging roof with a front porch below. Twin rocking chairs on the porch. Some stone, some Tudor beams, some Arts and Crafts influences, some Frank Lloyd Wright, Spanish tiles. A real confusion of styles in one very small building, but it worked. It had a lot of charm. And it was totally immaculate. The paint was perfect. It gleamed. The windows were clean. They shone. The yard was tidy. Green lawn, clipped. Bright flowers, no weeds. Short blacktop driveway, smooth as glass and swept clean. Calvin Franz had been a thorough and meticulous man, and Reacher felt he could see an expression of his old friend's whole personality displayed right there in a little piece of real estate.

Eventually a pretty lady two streets away pulled her Toyota Camry out of a kerbside spot and Neagley swerved the Mustang right in after her. She locked it up and they walked back together. It was late afternoon but still faintly warm. Reacher could smell the ocean.

He asked, 'How many widows have we been to see?'

'Too many,' Neagley said.

'Where do you live?'

'Lake Forest, Illinois.'

'I've heard of that. It's supposed to be a nice place.'

'It is.'

'Congratulations.'

'I worked hard for it.'

They turned together into Franz's street, and then into his driveway. They slowed a little on the short walk to the door. Reacher wasn't sure what they were going to find. In the past he had dealt with widows a lot fresher than one of seventeen days' vintage. Very often they hadn't even known they were widows until he had shown up and told them they were. He wasn't sure what difference the seventeen days were going to make. Didn't know where in the process she was going to be.

'What's her name?' he asked.

'Angela,' Neagley said.

'OK.'

'The kid is called Charlie. A boy.'

'OK.'

'Four years old.'

'OK.'

They stepped up on the porch and Neagley

found a bell push and laid a fingertip on it, gently, briefly, respectfully, as if the electric circuit could sense deference. Reacher heard the sound of a muted bell inside the house, and then nothing. He waited. About a minute and a half later the door was opened. Apparently by nobody. Then Reacher looked down and saw a little boy stretching up to the handle. The handle was high and the boy was small and his stretch was so extreme that the arc of the door's travel was pulling him off his tiptoes.

'You must be Charlie,' Reacher said.

'I am,' the boy said.

'I was a friend of your dad's.'

'My dad's dead.'

'I know. I'm very sad about that.'

'Me too.'

'Is it OK to be opening the door all by yourself?'

'Yes,' the boy said. 'It's OK.'

He looked exactly like Calvin Franz. The resemblance was uncanny. The face was the same. The body shape was the same. The short legs, the low waist, the long arms. The shoulders were just skin and bone under a child's T-shirt but somehow they already hinted at the simian bulk they would carry later. The eyes were Franz's own, exactly, dark, cool, calm, reassuring. Like the boy was saying, *Don't worry, everything will turn out fine*.

Neagley asked him, 'Charlie, is your mom home?'

The boy nodded.

'She's in back,' he said. He let the handle go

and stepped away to let them enter. Neagley went first. The house was too small for any one part of it to be really in back of any other part. It was like one generous room divided into four quadrants. Two small bedrooms on the right with a bathroom between, Reacher guessed. A small living room in the left front corner and a small kitchenette behind it. That was all. Tiny, but beautiful. Everything was off-white and pale yellow. There were flowers in vases. The windows were shaded with white wooden shutters. Floors were dark polished wood. Reacher turned and closed the door behind him and the street noise disappeared and silence clamped down over the house. A good feeling, once upon a time, he thought. Now maybe not so good.

A woman stepped out of the kitchen area, from behind a half-wide dividing wall so abbreviated that it couldn't have offered accidental concealment. Reacher felt she must have gone and hidden behind it, deliberately, when the doorbell rang. She looked a lot younger than him. A little younger than Neagley.

Younger than Franz had been.

She was a tall woman, white blonde, blue-eyed like a Scandinavian, and thin. She was wearing a light V-neck sweater and the bones showed in the front of her chest. She was clean and made up and perfumed and her hair was brushed. Perfectly composed, but not relaxed. Reacher could see wild bewilderment around her eyes, like a fright mask worn under the skin.

There was awkward silence for a moment and then Neagley stepped forward and said,

'Angela? I'm Frances Neagley. We spoke on the phone.'

Angela Franz smiled in an automatic way and offered her hand. Neagley took it and shook it briefly and then Reacher stepped forward and took his turn. He said, 'I'm Jack Reacher. I'm very sorry for your loss.' He took her hand, which felt cold and fragile in his.

'You've used those words more than a few times,' she said. 'Haven't you?'

'I'm afraid so,' Reacher said.

'You're on Calvin's list,' she said. 'You were an MP just like him.'

Reacher shook his head. 'Not just like him. Not nearly as good.'

'You're very kind.'

'It's how it was. I admired him tremendously.'

'He told me about you. All of you, I mean. Many times. Sometimes I felt like a second wife. Like he had been married before. To all of you.'

'It's how it was,' Reacher said again. 'The service was like a family. If you were lucky, that is, and we were.'

'Calvin said the same thing.'

'I think he got even luckier afterward.'

Angela smiled again, automatically. 'Maybe. But his luck ran out, didn't it?'

Charlie was watching them, Franz's eyes half open, appraising. Angela said, 'Thank you very much for coming.'

'Is there anything we can do for you?' Reacher asked.

'Can you raise the dead?'

Reacher said nothing.

'The way he used to talk about you, I wouldn't be surprised if you could.'

Neagley said, 'We could find out who did it. That's what we were good at. And that's as close as we can come to bringing him back. In a manner of speaking.'

'But it won't actually bring him back.'

'No, it won't. I'm very sorry.'

'Why are you here?'

'To give you our condolences.'

'But you don't know me. I came later. I wasn't a part of all that.' Angela moved away, toward the kitchen. Then she changed her mind and turned back and squeezed sideways between Reacher and Neagley and sat down in the living room. Laid her palms on the arms of her chair. Reacher saw her fingers moving. Just a slight imperceptible flutter, like she was typing or playing an invisible piano in her sleep.

'I wasn't part of the group,' she said. 'Sometimes I wished I had been. It meant so much to Calvin. He used to say, you do not mess with the special investigators. He used it like a catch-phrase, all the time. He would be watching football, and the quarterback would get sacked, something real spectacular, and he would say, yeah baby, you do not mess with the special investigators. He would say it to Charlie. He would tell Charlie to do something, and Charlie would moan, and Calvin would say, Charlie, you do not mess with the special investigators.'

Charlie looked up and smiled. 'You *do not* mess,' he said, in a little piping voice, but with his father's intonation, and then he stopped, as

59

if the longer words were too hard for him to say.

Angela said, 'You're here because of a slogan, aren't you?'

'Not really,' Reacher said. 'We're here because of what lay behind the slogan. We cared about each other. That's all. I'm here because Calvin would have been there for me, if the shoe was on the other foot.'

'Would he have been?'

'I think so.'

'He gave all of that up. When Charlie was born. No pressure from me. But he wanted to be a father. He gave it all up apart from the easy, safe stuff.'

'He can't have done.'

'No, I guess not.'

'What was he working on?'

'I'm sorry,' Angela said. 'I should have asked you to sit down.'

There was no sofa in the room. No space for one. Any kind of a normal-sized sofa would have blocked access to the bedrooms. There were two armchairs instead, plus a half-sized wooden rocker for Charlie. The armchairs were either side of a small fireplace that held pale dried flowers in a raw china jug. Charlie's rocker was to the left of the chimney. His name had been branded into the wood at the top of the back, with a hot poker or a soldering iron, seven letters, neat script. Tidy, but not a professional job. Franz's own work, probably. A gift, father to son. Reacher looked at it for a moment. Then he took the armchair opposite Angela's and

Neagley perched on the arm next to him, her thigh less than an inch from his body, but not touching it.

Charlie stepped over Reacher's feet and sat down in his wooden chair.

'What was Calvin working on?' Reacher asked again.

Angela Franz said, 'Charlie, you should go out and play.'

Charlie said, 'Mom, I want to stay here.'

Reacher asked, 'Angela, what was Calvin working on?'

'Since Charlie came along he only did background checks,' Angela said. 'It was a good business to be in. Especially here in LA. Everyone's worried about hiring a thief or a junkie. Or dating one, or marrying one. Someone would meet someone on the internet or in a bar and the first thing they would do is Google the person and the second thing is they would call a private detective.'

'Where did he work?'

'He had an office in Culver City. You know, just a rental, one room. Where Venice meets La Cienega. It was an easy hop on the 10. He liked it there. I guess I'll have to go and bring his things home.'

Neagley asked, 'Would you give us permission to search it first?'

'The deputies already searched it.'

'We should search it again.'

'Why?'

'Because he must have been working on something bigger than background checks.'

'Junkies kill people, don't they? And thieves, sometimes.'

Reacher glanced at Charlie, and saw Franz looking back at him. 'But not in the way that it seems to have happened.'

'OK. Search it again if you want.'

Neagley asked, 'Do you have a key?'

Angela got up slowly and stepped to the kitchen. Came back with two unmarked keys, one big, one small, on a steel split ring an inch in diameter. She cradled them in her palm for a moment and then she handed them to Neagley, a little reluctantly.

'I would like them back,' she said. 'This is his own personal set.'

Reacher asked, 'Did he keep stuff here? Notes, files, anything like that?'

'Here?' Angela said. 'How could he? He gave up wearing undershirts when we moved here, to save on drawer space.'

'When did you move here?'

Angela was still standing. A slight woman, but she seemed to fill the tiny space.

'Just after Charlie came along,' she said. 'We wanted a real home. We were very happy here. Small, but it was all we needed.'

'What happened the last time you saw him?'

'He went out in the morning, same as always. But he never came back.'

'When was that?'

'Five days before the deputies came over to tell me they had found his body.'

'Did he ever talk to you about his work?'

Angela said, 'Charlie, do you need a drink?'

62

Charlie said, 'I'm OK, mom.'

Reacher asked, 'Did Calvin ever talk to you about his work?'

'Not very much,' Angela said. 'Sometimes the studios would want an actor checked out, to find out what bodies were buried. He would give me the showbiz gossip. That's all, really.'

Reacher said, 'When we knew him he was a pretty blunt guy. He would say what was on his mind.'

'He stayed that way. You think he upset someone?'

'No, I just wondered whether he ever got around to toning it down. And if not, whether you liked it or not.'

'I loved it. I loved everything about him. I respect honesty and openness.'

'So would you mind if I was blunt?'

'Go right ahead.'

'I think there's something you're not telling us.'

ELEVEN

Angela Franz sat down again and asked, 'What do you think I'm not telling you?'

'Something useful,' Reacher said.

'Useful? What could possibly be useful to me now?'

'Not just to you. To us, too. Calvin was yours, because you married him, OK. But he was ours, too, because we worked with him. We have a right to find out what happened to him, even if you don't want to.'

'Why do you think I'm hiding something?'

'Because every time I get close to asking you a question, you duck it. I asked you what Calvin was working on, and you made a big fuss about sitting us down. I asked you again, and you talked to Charlie about going out to play. Not to spare him hearing your answer, because you used the time you gained to decide you don't have an answer.'

Angela looked across the tiny room, straight at him. 'Are you going to break my arm now? Calvin told me he saw you break someone's arm in an interview. Or was that Dave O'Donnell?'

'Me, probably,' Reacher said. 'O'Donnell was more of a leg breaker.'

'I promise you,' Angela said. 'I'm not hiding anything. Nothing at all. I don't know what Calvin was working on and he didn't tell me.'

Reacher looked back at her, deep into her bewildered blue eyes, and he believed her, just a little bit. She was hiding something, but it wasn't necessarily about Calvin Franz.

'OK,' he said. 'I apologize.'

He and Neagley left shortly after that, with directions to Franz's Culver City office, after further brief condolences and another shake of the cold, fragile hand.

The man called Thomas Brant watched them go. He was twenty yards from his Crown Victoria, which was parked forty yards west of Franz's house. He was walking up from a corner bodega with a cup of coffee. He slowed his gait and watched Reacher and Neagley from behind until they turned the corner a hundred yards ahead. Then he sipped his coffee and speed-dialled his boss, Curtis Mauney, one-handed, and left a voice mail describing what he had seen.

At that same moment the man in the dark blue suit was walking back to his dark blue Chrysler sedan. The sedan was parked in the Beverly Wilshire's valet lane. The man in the suit was poorer by the fifty bucks that the desk clerk had accepted as a bribe, and therefore correspondingly richer in new information, but he was puzzled by the new information's implications.

He called his boss on his cell and said, 'According to the hotel the big guy's name is Thomas Shannon, but there was no Thomas Shannon on our list.'

His boss said, 'I think we can be sure that our list was definitive.'

'I guess we can.'

'Therefore it's safe to assume that Thomas Shannon is a phony name. Obviously old habits die hard with these guys. So let's stay on it.'

Reacher waited until they were around the corner and out of Franz's street and said, 'Did you see a tan Crown Vic back there?'

'Parked,' Neagley said. 'Forty yards west of the house, on the opposite kerb. A base model '02.'

'I think I saw the same car outside of the Denny's we were in.'

'You sure?'

'Not certain.'

'Old Crown Vics are common cars. Taxis, gypsy cabs, rent-a-wrecks.'

'I guess.'

'It was empty anyway,' Neagley said. 'We don't need to worry about empty cars.'

'It wasn't empty outside of Denny's. There was a guy in it.'

'If it was the same car.'

Reacher stopped walking.

Neagley asked, 'You want to go back?'

Reacher paused a beat and shook his head and started walking again.

'No,' he said. 'It was probably nothing.'

* * *

The 10 was jammed eastbound. Neither one of them knew enough about LA geography to risk taking surface streets, so they covered the five freeway miles to Culver City slower than walking. They got to where Venice Boulevard crossed La Cienega Boulevard and from there Angela Franz's directions were good enough to take them straight to her late husband's office. It was a bland storefront place in a long low tan strip that was anchored by a small post office. Not a flagship USPS operation. Just a single-wide store. Reacher didn't know the terminology. A sub-office? A satellite? A postal delivery station? Next to it was a discount pharmacy, and then a nail salon and a dry cleaner. Then Franz's place. Franz's place had the door glass and the window painted over from the inside with tan paint that reached head-high and left just a narrow strip above for light to come through. The top of the paint was banded with a gold coach line edged in black. The legend *Calvin Franz Discreet Investigations* and a telephone number had been written on the door in the same gold-and-black style, plain letters, three lines, chest high, simple and to the point.

'Sad,' Reacher said. 'Isn't it? From the big green machine to this?'

'He was a father,' Neagley said. 'He was taking the easy money. It was his free choice. This was all he wanted now.'

'But I'm guessing your place in Chicago doesn't look like this.'

'No,' Neagley said. 'It doesn't.'

She took out the key ring Angela had parted

with so reluctantly. She selected the bigger key and tripped the lock and pulled the door. But she didn't go in.

Because the whole place was trashed from top to bottom.

It had been a plain square space, small for a store, large for an office. Whatever computers and telephones and other hardware it had contained was all long gone. The desk and the file cabinets had been searched and then smashed with hammers and every joint and sub-assembly had been torn apart in a quest for concealed hiding places. The chair had been ripped apart and the stuffing had been pulled out. The wall boards had been crowbarred off the studs and the insulation had been shredded. The ceiling had been torn down. The floor had been pulled up. The bathroom appliances had been smashed into porcelain shards. There was wreckage and paper strewn everywhere down in the crawl space, knee-high throughout and worse in places.

Trashed, from top to bottom. Like a bomb blast.

Reacher said, 'LA County deputies wouldn't be this thorough.'

'Not a chance,' Neagley said. 'Not even close. This was the bad guys tying up the loose ends. Retrieving whatever Franz had on them. Before the deputies even got here. Probably days before.'

'The deputies saw this and didn't tell Angela? She didn't know. She said she had to come over and bring his stuff home.'

'They wouldn't tell her. Why upset her more?'

Reacher backed away on the sidewalk. Stepped to his left and looked at the neat gold lettering on the door: *Calvin Franz Discreet Investigations*. He raised his hand and blocked out his old friend's name and in his mind tried *David O'Donnell* in its place. Then a pair of names: *Sanchez & Orozco*. Then: *Karla Dixon*.

'I wish those guys were answering their damn phones,' he said.

'This thing is not about us as a group,' Neagley said. 'It can't be. It's more than seventeen days old and nobody came after me yet.'

'Or me,' Reacher said. 'But then, neither did Franz.'

'What do you mean?'

'If Franz was in trouble, who would he call? The rest of us, that's who. But not you, because you're way upscale now and probably too busy. And not me, because nobody apart from you could ever find me. But suppose Franz got himself in deep shit and called the other guys? Because they were all more accessible than the two of us? Suppose they all came running out here to help? Suppose they're all in the same boat now?'

'Including Swan?'

'Swan was the closest. He would have gotten here first.'

'Possible.'

'Likely,' Reacher said. 'If Franz really needed someone, who else would he trust?'

'He should have called me,' Neagley said. 'I would have come.'

'Maybe you were next on the list. Maybe at

first he thought six people were enough.'

'But what kind of a thing can disappear six people? Six of *our* people?'

'I hate to think,' Reacher said, and then he went quiet. In the past he would have put his people up against anyone. Many times, he had. And they had always come through, against worse opponents than you normally find among the civilian population. Worse, because military training tended to enhance a criminal's repertoire in several important areas.

Neagley said, 'No point standing here. We're wasting time. We're not going to find anything. I think we can assume they got what they came for.'

Reacher said, 'I think we can assume they didn't.'

'Why?'

'Rule of thumb,' Reacher said. 'This place is trashed from top to bottom and side to side. Totally. And normally, when you find what you're looking for, you stop looking. But these guys never stopped looking. So if they found what they came for, by chance they found it in the very last place they chose to look. And how likely is that? Not very. So I think they never stopped looking because they never found what they wanted.'

'So where is it?'

'I don't know. What would it be?'

'Paperwork, a floppy disk, a CD-ROM, something like that.'

'Small,' Reacher said.

'He didn't take it home. I think he was separating home and work.'

Think like them. Be them. Reacher turned around and put his back to Franz's door as if he had just stepped out to the sidewalk. He cupped his hand and looked down at his empty palm. He had done plenty of paperwork in his life, but he had never used a computer disk or burned a CD-ROM. But he knew what one was. It was a five-inch round piece of polycarbonate. Often in a thin plastic case. A floppy disk was smaller. Square, about three inches, maybe? Letter-size paperwork would tri-fold down to eight and a half inches by about four.

Small.

But vital.

Where would Calvin Franz hide something small but vital?

Neagley said, 'Maybe it was in his car. He drove back and forth, apparently. So if it was a CD, he could have kept it in his auto-changer. Like hiding it in plain sight. You know, maybe the fourth slot, after the John Coltrane stuff.'

'Miles Davis,' Reacher said. 'He preferred Miles Davis. He only listened to John Coltrane on Miles Davis albums.'

'He could have made it look like stuff he had downloaded. You know, he could have written Miles Davis on it with a marker pen.'

'They'd have found it,' Reacher said. 'Guys this thorough, they'd have checked everything. And I think Franz would have wanted more security than that. Plain sight means it's right there in front of you all the time. You can't relax. And I think Franz wanted to relax. I think he wanted to

71

get home to Angela and Charlie and not have things on his mind.'

'So where? A safe deposit box?'

'I don't see a bank here,' Reacher said. 'And I don't think he would have wanted to take much of a detour. Not with this traffic. Not if there was some kind of urgency. And a bank's lobby hours don't necessarily suit a working stiff.'

'There are two keys on the ring,' Neagley said. 'Although it's possible the smaller one was for the desk.'

Reacher turned again and looked through the gloom at the drifts of trash and wreckage. The desk lock was in there somewhere, presumably. A small steel rectangle, torn out of the wood and dumped. He turned back and stepped to the kerb. Looked left, looked right. Cupped his hand again and looked down at his empty palm.

First: *What would I hide?*

'It's a computer file,' he said. 'Got to be. Because they knew to look for it. Any kind of handwritten paperwork, Franz wouldn't have told them anything about it. But probably they took his computers first and found some kind of traces that told them he'd been copying files. That happens, right? Computers leave traces of everything. But Franz wouldn't tell them where the copies were. Maybe that's why they broke his legs. But he kept quiet, which is why they had to come out here on this wild-assed search.'

'So where is it?'

Reacher looked down at his hand again.

Where would I hide something small and vital?

'Not under any old rock,' he said. 'I would want

72

somewhere structured. Maybe somewhere kind of custodial. I would want someone to be responsible.'

'A safe deposit box,' Neagley said again. 'In a bank. The small key has no markings. Banks do that.'

'I don't like banks,' Reacher said. 'I don't like the hours and I don't like the detour. Once, maybe, but not often. Which is the issue. Because there's some kind of regularity involved here. Isn't there? Isn't that what people do with computers? They back stuff up every night. So this wouldn't be a one-time thing. It would be a matter of routine. Which changes things somewhat. A one-time thing, you might go to extraordinary lengths. Every night, you need something safe but easy. And permanently available.'

'I e-mail stuff to myself,' Neagley said.

Reacher paused a beat. Smiled.

'There you go,' he said.

'You think that's what Franz did?'

'Not a chance,' Reacher said. 'E-mail would have come straight back to his computer, which the bad guys had. They'd have spent their time trying to break down his password instead of busting up his building.'

'So what did he do?'

Reacher turned and glanced along the row of stores. The dry cleaner, the nail salon, the pharmacy.

The post office.

'Not e-mail,' he said. 'Regular mail. That's what he did. He backed up his stuff onto some kind of a disk and every night he put it in an

73

envelope and dropped it in the mail. Addressed to himself. To his post office box. Because that's where he got his mail. In the post office. There's no slot in his door. Once the envelope was out of his hand it was safe. It was in the system. With a whole bunch of custodians looking after it all day and all night.'

'Slow,' Neagley said.

Reacher nodded. 'He must have had three or four disks in rotation. Any particular day two or three of them would be somewhere in the mail. But he went home every night knowing his latest stuff was safe. It's not easy to rob a mail box or make a clerk give you something that doesn't belong to you. USPS bureaucracy is about as safe as a Swiss bank.'

'The small key,' Neagley said. 'Not his desk. Not a safe deposit box.'

Reacher nodded again.

'His post office box,' he said.

TWELVE

But United States Postal Service bureaucracy cut two ways. It was late in the afternoon. The dry cleaner was still open. The nail salon was open. The pharmacy was open. But the post office was closed. Lobby hours had ended at four o'clock.

'Tomorrow,' Neagley said. 'We're going to be in the car all day. We have to get to Swan's place too. Unless we separate.'

'It's going to take two of us here,' Reacher said. 'But maybe one of the others will show up and do some work.'

'I wish they would. And not because I'm lazy.' For form's sake, like a little ritual, she pulled out her cell phone and checked the tiny screen.

No messages.

There were no messages at the hotel desk, either. No messages on the hotel voice mail. No e-mails on either one of Neagley's laptop computers.

Nothing.

'They can't just be ignoring us,' she said.

'No,' Reacher said. 'They wouldn't do that.'

'I'm getting a real bad feeling.'

'I've had a real bad feeling ever since I went to that ATM in Portland. I spent all my money taking someone to dinner. Twice. Now I wish we had stayed in and ordered pizza. She might have paid. I wouldn't know about any of this yet.'

'She?'

'Someone I met.'

'Cute?'

'As a button.'

'Cuter than Karla Dixon?'

'Comparable.'

'Cuter than me?'

'Is that even possible?'

'Did you sleep with her?'

'Who?'

'The woman in Portland.'

'Why do you want to know that?'

Neagley didn't answer. She just shuffled the five sheets of contact information like a card player and dealt Reacher two and kept three for herself. Reacher got Tony Swan and Karla Dixon. He used the landline on the credenza and tried Swan first. Thirty, forty rings, no answer. He dabbed the cradle and tried Dixon's number. A 212 area code, for New York City. No answer. Six rings, and straight to a machine. He listened to Dixon's familiar voice and waited for the beep and left her the same message he had left earlier: 'This is Jack Reacher with a ten-thirty from Frances Neagley at the Beverly Wilshire Hotel in Los Angeles, California. Get off your ass and call her back.' Then he paused a beat and added: 'Please, Karla. We really need to hear from you.'

Then he hung up. Neagley was closing her cell phone and shaking her head.

'Not good,' she said.

'They could all be on vacation.'

'At the same time?'

'They could all be in jail. We were a pretty rough bunch.'

'First thing I checked. They're not in jail.'

Reacher said nothing.

Neagley said, 'You really liked Karla, didn't you? You sounded positively tender there, on the phone.'

'I liked all of you.'

'But her especially. Did you ever sleep with her?'

Reacher said, 'No.'

'Why not?'

'I recruited her. I was her CO. Wouldn't have been right.'

'Was that the only reason?'

'Probably.'

'OK.'

Reacher asked, 'What do you know about their businesses? Is there any good reason why they should all be out of contact for days at a time?'

'I guess O'Donnell could have to travel overseas,' Neagley said. 'His practice is pretty general. Marital stuff could take him to hotels down in the islands, I guess. Or anyplace, if he's chasing unpaid alimony. Child abductions or custody issues could take him anywhere. People looking to adopt sometimes send detectives to Eastern Europe or China or wherever to make sure things are kosher. There are lots of possible reasons.'

'But?'

'I'd have to talk myself into really believing one of them.'

'What about Karla?'

'She could be down in the Caymans looking for someone's money, I guess. But I imagine she'd do that online from her office. It's not like the money is actually *there*.'

'So where is it?'

'It's notional. It's electricity in a computer.'

'What about Sanchez and Orozco?'

'They're in a closed world. I don't see why they would ever have to leave Vegas. Not professionally.'

'What do we know about Swan's company?'

'It exists. It does business. It files. It has an address. Apart from that, not much.'

'Presumably it has security issues, or Swan wouldn't have gotten hired.'

'All defence contractors have security issues. Or they think they ought to have, because they want to think what they do is important.'

Reacher said nothing to that. Just sat and stared out the window. It was getting dark. A long day, nearly over. He said, 'Franz didn't go to his office the morning he disappeared.'

'You think?'

'We know. Angela had his set of keys. He left them home. He was going somewhere else that day.'

Neagley said nothing.

'And the landlord at the strip mall saw the bad

guys,' Reacher said. 'Franz's lock wasn't broken. They didn't take Franz's key from him, because he didn't have it in his pocket. Therefore they scammed or bought one from the owner. Therefore the owner saw them. Therefore we need to find him tomorrow, along with everything else.'

'Franz should have called me,' Neagley said. 'I would have dropped everything.'

'I wish he had called you,' Reacher said. 'If you had been there, none of this bad stuff would have happened.'

Reacher and Neagley ate dinner in the downstairs restaurant, front corner of the lobby, where a bottle of still water from Norway cost eight dollars. Then they said goodnight and split up and headed for their separate rooms. Reacher's was a chintzy cube two floors below Neagley's suite. He stripped and showered and folded his clothes and put them under the mattress to press. He got into bed and folded his hands behind his head and stared up at the ceiling. Thought about Calvin Franz for a minute, in random flashing images, the same way a political candidate's biography is squeezed into a thirty-second television commercial. His memory made some of the pictures sepia and some of them washed out, but in all of them Franz was moving, talking, laughing, full of drive and energy. Then Karla Dixon joined the parade, petite, dark, sardonic, laughing with Franz. Dave O'Donnell was there, tall, fair, handsome, like a stockbroker with a switchblade. And Jorge Sanchez, durable, eyes narrowed, with a hint of a smile that showed a gold tooth and was as close as he ever came to showing contentment. And Tony Swan, as wide as he was high. And Manuel Orozco, opening and closing a Zippo lighter because he liked the sound so much. Even Stan Lowrey was there, shaking his head, drumming his fingers on a table to a rhythm only he could hear.

Then Reacher blinked all the pictures away and closed his eyes and fell asleep, ten thirty in the evening, a long day over.

Ten thirty in the evening in Los Angeles was one thirty the next morning in New York, and the last British Airways flight from London, delayed, had just landed at JFK. The delay meant that the last immigration watch in British Airways' own terminal had already gone off duty, so the plane taxied to Terminal Four and fed its passengers through the giant arrivals hall there. Third in the visitors' line was a first class passenger who had napped in seat 2K for most of the trip. He was medium height, medium weight, expensively dressed, and he radiated the kind of expansive self-confident courtesy typical of people who know how lucky they are to have been rich all their lives. He was perhaps forty years old. He had thick black hair, shiny, beautifully cut, and the kind of mid-brown skin and regular features that could have made him Indian, or Pakistani, or Iranian, or Syrian, or Lebanese, or Algerian, or even Israeli or Italian. His passport was British, and it passed the immigration agent's scrutiny with no trouble at all, as did its owner's manicured forefingers on the electronic fingerprint pad. Seventeen minutes after unclipping his seat belt the guy was out in the shiny New York night, walking briskly to the head of the cab line.

THIRTEEN

At six the next morning Reacher went up to Neagley's suite. He found her awake and showered and guessed she had been working out somewhere for an hour. Maybe in her room, maybe in the hotel gym. Maybe she had been out jogging. She looked sleek and pumped up and vital in a way that suggested there was a whole lot of oxygenated blood doing the rounds inside her.

They ordered room service breakfast and spent the waiting time on another fruitless round of phone calls. No answer from East LA, none from Nevada, none from New York, none from Washington D.C. They didn't leave messages. They didn't redial or try again. And when they hung up, they didn't talk about it. They just sat in silence until the waiter showed up and then they ate eggs and pancakes and bacon and drank coffee. Then Neagley called down to the valet station and ordered her car.

'Franz's place first?' she asked.

Reacher nodded. 'Franz is the focus here.'

So they rode the elevator down and got in the Mustang together and crawled south on La

Cienega to the post office at the tip of Culver City.

They parked right outside Franz's trashed office and walked back past the dry cleaner and the nail salon and the discount pharmacy. The post office was empty. A sign on the door said that the lobby had been open a half-hour. Clearly whatever initial rush there had been was over.

'We can't do this when it's empty,' Reacher said.

'So let's find the landlord first,' Neagley said.

They asked in the pharmacy. An old man in a short white coat was standing under an old-fashioned security camera behind the dispensing counter. He told them that the guy who owned the dry cleaner's store was the landlord. He spoke with the kind of guarded hostility that tenants always use about the people who get their rent cheques. He outlined a short success story in which his neighbour had come over from Korea and opened the cleaners and used the profits to leverage the whole strip mall. The American dream in action. Reacher and Neagley thanked him and walked past the nail salon and ducked into the cleaners and found the right guy imme-diately. He was rushing around in a crowded work area heavy with the stink of chemicals. Six big drum machines were churning away. Pressing tables were hissing. Racks of bagged clothes were winding around on a motorized conveyor above head height. The guy himself was sweating. Working hard. It looked like he deserved two strip malls. Or three. Maybe he already had them. Or more.

Reacher got straight to the point. Asked, 'When did you last see Calvin Franz?'

'I hardly ever saw him,' the guy answered. 'I couldn't see him. He painted over his window, first thing he ever did.' He said it like he had been annoyed about it. Like he had known he was going to have to get busy with a scraper before he could rent the unit again.

Reacher said, 'You must have seen him coming and going. I bet nobody here works longer hours than you.'

'I guess I saw him occasionally,' the guy said.

'When do you guess you stopped seeing him occasionally?'

'Three, four weeks ago.'

'Just before the guys came around and asked you for his key?'

'What guys?'

'The guys you gave his key to.'

'They were cops.'

'The second set of guys were cops.'

'So were the first.'

'Did they show you ID?'

'I'm sure they did.'

'I'm sure they didn't,' Reacher said. 'I'm sure they showed you a hundred dollar bill instead. Maybe two or three of them.'

'So what? It's my key and it's my building.'

'What did they look like?'

'Why should I tell you?'

'Because we were Mr Franz's friends.'

'Were?'

'He's dead. Someone threw him out of a helicopter.'

The dry cleaner just shrugged his shoulders.

'I don't remember the guys,' he said.

'They trashed your unit,' Reacher said. 'Whatever they paid you for the key won't cover the
damage.'

'Fixing the unit is my problem. It's my building.'

'Suppose it was your pile of smouldering ashes?
Suppose I came back tonight and burned the
whole place down?'

'You'd go to prison.'

'I don't think so. A guy with a memory as
bad as yours wouldn't have anything to tell the
police.'

The guy nodded. 'They were white men. Two
of them. Blue suits. A new car. They looked like
everybody else I see.'

'That's all?'

'Just white men. Not cops. Too clean and too
rich.'

'Nothing special about them?'

'I'd tell you if I could. They trashed my place.'

'OK.'

'I'm sorry about your friend. He seemed like a
nice guy.'

'He was,' Reacher said.

FOURTEEN

Reacher and Neagley walked back to the Post Office. It was a small, dusty place. Government décor. It had gotten moderately busy again. Normal morning business was in full swing. There was one clerk working and a short line of waiting customers. Neagley handed Reacher Franz's keys and joined the line. Reacher stepped to a shallow waist-high counter in back and took a random form out of a slot. It was a request for confirmation of delivery. He used a pen on a chain and bent down and pretended to fill out the form. He turned his body sideways and rested his elbow on the counter and kept his hand moving. Glanced at Neagley. She was maybe three minutes from the head of the line. He used the time to survey the rows of mail boxes.

They filled the whole end wall of the lobby. They came in three sizes. Small, medium, large. Six tiers of small, then below them four tiers of medium, then three tiers of large closest to the floor. Altogether one hundred eighty of the small size, ninety-six mediums, and fifty-four large. Total, three hundred thirty boxes.

Which one was Franz's?

One of the large ones, for sure. Franz had been running a business, and it had been the kind of business that would have generated a fair amount of incoming mail. Some of it would have been in the form of thick legal-sized packages. Credit reports, financial information, court transcripts, eight-by-ten photographs. Large, stiff envelopes. Professional journals. Therefore, a large box.

But which large box?

No way of telling. If Franz had been given a free choice, he would have picked the top row, three up from the floor, right hand end. Who wants to walk further than he needs to from the street door and then crouch all the way down on the linoleum? But Franz wouldn't have been given a free choice. You want a post office box, you take what's available at the time. Dead men's shoes. Someone dies or moves away, their box becomes free, you inherit it. Luck of the draw. A lottery. One chance in fifty-four.

Reacher put his left hand in his pocket and fingered Franz's key. He figured it would take between two and three seconds to test it in each lock. Worst case, almost three minutes of dancing along the array. Very exposed. Worse than worst case, he could be busy trying a box right in front of its legitimate owner who had just stepped in behind him. Questions, complaints, shouts, calls to the postal police, a potential federal case. Reacher had no doubt at all that he could get out of the lobby unharmed, but he didn't want to get out empty-handed.

He heard Neagley say: 'Good morning.'

87

He glanced left and saw her at the head of the counter line. Saw her leaning forward, commanding attention. Saw the counter clerk's eyes lock in on hers. He dropped the pen and took the key from his pocket. Stepped unobtrusively to the wall of boxes and tried the first lock on the left, three up from the floor.

Failure.

He rocked the key clockwise and counterclockwise. No movement. He pulled it out and tried the lock below. Failure. The one below that. Failure.

Neagley was asking a long complicated question about air mail rates. Her elbows were on the counter. She was making the clerk feel like the most important guy in the world. Reacher shuffled right and tried again, one box over, three up from the floor.

Failure.

Four down, fifty to go. Twelve seconds consumed, odds now improved from one point eight five chances in a hundred to two chances in a hundred. He tried the next box down. Failure. He crouched, and tried the box nearest to the floor.

Failure.

He stayed in a crouch and shuffled right. Started the next column from the bottom up. No luck with the lowest. No luck with the one above. No luck with the third up. Nine down, twenty-five seconds elapsed. Neagley was still talking. Then Reacher was aware of a woman squeezing in on his left. Opening her box, high up. Raking out a dense mass of curled junk. Sorting it, as she stood there. *Move*, he begged her. *Step away to the trash receptacle*. She backed away. He stepped to his right and tried the fourth row. Neagley was still talking. The clerk was still listening. The key didn't fit the top box. It didn't fit the middle box. It didn't fit the bottom box.

Twelve down. Odds now one in forty-two. Better, but not good. The key didn't fit anything in the fifth row. Nor the sixth. Eighteen down. One-third gone. Odds improving all the time. *Look on the bright side*. Neagley was still talking. He could hear her. He knew that behind her people in the line would be getting impatient. They would be shuffling their feet. They would be looking around, bored and inquisitive.

He started on the seventh row, at the top. Rocked the key. It didn't move. No go with the middle box. Nor the lowest. Neagley had stopped talking. The clerk was explaining something. She was pretending not to understand. Reacher moved right again. The eighth row. The key didn't fit the top box. The lobby was going quiet. Reacher could feel eyes on his back. He dropped his hand and tried the middle box in the eighth row.

Rocked the key. The small metallic sound was very loud.

Failure.

The lobby was silent.

Reacher tried the lowest box in the eighth row.

Rocked the key.

It moved.

The lock opened.

Reacher stepped back a foot and swung the little door all the way open and crouched down. The box was stuffed. Padded envelopes, big brown envelopes, big white envelopes, letters, catalogues, magazines wrapped in plastic, post-cards.

Sound came back to the lobby.

Reacher heard Neagley say, 'Thank you very much for your help.' He heard her footsteps on the tile. Heard the line behind her move up. Sensed people refocusing on their chances of getting their business done before they grew old and died. He slid his hand into the box and raked the contents forward. Butted everything together into a steady stack and clamped it between his palms and stood up. Jammed the stack under his arm and relocked the box and pocketed the key and walked away like the most natural thing in the world.

Neagley was waiting in the Mustang, three doors down. Reacher leaned in and dumped the stack of mail on the centre console and then followed it inside. Sorted through the stack and pulled out four small padded envelopes self-addressed in Franz's own familiar handwriting.

'Too small for CDs,' he said.

He arranged them in date order according to the postmarks. The most recent had been stamped the same morning that Franz had disap-peared.

'But mailed the night before,' he said.

He opened the envelope and shook out a small silver object. Metal, flat, two inches long, three-

90

quarters of an inch wide, thin, capped with plastic. Like something that would go on a key ring. It had *128 MB* printed on it.

'What is it?' he asked.

'Flash memory,' Neagley said. 'The new version of floppy disks. No moving parts and a hundred times the storage capacity.'

'What do we do with it?'

'We plug it into one of my computers and we see what's on it.'

'Just like that?'

'Unless it's password-protected. Which it probably will be.'

'Isn't there software to help with that?'

'There used to be. But not any more. Things get better all the time. Or worse, depending on your point of view.'

'So what do we do?'

'We spend the drive time making mental lists. Likely choices for his password. The old-fashioned way. My guess is we'll get three tries before the files erase themselves.'

She started the motor and eased away from the kerb. Pulled a neat U-turn in the strip mall's fire lane and headed back north to La Cienega.

The man in the dark blue suit watched them go. He was low down behind the wheel of his dark blue Chrysler sedan, forty yards away, in a slot that belonged to the pharmacy. He opened his cell phone and dialled his boss.

'This time they ignored Franz's place completely,' he said. 'They talked to the landlord instead. Then they were in the post office a long time. I think Franz must have been mailing the stuff to himself. That's why we couldn't find it. And they've probably got it now.'

FIFTEEN

Neagley plugged the flash memory into a socket on the side of her laptop computer. Reacher watched the screen. Nothing happened for a second and then an icon appeared. It looked like a stylized picture of the physical object she had just attached. It was labelled *No Name*. Neagley ran her forefinger over the touch pad and then tapped it twice.

The icon blossomed into a full-screen demand for a password.

'Damn,' she said.

'Inevitable,' he said.

'Ideas?'

Reacher had busted computer passwords many times before, back in the day. As always, the technique was to consider the person and think like them. *Be* them. Serious paranoids used long complex mixes of lower-case and upper-case letters and numbers that meant nothing to anyone including themselves. Those passwords were effectively unbreakable. But Franz had never been paranoid. He had been a relaxed guy, serious about but simultaneously a little amused by security demands. And he was a words guy, not a numbers guy. He was a man of interests and enthusiasms. Full of affections and loyalties. Middlebrow tastes. A memory like an elephant.

Reacher said, 'Angela, Charlie, Miles Davis, Dodgers, Koufax, Panama, Pfeiffer, MASH, Brooklyn, Heidi or Jennifer.'

Neagley wrote them all down on a new page in her spiral-bound notebook.

'Why those?' she asked.

'Angela and Charlie are obvious. His family.'

'Too obvious.'

'Maybe. Maybe not. Miles Davis was his favourite music, the Dodgers were his favourite team, and Sandy Koufax was his favourite player.'

'Possibilities. What's Panama?'

'Where he was deployed at the end of 1989. I think that was the place he had the most professional satisfaction. He'll have remembered it.'

'Pfeiffer as in Michelle Pfeiffer?'

'His favourite actress.'

'Angela looks a little like her, doesn't she?'

'There you go.'

'MASH?'

'His all-time favourite movie,' Reacher said.

'More than ten years ago, when you knew him,' Neagley said. 'There have been a lot of good movies since then.'

'Passwords come from down deep.'

'It's too short. Most software asks for a minimum of six characters now.'

'OK, scratch MASH.'

'Brooklyn?'

'Where he was born.'

'I didn't know that.'

'Not many people did. They moved west when he was little. That's what would make it a good password.'

'Heidi?'

'His first serious girlfriend. Hot as hell, apparently. Terrific in the sack. He was crazy about her.'

'I didn't know anything about that. Clearly I was excluded from the guy talk.'

'Clearly,' Reacher said. 'Karla Dixon was, too. We didn't want to look emotional.'

'I'm crossing Heidi off the list. Only five letters, and he was too much into Angela now anyway. He wouldn't have felt right using an old girlfriend's name for a password, however hot and terrific she was. I'm crossing Michelle Pfeiffer off for the same reason. And who was Jennifer? His second girlfriend? Was she hot too?'

'Jennifer was his dog,' Reacher said. 'When he was a kid. A little black mutt. Lived for eighteen years. Broke him up when it died.'

'Possibility, then. But that's six. We've only got three tries.'

'We've got twelve tries,' Reacher said. 'Four envelopes, four flash memories. If we start with the earliest postmark we can afford to burn the first three. That information is old anyway.'

Neagley laid the four flash memories on the hotel desk in strict date order. 'You sure he wouldn't have changed his password daily?'

'Franz?' Reacher said. 'Are you kidding? A

guy like Franz latches on to a word that means something to him and he sticks with it forever.'

Neagley clicked the oldest memory unit into the port and waited until the corresponding icon appeared on the screen. She clicked on it and tabbed the cursor straight to the password box.

'OK,' she said. 'You want to nominate a priority order?'

'Do the people names first. Then the place names. I think that's how it would have worked for him.'

'Is the Dodgers a people name?'

'Of course it is. Baseball is played by people.'

'OK. But we'll start with music.' She typed *MilesDavis* and hit *enter*. There was a short pause and then the screen redrew and came back with the dialogue box again and a note in red: *Your first attempt was incorrect.*

'One down,' she said. 'Now sports.'

She tried *Dodgers*.

Incorrect.

'Two down.' She typed *Koufax*.

The hard drive inside her laptop chattered and the screen went blank.

'What's happening?' Reacher asked.

'It's dumping the data,' she said. 'Erasing it. It wasn't Koufax. Three down.'

She pulled the flash memory out of the port and tossed it through a long silver arc into the trash can. Inserted the second unit in its place. Typed *Jennifer*.

Incorrect.

'Four down,' she said. 'Not his puppy.'

She tried *Panama*.

96

Incorrect.

'Five down.' She tried *Brooklyn*.

The screen went blank and the hard drive chattered.

'Six down,' she said. 'Not his old hood. You're zip for six, Reacher.'

The second unit clattered into the trash and she plugged in the third.

'Ideas?'

'Your turn. I seem to have lost my touch.'

'What about his old service number?'

'I doubt it. He was a words guy, not a numbers guy. And for me anyway my number was the same as my Social Security number. Same for him, probably, which would make it too obvious.'

'What would you use?'

'Me? I *am* a numbers guy. Top row of the keyboard, all in a line, easy to get to. No typing skills required.'

'What number would you use?'

'Six characters? I'd probably write out my birthday, month, day, year, and find the nearest prime number.' Then he thought for a second and said, 'Actually that would be a problem, because there would be two equally close, one exactly seven less and one exactly seven more. So I guess I'd use the square root instead, rounded to three decimal places. Ignore the decimal point, that would give me six numbers, all different.'

'Weird,' Neagley said. 'I think we can be sure Franz wouldn't do anything like that. Probably nobody else in the world would do anything like that.'

'Therefore it would be a good password.'

'What was his first car?'

'Some piece of shit, probably.'

'But guys like cars, right? What was his favourite car?'

'I don't like cars.'

'Think like him, Reacher. Did he like cars?'

'He always wanted a red Jaguar XKE.'

'Would that be worth a try?'

A man of interests and enthusiasms. Full of affections and loyalties.

'Maybe,' Reacher said. 'It's certainly going to be something special to him. Something talismanic, something that would give him a feeling of warmth just recalling the word. Either an early role model or a longstanding object of desire or affection. So the XKE might work.'

'Should I try it? We've only got six left.'

'I'd try it for sure if we had six hundred left.'

'Wait a minute,' Neagley said. 'What about what Angela told us? The way he kept on saying you do not mess with the special investigators?'

'That would make a hell of a long password.'

'So break it down. Either special investigators, or do not mess.'

A memory like an elephant. Reacher nodded. 'We had a good time back then, basically, didn't we? So remembering the old days might have given him a warm feeling. Especially stuck out there in Culver City, busy doing nothing much. People enjoy nostalgia, don't they? Like that song, "The Way We Were".'

'It was a movie too.'

'There you go. It's a universal feeling.'

'Which should we try first?'

Reacher heard Charlie in his mind, the little boy's piping treble: *You do not mess.*

'Do not mess,' he said. 'Nine letters.'

Neagley typed *donotmess.*

Hit *enter.*

Incorrect.

'Shit,' she said.

She typed *specialinvestigators.* Held her finger over the enter key.

'That's very long,' Reacher said.

'Yes or no?'

'Try it.'

Incorrect.

Neagley said, 'Damn,' and went quiet.

Charlie was still in Reacher's mind. And his tiny chair, with the neat branded name at the top. He could see Franz's steady hand at work. He could smell the smoking wood. A gift, father to son. Probably intended to be the first of many. Love, pride, commitment.

'I like Charlie,' he said.

'Me too,' Neagley said. 'He's a cute kid.'

'No, for the password.'

'Too obvious.'

'He didn't take this kind of stuff very seriously. He was going through the motions. Easier to put in any old thing than to reprogram the software to get around it.'

'Still too obvious. And he had to be taking it seriously. At least this time. He was in big trouble and he was mailing stuff to himself.'

'So it could be a double bluff. It's obvious but it's the last thing anyone would think of trying. That makes for a very effective password.'

'Possible but unlikely.'

'What are we going to find on there anyway?'

'Something we really need to see.'

'Try Charlie for me.'

Neagley shrugged and typed *Charlie*.

Hit *enter*.

Incorrect.

The hard disk spun up and the memory unit erased itself.

'Nine down,' Neagley said. She pitched the third unit into the trash and plugged the fourth one in. The last one. 'Three to go.'

Reacher asked, 'Who did he love before Charlie?'

'Angela,' Neagley said. 'Way too obvious.'

'Try it.'

'Are you sure?'

'I'm a gambler.'

'We're down to our last three chances.'

'Try it,' he said again.

She typed *Angela*.

Hit *enter*.

Incorrect.

'Ten down,' she said. 'Two to go.'

'What about Angela Franz?'

'That's even worse.'

'What about her unmarried name?'

'I don't know what it was.'

'Call her and ask.'

'Are you serious?'

'At least let's find out.'

So Neagley thumbed through her notebook and found the number and fired up her cell phone. Introduced herself again. Small-talked for a moment. Then Reacher heard her ask the question. He didn't hear Angela's answer. But he saw Neagley's eyes widen a fraction, which for her was about the same thing as falling on the floor with shock.

She hung up.

'It was Pfeiffer,' she said.

'Interesting.'

'Very.'

'Are they related?'

'She didn't say.'

'So try it. It's a perfect twofer. He feels good twice over and doesn't have to feel disloyal at all.'

Neagley typed *Pfeiffer*.

Hit *enter*.

Incorrect.

SIXTEEN

The room was hot and stuffy. No air in it. And it seemed to have gotten smaller. Neagley said, 'Eleven down. One to go. Do or die. Last chance.'

Reacher asked, 'What happens if we don't do anything?'

'Then we don't get to see what's on the file.'

'No, I mean do we have to do it right now? Or can it keep?'

'It's not going anywhere.'

'So we should take a break. Come back to it later. One to go, we've got to pay attention.'

'Weren't we already?'

'Clearly not the right kind of attention. We'll go out to East LA and look for Swan. If we find him, he might have ideas. If not, then at least we'll come back to this fresh.'

Neagley called down to the valet station again and ten minutes later they were in the Mustang heading east on Wilshire. Through Wilshire Center, through Westlake, through a dog-leg south that took them straight through Macarthur Park. Then north and east on the Pasadena

Freeway, past the concrete bulk of Dodger Stadium all alone in acres of empty parking. Then deep into a rats' nest of surface streets bounded by Boyle Heights, Monterey Park, Alhambra, and South Pasadena. There were science parks and business parks and strip malls and old housing and new housing. The kerbs were thick with parked cars and there was traffic everywhere, moving slow. A brown sky. Neagley had an austere Rand McNally map in the glove box. Looking at it was like looking at the surface of the earth from fifty miles up. Reacher squinted and followed the faint grey lines. Matched the street names on signposts to the street names on the map and pinpointed specific junctions about thirty seconds after they blew through them. He had his thumb on New Age's location and steered Neagley toward it in a wide ragged spiral.

When they got there they found a low sign of chiselled granite and a big prosperous mirror-glass cube set behind a tall hurricane fence topped with coils of razor wire. The fence was impressive at first sight, but only semi-serious in that ten seconds and a pair of bolt cutters would get a person through it unscathed. The building itself was surrounded by a wide parking lot studded with specimen trees. The way the mirror glass reflected the trees and the sky made the building look like it was there and not there simultaneously.

The main gate was lightweight and standing wide open and there was no sentry post next to it. It was just a gate. Beyond it the lot was about half full of parked cars. Neagley paused to let a photocopier truck out and then drove in and put the Mustang in a visitor slot near the entrance lobby. She and Reacher got out and stood for a moment. It was the middle of the morning and the air was warm and heavy. The neighbourhood was quiet. It sounded like a whole lot of people were concentrating very hard, or else no one was doing very much of anything.

The reception entrance had a shallow step up to double glass doors that opened for them automatically and admitted them to a large square lobby that had a slate floor and aluminum walls. There were leather chairs and a long reception counter in back. Behind the counter was a blonde woman of about thirty. She was wearing a corporate polo shirt with *New Age Defense Systems* embroidered above her small left breast. Clearly she had heard the doors open but she waited until Reacher and Neagley were halfway across the floor before she looked up.

'Can I help you?' she asked.

'We're here to see Tony Swan,' Reacher said.

The woman smiled automatically and asked, 'May I know your names?'

'Jack Reacher and Frances Neagley. We were good friends of his in the service.'

'Then please take a seat.' The woman picked up her desk phone and Reacher and Neagley stepped away to the leather chairs. Neagley sat down but Reacher stayed on his feet. He watched the dull aluminum reflection of the woman on the phone and heard her say, 'Two friends of Tony Swan to see him.' Then she put the phone down and smiled in Reacher's direction even though he wasn't looking directly at her. Then the lobby went quiet.

It stayed quiet for about four minutes and then Reacher heard the click of shoes on slate from a corridor that entered the lobby to the side of and behind the desk. A measured stride, no hurry, a person of medium height and medium weight. He watched the mouth of the corridor and saw a woman step into view. About forty years old, slim, brown hair stylishly cut. She was in a tailored black pant suit and a white blouse. She looked swift and efficient and had an open and welcoming expression on her face. She smiled a token thank you to the receptionist and walked straight past her toward Reacher and Neagley. Held out her hand and said, 'I'm Margaret Berenson.'

Neagley stood up and she and Reacher said their names and shook hands with her. Up close she had old looping car crash scars under her makeup and the chilly breath of a big-time gum chewer. She was wearing decent jewellery, but no wedding band.

'We're looking for Tony Swan,' Reacher said.

'I know,' the woman said. 'Let's find somewhere to talk.'

One of the aluminum wall panels was a door that led to a small rectangular conference room directly off the lobby. Clearly it was designed for discussions with visitors who didn't merit admission into the inner sanctums. It was a cool spare space with a table and four chairs and floor to ceiling windows that gave directly on to the parking lot. The front bumper of Neagley's Mustang was about five feet away.

'I'm Margaret Berenson,' the woman said again. 'I'm New Age's human resources director. I'll get straight to the point, which is that Mr Swan isn't with us any more.'

Reacher asked, 'Since when?'

'A little over three weeks ago,' Berenson said.

'What happened?'

'I'd feel more comfortable talking about it if I knew for sure you have a connection with him. Anyone can walk up to a reception counter and claim to be old friends.'

'I'm not sure how we could prove it.'

'What did he look like?'

'About five-nine tall and about five-eight wide.'

Berenson smiled. 'If I told you he used a piece of stone as a paperweight, could you tell me where that piece of stone came from?'

'The Berlin Wall,' Reacher said. 'He was in Germany when it came down. I saw him there just afterward. He took the train up and got himself a souvenir. And it's concrete, not stone. There's a trace of graffiti on it.'

Berenson nodded.

'That's the story I heard,' she said. 'And that's the object I've seen.'

'So what happened?' Reacher asked. 'He quit?'

Berenson shook her head.

'Not exactly,' she said. 'We had to let him go. Not just him. You have to understand, this is a new company. It was always speculative, and there was always risk. In terms of our business plan, we're not where we want to be. Not yet, anyway. So we reached the stage where we had to

106

revise our staffing levels. Downward, unfortunately. We operated a last in, first out policy, and basically that meant we had to let the whole assistant management level go. I lost my own assistant director. Mr Swan was assistant director of security, so unfortunately the policy swept him away too. We were very sorry to see him go, because he was a real asset. If things pick up, we'll beg him to come back. But I'm sure he'll have secured another position by then.'

Reacher glanced through the window at the half-empty parking lot. Listened to the quiet of the building. It sounded half empty, too.

'OK,' he said.

'Not OK,' Neagley said. 'I've been calling his office over and over for the last three days and every time I was told he had just stepped out for a minute. That doesn't add up.'

Berenson nodded again. 'That's a professional courtesy that I insist upon. With this calibre of management it would be a disaster for an individual if his personal network of contacts heard the news secondhand. Much better if Mr Swan can inform people himself, directly. Then he can spin it however he wants. So I insist that the remaining secretarial staff tell little white lies during the readjustment period. I don't apologize for it, but I do hope you understand. It's the least I can do for the people we've lost. If Mr Swan can approach a new employer as if it were a voluntary move, he's in a far better position than if everyone knew he'd been let go from here.'

Neagley thought about it for a moment, and then she nodded.

'OK,' she said. 'I can see your point.'

'Especially in Mr Swan's case,' Berenson said. 'We all liked him very much.'

'What about the ones you didn't like?'

'There weren't any. We would never hire people we didn't believe in.'

Reacher said, 'I called Swan and nobody answered at all.'

Berenson nodded again, still patient and professional. 'We had to cut the secretarial pool too. The ones we kept on are covering five or six phones each. Sometimes they can't get to every call.'

Reacher asked, 'So what's up with your business plan?'

'I really can't discuss that in detail. But I'm sure you understand. You were in the army.'

'We both were.'

'Then you know how many new weapons systems work straight out of the gate.'

'Not many.'

'Not *any*. Ours is taking a little longer than we hoped.'

'What kind of a weapon is it?'

'I really can't discuss that.'

'Where is it made?'

'Right here.'

Reacher shook his head. 'No, it isn't. You've got a fence a three-year-old could walk through and no guard shack at the gate and an unsecured lobby. Tony Swan wouldn't have let you get away with that if anything sensitive was happening here.'

'I really can't comment on our procedures.'

'Who was Swan's boss?'

'Our director of security? He's a retired LAPD lieutenant.'

'And you kept him and let Swan go? Your last-in-first-out policy didn't do you any favours there.'

'They're all great people, the ones who stayed and the ones who went. We hated making the cut. But it was an absolute necessity.'

Two minutes later Reacher and Neagley were back in the Mustang, sitting in New Age's parking lot, engine idling to run the air, with the full scope of the disaster plain to both of them.

'Really bad timing,' Reacher said. 'Suddenly Swan is at loose ends, Franz calls him with a problem, what else is Swan going to do? He's going to run right over there. It's twenty minutes down the road.'

'He'd have gone anyway, unemployed or not.'

'They all would. And I guess they all did.'

'So are they all dead now?'

'Hope for the best, plan for the worst.'

'You got what you wanted, Reacher. It's just the two of us.'

'I didn't want it for these reasons.'

'I just can't believe it. *All* of them?'

'Someone's going to pay.'

'You think? We've got nothing. We've got one last chance with a password. Which by definition we'll be too nervous to take.'

'This is no kind of a time to be getting nervous.'

'So tell me what to type.'

Reacher said nothing.

They retraced their route through the surface streets. Neagley drove in silence and Reacher pictured Tony Swan making the same drive more than three weeks earlier. Maybe with the contents of his New Age desk boxed up in his trunk, his pens and pencils and his chip of Soviet concrete. On his way to help his old buddy. Other old buddies pouring in down spokes of an invisible wheel. Sanchez and Orozco hustling over from Vegas on the 15. O'Donnell and Dixon coming in on planes from the East Coast, toting luggage, taking taxis, assembling.

Meeting and greeting.

Running into some kind of a brick wall.

Then their images faded away and he was alone again with Neagley in the car. *Just the two of us*. Facts were to be faced, not fought.

Neagley left the car with the Beverly Wilshire valets and they entered the lobby from the rear through the crooked corridor. They rode up in the elevator in silence. Neagley used her key and pushed open her door.

Then she stopped dead.

Because sitting in her chair by the window, reading Calvin Franz's autopsy report, was a man in a suit.

Tall, fair, aristocratic, relaxed.

David O'Donnell.

SEVENTEEN

O'Donnell looked up, sombre. 'I was going to enquire as to the meaning of all those rude and abusive messages on my answering machine.' Then he raised the autopsy report, an explanatory gesture. 'But now I understand.'

Neagley asked, 'How did you get in here?'

O'Donnell just said, 'Oh, please.'

'Where the hell were you?' Reacher asked.

'I was in New Jersey,' O'Donnell said. 'My sister was sick.'

'How sick?'

'Very sick.'

'Did she die?'

'No, she recovered.'

'Then you should have been here days ago.'

'Thanks for your concern.'

'We were worried,' Neagley said. 'We thought they got you too.'

O'Donnell nodded. 'You should be worried. You should stay worried. It's a worrying situation. I had to wait four hours for a flight. I used the time making calls. No answer from Franz, obviously. Now I know why, of course. No answer from Swan or Dixon or Orozco or Sanchez either. My conclusion was that one of them had gotten all the others together and they had run into a problem. Not you or Reacher, because you're too busy in Chicago and who the hell could ever find Reacher? And not me, because I was temporarily off the grid in New Jersey.'

'I wasn't too busy,' Neagley said. 'How could anyone think that? I'd have dropped everything and come running.'

O'Donnell nodded again. 'At first that was the only thing that gave me hope. I figured they would have called you.'

'So why didn't they? Don't they like me?'

'If they hated you they'd still have called you. Without you it would have been like fighting with one hand behind their backs. Who would do that voluntarily? But in the end it's perception that counts, not reality. You're very high grade now compared to the rest of us. I think they might have hesitated with you. Maybe until it was too late.'

'So what are you saying?'

'I'm saying that one of them, and now I see that it would have been Franz, was in trouble, and he called all of us that he perceived as readily available. Which excluded you and Reacher by definition, and me also, by bad luck, because I wasn't where I normally am.'

'That's how we saw it too. Except you're a bonus. Your sister being sick was a stroke of luck for us. And for you, maybe.'

'But not for her.'

'Stop whining,' Reacher said. 'She's alive, isn't she?'

'Nice to see you too,' O'Donnell said. 'After all these years.'

'How *did* you get in here?' Neagley asked.

O'Donnell shifted in his seat and took a switchblade from one coat pocket and a set of brass knuckles from the other. 'A guy who can get these through airport security can get into a hotel room, believe me.'

'How did you get those through an airport?'

'My secret,' O'Donnell said.

'Ceramic,' Reacher said. 'They don't make them any more. Because they don't set the metal detector off.'

'Correct,' O'Donnell said. 'No metal at all, apart from the switchblade spring, which is still steel. But that's very small.'

'It's good to see you again, David,' Reacher said.

'Likewise. But I wish it was in happier circumstances.'

'The circumstances just got fifty per cent happier. We thought it was just the two of us. Now it's the three of us.'

'What have we got?'

'Very little. You've seen what's in his autopsy report. Apart from that we've got two generic white men who tossed his office. Didn't find anything, because he was mailing stuff to himself in a permanent loop. We found his mail box and picked up four flash memories and we're down to the last try at a password.'

'So start thinking about computer security,' Neagley said.

O'Donnell took a deep breath and held it

113

longer than seemed humanly possible. Then he exhaled, gently. It was an old habit.

'Tell me what words you've tried so far,' he said.

Neagley opened her notebook to the relevant page and handed it over. O'Donnell put a finger to his lips and read. Reacher watched him. He hadn't seen him in eleven years, but he hadn't changed much. He had the kind of corn-coloured hair that would never show grey. He had the kind of greyhound's body that would never show fat. His suit was beautifully cut. In the same way as Neagley he looked settled and prosperous and successful. Like he was making it.

'Koufax didn't work?' he asked.

Neagley shook her head. 'That was our third try.'

'Should have been your first, out of this list. Franz related to icons, gods, people he admired, performances he idolized. Koufax is the only one of these that really fits the bill. The others are merely sentimental. Miles Davis perhaps, because he loved music, but ultimately he thought music was inessential.'

'Music is inessential and baseball isn't?'

'Baseball is a metaphor,' O'Donnell said. 'An ace pitcher like Sandy Koufax, a man of great integrity, all alone on the mound, the World Series, stakes high, that's how Franz wanted to see himself. He probably wouldn't have articulated it exactly that way, but I can tell you his password would have to be a worthy repository for his devotion. And it would be expressed in a brusque,

114

masculine fashion, which would mean a surname only.'

'So what would you vote for?'

'It's tough, with only one try left. I'd look like a real fool if I was wrong. What are we going to find on there anyway?'

'Something he felt was worth hiding.'

Reacher said, 'Something he got his legs broken for. He didn't give anything up. He drove them into a fury. His office looks like a tornado hit it.'

'What's our ultimate aim here?'

'Seek and destroy. Is that good enough for you?'

O'Donnell shook his head.

'No,' he said. 'I want to kill their families and piss on their ancestors' graves.'

'You haven't changed.'

'I've gotten worse. Have you changed?'

'If I have I'm ready to change back.'

O'Donnell smiled, briefly. 'Neagley, what don't you do?'

Neagley said, 'You don't mess with the special investigators.'

'Correct,' O'Donnell said. 'You do not. Can we get some room service coffee?'

They drank thick strong coffee out of the kind of battered electroplated jugs found only in old hotels. They kept pretty quiet, but each of them knew the others were tracing the same mental circles, shying away from the last attempt at the password, examining the vector, trying to find another avenue forward, failing to, and starting all over again. Finally O'Donnell put his cup down and said, 'Time to shit or get off the pot. Or fish or cut bait. Or however else you want to express it. Let's hear your ideas.'

Neagley said, 'I don't have any.'

Reacher said, 'You do it, Dave. You've got something in mind. I can tell.'

'Do you trust me?'

'As far as I could throw you. Which would be pretty damn far, as skinny as you are. Exactly how far, you'll find out if you screw up.'

O'Donnell got out of his chair and flexed his fingers and stepped over to the laptop on the desk. Put the cursor in the box on the screen and typed seven letters.

Took a breath and held it.

Paused.

Waited.

Hit *enter*.

The laptop screen redrew.

A file directory appeared. A table of contents. Big, bold, clear and obvious.

O'Donnell breathed out.

He had typed: *Reacher*.

EIGHTEEN

Reacher spun away from the computer like he had been slapped and said, 'Ah, man, that ain't fair.'

'He liked you,' O'Donnell said. 'He admired you.'

'It's like a voice from the grave. Like a call.'

'You were here anyway.'

'It doubles everything. Now I can't let him down.'

'You weren't going to in the first place.'

'Too much pressure.'

'No such thing as too much pressure. We like pressure. We thrive on pressure.'

Neagley was at the desk, fingers on the laptop's keyboard, staring at the screen.

'Eight separate files,' she said. 'Seven of them are a bunch of numbers and the eighth is a list of names.'

'Show me the names,' O'Donnell said.

Neagley clicked on an icon and a word processor page opened. It contained a vertical list of five names. At the top, typed in bold and underlined, was *Azhari Mahmoud*. Then came four

Western names: *Adrian Mount*, *Alan Mason*, *Andrew MacBride*, and *Anthony Matthews*.

'Initials are all the same,' O'Donnell said. 'Top one is Arab, anywhere from Morocco to Pakistan.'

'Syrian,' Neagley said. 'That would be my guess.'

'Last four names feel British,' Reacher said. 'Don't you think? Rather than American? English or Scottish.'

'Significance?' O'Donnell asked.

Reacher said, 'At first glance I would say one of Franz's background checks came up with a Syrian guy with four known aliases. Because of the five sets of common initials. Clumsy, but indicative. Maybe he's got monogrammed shirts. And maybe the phony names are British because the paperwork is British, which would get around the kind of scrutiny that American paperwork would invite over here.'

'Possible,' O'Donnell said.

Reacher said, 'Show me the numbers.'

Neagley closed the word processor document and opened the first of seven spreadsheets. It was nothing more than a page-long vertical list of fractions. At the top was *10/12*. At the bottom was *11/12*. In between were twenty-some similar numbers, including a repeated *10/12* and a *12/13* and a *9/10*.

'Next,' Reacher said.

The next spreadsheet was essentially identical. A long vertical column, starting with *13/14* and ending with *8/9*. Twenty-some similar numbers in between.

118

'Next,' Reacher said.

The third spreadsheet showed more or less exactly the same thing.

'Are they dates?' O'Donnell said.

'No,' Reacher said. 'Thirteen-fourteen isn't a date whether it's month-day or day-month.'

'So what are they? Just fractions?'

'Not really. Ten over twelve would be written five over six if it was a regular fraction.'

'They're like box scores, then.'

'For the game from hell. Thirteen for fourteen and twelve for thirteen would imply lots of extra innings and a three-figure final score, probably.'

'So what are they?'

'Show me the next one.'

The fourth spreadsheet showed the same long vertical list of fractions. The denominators were pretty much the same as in the first three, twelves and tens and thirteens. But the numerators were generally smaller. There was a *9/12*, and an *8/13*. Even a *5/14*.

O'Donnell said, 'If these are box scores, someone's slumping.'

'Next,' Reacher said.

The trend continued. The fifth sheet had a *3/12*, and a *4/13*. The best was a *6/11*.

'Someone's heading back to the minor leagues,' O'Donnell said.

The sixth list had *5/13* as its best score and *3/13* as its worst. The seventh and last was about the same, varying between *4/11* and *3/12*.

Neagley looked up at Reacher and said, 'You figure it out. You're the numbers guy. And Franz addressed all of this to you, after all.'

'I was his password,' Reacher said. 'That's all. He didn't address anything to anyone. These aren't messages. He'd have made it clearer if he was trying to communicate. These are working notes.'

'Very cryptic working notes.'

'Can you print them out for me? I can't think without seeing them on paper.'

'I can print them in the business centre downstairs. That's why I stay in places like this now.'

O'Donnell asked, 'Why would they trash an office to look for a list of numbers?'

'Maybe they didn't,' Reacher said. 'Maybe they were looking for the list of names.'

Neagley shut down the spreadsheets and reopened the word processor document. *Azhari Mahmoud*, *Adrian Mount*, *Alan Mason*, *Andrew MacBride*, *Anthony Matthews*.

'So who is this guy?' Reacher said.

Three time zones away in New York City it was three hours later in the day and the dark-haired forty-year-old man who could have been Indian, or Pakistani, or Iranian, or Syrian, or Lebanese, or Algerian, or Israeli, or Italian was crouching on a bathroom floor inside an expensive Madison Avenue hotel room. The door was closed. There was no smoke detector in the bathroom, but there was an extractor fan. The British passport issued to Adrian Mount was burning in the toilet pan. As always the inside pages went up easily. The stiff red covers burned more slowly. Page 31 was the laminated ID page. It burned slowest of all. The plastic curled and twisted and melted. The man used the hairdryer from the bathroom wall at a distance to fan the flames. Then he used the butt end of his toothbrush to stir the ashes and the unburned flakes of paper. He lit another match and went after anything that was still recognizable.

Five minutes later Adrian Mount was flushed away and Alan Mason was on his way down to the street in the elevator.

NINETEEN

Neagley detoured to the Beverly Wilshire's basement business centre and printed out all eight of Franz's secret files. Then she joined O'Donnell and Reacher for lunch in the lobby restaurant. She sat between the two of them with the kind of look on her face that made Reacher think she was reliving a hundred similar meals.

And Reacher was doing the same thing himself. But back in the day they had been in creased BDUs and they had eaten in O Clubs or grimy off-post diners or had shared sandwiches and pizza around battered metal desks. Now the déjà vu was corrupted by the new context. The room was dim and tall and stylish and full of people who could have been movie agents or executives. Actors, even. Neagley and O'Donnell looked right at home. Neagley was wearing baggy black high-waisted pants and a cotton T shirt that fitted her like a second skin. Her face was tan and flawless and her makeup was so subtle it was like she was wearing none at all. O'Donnell's suit was grey with a slight sheen to it and his shirt was white and crisp and immaculate even though he must have put it on three thousand miles away. His tie was striped and regimental and perfectly knotted.

Reacher was in a shirt a size too small with a tear in the sleeve and a stain on the front. His hair was long and his jeans were cheap and his shoes were scuffed and he couldn't afford to pay for the dish he had ordered. He couldn't even afford to pay for the Norwegian water he was drinking.

Sad, he had said about Franz, when he had seen the strip mall office. *From the big green machine to this?*

What were Neagley and O'Donnell thinking about him?

'Show me the pages with the numbers,' he said.

Neagley passed seven sheets of paper across the table. She had marked them in pencil, top right-hand corner, to indicate their order. He scanned them all, one through seven, quickly, looking for overall impressions. A total of 183 proper fractions, not cancelled. Proper, in that the numerator, the top number, was always smaller than the denominator, the bottom number. Not cancelled, in that *10/12* and *8/10* were not expressed as *5/6* and *4/5*, which they would have been if the arithmetic convention had been properly followed.

Therefore, they were not really fractions at all. They were scores, or results, or performance assessments. They were saying *ten times out of twelve* or *eight times out of ten, something happened.*

Or didn't happen.

123

There were consistently twenty-six scores on each page, except for the fourth sheet, where there were twenty-seven.

The scores or the results or the ratios or whatever they were on the first three sheets looked pretty healthy. Expressed like a batting average or a win percentage they hovered between a fine .870 and an excellent .907. Then there was a dramatic fall on the fourth sheet, where the overall average looked like a .574. The fifth, sixth, and seventh sheets got progressively more and more dismal, with a .368, a .308, and a .307.

'Got it yet?' Neagley asked.

'No clue,' Reacher said. 'I wish Franz was here to explain it.'

'If he was here, we wouldn't be here.'

'We could have been. We could have all gotten together from time to time.'

'Like a class reunion?'

'It might have been fun.'

O'Donnell raised his glass and said, 'Absent friends.'

Neagley raised her glass. Reacher raised his. They drank water that had frozen at the top of a Scandinavian glacier ten thousand years ago and then inched downward over centuries before melting into mountain springs and streams, to the memory of four friends, five including Stan Lowrey, whom they assumed they would never see again.

But they assumed wrong. One of their friends had just gotten on a plane in Las Vegas.

TWENTY

A waiter brought their food. Salmon for Neagley, chicken for Reacher, tuna for O'Donnell, who said, 'I assume you've been to Franz's house.'

'Yesterday,' Neagley said. 'Santa Monica.'

'Anything there?'

'A widow and a fatherless child.'

'Anything else?'

'Nothing that meant anything.'

'We should go to all the houses. Swan's first, because it'll be the closest.'

'We don't have his address.'

'Didn't you ask the New Age lady?'

'Not worth it. She wouldn't have told us. She was very correct.'

'You could have broken her leg.'

'Those were the days.'

Reacher asked, 'Was Swan married?'

'I don't think so,' Neagley said.

'Too ugly,' O'Donnell said.

'Are you married?' Neagley asked him.

'No.'

'Well, then.'

'But for the opposite reason. It would upset too many other innocent parties.'

Reacher said, 'We could try that UPS thing again. Swan probably got packages at home. If he wasn't married he probably furnished his place from catalogues. I can't see him shopping for chairs or tables or knives and forks.'

'OK,' Neagley said. She used her cell to call Chicago, right there at the table, and looked more like a movie executive than ever. O'Donnell leaned forward and looked across her to Reacher and said, 'Go over the time line for me.'

'The dragon lady at New Age said Swan got fired more than three weeks ago. Call it twenty-four or twenty-five days. Twenty-three days ago Franz went out and never came back. His wife called Neagley fourteen days after the body was found.'

'For what reason?'

'Notification, pure and simple. She's relying on the deputies from up where it happened.'

'What's she like?'

'She's a civilian. She looks like Michelle Pfeiffer. She's halfway resentful of us for having been such good friends with her husband. Their son looks just like him.'

'Poor kid.'

Neagley covered her phone with her hand and said, 'We got cell numbers for Sanchez, Orozco and Swan.' She fumbled one-handed and took paper and pen from her purse. Wrote three numbers, ten digits each.

'Use them to get addresses,' Reacher said.

Neagley shook her head. 'They don't help.

Sanchez and Orozco's are corporate and Swan's comes back to New Age.' She clicked off with her guy in Chicago and dialled the numbers she had listed, one after another.

'Straight to voice mail,' she said. 'Switched off, all of them.'

'Inevitable,' Reacher said. 'All the batteries ran out three weeks ago.'

'I really hate hearing their voices,' she said. 'You know, you record your mailbox greeting, you have absolutely no idea what's going to happen to you.'

'A little bit of immortality,' O'Donnell said.

A busboy took their plates away. Their waiter came back with dessert menus. Reacher scanned a list of confections priced higher than a night in a motel in most parts of the United States.

'Nothing for me,' he said. He thought Neagley was going to press him, but her cell phone rang. She answered it and listened and wrote some more on her slip of paper.

'Swan's address,' she said. 'Santa Ana, near the zoo.'

O'Donnell said, 'Let's hit the road.'

They used his car, a Hertz four-door with GPS navigation, and started the slow crawl south and east to the 5.

The man called Thomas Brant watched them go. His Crown Vic was parked a block away and he was sitting on a bench in the mouth of Rodeo Drive, surrounded by two hundred tourists. He used his cell and called Curtis Mauney, his boss. Said, 'There are three of them now. It's

127

working like a charm. It's like the gathering of the clans.'

Forty yards west the man in the blue suit watched them go, too. He was slumped low in his blue Chrysler in a hairdresser's lot on Wilshire. He dialled his boss and said, 'There are three of them now. I think the new one must be O'Donnell. Therefore the bum is Reacher. They look like they've got the bit between their teeth.'

And three thousand miles away in New York City the dark-haired forty-year-old was in the shared airline offices at Park and 42nd. He was buying an open round-trip ticket from La Guardia to Denver, Colorado. He was paying for it with a platinum Visa card in the name of Alan Mason.

TWENTY-ONE

Santa Ana was way south and east, past Anaheim, down in Orange County. The township itself was twenty miles west of the Santa Ana Mountains, where the infamous winds came from. Time to time they blew in, dry, warm, steady, and they sent the whole of LA crazy. Reacher had seen their effects a couple of times. Once he had been in town after liaising with the jarheads at Camp Pendleton. Once he had been on a weekend pass from Fort Irwin. He had seen minor barroom brawls end up as multiple first-degree homicides. He had seen burned toast end up in wife-beating and prison and divorce. He had seen a guy get bludgeoned to the ground for walking too slow on the sidewalk.

But the winds weren't blowing that day. The air was hot and still and brown and heavy. O'Donnell's rented GPS had a polite insistent female voice that took them off the 5 south of the zoo, opposite Tustin. Then it led them through the spacious grid of streets toward the Orange County Museum of Art. Before they got there it turned them left and right and left again and told them they were approaching their destination. Then it told them they had arrived.

Which they clearly had.

O'Donnell coasted to a stop next to a kerbside mailbox tricked out to look like a swan. The box was a standard USPS-approved metal item set on a post and painted bright white. Along the spine at the top was attached a vertical shape jig-sawed from a wooden board. The shape had a long graceful neck and a scalloped back and a kicked-up tail. It was painted white too, except for the beak, which was dark orange, and the eye, which was black. With the bulk of the box suggesting the swell of the bird's body it was a pretty good representation.

O'Donnell said, 'Tell me Swan didn't make that.'

'Nephew or niece,' Neagley said. 'Probably a housewarming gift.'

'Which he had to use in case they visited.'

'I think it's nice.'

Behind the box a cast concrete driveway led to a double gate in a four-foot fence. Parallel to the driveway was a narrower concrete walkway that led to a single gate. The fence was made of green plastic-coated wire. All four gateposts were topped with tiny alloy pineapples. Both gates were closed. Both had store-bought *Beware Of The Dog* signs on them. The driveway led to an attached one-car garage. The walkway led to the front door of a small plain stucco bungalow painted a sun-baked tan. The windows had corrugated metal awnings over them, like eyebrows. The door had a similar thing, narrower, set high. As a whole the place was serious, severe, adequate, unfrivolous. Masculine.

And quiet, and still.

'Feels empty,' Neagley said. 'Like there's nobody home.'

Reacher nodded. The front yard was grass only. No plantings. No flowers. No shrubs. The grass looked dry and slightly long, like a meticulous owner had stopped watering it and mowing it about three weeks ago.

There was no visible alarm system.

'Let's check it out,' Reacher said.

They got out of the car and walked to the single gate. It wasn't locked or chained. They walked to the door. Reacher pushed the bell. Waited. No response. There was a slab path around the perimeter of the building. They followed it counterclockwise. There was a personnel door in the side of the garage. It was locked. There was a kitchen door in the back wall of the house. It was locked too. The top half of it was a single glass panel. Through it was visible a small kitchen, old-fashioned, unrenovated in maybe forty years, but clean and efficient. No mess. No dirty dishes. Appliances in speckled green enamel. A small table and two chairs. Empty dog bowls neatly side by side on a green linoleum floor.

Beyond the kitchen door was a slider with a step down to a small concrete patio. The patio was empty. The slider was locked. Behind it drapes were partially drawn. A bedroom, maybe used as a den.

The neighbourhood was quiet. The house was still and silent, except for a tiny subliminal hum that raised the hairs on Reacher's arms and sounded a faint alarm in the back of his mind.

'Kitchen door?' O'Donnell asked.

Reacher nodded. O'Donnell put his hand in his pocket and came out with his brass knuckles. Ceramic knuckles, technically. But they didn't have much in common with cups and saucers. They were made from some kind of a complex mineral powder, moulded under tremendous pressure and bound with epoxy adhesives. They were probably stronger than steel and certainly they were harder than brass. And the moulding process allowed wicked shapes in the striking surfaces. Being hit by a set wielded by a guy as big as David O'Donnell would be like being hit by a bowling ball studded with sharks' teeth.

O'Donnell fitted them to his hand and balled his fist. He stepped to the kitchen door and tapped the glass backhand, quite gently, like he was trying to attract an occupant's attention without startling him. The glass broke and a triangular shard fell backward into the kitchen. O'Donnell's coordination was so good that his real knuckles stopped before they reached the jagged edges. He tapped twice more and cleared a hole big enough to get a hand through. Then he slipped the knuckles off and pushed his sleeve up on his forearm and threaded his hand through and turned the inside handle.

The door sagged open.

No alarm.

Reacher went in first. Took two steps and stopped. Inside, the hum he had sensed was louder. And there was a smell in the air. Both

132

were unmistakable. He had heard similar sounds and smelled similar smells more times than he wanted to remember.

The hum was a million flies going crazy.

The smell was dead flesh, rotting and decomposing, leaking putrid fluids and gases.

Neagley and O'Donnell crowded in behind him. And stopped.

'We knew anyway,' O'Donnell said, maybe to himself. 'This is not a shock.'

'It's always a shock,' Neagley said. 'I hope it always will be.'

She covered her mouth and nose. Reacher stepped to the kitchen door. There was nothing on the hallway floor. But the smell was worse out there, and the noise was louder. There were stray flies in the air, big and blue and shiny, buzzing and darting and hitting the walls with tiny papery sounds. They were in and out of a door that was standing partially open.

'The bathroom,' Reacher said.

The house was laid out like Calvin Franz's, but it was bigger because the lots were larger in Santa Ana than they had been in Santa Monica. Cheaper real estate, more scope. There was a centre hallway and each room was a real room, not just a corner of an open-plan space. Kitchen in back, living room in front, separated by a walk-in closet. On the other side of the hallway, two bedrooms separated by a bathroom.

Impossible to say where the smell was coming from. It filled the house.

But the flies were interested in the bathroom.

The air was hot and foul. No sound, except the

insane thrashing of the flies. On porcelain, on tile, on papered walls, on the hollow wood of the door.

'Stay there,' Reacher said.

He walked down the hallway. Two paces. Three. He stopped outside the bathroom. Nudged the door with his foot. An angry black cloud of flies billowed out at him. He turned away and batted the air. Turned back. Used his foot again and pushed the door all the way open. Fanned the air and peered through the buzzing insects.

There was a body on the floor.

It was a dog.

Once it had been a German shepherd, big, beautiful, maybe a hundred pounds, maybe a hundred and ten. It was lying on its side. Its hair was dead and matted. Its mouth was open. Flies were feasting on its tongue and its nose and its eyes.

Reacher stepped right into the bathroom. Flies swarmed around his shins. There was nothing in the tub. The toilet was empty. All the water was gone from the throat. There were towels undisturbed on the rails. Dried brown stains on the floor. Not blood. Just leakage from failed sphincters.

Reacher backed out of the bathroom.

'It's his dog,' he said. 'Check the other rooms and the garage.'

There was nothing in the other rooms or the garage. No signs of struggle or disturbance, no sign of Swan himself. They regrouped in the hallway. The flies had settled back to their business in the bathroom.

'What happened here?' Neagley asked.

'Swan went out,' O'Donnell said. 'Didn't come back. The dog starved to death.'

'It died of thirst,' Reacher said.

Nobody spoke.

'The water bowl in the kitchen is dry,' Reacher said. 'Then it drank what it could from the toilet. Probably lasted about a week.'

'Awful,' Neagley said.

'You bet. I like dogs. If I lived anywhere I'd have three or four. We're going to rent a helicopter and we're going to throw these guys out one by one in little pieces.'

'When?'

'Soon.'

O'Donnell said, 'We're going to need more than we've got now.'

Reacher said, 'So let's start looking.'

They took scraps of paper towel from the kitchen and balled them up and shoved them up their noses to combat the smell. Settled down to a long and serious search. O'Donnell took the kitchen. Neagley took the living room. Reacher took Swan's bedroom.

They found nothing of any significance in any of those three places. Quite apart from the dog's predicament it was clear that Swan had gone out expecting to return. The dishwasher was half loaded and had not been run. There was food in the refrigerator and trash in the kitchen pail. Pyjamas were folded under the pillow. A half-finished book was resting on the night table. It had one of Swan's own business cards jammed in it as a placeholder: *Anthony Swan, U.S. Army (Retired), Assistant Director of Corporate Security, New Age Defense Systems, Los Angeles, California.* On the bottom of the card was an e-mail address and the same direct-line phone number that Reacher and Neagley had tried so many times.

'What exactly does New Age make?' O'Donnell asked.

'Money,' Reacher said. 'Although less than it used to, I guess.'

'Does it have a product or is it all research?'

'The woman we saw claimed they're manufacturing something somewhere.'

'What exactly?'

'We have no idea.'

The three of them tackled the second bedroom together. The one at the back of the house, with the draped slider and the step down to the empty patio. The room had a bed in it but was clearly used as a den most of the time. There was a desk and a phone and a file cabinet and a wall of shelves piled high with the kind of junk that a sentimental person accumulates.

They started with the desk. Three pairs of eyes, three separate assessments. They found nothing. They moved on to the file cabinet. It was full of the kind of routine paperwork any homeowner has. Property taxes, insurance, cancelled cheques, paid bills, receipts. There was a personal section. Social Security, state and federal income taxes, a contract of employment from New Age Defense Systems, paycheque stubs. It looked like Swan had made a decent living. In a month he had

136

pulled down what Reacher could make last a year and a half.

There was stuff from a veterinarian. The dog had been female. Her name had been Maisi and her shots had all been up to date. She had been old but in good health. There was stuff from an organization called People for the Ethical Treatment of Animals. Swan had been a contributor. Big money. Therefore a worthwhile cause, Reacher guessed. Swan was nobody's fool.

They checked the shelves. Found a shoe box full of photographs. They were random snaps from Swan's life and career. Maisi the dog was in some of them. Reacher and Neagley and O'Donnell were in others, and Franz, and Karla Dixon, and Sanchez and Orozco, and Stan Lowrey. All of them long ago in the past, younger, different in crucial ways, blazing with youth and vigour and preoccupation. There were random pairings and trios from offices and squad rooms all over the world. One was a formal group portrait, all nine of them in Class A uniforms after a ceremony for a unit citation. Reacher didn't remember who had taken the picture. An official photographer, probably. He didn't remember what the citation had been for, either.

'We need to get going,' Neagley said. 'Neighbours might have seen us.'

'We've got probable cause,' O'Donnell said. 'A friend who lives alone, no answer when we knocked on the door, a bad smell from inside.'

Reacher stepped to the desk and picked up the phone. Hit redial. There was a rapid sequence of electronic blips as the circuit remembered the last number called. Then a purring ring tone. Then Angela Franz answered. Reacher could hear Charlie in the background. He put the phone down.

'The last call he made was to Franz,' he said. 'At home in Santa Monica.'

'Reporting for duty,' O'Donnell said. 'We knew that already. Doesn't help us.'

'Nothing here helps us,' Neagley said.

'But what isn't here might,' Reacher said. 'His piece of the Berlin Wall isn't here. There's no box of stuff from his desk at New Age.'

'How does that help us?'

'It might establish a time line. You get canned, you box up your stuff, you throw it in the trunk of your car, how long do you leave it there before you bring it in the house and deal with it?'

'A day or two, maybe,' O'Donnell said. 'A guy like Swan, he's extremely pissed when it happens, but fundamentally he's a squared-away personality. He'd suck it up and move on fast enough.'

'Two days?'

'Max.'

'So all of this went down within two days of when New Age let him go.'

'How does that help us?' Neagley asked again.

'No idea,' Reacher said. 'But the more we know the luckier we'll get.'

They left through the kitchen and closed the door but didn't relock it. No point. The broken glass made it superfluous. They followed the slab path around the side of the garage to the driveway.

Headed back to the kerb. It was a quiet neighbourhood. A dormitory. Nothing was moving. Reacher scanned left and right for signs of nosy neighbours and saw none. No onlookers, no furtive eyes behind twitching drapes.

But he did see a tan Crown Victoria parked forty yards away.

Facing them.

A guy behind the wheel.

TWENTY-TWO

Reacher said, 'Come to a casual stop and turn around like you're taking one last look at the house. Make conversation.'

O'Donnell turned.

'Looks like the married officers' quarters at Fort Hood,' he said.

'Apart from the mailbox,' Reacher said.

Neagley turned.

'I like it,' she said. 'The mailbox, I mean.'

Reacher said, 'There's a tan Crown Vic parked on the kerb forty yards west. It's tailing us. Tailing Neagley, to be precise. It was there when I met her on Sunset and it was there again outside Franz's place. Now it's here.'

O'Donnell asked, 'Any idea who it is?'

'None at all,' Reacher said. 'But I think it's time to find out.'

'Like we used to?'

Reacher nodded. 'Exactly like we used to. I'll drive.'

They took one last look at Swan's house and then they turned and walked slowly back to the kerb. They slid into O'Donnell's rental, Reacher in the driver's seat, Neagley next to him in the front, O'Donnell behind him in the back. No seat belts.

'Don't hurt my car,' O'Donnell said. 'I didn't get the extra insurance.'

'You should have,' Reacher said. 'Always a wise precaution.'

He started the engine and eased away from the kerb. Checked the view ahead, checked the mirror.

Nothing coming.

He spun the wheel and stamped on the gas and pulled a fast U-turn across the width of the road. Hit the gas again and accelerated thirty yards. Jammed on the brakes and O'Donnell jumped out a yard in front of the Crown Vic and Reacher hit the gas and then the brake again and stopped dead level with the Crown Vic's driver's door. O'Donnell was already at the passenger window. Reacher jumped out and O'Donnell shattered the passenger glass with his knuckles and chased the driver out the other side of the car straight into Reacher's arms. Reacher hit him once in the gut and then again in the face. Fast and hard. The guy slammed back against the side of his car and went down on his knees. Reacher picked his spot and hit him a third time, a solid elbow against the side of his head. The guy fell sideways, slowly, like a bulldozed tree. He finished up jammed in the space between the Crown Vic's sill and the road. Sprawled out on his back, inert, unconscious, bleeding heavily from a broken nose.

'Well, that still works,' O'Donnell said.

'As long as I do the hard part,' Reacher said.

141

Neagley took hold of the loose folds of the guy's sport coat and flipped him on his side, so that the blood from his nose would pool on the blacktop rather than in the back of his throat. No point in drowning him. Then she pulled the flap of his coat open, looking for a pocket.

And then she stopped.

Because the guy was wearing a shoulder holster. An old well-used item, made of worn black leather. There was a Glock 17 in it. He was wearing a belt. The belt had a pouch for a spare magazine on it. And a pancake holder with a pair of stainless steel handcuffs in it.

Police issue.

Reacher glanced inside the Crown Vic. There were pebbles of broken glass all over the passenger seat. There was a radio mounted under the dash.

Not a taxicab radio.

'Shit,' Reacher said. 'We just took down a cop.'

'You did the hard part,' O'Donnell said.

Reacher crouched and put his fingers against the guy's neck. Felt for his pulse. It was there, strong and regular. The guy was breathing. His nose was busted bad, which would be an aesthetic problem later, but he hadn't been very good-looking to start with.

'Why was he tailing us?' Neagley said.

'We'll work that out later,' Reacher said. 'When we're a long way from here.'

'Why did you hit him so hard?'

'I was upset about the dog.'

'This guy didn't do that.'

'I know that now.'

Neagley dug through the guy's pockets. Came out with a leather ID folder. There was a chrome-plated badge pinned inside it, opposite a laminated card behind a milky plastic window.

'His name is Thomas Brant,' she said. 'He's an LA County deputy.'

'This is Orange County,' O'Donnell said. 'He's outside of his jurisdiction. As he was on Sunset and in Santa Monica.'

'Think that will help us?'

'Not very much.'

Reacher said, 'Let's get him comfortable and get the hell out of here.'

O'Donnell took Brant's feet and Reacher took his shoulders and they piled him into the rear seat of his car. They stretched him out and arranged him and left him in what medics call the recovery position, on his side, one leg drawn up, able to breathe, unlikely to choke. The Crown Vic was spacious. The engine was off and there was plenty of fresh air coming in through the broken window.

'He'll be OK,' O'Donnell said.

'He'll have to be,' Reacher said.

They closed the door on him and turned back to O'Donnell's rental. It was still right there in the middle of the street, three doors open, engine still running. Reacher got in the back. O'Donnell drove. Neagley sat next to him. The polite voice inside the GPS set about guiding them back toward the freeway.

'We should return this car,' Neagley said. 'Right now. And then my Mustang. He'll have gotten both the plate numbers.'

'And then do what for transport?' Reacher asked.

'Your turn to rent something.'

'I don't have a driver's licence.'

'Then we'll have to take cabs. We have to break the link.'

'That means changing hotels too.'

'So be it.'

The GPS wouldn't allow adjustment on the fly. A liability issue. O'Donnell pulled over and stopped and altered the destination from the Beverly Wilshire to the Hertz lot at LAX. The unit took the change in its stride. There was a second's delay while a *Calculating Route* bar spooled up and then the patient voice came back and told O'Donnell to turn around and head west instead of east, toward the 405 instead of the 5. Traffic was OK through the subdivisions and heavy on the freeway. Progress was slow.

'Tell me about yesterday,' Reacher said to Neagley.

'What about it?'

'What you did.'

'I flew into LAX and rented the car. Drove to the hotel on Wilshire. Checked in. Worked for an hour. Then I drove up to the Denny's on Sunset. Waited for you.'

'You must have been tailed all the way from the airport.'

'Clearly. The question is why.'

'No, that's the second question. The first question is *how*. Who knew when and where you were coming in?'

'The cop, obviously. He put a flag against my name and Homeland Security tipped him off as soon as I bought my ticket.'

'OK, why?'

'He's working on Franz. LA County deputies. I'm a known associate.'

'We all are.'

'I was the first to arrive.'

'So are we suspects?'

'Maybe. In the absence of any others.'

'How stupid are they?'

'They're about normal. Even we looked at known associates if we struck out everywhere else.'

Reacher said, 'You do not mess with the special investigators.'

'Correct,' Neagley said. 'But we just messed with the LA County deputies. Big time. I hope they don't have a similar slogan.'

'You can bet your ass they do.'

LAX was a gigantic, sprawling mess. Like every airport Reacher had ever seen it was permanently half finished. O'Donnell threaded through construction zones and perimeter roads and made it to the car rental returns. The different organizations were all lined up, the red one, the green one, the blue one, and finally the Hertz yellow. O'Donnell parked on the end of a long nose-to-tail line and a guy in a company jacket rushed up and scanned a barcode in the rear window with a handheld reader. That was it, vehicle returned, rental over. Chain broken.

'Now what?' O'Donnell said.

Neagley said, 'Now we take the shuttle bus to the terminal and we find a cab. Then we check out of the hotel and the two of us come back here with my Mustang. Reacher can find a new hotel and start work on those numbers. OK?'

But Reacher didn't reply. He was staring across the lot, through the rental office's plate glass windows. At the line of people inside.

He was smiling.

'What?' Neagley said. 'Reacher, what?'

'In there,' Reacher said. 'Fourth in line. See her?'

'Who?'

'Small woman, dark hair? I'm pretty sure that's Karla Dixon.'

TWENTY-THREE

Reacher and Neagley and O'Donnell hurried across the lot, getting surer with every step. By the time they were ten feet from the office windows they were absolutely certain. It was Karla Dixon. She was unmistakable. *Dark and comparatively small, a happy woman who thought the worst of people.* She was right there, now third in line. Her body language said she was simultaneously impatient with and resigned to the wait. As always she looked relaxed but never quite still, always burning energy, always giving the impression that twenty-four hours in the day were not enough for her. She was thinner than Reacher remembered. She was dressed in tight black jeans and a black leather jacket. Her thick black hair was cut short. She had a black leather Tumi roll-on next to her and a black leather briefcase slung across her shoulder.

Then as if she felt their gazes on her back she turned around and looked straight at them, nothing much in her face, as if she had last seen them minutes ago instead of years ago. She smiled a brief smile. The smile was a little sad, as if she already knew what was happening. Then she jerked her head at the clerks behind the counter as if to say, *I'll be right there but you know how it is with civilians*. Reacher pointed at himself and Neagley and O'Donnell and held up four fingers and mouthed, *Get a four-seat car*. Dixon nodded again and turned back to wait.

Neagley said, 'This is kind of biblical. People keep coming back to life.'

'Nothing biblical about it,' Reacher said. 'Our assumptions were wrong, is all.'

A fourth clerk came out of a back office and took up station behind the counter. Dixon went from being third in line to being served within about thirty seconds. Reacher saw the pink flash of a New York driver's licence and the platinum flash of a credit card changing hands. The clerk typed and Dixon signed a bunch of stuff and then received a fat yellow packet and a key. She hoisted her briefcase and grabbed her roll-on and headed for the exit. She stepped out to the side-walk. She stood in front of Reacher and Neagley and O'Donnell and looked at each of them in turn with a level, serious gaze. Said, 'Sorry I'm late to the party. But then, it's not really much of a party, is it?'

'What do you know so far?' Reacher asked her.

Dixon said, 'I only just got your messages. I didn't want to wait around in New York for a direct flight. I wanted to be on the move. First flight out was through Las Vegas. I had a two-hour layover there. So I made some calls and did some running around. Some checking. And I found out that Sanchez and Orozco are missing. It seems that about three weeks ago they just vanished off the face of the earth.'

TWENTY-FOUR

Hertz had given Dixon a Ford 500, which was a decent-sized four-seat sedan. She put her bags in the trunk and climbed in the driver's seat. Neagley sat next to her in the front and Reacher and O'Donnell squeezed in the back. Dixon started up and left the airport heading north on Sepulveda. She talked for the first five minutes. She had been working undercover as a new hire at a Wall Street brokerage house. Her client was a major institutional investor worried about illegalities. Like all undercover operatives who want to survive, she had stuck religiously to her cover, which meant she could afford no contact with her regular life. She couldn't call her office on her brokerage-supplied cell or on her brokerage-supplied landline from her brokerage-supplied corporate apartment, or get her e-mail on her brokerage-supplied Blackberry. Eventually she had checked in clandestinely from a Port Authority pay phone and found the long string of increasingly desperate 10-30s on her machine. So she had ditched her job and her client and headed straight for JFK and jumped on America West. From the Vegas airport she had called Sanchez and Orozco and gotten no reply. Worse, their voice mail was full, which was a bad sign. So she had cabbed over to their offices and found them deserted with three weeks' worth of mail backed up behind the door. Their neighbours hadn't seen them in a long time.

'So that's it,' Reacher said. 'Now we know for sure. It's just the four of us left.'

Then Neagley talked for five minutes. She gave the same kind of clear concise briefing she had given a thousand times before. No wasted words, no omitted details. She covered all the hard intelligence and all the speculation from Angela Franz's first phone call onward. The autopsy report, the small house in Santa Monica, the trashed Culver City office, the flash memories, the New Age building, O'Donnell's arrival, the dead dog, the unfortunate attack on the LA County deputy outside Swan's house in Santa Ana, the subsequent decision to ditch the Hertz cars to derail the inevitable pursuit.

'Well, that part is taken care of at least,' Dixon said. 'Nobody is following us now, so this car is clean for the time being.'

'Conclusions?' Reacher asked.

Dixon thought for three hundred yards of slow boulevard traffic. Then she slid onto the 405, the San Diego Freeway, but heading north, away from San Diego, toward Sherman Oaks and Van Nuys.

'One conclusion, mainly,' she said. 'This wasn't about Franz calling only some of us because he

151

assumed only some of us would be available. And it wasn't about him calling only some of us because he underestimated the extent of his problem. Franz was way too smart for that. And too cautious now, apparently, what with the kid and all. So we need to shift the paradigm. Look at who's here and who isn't. I think this was about Franz calling only those of us who could get to him in a big hurry. Real fast. Swan, obviously, because he was right here in town, and then Sanchez and Orozco because they were only an hour or so away in Vegas. The rest of us were no good to him. Because we were all at least a day away. So this is about speed and panic and urgency. The kind of thing where half a day makes a difference.'

'Specifically?' Reacher asked.

'No idea. It's a shame you burned the first eleven passwords. We could have seen what information was new or different.'

O'Donnell said, 'It's got to be the names. They were the only hard data.'

'Numbers can be hard data too,' Dixon said.

'You'll go blind figuring them out.'

'Maybe. Maybe not. Sometimes numbers speak to me.'

'These won't.'

There was quiet in the car for a moment. Traffic was moving OK. Dixon stayed on the 405 and blew through the intersection with the 10.

'Where are we headed?' she asked.

Neagley said, 'Let's go to the Chateau Marmont. It's out of the way and discreet.'

'And expensive,' Reacher said. Something in his tone made Dixon take her eyes off the road and glance behind her.

Neagley said, 'Reacher's broke.'

'I'm not surprised,' Dixon said. 'He hasn't worked in nine years.'

'He didn't do much when he was in the army, either,' O'Donnell said. 'Why change the habit of a lifetime?'

'He's sensitive about other people paying for him,' Neagley said.

'Poor baby,' Dixon said.

Reacher said, 'I'm just trying to be polite.'

Dixon stayed on the 405 until Santa Monica Boulevard. Then she struck out north and east, aiming to pass through Beverly Hills and West Hollywood and to hit Sunset right at the base of Laurel Canyon.

'Mission statement,' she said. 'You do not mess with the special investigators. The four of us here have to make that stick. On behalf of the four of us who aren't here. So we need a command structure and a plan and a budget.'

Neagley said, 'I'll take care of the budget.'

'Can you?'

'This year alone there's seven billion dollars of Homeland Security money washing around the private system. Some of it comes our way in Chicago and I own half of whatever part of it sticks in our books.'

'So are you rich?'

'Richer than I was when I was a sergeant.'

'We'll get it back anyway,' O'Donnell said. 'People get killed for love or money, and our guys sure as hell didn't get killed for love. So there's money in this somewhere.'

'So are we agreed on Neagley staking the budget?' Dixon asked.

'What is this, a democracy?' Reacher said.

'Temporarily. Are we agreed?'

Four raised hands. Two majors and a captain, letting a sergeant pick up the tab.

'OK, the plan,' Dixon said.

'Command structure first,' O'Donnell said. 'Can't put the cart before the horse.'

'OK,' Dixon said. 'I nominate Reacher for CO.'

'Me too,' O'Donnell said.

'Me three,' Neagley said. 'Like it always was.'

'Can't do it,' Reacher said. 'I hit that cop. If it comes to it, I'm going to have to put my hands up for it and leave the rest of you to carry on without me. Can't have a CO in that position.'

Dixon said, 'Let's cross that bridge if we come to it.'

'We're coming to it,' Reacher said. 'For sure. Tomorrow or the next day at the latest.'

'Maybe they'll let it go.'

'Dream on. Would we have let it go?'

'Maybe he'll be too shamefaced to report it.'

'He doesn't have to report it. People will notice. He's got a busted window and a busted nose.'

'Does he even know who you are?'

'He put Neagley's name in the machine. He was tailing us. He knows who we are.'

'You can't put your hands up for it,' O'Donnell said. 'You'll go to jail. If it comes to it, you'll have to get out of town.'

'Can't do that. If they don't get me, they'll come after you and Neagley as accessories. We don't want that. We need boots on the ground here.'

'We'll get you a lawyer. A cheap one.'

'No, a good one,' Dixon said.

'Whatever, I'll still be preoccupied,' Reacher said.

Nobody spoke.

Reacher said, 'Neagley should be CO.'

'I decline,' Neagley said.

'You can't decline. It's an order.'

'It can't be an order until you're CO.'

'Dixon, then.'

'Declined,' Dixon said.

'OK, O'Donnell.'

'Pass.'

Dixon said, 'Reacher until he goes to jail. Then Neagley. All in favour?'

Three hands went up.

'You'll regret this,' Reacher said. 'I'll make you regret it.'

'So what's the plan, boss?' Dixon asked, and the question sent Reacher spinning nine years into the past, to the last time he had heard anyone ask it.

'Same as ever,' he said. 'We investigate, we prepare, we execute. We find them, we take them down, and then we piss on their ancestors' graves.'

TWENTY-FIVE

The Chateau Marmont was a bohemian old pile on Sunset near the foot of Laurel Canyon. All kinds of movie stars and rock stars had stayed there. There were plenty of photographs on the walls. Errol Flynn, Clark Gable, Marilyn Monroe, Greta Garbo, James Dean, John Lennon, Mick Jagger, Bob Dylan, Jim Morrison. Led Zeppelin and Jefferson Airplane had booked in there. John Belushi had died in there, after speedballing enough heroin and cocaine to take down every guest in the hotel. There were no photographs of him.

The desk clerk wanted IDs along with Neagley's platinum card, so they all checked in under their real names. No choice. Then the guy told them there were only three rooms available. Neagley had to be alone, so Reacher and O'Donnell bunked together and let the women have a room each. Then O'Donnell drove Neagley back to the Beverly Wilshire in Dixon's car to pick up their bags and check out. Then Neagley would take the Mustang back to LAX and O'Donnell would follow her in convoy to bring her back. It would be a three-hour hiatus. Reacher and Dixon would stay behind and spend the three hours working on the numbers.

They set up in Dixon's room. According to the desk guy Leonardo diCaprio had been in there once, but there was no remaining sign of him. Reacher laid the seven spreadsheets side by side on the bed and watched as Dixon bent down and scanned them, the same way some people read music or poetry.

'Two key issues,' she said immediately. 'There are no hundred per cent scores. No ten out of ten, no nine out of nine.'

'And?'

'The first three sheets have twenty-six numbers, the fourth has twenty-seven, and the last three all have twenty-six again.'

'Which means what?'

'I don't know. But none of the sheets is full. Therefore the twenty-six and twenty-seven thing must mean something. It's deliberate, not accidental. It's not just a continuous list of numbers with page breaks. If it was, Franz could have gotten them on to six sheets, not seven. So it's seven separate categories of something.'

'Separate but similar,' Reacher said. 'It's a descriptive sequence.'

'The scores get worse,' Dixon said.

'Radically.'

'And quite suddenly. They're OK, and then they fall off a cliff.'

'But what are they?'

'No idea.'

Reacher asked, 'What can be measured like that, repetitively?'

'Anything can, I guess. Could be mental health, answers to simple questions. Could be physical performance, coordination tasks. It could be that errors are being recorded, in which case the numbers are actually getting better, not worse.'

'What are the categories? What are we looking at? Seven of what?'

Dixon nodded. 'That's the key. We need to understand that first.'

'Can't be medical tests. Can't be any kind of tests. Why stick twenty-seven questions in the middle of a sequence where everything else is twenty-six questions? That would destroy consistency.'

Dixon shrugged and stood up straight. She took off her jacket and dumped it on a chair. Walked to the window and pulled a faded drape aside and looked out and down. Then up at the hills.

'I like LA,' she said.

'Me too, I guess,' Reacher said.

'I like New York better.'

'Me too, probably.'

'But the contrast is nice.'

'I guess.'

'Shitty circumstances, but it's great to see you again, Reacher. Really great.'

Reacher nodded. 'Likewise. We thought we'd lost you. Didn't feel good.'

'Can I hug you?'

'You want to hug me?'

'I wanted to hug all of you at the Hertz office.

But I didn't, because Neagley wouldn't have liked it.'

'She shook Angela Franz's hand. And the dragon lady's, at New Age.'

'That's progress,' Dixon said.

'A little,' Reacher said.

'She was abused, way back. That was always my guess.'

'She'll never talk about it,' Reacher said.

'It's sad.'

'You bet.'

Karla Dixon turned to him and Reacher took her in his arms and hugged her hard. She was fragrant. Her hair smelled of shampoo. He lifted her off her feet and spun her around, a complete slow circle. She felt light and thin and fragile. Her back was narrow. She was wearing a black silk shirt, and her skin felt warm underneath it. He set her back on her feet and she stretched up tall and kissed his cheek.

'I've missed you,' she said. 'Missed you all, I mean.'

'Me too,' he said. 'I didn't realize how much.'

'You like life after the army?' she asked.

'Yes, I like it fine.'

'I don't. But maybe you're reacting better than me.'

'I don't know how I'm reacting. I don't know whether I'm reacting at all. I look at you people and I feel like I'm just treading water. Or drowning. You all are swimming.'

'Are you really broke?'

'Almost penniless.'

'Me too,' she said. 'I earn three hundred grand

159

a year and I'm on the breadline. That's life. You're well out of it.'

'I feel that way, usually. Until I have to get back in it. Neagley put a thousand and thirty bucks in my bank account.'

'Like a ten-thirty radio code? Smart girl.'

'And for my air fare. Without that I'd still be on my way down here, hitch-hiking.'

'You'd be walking. Nobody in their right mind would pick you up.'

Reacher glanced at himself in an old spotted mirror. Six-five, two-fifty, hands as big as frozen turkeys, hair all over the place, unshaven, torn shirt cuffs up on his forearms like Frankenstein's monster.

A bum.

From the big green machine to this.

Dixon said, 'Can I ask you a question?'

'Go ahead.'

'I always wished we had done more than just work together.'

'Who?'

'You and me.'

'That was a statement, not a question.'

'Did you feel the same way?'

'Honestly?'

'Please.'

'Yes, I did.'

'So why didn't we do more?'

'Wouldn't have been right.'

'We ignored all kinds of other regulations.'

'It would have wrecked the unit. The others would have been jealous.'

'Including Neagley?'

'In her way.'

'We could have kept it a secret.'

Reacher said, 'Dream on.'

'We could keep it a secret now. We've got three hours.'

Reacher said nothing.

Dixon said, 'I'm sorry. It's just that all of this bad stuff makes me feel that life is so short.'

Reacher said, 'And the unit is wrecked now anyway.'

'Exactly.'

'Don't you have a boyfriend back East?'

'Not right now.'

Reacher stepped back to the bed. Karla Dixon came over and stood right next to him, her hip against his thigh. The seven sheets of paper were still laid out in a line.

'Want to look at these some more?' Reacher asked.

'Not right now,' Dixon said.

'Me either.' He gathered them up and butted them together. Placed them on the night stand and trapped them under the phone. Asked, 'You sure about this?'

'I've been sure for fifteen years.'

'Me too. But it has to stay a secret.'

'Agreed.'

He took her in his arms and kissed her mouth. The shape of her teeth was new to his tongue. The buttons on her shirt were small and awkward.

TWENTY-SIX

Afterwards they lay in bed together and Dixon said, 'We need to get back to work.' Reacher rolled over to take the stack of papers off the night stand but Dixon said, 'No, let's do it in our heads. We'll see more that way.'

'Will we?'

'Total of one hundred and eighty-three numbers,' she said. 'Tell me about one hundred and eighty-three, *as* a number.'

'Not prime,' Reacher said. 'It's divisible by three and sixty-one.'

'I don't care whether it's prime or not.'

'Multiply it by two and you get three hundred and sixty-six, which is the number of days in a leap year.'

'So is this half a leap year?'

'Not with seven lists,' Reacher said. 'Half of any kind of a year would be six months and six lists.'

Dixon went quiet.

Reacher thought: *Half a year.*

Half.

More than one way to skin a cat.

Twenty-six, twenty-seven.

He said, 'How many days are there in half a year?'

'A regular year? Depends which half. Either one hundred and eighty-two or one hundred and eighty-three.'

'How do you make half?'

'Divide by two.'

'Suppose you multiplied by seven over twelve?'

'That's more than half.'

'Then again by six over seven?'

'That would bring it back to exactly half. Forty-two over eighty-four.'

'There you go.'

'I don't follow.'

'How many weeks in a year?'

'Fifty-two.'

'How many working days?'

'Two hundred sixty for five-day weeks, three hundred twelve for six-day weeks.'

'So how many days would there be in seven months' worth of six-day working weeks?'

Dixon thought for a second. 'Depends on which seven months you pick. Depends on where the Sundays fall. Depends on what day of the week January first is. Depends on whether you're looking at a continuous run of months or cherry-picking.'

'Run the numbers, Karla. There are only two possible answers.'

Dixon paused a beat. 'One hundred and eighty-two or one hundred and eighty-three.'

'Exactly,' Reacher said. 'Those seven sheets are seven months' worth of six-day working

163

weeks. One of the long months only had four Sundays. Hence the twenty-seven day anomaly.'

Dixon slid out from under the sheet and walked naked to where she had left her briefcase and came back with a leather Filofax diary. She opened it out and put it on the bed and took the papers off the night stand and arranged them in a line below the diary. Her eyes flicked back and forth, seven times.

'It's this year,' she said. 'It's the last seven calendar months. Right up to the end of last month. Take out the Sundays, you get three twenty-six-day months, then one twenty-seven-day month, and then three more twenty-six-day months.'

'There you go,' Reacher said. 'Some kind of six-day-a-week figures got worse and worse over the last seven months. Some kind of results. We're halfway there.'

'The easy half,' Dixon said. 'Now tell me what the figures mean.'

'Something was supposed to happen nine or ten or twelve or thirteen times a day Monday through Saturday and didn't always come out right.'

'What kind of something?'

'I don't know. What kind of a thing happens ten or twelve times a day?'

'Not Model-T Ford production, that's for sure. It's got to be something small scale. Or professional. Like a dentist's appointments. Or a lawyer's. Or a hairdresser's.'

'There was a nail salon near Franz's office.'

'They do more than that in a day. And how

164

would nails relate to four people disappearing and a Syrian with four aliases?'

'I don't know,' Reacher said.

'Me either,' Dixon said.

'We should shower and get dressed.'

'After.'

'After what?'

Dixon didn't answer. Just walked back to the bed and pinned him to the pillow and kissed him again.

Two thousand horizontal and seven vertical miles away from them the dark-haired forty-year-old currently calling himself Alan Mason was in the front cabin of a United Airlines Boeing 757, en route from La Guardia, New York, to Denver, Colorado. He was in seat 3A, with a glass of sparkling mineral water beside him on the armrest tray and a newspaper open on his lap. But he wasn't reading it. He was gazing out of the window instead, at the bright white clouds below.

And eight miles south of them the man in the dark blue suit in the dark blue Chrysler was tailing O'Donnell and Neagley back from the LAX Hertz lot. He had picked them up leaving the Beverly Wilshire. He had guessed they were flying out, so he had positioned himself to follow them to the airport terminals. When O'Donnell had swung back north on Sepulveda he had needed to scramble fast to get behind them. As a result he was ten cars back all the way. Which was good, he figured, in terms of inconspicuous surveillance.

TWENTY-SEVEN

O'Donnell said, 'We're nowhere at all,' and Neagley said, 'We need to face facts. The trail is stone cold and we have virtually no useful data.'

They were in Karla Dixon's bedroom. Leonardo diCaprio's old crib. The bed was made. Reacher and Dixon were showered and dressed and their hair was dry. They were standing well apart from one another. The seven spreadsheets were laid out on the dresser with the diary next to them. No one disputed that they represented the last seven calendar months. But no one saw how that information helped them, either.

Dixon looked at Reacher and asked, 'What do you want to do, boss?'

'Take a break,' Reacher said. 'We're missing something. We're not thinking straight. We should take a break and come back to it.'

'We never used to take breaks.'

'We used to have five more pairs of eyes.'

The man in the dark blue suit called it in: 'They moved to the Chateau Marmont. And there's four of them now. Karla Dixon showed up. So

166

they're all present and correct and accounted for.'
Then he listened to his boss's reply, and pictured
him smoothing his tie over the front of his shirt.

Reacher went for a walk west on Sunset, alone.
Solitude was still his natural condition. He took
his money out of his pocket and counted it. Not
much left. He ducked into a souvenir store and
found a rail of discounted shirts. Last year's
styles. Or the last decade's. On one end of the rail
was a bunch of blue items with white patterns,
shiny, some kind of a man-made material. Spread
collars, short sleeves, square hems. He picked one
out. It was like something his father might have
worn to go bowling in the 1950s. Except three
sizes larger. Reacher was much bigger than his
father had been. He found a mirror and jammed
the hanger up under his chin. The shirt looked
like it might fit him. It was probably wide enough
in the shoulders. The short sleeves would solve
the problem of trying to find something to accommodate the length of his arms. His arms were like
a gorilla's, only longer and thicker.

With tax the garment cost nearly twenty-one
dollars. Reacher paid the guy at the register and
then bit off the tags and stripped off his old shirt
and put the new one on right there and then. Left
it untucked. Tugged it down at the bottom and
rolled his shoulders. With the top button open it
fit pretty well. The sleeves were tight around his
biceps but not so bad that his blood flow was
imperilled.

'Got a trash can?' he asked.

The guy ducked down and came back with a

round metal canister lined with a white plastic bag. Reacher balled up his old shirt and tossed it in.

'Barbershop near here?' he asked.

'Two blocks north,' the guy said. 'Up the hill. Shoeshines and haircuts in the corner of the grocery store.'

Reacher said nothing.

'Laurel Canyon,' the guy said, like an explanation.

The grocery store sold beer out of ice chests and coffee out of press-top flasks. Reacher took a medium cup of house blend, black, and headed for the barber's chair. It was an old-fashioned thing covered in red speckled vinyl. There were straight razors on the sink and a shoeshine chair nearby. A thin guy in a white wife-beater was sitting in it. He had needle tracks up and down his arms. He looked up and concentrated, like he was assessing the size of the task ahead of him.

'Let me guess,' he said. 'Shave and a haircut?'

'Two bits?' Reacher said.

'Eight dollars,' the guy said.

Reacher checked his pocket again.

'Ten,' he said. 'To include a shoeshine and the coffee.'

'That all would be twelve.'

'Ten is what I've got.'

The guy shrugged and said, 'Whatever.'

Laurel Canyon, Reacher thought. Thirty minutes later he was down to his last dollar but his shoes were clean and his face was as smooth as it had ever been. His head was shaved almost as close. He had asked for a standard army buzz cut but the guy had given him something a whole lot closer to the Marine Corps version. Clearly not a veteran. Reacher paused a beat and checked the guy's arms again.

He asked, 'Where can a person score around here?'

'You're not a user,' the guy said.

'For a friend.'

'You don't have any money.'

'I can get some.'

The guy in the wife-beater shrugged and said, 'There's usually a crew behind the wax museum.'

Reacher walked back to the hotel by staying in the low canyon streets for two blocks and then coming on it from the rear. Along the way he passed a dark blue Chrysler 300C parked on the kerb. A guy in a dark blue suit was behind the wheel. The suit matched the sheet metal, more or less exactly. The engine was off and the guy was just waiting. Reacher assumed it was a livery car. A limo. He figured some enterprising car service owner had gotten a better price from the Chrysler dealership than the Lincoln dealership and had switched away from Town Cars. Figured he had dressed the drivers in matching suits, looking for an edge. Reacher knew that LA was a tough market, in the limousine business. He had read about it somewhere.

Dixon and Neagley were polite about his new shirt but O'Donnell laughed at it. They all laughed at his haircut. Reacher didn't care. He caught sight of it in Dixon's spotted old mirror and had to agree it was a little extreme. It was a real whitewall. And he was happy to provide a moment of levity. They weren't going to get any light relief anyplace else, that was for sure. Together they had handled two years' worth of crimes, some of them gruesome, some of them merely venal, some of them cruel, some of them appalling, and they had joked their way through like cops everywhere. Black humour. The universal refuge. One time they had found a partially decomposed dead guy with a gardening shovel buried in what was left of his head and immediately rechristened the corpse Doug and laughed like drains. Later in a court martial proceeding Stan Lowrey had slipped and used the nickname instead of the real name. A JAG defender hadn't understood the reference. Lowrey had laughed all over again on the witness stand and said, *Like, dug? Shovel in his head? Get it?*

No one was laughing now. It was different when it was your own.

The spreadsheets were back on the bed. One hundred and eighty-three days over a seven-month span. A total of 2,197 events. There was a new page next to them in Dixon's handwriting. She had extrapolated the numbers out to three hundred and fourteen days and 3,766 events in a complete year. Reacher guessed she had invited the others to brainstorm about what kind of a thing happens 3,766 times over three hundred and fourteen days in a year. But the rest of the page was blank. Nobody had come up with anything.

The sheet with the five names was on the pillow. It was lying at a careless angle, like someone had been studying it and then thrown it down in frustration.

'There must be more than this,' O'Donnell said.

'What exactly do you want?' Reacher said back. 'Cliff Notes?'

'I'm saying there isn't enough here for four people to have died for it.'

Reacher nodded.

'I agree,' he said. 'It ain't much. Because the bad guys got practically everything. His computers, his Rolodex, his client list, his phone book. All we've got is the tip of the iceberg. Fragments. Like archaeological remains. But we better get used to it, because this kind of thing is all we're ever going to get.'

'So what do we do?'

'Break the habit.'

'What habit?'

'Asking me what to do. I might not be here tomorrow. I imagine those deputies are gearing up right now. You're going to have to start thinking for yourselves.'

'Until then what do we do?'

Reacher ignored the question. Turned instead to Karla Dixon and asked, 'When you rented your car, did you get the extra insurance?'

She nodded.

'OK,' Reacher said. 'Take another break. Then we'll go get some dinner. My treat. Maybe like the last supper. I'll meet you in the lobby in an hour.'

171

Reacher got Dixon's Ford from the valets and drove east on Hollywood Boulevard. He passed the Entertainment Museum and Mann's Chinese Theater. Made the left on Highland. He was two blocks west of Hollywood and Vine, which was where the bad stuff had traditionally been. Now the bad stuff seemed to have migrated, which was usually the way. Law enforcement never really won. It just shoved stuff around, a block here, a block there.

Reacher pulled into the kerb. There was a wide alley behind the wax museum. Really a vacant half-lot, gravel surface, unfenced, colonized by cars into a turning loop, recolonized by dealers into a drive-through facility. The operation was organized in the conventional triangulated manner. A buyer would drive in and slow up. A kid not more than eleven years old would approach. The driver would place his order and hand over his cash. The kid would run the cash to a bag man and then continue to a stash man and pick up the product. Meanwhile the driver would be crawling through a slow half-circle, ready to meet the kid again on the other side of the lot. Whereupon the transfer would be made and the driver would leave. The kid would run back to where he began and wait to start all over again.

A smart system. Complete separation of product and money, easy instant dispersal in three different directions if necessary, and no one was seen with anything except someone way too young to be prosecuted. The stash would be refreshed often, leaving the stash man holding the

172

bare minimum at any one time. The cash bag would be emptied frequently, reducing potential losses and the bag man's vulnerability.

A smart system.

A system Reacher had seen before.

A system he had exploited before.

The bag man was literally a bag man. He was sitting on a concrete block in the middle of the lot with a black vinyl duffel at his feet. He was wearing sunglasses and would be armed with whatever was the handgun of choice that week.

Reacher waited.

A black Mercedes ML slowed and pulled into the lot. A pretty SUV, tinted windows, California vanity plates spelling out an acronym Reacher didn't understand. It paused at the entry and the kid ran up. His head barely reached the driver's window. But his hand did. It snaked up and came back down with a folded wad. The Mercedes eased forward and the kid ran over to the bag man. The wad went into the bag and the kid headed for the stash man. The Mercedes was beginning to turn its slow half-circle.

Reacher put Dixon's Ford in gear. Checked north, checked south. Hit the gas and turned the wheel and slammed into the lot. Ignored the worn circular path and aimed straight for the centre of the space.

Straight for the bag man, accelerating, front wheels spraying gravel.

The bag man froze.

Ten feet before hitting him head-on Reacher did three things. He twitched the wheel. He stamped on the brake. And he opened his door.

The car slewed right and the front wheels washed into the loose stones and the door swung out through a moving arc and caught the guy like a full-on punch. It smacked him solidly from his waist up to his face. He went over backward and the car stopped dead and Reacher leaned down and grabbed the vinyl duffel left-handed from the floor. Pitched it into the passenger seat and hit the gas and slammed his door shut and pulled a tight U-turn inside the slow Mercedes. Roared back out of the lot and bounced over the kerb onto Highland. In the mirror he saw dust in the air and confusion and the bag man flat on his back and two guys running. Ten yards later he was behind the bulk of the wax museum. Then he was through the light, back on Hollywood Boulevard.

Twelve seconds, beginning to end.

No reaction. No gunshots. No pursuit.

Nor would there be any, Reacher guessed. They would have clocked the plain-vanilla Ford and the appalling shirt and the short hair and put it down to an LAPD freelance looking to supplement his pension fund. The cost of doing business. And the Mercedes driver couldn't afford to say a word to anyone.

Yeah baby, you do not mess *with the special investigators.*

Reacher slowed and caught his breath and made a right and drove a complete counter-clockwise scenic circle. Nichols Canyon Road, Woodrow Wilson Drive, and back on Laurel Canyon Boulevard. Nobody was behind him. He stopped on a deserted hairpin up high and emptied the bag and ditched it on the shoulder. Then he counted the money. Close to nine hundred dollars, mostly in twenties and tens. Enough for dinner. Even with Norwegian water. And a tip.

He got out and checked the car. The driver's door was a little dented, right in the centre. The bag man's face. No blood. He got back in and buckled up. Ten minutes later he was in the Chateau Marmont's lobby, sitting in a faded velvet armchair, waiting for the others.

Twelve hundred miles northeast of the Chateau Marmont the dark-haired forty-year-old calling himself Alan Mason was riding the underground train from his arrival gate to the Denver airport's main terminal. He was alone in the car, sitting down, tired, but smiling all the same at the crazy bursts of jug-band music that preceded the station announcements. He figured they had been specified by a psychologist to reduce travel stress. In which case they were working. He felt fine. A lot more relaxed than he had any right to be.

TWENTY-EIGHT

In the event dinner cost Reacher way less than nine hundred bucks. Either out of taste or preference or respect for the context or deference to his economic predicament the others opted for a noisy hamburger barn on Sunset, just east of the Mondrian Hotel. There was no Norwegian water on offer. Just tap and domestic beer and thick juicy patties and pickles and loud vintage rhythm and blues. Reacher looked right at home, in a Fifties kind of a way. The others looked a little out of place. They were at a round table set for four. Conversation stopped and started as the pleasure of being among old friends was overtaken by memories of the others who were missing. Reacher mostly listened. The dynamic of the round table meant that no one person was dominant. The centre of attention bounced back and forth randomly. After thirty minutes of reminiscence and catch-up the talk turned back to Franz.

O'Donnell said, 'Start at the very beginning. If we believe his wife, he quit everything except routine database mining more than four years ago. So why would he suddenly launch into something this serious?'

Dixon said, 'Because someone asked him to.'

'Exactly,' O'Donnell said. 'This thing starts with his client. So who was it?'

'Could have been anybody.'

'No,' O'Donnell said. 'It was someone special. He went the extra mile here. He broke a four-year habit for this guy. Kind of broke faith with his wife and son, too.'

Neagley said, 'It could have been a big payer.'

'Or someone he was obligated to somehow,' Dixon said.

Neagley said, 'Or it might have looked routine at the get-go. Maybe he had no idea where it was leading. Maybe the client didn't, either.'

Reacher listened. *It was someone special. Someone he was obligated to somehow.* He watched as O'Donnell took the floor, then Dixon, then Neagley. The vector bounced around between them and traced a heavy triangle in the air. Something stirred in the back of his mind. Something Dixon had said, hours ago, in the car leaving LAX. He closed his eyes, but he couldn't get it. He spoke up and the triangle changed to a square, to include him.

'We should ask Angela,' he said. 'If he had some kind of a longstanding big-deal client, he might have mentioned him at home.'

'I'd like to meet Charlie,' O'Donnell said.

'We'll go tomorrow,' Reacher said. 'Unless the deputies come for me. In which case you can go on ahead without me.'

'Look on the bright side,' Dixon said. 'Maybe

177

you gave the guy a concussion. Maybe he doesn't remember who he is, let alone who you are.'

They walked back to the hotel and split up in the lobby. No appetite for a nightcap. Just an unspoken agreement to get some sleep and start work again bright and early. Reacher and O'Donnell headed up together. Didn't talk much. Reacher was asleep five seconds after his head hit the pillow.

He woke up again at seven o'clock in the morning. Early sun was coming in the window. David O'Donnell was coming in the door. In a hurry. Fully dressed, a newspaper under his arm, cardboard cups of coffee in both hands.

'I went for a walk,' he said.

'And?'

'You're in trouble,' he said. 'I think.'

'Who?'

'That deputy. He's parked a hundred yards from here.'

'The same guy?'

'The same guy and the same car. He's got a metal splint on his face and a garbage bag taped across his window.'

'Did he see you?'

'No.'

'What's he doing?'

'Just sitting there. Like he's waiting.'

TWENTY-NINE

They ordered breakfast in Dixon's room. First rule, learned a long time ago: eat when you can, because you never know when the next chance will come. Especially when you're about to disappear into the system. Reacher shovelled eggs and bacon and toast down his throat and followed it with plenty of coffee. He was calm, but frustrated.

'I should have stayed in Portland,' he said. 'I might as well have.'

'How did they find us so fast?' Dixon asked.

'Computers,' Neagley said. 'Homeland Security and the Patriot Act. They can search hotel registers any time they want now. This is a police state.'

'We are the police,' O'Donnell said.

'We used to be.'

'I wish we still were. You'd hardly have to break a sweat any more.'

'You guys get going,' Reacher said. 'I don't want you to get snarled up in this. We can't spare the time. So don't let the deputy see you leave. Go visit with Angela Franz. Chase the client. I'll get back to you when I can.'

He drained the last of his coffee and headed back to his room. Put his folding toothbrush in his pocket and hid his passport and his ATM card and seven hundred of his remaining eight hundred dollars in O'Donnell's suit carrier. Because certain things can go missing, after an arrest. Then he took the elevator down to the lobby. Just sat in an armchair and waited. No need to turn the whole thing into a big drama, running up and down hotel corridors. Because, second rule, learned from a lifetime of bad luck and trouble: maintain a little dignity.

He waited.

Thirty minutes. Sixty. The lobby had three morning papers, and he read them all. Every word. Sports, features, editorials, national, international. And business. There was a story about Homeland Security's financial impact on the private sector. It quoted the same seven-billion-dollar figure that Neagley had mentioned. A lot of money. Surpassed only, the article said, by the bonanza for the defence contractors. The Pentagon still had more cash than anyone else, and it was still spreading it around like crazy.

Ninety minutes.

Nothing happened.

At the two-hour point Reacher got up and put the papers back on the rack. Stepped to the door and looked outside. Bright sun, blue sky, not much smog. A light wind tossing exotic trees. Waxed cars rolling past, slow and glittering. A fine day. The twenty-fourth day Calvin Franz hadn't been around to see. Nearly four whole weeks. Same for Tony Swan and Jorge Sanchez and Manuel Orozco, presumably.

There are dead men walking, as of right now. You don't throw my friends out of helicopters and live to tell the tale.

Reacher stepped outside. Stood for a second, exposed, like he was expecting sniper fire. Certainly there had been time to get whole SWAT teams into position. But the sidewalk was quiet. No parked vehicles. No innocuous florists' trucks. No bogus telephone linemen. No surveillance. He turned left on Sunset. Left again on Laurel Canyon Boulevard. Walked slow and kept close to hedges and plantings. Turned left again on the winding canyon road that ran behind the hotel.

The tan Crown Vic was dead ahead.

It was parked on the far kerb, alone, isolated, a hundred yards away. Still, inert, engine off. Like O'Donnell had said, its broken front passenger window was taped over with a black garbage bag, pulled taut. The driver was in the seat. Just sitting there. Not moving, except for regular turns of his head. Rear view mirror, straight ahead, door mirror. The guy had a real rhythm going. Hypnotic. Rear view mirror, straight ahead, door mirror. Reacher caught a flash of an aluminum splint fixed across his nose.

The car looked low and cold, like it hadn't been run for many hours.

The guy was on his own, just watching and waiting.

But for what?

Reacher turned around and backtracked the way he had come. Made it back to the lobby and

181

back to his chair. Sat down again, with the seed of a germ of a new theory in his mind.

His wife called me, Neagley had said.

What did she want you to do?

Nothing, Neagley had said. *She was just telling me.*

Just telling me.

And then: Charlie swinging on the door handle. Reacher had asked: *Is it OK to be opening the door all by yourself?* And the little boy had said: *Yes, it's OK.*

And then: *Charlie, you should go out and play.*

And then: *I think there's something you're not telling us.*

The cost of doing business.

Reacher sat in the Chateau Marmont's velvet lobby armchair, thinking, waiting to be proved right or wrong by whoever came through the street door first, his old unit or a bunch of fired-up LA County deputies.

THIRTY

His old unit came through the door first. What was left of it, anyway. The remnant. O'Donnell and Neagley and Dixon, all of them fast and anxious. They stopped dead in surprise when they saw him and he raised a hand in greeting.

'You're still here,' O'Donnell said.

'No, I'm an optical illusion.'

'Outstanding.'

'What did Angela say?'

'Nothing. She doesn't know anything about his clients.'

'How was she?'

'Like a woman whose husband just died.'

'What did you think of Charlie?'

'Nice kid. Like his dad. Franz lives on, in a way.'

Dixon said, 'Why are you still here?'

'That's a very good question,' Reacher said.

'What's the answer?'

'Is the deputy still out there?'

Dixon nodded. 'We saw him from the end of the street.'

'Let's go upstairs.'

*   *   *

They used the room that Reacher and O'Donnell were in. It was a little bigger than Dixon's, because it was a double. The first thing Reacher did was retrieve his money and his passport and his ATM card from O'Donnell's bag.

O'Donnell said, 'Looks like you think you're sticking around.'

'I think I am,' Reacher said.

'Why?'

'Because Charlie opened the door all by himself.'

'Which means?'

'Seems to me that Angela is a pretty good mom. Normal, at worst. Charlie was clean, well fed, well dressed, well balanced, well cared for, well looked after. So we can conclude that Angela is doing a conscientious job with the parenting thing. Yet she let the kid open the door to a couple of complete strangers.'

Dixon said, 'Her husband was just killed. Maybe she was distracted.'

'More likely the opposite. Her husband was killed more than three weeks ago. My guess is she's over whatever initial reaction she had. Now she's clinging to Charlie more than ever because he's all she's got left. Yet she let the kid get the door. Then she told him to go out to play. She didn't say, go play in his room. She said, go out. In Santa Monica? In a yard on a busy street full of passers-by? Why would she do that?'

'I don't know.'

'Because she knew it was safe.'

'How?'

184

'Because she knew that deputy was watching the house.'

'You think?'

'Why did she wait fourteen days before calling Neagley?'

'She was distracted,' Dixon said again.

'Possibly,' Reacher said. 'But maybe there's another reason. Maybe she wasn't going to call us at all. We were ancient history. She liked Franz's current life better. Naturally, because she *was* Franz's current life. We represented the bad old days, rough, dangerous, uncouth. I think she was disapproving. Or if not, then a little jealous.'

'I agree,' Neagley said. 'That's the impression I got.'

'So why did she call you?'

'I don't know.'

'Think about it from the deputies' point of view. Small department, limited resources. They find a dead guy in the desert, they ID him, they set the wheels in motion. They do it by the book. First thing they do is profile the victim. Along the way they find out that he used to be a part of a shit-hot investigative team in the military. And they find out that all but one of his old buddies are supposedly still around somewhere.'

'And they suspect us?'

'No, I think they dismiss us as suspects and they move right along. But they get nowhere. No clues, no leads, no breaks. They're stuck.'

'So?'

'So after two weeks of frustration they get an idea. Angela has told them all about the unit and the loyalty and the old slogan, and they see an opportunity. Effectively they've got a freelance investigative team waiting in the wings. One that's smart and experienced and above all one that's going to be very highly motivated. So they prompt Angela to call us. Just to tell us, nothing more. Because they know that's the exact same thing as winding up the Energizer Bunny. They know we're going to get down here pretty damn fast. They know we're going to look for answers. They know they can just stay in the shadows and watch us and piggy-back on whatever we do.'

'That's ridiculous,' O'Donnell said.

'But I think it's exactly what happened,' Reacher said. 'Angela told them it was Neagley she had gotten on the phone, they put Neagley's name on a watch list, they picked her up when she got to town, they tailed her and lay back in the weeds and watched the rest of us show up one by one. And they've been watching everything we've been doing ever since. Police work by proxy. That's what Angela wasn't telling us. The deputies asked her to set us up as stalking horses and she agreed. And that's why I'm still here. There's no other explanation. They figure a busted nose is the price of doing business.'

'That's nuts.'

'Only one way to find out. Take a walk around the block and talk to the deputy.'

'You think?'

'Dixon should go. She wasn't with us in Santa Ana. So if I'm wrong the guy probably won't shoot her.'

186

THIRTY-ONE

Dixon went. She left the room without a word. O'Donnell said, 'I don't think Angela was hiding anything today. So I don't think Franz had a client at all.'

'How hard did you press her?' Reacher asked.

'We didn't need to press her. It was all right out there. She had nothing to tell us. It's inconceivable that Franz would have gotten into a thing like this for anyone except a big-deal regular customer who went back years, and it's inconceivable he could have had such a guy without Angela at least hearing a name.'

Reacher nodded. Then he smiled, briefly. He liked his old team. He could rely on them, absolutely. No second guessing. If Neagley and Dixon and O'Donnell went out with questions, they came back with answers. Always, whatever the issue, whatever it took. He could send them to Atlanta and they would come back with the Coke recipe.

Neagley asked, 'What next?'

'Let's talk to the deputies first,' Reacher said. 'Specifically let's see if they went out to Vegas.'

'To Sanchez and Orozco's office? Dixon was just there. It hadn't been disturbed.'

'She didn't check their homes.'

Dixon came back thirty minutes later. Said, 'He didn't shoot me.'

'That's good,' Reacher said.

'I certainly thought so.'

'Did he 'fess up to anything?'

'He didn't confirm or deny.'

'Is he mad about his face?'

'Livid.'

'So what's the story?'

'He called his boss. They want to meet with us. Here, an hour from now.'

'Who's his boss?'

'A guy called Curtis Mauney. LA County Sheriff's Department.'

'OK,' Reacher said. 'We can do that. We'll see what the guy has got. We'll treat him like some asshole provost marshal. All take and no give.'

They waited the hour downstairs in the lobby. No stress, no strain. Military service teaches a person how to wait. O'Donnell sprawled on a sofa and cleaned his fingernails with his switchblade. Dixon read the seven spreadsheets over and over and then put them away and closed her eyes. Neagley sat alone in a chair against a wall. Reacher sat under an old framed photograph of Raquel Welch. The picture had been taken outside the hotel late in the afternoon and the light was as golden as her skin. The magic hour, photographers called it. Brief, glowing, lovely. Like fame itself, Reacher figured.

The dark-haired forty-year-old calling himself Alan Mason was waiting, too. He was waiting to take a clandestine meeting in his room in the Brown Palace Hotel in downtown Denver. He was uncharacteristically nervous and out of sorts. Three reasons. First, his room was dim and shabby. Not at all what he had been expecting. Second, he had a suitcase stacked against the wall. It was a dark grey hard-shell Samsonite, carefully selected like all his accessories, expensive enough to blend with his air of affluence but not ostentatious enough to attract undue attention. Inside it were bearer bonds and cut diamonds and Swiss bank access codes worth a lot of money. Sixty-five million U.S. dollars, to be exact, and the people he was going to be meeting with were not the kind of people a prudent person would trust around portable and untraceable assets.

And third, he hadn't slept well. The night air had been full of an unpleasant smell. He had run through a mental checklist until he had identified it as dog food. Clearly there was a factory nearby and the wind was blowing in an unfortunate direction. Then he had lain awake and worried about the dog food's ingredients. Meat, obviously. But he knew that smell was a physical mechanism that depended on the impact of actual molecules on the nasal lining. Therefore, technically, actual fragments of meat were entering his nostrils. They were in contact with his body. And there were certain meats that Azhari Mahmoud should not be in contact with, ever, under any circumstances.

He stepped to the bathroom. Washed his face for the fifth time that day. Looked at himself in the mirror. Clamped his jaw. He wasn't Azhari Mahmoud. Not right then. He was Alan Mason, a Westerner, and there was a job to be done.

First in through the Chateau Marmont's lobby door was the banged-up deputy himself, Thomas Brant. He had a vivid bruise on the side of his forehead and the sculptured metal splint on his face was taped to his cheekbones so tight that the skin around his eyes was distorted. He was walking like he hurt. He looked about one-third mad as hell that he had been taken down and one-third sheepish that he had let it happen and one-third pissed that he had to swallow his feelings for the sake of the job. He was followed in by an older guy who had to be his boss, Curtis Mauney. Mauney looked to be approaching fifty. He was short and solid and had the kind of worn look a guy gets when he has been in the same line of work too long. His hair was dyed a dull black that didn't match his eyebrows. He was carrying a battered leather briefcase. He asked, 'Which one of you assholes hit my guy?'

'Does it matter?' Reacher said.

'Shouldn't have happened.'

'Don't feel bad about it. He didn't stand a chance. It was three on one. Even though one of the three was a girl.'

Neagley gave him a look that would have

blinded him if looks were knives. Mauney shook his head and said, 'I'm not criticizing my guy's self-defence capabilities. I'm saying you don't come down here and start hitting cops.'

Reacher said, 'He was outside of his jurisdiction, he hadn't identified himself, and he was acting in a suspicious manner. He was asking for it.'

'Why are you here anyway?'

'For our friend's funeral.'

'The body hasn't been released yet.'

'So we'll wait.'

'Was it you who hit my guy?'

Reacher nodded. 'I apologize. But all you had to do was ask.'

'For what?'

'For our help.'

Mauney looked blank. 'You think we brought you here to help?'

'Didn't you?'

Mauney shook his head.

'No,' he said. 'We brought you here as bait.'

THIRTY-TWO

Thomas Brant stayed on his feet, surly, unwilling to make the kind of social gesture that sitting down as part of the group would represent. But his boss Curtis Mauney took a chair. He sat down and tucked his briefcase between his ankles and put his elbows on his knees.

'Let's get a couple of things straight,' he said. 'We're LA County sheriffs. We're not hicks from the sticks, we're not idiots, and we're nobody's poor relations. We're fast and smart and pro-active and light on our feet. We knew every detail of Calvin Franz's life within twelve hours of finding his body. Including the fact that he was one of eight survivors of an elite military unit. And within twenty-four hours we knew for sure that three other members of that unit were missing also. One from right here in LA, and two from Vegas. Which calls into question exactly how elite you all were, wouldn't you say? You're fifty per cent MIA in the blink of an eye.'

Reacher said, 'I would need to know who the opposition was before I came to any performance conclusions.'

'Whoever, it wasn't the Red Army.'

'We never fought the Red Army. We fought the U.S. Army.'

'So I'll ask around,' Mauney said. 'I'll check if the 81st Airborne just won any major victories.'

'Your thesis is someone's hunting all eight of us?'

'I don't know what my thesis is. But that's certainly a possibility. Therefore flushing you four out was a win-win for me. If you don't show up, maybe they've already got you, which adds pieces to the puzzle. If you do show up, then you're bait, and maybe I can use you to flush *them* out.'

'What if they're not hunting all eight of us?'

'Then you can hang around here and wait for the funeral. No skin off my nose.'

'Did you go to Vegas?'

'No.'

'Then how do you know the two from Vegas are missing?'

'Because I called,' Mauney said. 'We work with the Nevada staties a lot, and they work with the Vegas cops a lot, and your guys Sanchez and Orozco went missing three weeks ago and both their apartments have been royally trashed. So that's how I know. The telephone system. Useful technology.'

'Trashed as bad as Franz's office?'

'Similar handiwork.'

'They miss anything?'

'Why would they?'

'People miss things.'

'Did they miss something at Franz's place? Did we?'

Reacher had said: *We'll treat him like some asshole provost marshal. All take and no give.* But Mauney was better than any asshole provost marshal. That was clear. He looked like a pretty good cop. Not dumb. But maybe playable. So Reacher nodded and said, 'Franz was mailing computer files back and forth to himself for security. They missed them. You missed them. We got them.'

'From out of his post office box?'

Reacher nodded.

'That's a federal crime,' Mauney said. 'You should have gotten a warrant.'

'I couldn't have,' Reacher said. 'I'm retired.'

'Then you should have butted out.'

'So arrest me.'

'I can't,' Mauney said. 'I'm not federal.'

'What did they miss in Vegas?'

'Are we trading here?'

Reacher nodded. 'But you go first.'

'OK,' Mauney said. 'In Vegas they missed a napkin with writing on it. It was the kind of paper napkin you get with Chinese delivery. It was balled up and greasy in Sanchez's kitchen trash. My guess is Sanchez was eating and the phone rang. He scribbled down a note to himself and transferred it later to a book or a file that we don't have. Then he threw the napkin in the trash because he didn't need it any more.'

'How do we know it's got anything to do with anything?'

'We don't,' Mauney said. 'But the timing is suggestive. Ordering that Chinese delivery seems

194

to be about the last thing Sanchez ever did in Las Vegas.'

'What does the note say?'

Mauney bent down and hauled his battered briefcase up on his knees and clicked the latches. Lifted the lid. Took out a clear plastic page protector with a colour photocopy in it. The photocopy was edged with smudged black where the napkin hadn't filled the platen. It showed the creases and the grease stains and the pimpled paper texture. And a scrawled half-line in Jorge Sanchez's familiar handwriting: *650 at $100k per*. Bold, confident, forward-leaning, done with a blue fibre-tipped pen, vivid against the unbleached beige of the paper.

650 at $100k per.

Mauney asked, 'What does it mean?'

Reacher said, 'Your guess is as good as mine.' He was looking at the numbers, and he knew Dixon would be, too. The *k* abbreviation meant *thousand* and was fairly standard among U.S. Army personnel of Sanchez's generation, coming either from math or engineering school or from having served long years overseas where distances were measured in kilometres instead of miles. A kilometre was nicknamed a *klick* and measured a thousand metres, about 60 per cent of a mile. Therefore *$100k* meant *one hundred thousand dollars*. The *per* was a standard Latin preposition meaning *for each*, as in miles per gallon or miles per hour.

'I think it's an offer or a bid,' Mauney said. 'Like, you can have six hundred and fifty of something for a hundred grand each.'

'Or a market report,' O'Donnell said. 'Like six hundred and fifty of something were sold at a hundred grand each. Overall value, sixty-five million dollars. Some kind of a fairly big deal. Certainly big enough for people to get killed over.'

'People can get killed for sixty-five cents,' Mauney said. 'Doesn't always take millions of dollars.'

Karla Dixon was silent. Still, quiet, preoccupied. Reacher knew she had seen something in the number 650 that he hadn't. He couldn't imagine what. It wasn't an interesting number.

650 at $100k per.

'No bright ideas?' Mauney asked.

Nobody spoke.

Mauney said, 'What did you get from Franz's post office box?'

'A flash memory chip,' Reacher said. 'For a computer.'

'What's on it?'

'We don't know. We can't break the password.'

'We could try,' Mauney said. 'There's a lab we use.'

'I don't know. We're down to the last attempt.'

'Actually you don't have a choice. It's evidence, and therefore it's ours.'

'Will you share the information?'

Mauney nodded. 'We're in sharing mode here, apparently.'

'OK,' Reacher said. He nodded to Neagley. She put her hand in her tote bag and came out with the silver plastic sliver. Tossed it underhand to him. He caught it and passed it to Mauney.

'Good luck,' he said.

'Pointers?' Mauney asked.

'It'll be numbers,' Reacher said. 'Franz was a numbers type of guy.'

'OK.'

'It wasn't an airplane, you know.'

'I know,' Mauney said. 'That was just hick stuff to get you interested. It was a helicopter. You know how many private helicopters there are within cruise range of the place we found him?'

'No.'

'More than nine thousand.'

'Did you check Swan's office?'

'He was canned. He didn't have an office.'

'Did you check his house?'

'Through the windows,' Mauney said. 'It hadn't been tossed.'

'Bathroom window?'

'Pebbled glass.'

'So one last question,' Reacher said. 'You checked on Swan and sent the Nevada staties after Sanchez and Orozco. Why didn't you call D.C. and New York and Illinois about the rest of us?'

'Because at that point I was dealing with what I had.'

'Which was what?'

'I had all four of them on tape. Franz, Swan, Sanchez, and Orozco. All four of them together. Video surveillance, the night before Franz went out and didn't come back.'

THIRTY-THREE

Curtis Mauney didn't wait to be asked. He raised the lid of his briefcase again and took out another clear plastic page protector. In it was a copy of a still frame from a black and white surveillance tape. Four men, shoulder to shoulder in front of some kind of a store counter. Upside down and from a distance Reacher couldn't make out much detail.

Mauney said, 'I made the IDs by comparing a bunch of old snapshots from a shoebox in Franz's bedroom closet.' Then he passed the photograph to his right, to Neagley. She studied it for a moment, nothing in her face except light reflected off the shiny plastic. She passed it counterclockwise, to Dixon. Dixon looked at it for ten long seconds and blinked once and passed it to O'Donnell. O'Donnell took it and studied it and shook his head and passed it to Reacher.

Manuel Orozco was on the left of the frame, glancing to his right, caught by the camera in his perpetual state of restlessness. Then came Calvin Franz, hands in his pockets, patience on his face. Then came Tony Swan, front and centre, looking straight ahead. On the right was Jorge Sanchez, in a buttoned-up shirt, no tie, with a finger hooked under his collar. Reacher knew that pose. He had seen it a thousand times before. It meant that Sanchez had shaved about ten hours previously, and the stubble on his throat was growing back and beginning to irritate him. Even without the time code burned into the lower right of the shot Reacher would have known he was looking at a picture taken early in the evening.

They all looked a little older. Orozco's hair was grey at the temples and his eyes were lined and weary. Franz had maybe lost a little weight. Some of the muscle was gone from his shoulders. Swan was as wide as ever, barrel-chested, thicker in the gut. His hair was short and had crept backward maybe half an inch. Sanchez's scowl had settled into a tracery of permanent down-turned lines running from his nose to his chin and framing his mouth.

Older, but maybe a little wiser, too. There was a lot of talent and experience and capability right there in the picture. And an easy camaraderie and a mutual trust still floating on recent renewal. Four tough guys. In Reacher's opinion, four of the best eight in the world.

Who or what had beaten them?

Behind them, running away from the camera, were narrow store aisles that looked familiar.

'Where is this?' Reacher asked.

Mauney said, 'The pharmacy in Culver City. Next to Franz's office. The guy behind the counter remembered them. Swan was buying aspirin.'

'That doesn't sound like Swan.'

199

'For his dog. It had arthritis in its hips. He gave it a quarter-tab of aspirin a day. The pharmacist said that's a pretty common practice with dogs. Especially big dogs.'

'How much aspirin did he buy?'

'The economy bottle. Ninety-six pills, generic.'

Dixon said, 'At a quarter-tab a day, that's a year and nineteen days' worth.'

Reacher looked at the picture again. Four guys, relaxed poses, no urgency, all the time in the world, a routine purchase, a provision on behalf of a pet animal designed to stretch more than a year into the future.

They never even saw it coming.

Who or what had beaten them?

'Can I keep this picture?' he asked.

'Why?' Mauney said. 'You see something in it?'

'Four of my old friends.'

Mauney nodded. 'So keep it. It's a copy.'

'What next?'

'Stay here,' Mauney said. He dropped the lid of his case and clicked the latches, loud in the silence. 'Stay visible, and call me if you see anyone sniffing around. No more independent action, OK?'

'We're just here for the funeral,' Reacher said.

'But whose funeral?'

Reacher didn't reply to that. Just stood up and turned and looked at Raquel Welch's picture again. The glass in the frame was reflective and behind him he saw Mauney getting out of his chair, and the others standing up with him. When a seated person stands up, he slides forward to do it, so that when a seated group stands up they all

200

end up temporarily closer to one another than they were when they were sitting down. Therefore their next communal move is to shuffle backward, turning, dispersing, widening the circle, respecting space. Neagley was first and fastest, of course. Mauney turned toward the door and set himself to thread through the limited space between the chairs. O'Donnell stepped the other way, toward the interior of the hotel. Dixon paralleled him, small, deft, nimble, side-stepping a coffee table.

But Thomas Brant moved the other way.

Inward.

Reacher kept his eye on the glass in front of Raquel. Watched Brant's tan reflection. He knew instantly what was going to happen. Brant was going to tap him on his right shoulder with his left hand. Whereupon Reacher was supposed to turn enquiringly and take a massive straight right to the face.

Brant stepped closer. Reacher focused on the gold ring between the two halves of Raquel's bikini top. Brant's left hand snaked forward and his right hand eased back. His left hand had the index finger extended and his right hand was bunched into a fist the size of a softball. Good but not great technique. Reacher sensed that Brant's feet were not perfectly placed. Brant was a brawler, not a fighter. He was hobbling himself about 50 per cent.

Brant tapped Reacher on the shoulder.

Because he was expecting it Reacher turned much faster than he might have done and caught the incoming straight right in his left palm a foot in front of his face. Like snaring a line drive barehanded in the infield. It was a hefty blow. A lot of weight behind it. It made a hell of a smack. It stung Reacher's palm all the way down to the tendons.

Then it was all about superhuman self-control.

Every ounce of Reacher's animal instinct and muscle memory dictated a head butt to Brant's damaged nose. It was a no-brainer. Use the adrenalin. Jerk forward from the waist, plenty of snap, bury that forehead deep. A move that Reacher had perfected at the age of five. A reaction that was almost mandatory a lifetime later.

But Reacher held off.

He just stood still, gripping Brant's bunched fist. He looked into Brant's eyes, breathed out, and shook his head.

'I apologized once,' he said. 'And I'm apologizing again, right now. If that's not good enough for you, then wait until after this is all over, OK? I'll stick around. You can get a couple of buddies and jump me three on one when I'm not looking for it. That's fair, right?'

'Maybe I'll do that,' Brant said.

'You should. But choose your buddies carefully. Don't pick anyone who can't afford six months in the hospital.'

'Tough guy.'

'I ain't the one wearing the splint here.'

Curtis Mauney came over and said, 'No fighting. Not now, not ever.' He hauled Brant away by the collar. Reacher waited until they were both out the door and then grimaced and shook his left hand wildly and said, 'Damn, that stings.'

'Put some ice on it,' Neagley said.

'Wrap it around a cold beer,' O'Donnell said.

'Get over it and let me tell you about the number six hundred and fifty,' Dixon said.

THIRTY-FOUR

They went up to Dixon's room and she arranged the seven spreadsheets neatly on the bed. Said, 'OK, what we have here is a sequence of seven calendar months. Some kind of a performance analysis. For simplicity's sake let's just call them hits and misses. The first three months are pretty good. Plenty of hits, not too many misses. An average success rate of approximately ninety per cent. A hair over eighty-nine point four per cent, to be precise, which I know you want me to be.'

'Move along,' O'Donnell said.

'Then in the fourth month we fall off a cliff and we get worse.'

'We know that already,' Neagley said.

'So for the sake of argument let's take the first three months as a baseline. We know they can hit ninety per cent, give or take. They're capable of it. Let's say they could have or should have continued that level of performance indefinitely.'

'But they didn't,' O'Donnell said.

'Exactly. They could have, but they didn't. What's the result?'

Neagley said, 'More misses later than earlier.'

'How many more?'

'I don't know.'

'I do,' Dixon said. 'On this volume if they had continued their baseline success rate through the final four months they would have saved themselves exactly six hundred and fifty extra misses.'

'Really?'

'Really,' Dixon said. 'Numbers don't lie, and percentages are numbers. Something happened at the end of month three that went on to cost them six hundred and fifty avoidable future failures.'

Reacher nodded. A total of 183 days, a total of 2,197 events, a total of 1,314 successes and 883 failures. But with markedly unequal distribution. The first three months, 897 events, 802 successes, 95 failures. The next four months, 1,300 events, a miserable 512 successes, a catastrophic 788 failures, 650 of which wouldn't have happened if something hadn't changed.

'I wish we knew what we were looking at,' he said.

'Sabotage,' O'Donnell said. 'Someone got paid to screw something up.'

'At a hundred grand a time?' Neagley said. 'Six hundred and fifty times over? That's nice work if you can get it.'

'Can't be sabotage,' Reacher said. 'You could get a whole factory or office or whatever torched for a hundred grand, easy. Probably a whole town. You wouldn't have to pay per occasion.'

'So what is it?'

'I don't know.'

'But it ties in,' Dixon said. 'Doesn't it? There

205

was a definite mathematical relationship between what Franz knew and what Sanchez knew.'

A minute later Reacher stepped to Dixon's window and looked out at the view. Asked, 'Would it be fair to assume that Orozco knew whatever Sanchez knew?'

'Totally,' O'Donnell said. 'And vice versa, certainly. They were friends. They worked together. They must have talked all the time.'

'So all we're missing is what Swan knew. We've got fragments from the other three. Nothing from him.'

'His house was clean. Nothing there.'

'So it's at his office.'

'He didn't have an office. He was canned.'

'But only very recently. So his office is just sitting there empty. They're shedding staff, not hiring. So there's no pressure on space. His office is mothballed. With his computer still right there on his desk. And maybe there are notes in the desk drawers, stuff like that.'

Neagley said, 'You want to go see the dragon lady again?'

'I think we have to.'

'We should call before we drive all the way out there.'

'Better if we just show up.'

'I'd like to see where Swan worked,' O'Donnell said.

'Me too,' Dixon said.

Dixon drove. Her rental, her responsibility. She headed east on Sunset, hunting the 101. Neagley told her what she was going to have to do after that. A complex route. Slow traffic. But the ride through Hollywood itself was picturesque. Dixon seemed to enjoy it. She liked LA.

The man in the dark blue suit in the dark blue Chrysler tailed them all the way. Outside the KTLA studios, just before the freeway, he dialled his phone. Told his boss, 'They're heading east. All four of them together in the car.'

His boss said, 'I'm still in Colorado. Watch them for me, OK?'

THIRTY-FIVE

Dixon turned in through New Age's open gate and parked in the same visitor slot Neagley had used, head-on against the shiny corporate cube. The lot was still half empty. The specimen trees were motionless in the heavy air. The same receptionist was on duty. Same polo shirt, same slow response. She heard the doors open but didn't look up until Reacher put his hand on the counter.

'Help you?' she said.

'We need to see Ms Berenson again,' Reacher said. 'The human resources person.'

'I'll see if she's available,' the receptionist said. 'Please take a seat.'

O'Donnell and Neagley sat down but Reacher and Dixon stayed on their feet. Dixon was too restless to spend more of the day in a chair. Reacher stood because if he sat next to Neagley he would crowd her and if he sat somewhere else she would wonder why.

They waited the same four minutes before they heard the click of Berenson's heels on the slate. She came out of the corridor and around the corner and didn't hesitate. Just gave the receptionist a nod of thanks and passed her by and headed on out. She gave up two types of smiles, one kind to Reacher and Neagley because she had met them before, and another kind to O'Donnell and Dixon because she hadn't. She shook hands all around. Same scars under the makeup, same icy breath. She opened the aluminum door and stood still until everyone had filed past her into the conference room.

With five people in it the room was short one chair, so Berenson stood by the window. Polite, but also psychologically dominating. It made her visitors look upward at her and it made them squint against the light behind her. She said, 'How may I help you today?' There was a little condescension in her voice. A little irritation. A slight emphasis on *today*.

'Tony Swan is missing,' Reacher said.

'Missing?'

'As in, we can't find him.'

'I don't understand.'

'It's not a difficult concept to grasp.'

'But he could be anywhere. A new job, out of state. Or a long-delayed vacation. Somewhere he always wanted to go. People sometimes do that, in Mr Swan's circumstances. Like a silver lining.'

O'Donnell said, 'His dog died of thirst trapped inside his house. No silver lining there. All cloud. Swan didn't go anywhere he planned to go.'

'His dog? How awful.'

'Roger that,' Dixon said.

'Her name was Maisi,' Neagley said.

'I don't see how I can help,' Berenson said. 'Mr

Swan left here more than three weeks ago. Isn't this a matter for the police?'

'They're working on it,' Reacher said. 'We're working on it too.'

'I don't see how I can help.'

'We'd like to see his desk. And his computer. And his diary. There might be notes. Or information, or appointments.'

'Notes about what?'

'About whatever has caused him to be missing.'

'He's not missing because of New Age.'

'Maybe not. But people have been known to conduct private business during office hours. People have been known to jot down notes about things from their outside lives.'

'Not here.'

'Why not? You're all business all the time?'

'There are no notes here. No paper at all. No pens or pencils. Basic security. This is a completely paperless environment. Much safer. It's a rule. Anyone even thinks about breaking it, they get fired. Everything is done on computers here. We have an in-house network with secure firewalls and automatic random data monitoring.'

'Can we see his computer, then?' Neagley asked.

'I guess you could *see* it,' Berenson said. 'But it won't do you any good. Someone leaves here, within thirty minutes their desktop hard drive is taken out and destroyed. Smashed. Physically. With hammers. It's another security rule.'

'With hammers?' Reacher said.

'It's the only definitive method. Data can be recovered otherwise.'

'So there's no trace of him left?'

'None at all, I'm afraid.'

'You've got some pretty heavy rules here.'

'I know. Mr Swan designed them himself. In his first week. They were his first major contribution.'

'Did he talk to anybody?' Dixon asked. 'Water cooler buddies? Is there anyone he would have shared a concern with?'

'Personal issues?' Berenson said. 'I doubt it. The dynamic wouldn't have been appropriate. He had to play a cop's role here. He had to keep himself a little unapproachable, to be effective.'

'What about his boss?' O'Donnell said. 'They might have shared. They were in the same boat, professionally.'

'I'll certainly ask him,' Berenson said.

'What's his name?'

'I can't tell you that.'

'You're very discreet.'

'Mr Swan insisted on it.'

'Can we meet with the guy?'

'He's out of town right now.'

'So who's minding the store?'

'Mr Swan is, in a way. His procedures are all still in place.'

'Did he talk to you?'

'About personal things? No, he really didn't.'

'Was he upset or worried the week he left?'

'Not that I saw.'

'Was he making a lot of phone calls?'

'I'm sure he was. We all do.'

'What do you think might have happened to him?'

'Me?' Berenson said. 'I really have no idea. I walked him to his car, and I said when things pick up again I'll be on the phone begging him to come back, and he said he'd look forward to my call. That was the last I saw of him.'

They got back in Dixon's car and reversed away from the mirror glass. Reacher watched the Ford's reflection get smaller and smaller.

Neagley said, 'Wasted trip. I told you we should have called.'

Dixon said, 'I wanted to see where he worked.'

O'Donnell said, 'Worked is the wrong word. They were using him there, that's all. They picked his brains for a year and then kicked him out. They were buying his ideas, not giving him a job.'

'Sure looks that way,' Neagley said.

'They're not making anything there. It's an unsecured building.'

'Obviously. They must have a third place somewhere. A remote plant for manufacturing.'

'So why didn't UPS get that address too?'

'Maybe it's secret. Maybe they don't get mail there.'

'I'd like to know what they make.'

'Why?' Dixon asked.

'Just curious. The more we know the luckier we get.'

Reacher said, 'So go ahead and find out.'

'I don't know anyone to ask.'

'I do,' Neagley said. 'I know a guy in Pentagon procurement.'

Reacher said, 'Call him.'

* * *

In his room in his Denver hotel the dark-haired forty-year-old calling himself Alan Mason was concluding his meeting. His guest had shown up exactly on time and had been accompanied by a single bodyguard. Mason had taken both of those facts as positive signs. He appreciated punctuality in business. And being outnumbered only two to one was a luxury. Often he was alone with as many as six or ten on the other side of the deal.

So, a good start. It had been followed by substantive progress. No lame excuses about late delivery or lowered numbers or other difficulties. No bait and switch. No attempt to renegotiate. No jacked-up prices. Just the sale as previously discussed, six hundred and fifty units at a hundred thousand dollars each.

Mason had opened his suitcase and his client had started the long process of totalling the consideration inside. The Swiss bank balances and the bearer bonds were uncontroversial. They had reliable face values. The diamonds were more subjective. Carat weight was a given, of course, but much depended on cut and clarity. Mason's people had in fact underestimated in order to build in a horse trading margin. Mason's guest quickly understood. He pronounced himself entirely satisfied and agreed that the suitcase did indeed contain sixty-five million dollars.

At which point it became his suitcase.

In exchange Mason received a key and a piece of paper.

The key was small, old, scratched and worn, plain and unlabelled. It looked like the kind of thing a hardware store cuts while a person waits.

Mason was told it was the key to a padlock currently securing a shipping container waiting at the Los Angeles docks.

The piece of paper was a bill of lading, describing the shipping container's contents as six hundred and fifty DVD players.

Mason's guest and his bodyguard left, and Mason stepped into the bathroom and set fire to his passport in the toilet pan. A half-hour later Andrew MacBride left the hotel and headed back to the airport. He was surprised to realize that he was looking forward to hearing the jug-band music again.

Frances Neagley called Chicago from the back of Dixon's car. She told her assistant to e-mail her contact at the Pentagon and explain that she was out of the office, in California, away from a secure phone, and that she had an enquiry about New Age's product. She knew her guy would feel better about responding by e-mail than talking on an unsecured cell network.

O'Donnell said, 'You have secure phones in your office?'

'Sure.'

'Outstanding. Who's the guy?'

'Just a guy,' Neagley said. 'Who owes me big.'

'Big enough to deliver?'

'Always.'

Dixon came off the 101 at Sunset and headed west to the hotel. The traffic was slow. Less than three miles, but a jogger could have covered them faster. When they eventually arrived they found a Crown Vic waiting out front. An unmarked cop car. Not Thomas Brant's. This one was newer and intact and a different colour.

It was Curtis Mauney's car.

He climbed out as soon as Dixon got parked. He walked over, short, solid, worn, tired. He stopped directly in front of Reacher and paused a beat. Then he asked, 'Did one of your friends have a tattoo on his back?'

A gentle tone of voice.

Quiet.

Sympathetic.

Reacher said, 'Ah, Christ.'

THIRTY-SIX

Manuel Orozco had gone through four years of college on army money and had assumed he would wind up a combat infantry officer. His baby sister had gone through a major irrational panic and had assumed he would wind up KIA with serious disfiguring facial wounds such that his body would not be identified on recovery. She would never know what had happened to him. He told her about dog tags. She said they might get blown off or lost. He told her about fingerprints. She said he might lose limbs. He told her about dental identification. She said his whole jaw might get exploded. Later he realized she was worrying on a deeper level but at the time he thought the answer to her fears was to get a big tattoo across his upper back that said *Orozco, M.* in large black letters with his service number equally large below. He had gotten home and peeled off his shirt in triumph and had been mystified when the kid had cried even harder.

Ultimately he had avoided the infantry and ended up a key part of the 110th MP, where Reacher had immediately rechristened him Kit

Bag because his broad olive back looked like a GI duffel with its name-and-number stencil. Now fifteen years later Reacher stood in the Chateau Marmont's sunblasted parking lot and said, 'You found another body.'

'I'm afraid we did,' Mauney said.

'Where?'

'Same general area. In a gully.'

'Helicopter?'

'Probably.'

'Orozco,' Reacher said.

'That's the name on his back,' Mauney said.

'So why ask?'

'We have to be sure.'

'All corpses should be so convenient.'

'Who's the next of kin?'

'He has a sister somewhere. Younger.'

'So you should make the formal ID. If you would. This really isn't the kind of thing a younger sister should see.'

'How long was he in the gully?'

'A long time.'

They got back in the car and Dixon followed Mauney all the way to a county facility north of Glendale. Nobody spoke. Reacher sat in the back next to O'Donnell and did what he was pretty sure O'Donnell was doing too, which was to run through a long involuntary sequence of remembered Orozco moments. The guy had been a comedian, part on purpose, part unwitting. He had been of Mexican descent, born in Texas and raised in New Mexico, but for many years had pretended to be a white Australian. He had called

217

everyone *mate*. As an officer his command skills had been first rate, but he had never really issued orders. He would wait until a junior officer or a grunt had grasped the general consensus and then he would say, *If you wouldn't mind, mate, please.* It had become a group catchphrase every bit as ubiquitous as *You do not mess.*

Coffee?

If you wouldn't mind, mate, please.

Cigarette?

If you wouldn't mind, mate, please.

Want me to shoot this mother?

If you wouldn't mind, mate, please.

O'Donnell said, 'We knew already. This is not a surprise.'

Nobody answered him.

The county facility turned out to be a brand new medical centre with a hospital on one side of a wide new street. On the other side was a state-of-the-art receiving station for townships without morgues of their own. It was a white concrete cube set on stilts a storey high. Meat wagons could roll right under the bulk of the building to hidden elevator doors. Neat, clean, discreet. Californian. Mauney parked in a line of visitor slots near some trees. Dixon parked right next to him. Everyone got out and stood for a moment, stretching, looking around, wasting time.

Nobody's favourite trip.

Mauney led the way. There was a personnel elevator opening off a cross-hatched walkway. Mauney hit the call button and the elevator door slid back and cold chemical air spilled out. Mauney stepped in, then Reacher, then O'Donnell, then Dixon, then Neagley.

Mauney pressed four.

The fourth floor was as cold as a meat locker. There was a miserable public viewing area with a wide internal window backed by a venetian blind. Mauney passed it by and headed through a door to a storage area. Three walls showed the fronts of refrigerated drawers. Dozens of them. The air was bitter with cold and heavy with smells and noisy from reflections off stainless steel. Mauney pulled a drawer. It came out easily on ball bearing runners. Full length. It smacked all the way open against end stops made of rubber.

Inside was a refrigerated corpse. Male. Hispanic. The wrists and the ankles were tied with rough twine that had bitten deep. The arms were behind the back. The head and the shoulders were grievously damaged. Almost unrecognizable as human.

'He fell head first,' Reacher said, softly. 'He would, I guess, tied up like that. If you're right about the helicopter.'

'No tracks to or from,' Mauney said.

Further medical details were hard to discern. Decomposition was well advanced, but due to the desert heat and dryness it looked more like mummification. The body was shrunken, diminished, collapsed, leathery. It looked empty. There was some animal damage, but not much. Contact with the gully's walls had prevented more.

Mauney asked, 'Do you recognize him?'

'Not really,' Reacher said.

'Check the tattoo.'

Reacher just stood there.

Mauney said, 'Want me to call an orderly?'

Reacher shook his head and put a hand under the corpse's icy shoulder. Lifted. The body rolled awkwardly, all of a piece, stiff, like a log or a stump. It settled face down, the arms flung upward, tied and contorted as if the desperate struggle for freedom had continued until the very last.

Which it undoubtedly had, Reacher thought.

The tattoo was a little folded and creased and wrinkled by the sloughing looseness of the skin and the unnatural inward pressure of the upper arms.

It was a little faded by time.

But it was unmistakable.

It said: *Orozco, M.*

Under it was a nine-digit service number.

'It's him,' Reacher said. 'It's Manuel Orozco.'

Mauney said, 'I'm very sorry.'

There was silence for a moment. Nothing to hear, except cooled air forcing its way through aluminum vents. Reacher asked, 'Are you still searching the area?'

'For the others?' Mauney said. 'Not actively. It's not like we've got a missing child.'

'Is Franz in here too? In one of these damn drawers?'

'You want to see him?' Mauney asked.

'No,' Reacher said. Then he looked back at Orozco and asked, 'When is the autopsy?'

'Soon.'

'Is the string going to tell us anything?'

'It's probably too common.'

'Do we have an estimate on when he died?'

Mauney half smiled, cop to cop. 'When he hit the ground.'

'Which was when?'

'Three, four weeks ago. Before Franz, we think. But we may never know for sure.'

'We will,' Reacher said.

'How?' Mauney asked.

'I'll ask whoever did it. And he'll tell me. By that point he'll be begging to.'

'No independent action, remember?'

'In your dreams.'

Mauney stayed to process paperwork and Reacher and Neagley and Dixon and O'Donnell took the elevator back down to warmth and sunlight. They stood in the lot, saying nothing. Doing nothing. Just crackling and trembling and twitching with suppressed rage. It was a given that soldiers contemplate death. They live with it, they accept it. They expect it. Some of them even want it. But deep down they want it to be *fair*. Me against him, may the best man win. They want it to be *noble*. Win or lose, they want it to arrive with significance.

A soldier dead with his arms tied behind him was the worst kind of outrage. It was about helplessness and submission and abuse. It was about powerlessness.

It took away all the illusions.

'Let's go,' Dixon said. 'We're wasting time.'

221

THIRTY-SEVEN

At the hotel Reacher sat for a moment with the photograph Mauney had given him. The video surveillance frame. The pharmacy. Four men in front of the counter. Manuel Orozco on the left, glancing right, restless. Then Calvin Franz, hands in his pockets, patience on his face. Then Tony Swan, looking straight ahead. Then Jorge Sanchez, on the right, his finger hooked under his collar.

Four friends.

Two down for sure.

Presumably all four down.

'Shit happens,' O'Donnell said.

Reacher nodded. 'And we get over it.'

'Do we?' Neagley said. 'Will we this time?'

'We always have before.'

'This never happened before.'

'My brother died.'

'I know. But this is worse.'

Reacher nodded again. 'Yes, it is.'

'I was hoping the other three were still OK somehow.'

'We all were.'

'But they're not. They're all gone.'

'Looks that way.'

'We need to work,' Dixon said. 'That's all we've got now.'

They went up to Dixon's room, but work was a relative term. They were dead-ended. They had nothing to go on. Those feelings didn't improve any when they transferred to Neagley's room and found an e-mail response from her Pentagon contact: *Sorry, no way. New Age is classified.* Just seven words, blank and dismissive.

'Seems he doesn't owe you all that big,' O'Donnell said.

'He does,' Neagley said. 'Bigger than you could imagine. This says more about New Age than him and me.'

She scrolled on through her inbox. Then she stopped. There was another message from the same guy. Different version of his name, different e-mail address.

'Disposable,' Neagley said. 'That's a one-time free account.'

She clicked on the message. It said: *Frances, great to hear from you. We should get together. Dinner and a movie? And I need to return your Hendrix CDs. Thanks so much for the loan. I loved them all. The sixth track on the second album is dynamically brilliant. Let me know when you're next in Washington. Please call soonest.*

Reacher said, 'You own CDs?'

'No,' Neagley said. 'I especially don't own Jimi Hendrix CDs. I don't like him.'

O'Donnell said, 'You've been to movies and dinner with this guy?'

'Never,' Neagley said.

'So he's confusing you with some other woman.'

'Unlikely,' Reacher said.

'It's coded,' Neagley said. 'That's what it is. It's the answer to my question. Got to be. A kosher reply from his official address, and then a coded follow-up from an unofficial address. His ass is covered both ways.'

Dixon asked, 'What's the code?'

'Something to do with the sixth track on the second Hendrix album.'

Reacher said, 'What was the second Hendrix album?'

O'Donnell said, '*Electric Ladyland*?'

'That was later,' Dixon said. 'The first was *Are You Experienced?*'

'Which one had the naked women on the cover?'

'That was *Electric Ladyland*.'

'I loved that cover.'

'You're disgusting. You were eight years old.'

'Nearly nine.'

'That's still disgusting.'

Reacher said, '*Axis Bold As Love*. That was the second album.'

'What was the sixth track?' Dixon asked.

'I have no idea.'

O'Donnell said, 'When the going gets tough, the tough go shopping.'

*   *   *

224

They walked a long way east on Sunset, until they found a record store. They went inside and found cool air and young people and loud music and the H section in the Rock/Pop aisles. There was a dense foot and a half of Jimi Hendrix albums. Four old titles that Reacher recognized, plus a bunch of posthumous stuff. *Axis Bold As Love* was right there, three copies. Reacher pulled one and flipped it. It was wrapped in plastic and the store's barcode label was stuck over the second half of the track listings.

Same for the second copy.

Same for the third.

'Rip it off,' O'Donnell said.

'Steal it?'

'No, rip the plastic off.'

'Can't do that. It's not ours.'

'You smack cops around but you won't damage a store's wrapper?'

'It's different.'

'So what are you going to do?'

'I'm going to buy it. We can play it in the car. Cars have CD players, right?'

'For the last hundred years,' Dixon said.

Reacher took the CD and lined up behind a girl with more metal punched through her face than a grenade victim. He made it to the register and peeled off thirteen of his remaining eight hundred dollars and for the first time in his life became the owner of a digital product.

'Unwrap it,' O'Donnell said.

It was wrapped tight. Reacher used his finger-nails to scrape up a corner and then his teeth to tear the plastic. When he got it all off he turned the CD over and ran his finger down the track list.

'Little Wing,' he said.

O'Donnell shrugged. Neagley looked blank.

'Doesn't help,' Dixon said.

'I know the song,' Reacher said.

'Please don't sing it,' Neagley said.

'So what does it mean?' O'Donnell said.

Reacher said, 'It means New Age makes a weapons system called Little Wing.'

'Obviously. But that doesn't help us if we don't know what Little Wing *is*.'

'Sounds aeronautical. Like a drone plane or something.'

'Nobody heard of it?' Dixon asked. 'Anybody?'

O'Donnell shook his head.

'Not me,' Neagley said.

'So it really is super-secret,' Dixon said. 'No loose lips in D.C. or on Wall Street or among all of Neagley's connections.'

Reacher tried to open the CD box but found it taped shut with a title label that ran all the way across the top seam. He picked at it with his nails and it came off in small sticky fragments.

'No wonder the record business is in trouble,' he said. 'They don't make these things very easy to enjoy.'

Dixon asked, 'What are we going to do?'

'What did the e-mail say?'

'You know what it said.'

'But do you?'

'What do you mean?'

'What did it say?'

'Find the sixth track on the second Hendrix album.'

'And?'

'And nothing.'

'No, it said please call soonest.'

'That's ridiculous,' Neagley said. 'If he won't tell me by e-mail, why would he tell me on the phone?'

'It didn't say please call *me*. A coded note like that, every word counts.'

'So who am I supposed to call?'

'There must be somebody. He knows you know somebody that can help.'

'Who's going to help with a thing like this? If he won't?'

'Who does he know you know? Maybe from Washington, since he used that word, and every word counts?'

Neagley opened her mouth to say *nobody*. Reacher saw the denial forming in her throat. But then she paused.

'There's a woman,' she said. 'She's called Diana Bond. We both know her. She's a staffer for a guy on the Hill. The guy is on the House Defense Committee.'

'There you go. Who's the guy?'

Neagley said a familiar but unloved name.

'You've got a friend who works for that asshole?'

'Not exactly a friend.'

'I should hope not.'

'Everyone needs a job, Reacher. Except you, apparently.'

'Whatever, her boss is signing the cheques, so

227

he'll have been briefed. He'll know what Little Wing is. Therefore she will too.'

'Not if it's secret.'

'That guy can't spell his own name without help. Believe me, if he knows, she knows too.'

'She's not going to tell me.'

'She is. Because you're going to play hardball. You're going to call her and tell her that Little Wing's name is out there, and you're about to tell the papers that the leak came from her boss's office, and the price of your silence is everything she knows about it.'

'That's dirty.'

'That's politics. She can't be exactly unfamiliar with the process, working for that guy.'

'Do we really need to do this? Is it relevant?'

'The more we know the luckier we get.'

'I don't want to involve her.'

'Your Pentagon buddy wants you to,' O'Donnell said.

'That's just Reacher's guess.'

'No, it's more than that. Think about the e-mail. He said the sixth track was dynamically brilliant. That's a weird phrase. He could have just said it was great. Or amazing. Or brilliant on its own. But he said dynamically brilliant, which is the letters *d* and *b*. Like this Diana Bond woman's initials.'

THIRTY-EIGHT

Neagley insisted on making the call to Diana Bond alone. When they got back to the hotel she parked herself in a far corner of the lobby and did a whole lot of dialling and redialling. Then some serious talking. She came back a long twenty minutes later. Slight distaste on her face. Slight discomfort in her body language. But a measure of excitement, too.

'Took me some time to track her down,' she said. 'Turns out she's not far away. She's up at Edwards Air Force Base for a few days. Some big presentation.'

O'Donnell said, 'That's why your guy said call her soonest. He knew she was in California. Every word counts.'

'What did she say?' Reacher asked.

'She's coming down here,' Neagley said. 'She wants to meet face to face.'

'Really?' Reacher said. 'When?'

'Just as soon as she can get away.'

'That's impressive.'

'You bet your ass it is. Little Wing must be important.'

'Feel bad about the call?'

Neagley nodded. 'I feel bad about every-thing.'

They went up to Neagley's room and looked at maps and figured out Diana Bond's earliest possible arrival time. Edwards was on the other side of the San Gabriel Mountains, out in the Mojave, about seventy miles north and east, past Palmdale and Lancaster, about halfway to Fort Irwin. A two-hour wait, minimum, if Bond got away immediately. Longer if she didn't.

'I'm going for a walk,' Reacher said.

O'Donnell said, 'I'll come with you.'

They headed east on Sunset again to where West Hollywood met regular Hollywood. It was early afternoon and Reacher felt the sun burning his head through his shaved hair. It was like the rays had extra intensity after bouncing around through glittering particles of air pollution.

'I should buy a hat,' he said.

'You should buy a better shirt,' O'Donnell said. 'You can afford one now.'

'Maybe I will.'

They saw a store they had passed on the way to Tower Records. It was some kind of a popular chain. It had an artfully pale and uncrowded window, but it wasn't expensive. It sold cotton stuff, jeans, chinos, shirts and T-shirts. And ball caps. They were brand new but looked like they had been worn and washed a thousand times already. Reacher picked one out, blue, no writing on it. He never bought anything with writing on it. He had spent too long in uniform. Name tapes and badges and alphabet soup all over him for thirteen long years.

He loosened the strap at the back of the cap and tried it on.

'What do you think?' he asked.

O'Donnell said, 'Find a mirror.'

'Doesn't matter what I see in a mirror. You're the one laughing at how I look.'

'It's a nice hat.'

Reacher kept it on and moved across the store to a low table piled high with T-shirts. In the centre of the table was a mannequin torso wearing two of them, one under the other, pale green and dark green. The underneath shirt showed at the hem and the sleeves and the collar. Together the two layers were reassuringly thick and hefty.

Reacher asked, 'What do you think?'

'It's a look,' O'Donnell said.

'Do they need to be different sizes?'

'Probably not.'

Reacher picked a light blue and a dark blue, both XXLs. He took off the hat and carried the three items to the register. Refused a bag and bit off the tags and stripped off his bowling shirt right there in the middle of the store. Stood and waited, naked to the waist in the chill of the air conditioning.

'Got a trash can?' he asked.

The girl behind the counter bent down and came back with a plastic item with a liner. Reacher tossed his old shirt in and put his new shirts on, one after the other. Tugged them around and rolled his shoulders to get them comfortable and jammed the

231

cap on his head. Then he headed back to the street. Turned east.

O'Donnell asked, 'What are you running from?'

'I'm not running from anything.'

'You could have kept the old shirt.'

'Slippery slope,' Reacher said. 'I carry a spare shirt, pretty soon I'm carrying spare pants. Then I'd need a suitcase. Next thing I know, I've got a house and a car and a savings plan and I'm filling out all kinds of forms.'

'People do that.'

'Not me.'

'So like I said, what are you running from?'

'From being like people, I guess.'

'I'm like people. I've got a house and a car and a savings plan. I fill out forms.'

'Whatever works for you.'

'Do you think I'm ordinary?'

Reacher nodded. 'In that respect.'

'Not everyone can be like you.'

'That's ass-backward. The fact is a few of us can't be like you.'

'You want to be?'

'It's not about wanting. It just can't be done.'

'Why not?'

'OK, I'm running.'

'From what? Being like me?'

'From being different than I used to be.'

'We're all different than we used to be.'

'We don't all have to like it.'

'I don't like it,' O'Donnell said. 'But I deal with it.'

Reacher nodded. 'You're doing great, Dave. I

mean it. It's me that I worry about. I've been looking at you and Neagley and Karla and feeling like a loser.'

'Really?'

'Look at me.'

'All that we've got that you don't is suitcases.'

'But what have I got that you don't?'

O'Donnell didn't answer. They turned north on Vine, middle of the afternoon in America's second largest city, and saw two guys with pistols in their hands jumping out of a moving car.

THIRTY-NINE

The car was a black Lexus sedan, brand new. It took off again immediately, leaving the two guys alone on the sidewalk maybe thirty yards ahead. They were the bag man and the stash man from the vacant lot behind the wax museum. The pistols were AMT Hardballers, which were stainless steel copies of Colt Government 1911 .45 automatics. The hands holding them were shaking a little and moving up level and rotating through ninety degrees into flat movie-approved bad-boy grips.

O'Donnell's own hands went straight to his pockets.

'They want us?' he said.

'They want me,' Reacher said. He glanced back at what was behind him. He wasn't very worried about being hit by a badly held .45 from thirty yards away. He was a big target but statistics were on his side. Handguns were in-room weapons. Under expert control in high-pressure situations the average range for a successful engagement was about eleven feet. But even if Reacher himself wasn't hit, someone else might be. Or something else. A person a block away, or a low-flying plane, maybe. Collateral damage. The street was thick with potential targets. Men, women, children, plus other folks Reacher wasn't entirely sure how to categorize.

He turned to face front again. The two guys hadn't moved far. Not more than a couple of steps. O'Donnell's eyes were locked hard on them.

'We should take this off the street, Dave,' Reacher said.

O'Donnell said, 'Roger that.'

'Moving left,' Reacher said. He crabbed sideways and risked a glance to his left. The nearest door was a narrow tarot reader's dive. His mind was working with a kind of icy high-pressure speed. He was moving normally, but the world around him had slowed. The sidewalk had become a four-dimensional diagram. Forward, backward, sideways, time.

'Break back a yard and left, Dave,' he said.

O'Donnell was like a blind man. His eyes were tight on the two guys and wouldn't leave them. He heard Reacher's voice and tracked backward and left, fast. Reacher pulled the tarot reader's door and held it open and let O'Donnell loop in around him. The two guys were following. Now twenty yards away. Reacher crowded inside after O'Donnell. The tarot parlour was empty apart from a woman of about nineteen sitting alone at a table. The table was a dining room item about seven feet long, draped to the floor with red cloth. Packs of cards all over it. The woman had long dark hair and was wearing a purple cheesecloth dress that was probably leaking vegetable dye all over her skin.

'Got a back room?' Reacher asked her.

'Just a toilet,' she said.

'Go in there and lie down on the floor, right now.'

'What's up?'

'You tell me.'

The woman didn't move until O'Donnell's hands came out of his pockets. The knuckles were on his right fist like a shark's smile. The switch-blade was in his left hand. It was closed. Then it popped open with a sound like a bone breaking. The woman jumped up and fled. An Angelina, who worked on Vine. She knew the rules of the game.

O'Donnell said, 'Who are these guys?'

'They just bought me these shirts.'

'Is this going to be a problem?'

'Possibly.'

'Plan?'

'You like the Hardballer?'

'Better than nothing.'

'OK then.' Reacher flipped up the edge of the tablecloth and crouched down and backed under the table on his knees. O'Donnell followed him to his left and dragged the cloth back into position. He touched it with his knife, a short gentle side-ways stroke, and a slit appeared in front of him. He widened it to the shape of an eye with his fingers. Then he did the same in front of Reacher. Reacher braced the flat of his hands against the underside of the table. O'Donnell swapped the knife into his right hand and braced his left the same way as Reacher's.

Then they waited.

The guys were at the door within about eight seconds. They paused and peered in through the glass and then they pulled the door and came inside. Paused again, six feet in front of the table, guns pointed straight out with the butts twisted parallel to the floor.

They took a cautious step forward.

Paused again.

O'Donnell's right hand was wrapped with the knuckles and was gripping the knife but it was the only free hand under the table. He used it to count down. Thumb, index finger, middle finger. One, two, three.

On three Reacher and O'Donnell heaved the table up and out. They powered it through an explosive quarter-circle, three feet in the air, three feet forward. The flat of the top tipped vertical and collected the guns first and then moved on and smacked the two guys full in the chests and faces. It was a heavy table. Solid wood. Maybe oak. It put the guys straight down with no trouble at all. They went over on their backs in a cloud of tarot cards and lay still under the slab in a tangle of red cloth. Reacher got up and stepped onto the upside-down table and rode it like a surfboard. Then he jumped up and down a couple of times. O'Donnell timed it for when Reacher's weight was off it and kicked the table backward six inches until the two guys were exposed to the waist and their gun hands were accessible. He took the Hardballers and used his switchblade to slice the webs of the two guys' thumbs. Painful, and a real disincentive against holding pistols

again until they healed, which could be a long time, depending on their approach to nutrition and antisepsis. Reacher smiled, briefly. The technique had been a part of his unit's SOP. Then he stopped smiling, because he recalled that Jorge Sanchez had developed it, and Jorge Sanchez was dead in the desert somewhere.

'Not too much of a problem,' O'Donnell said.

'We've still got the good stuff,' Reacher said.

O'Donnell put his ceramic collection back in his pockets and tucked a Hardballer into his waistband under his suit coat. Handed the second gun to Reacher who shoved it in his pants pocket and draped his T-shirts over it. Then they stepped out to the sunshine and headed north on Vine again and turned west on Hollywood Boulevard.

Karla Dixon was waiting for them in the Chateau Marmont's lobby.

'Curtis Mauney called,' she said. 'He liked that thing you did with Franz's mail. So he got the Vegas PD to check through the stuff in Sanchez and Orozco's office. And they found something.'

FORTY

Mauney showed up in person thirty minutes later. He stepped through the lobby door, still tired, still carrying his battered leather briefcase. He sat down and asked, 'Who is Adrian Mount?'

Reacher looked up. *Azhari Mahmoud, Adrian Mount, Alan Mason, Andrew MacBride, Anthony Matthews.* The Syrian and his four aliases. Information Mauney didn't know they had.

'No idea,' he said.

'You sure?'

'Pretty much.'

Mauney balanced his briefcase on his knees and opened the lid and took out a sheet of paper. Handed it over. It was blurred and indistinct. It looked like a fax of a copy of a copy of a fax. At the top it said *Department of Homeland Security.* But not in the style of an official letterhead. It looked more like content hacked out of a computer file. Plain DOS script. It related to an airline booking that a guy called Adrian Mount had made on British Airways, London to New York. The booking had been finalized two weeks ago for a flight three days ago. First class, one way, Heathrow to JFK, seat 2K, last departure of the evening, expensive, paid for with a legitimate credit card. Booked through British Airways' UK web site, although it was impossible to say exactly where in the world the mouse had been physically clicked.

'This came in the mail?' Reacher asked.

Mauney said, 'It was stored in their fax machine's memory. It came in two weeks ago. The machine was out of paper. But we know that Sanchez and Orozco weren't around two weeks ago. Therefore this must be a response to a request they made at least a week earlier. We think they put a bunch of names on an unofficial watch list.'

'A bunch of names?'

'We found what we think is the original request. They had notes circulating in the mail, just like Franz. Four names.' Mauney pulled a second sheet of paper from his case. It was a photocopy of a sheet of blank paper with Manuel Orozco's spidery handwriting all over it. *Adrian Mount, Alan Mason, Andrew MacBride, Anthony Matthews, check w. DHS for arrival.* Fast untidy scrawl, written in a hurry, not that Orozco's penmanship had ever been neat.

Four names. Not five. Azhari Mahmoud's real name wasn't there. Reacher figured that Orozco knew that whoever the hell Mahmoud was, he would be travelling under an alias. No point in having aliases if you didn't use them.

'DHS,' Mauney said. 'The Department of Homeland Security. You know how hard it is for a civilian to get co-operation out of Homeland

240

Security? Your pal Orozco must have called in a shitload of favours. Or spent a shitload of bribe money. I need to know why.'

'Casino business, maybe.'

'Possible. Although Vegas security doesn't necessarily worry if bad guys show up in New York. New York arrivals are more likely headed for Atlantic City. Someone else's problem.'

'Maybe they share. Maybe there's a network. Guys can hit Jersey first and Vegas second.'

'Possible,' Mauney said again.

'Did this Adrian Mount guy actually arrive in New York?'

Mauney nodded. 'The INS computer has him entering through Terminal Four. Terminal Seven had already closed for the night. The flight was delayed.'

'And then what?'

'He checks in at a Madison Avenue hotel.'

'And then?'

'He disappears. No further trace.'

'But?'

'We move on down the list. Alan Mason flies to Denver, Colorado. Takes a room at a downtown hotel.'

'And then?'

'We don't know yet. We're still checking.'

'But you think they're all the same guy?'

'Obviously they're all the same guy. The initials are a dead giveaway.'

Reacher said, 'That makes me Chief Justice of the Supreme Court.'

'You sure act like it.'

'So who is he?'

241

'I have no idea. The INS inspector won't remember him. Those Terminal Four guys see ten thousand faces a day. The New York hotel people won't remember him. We haven't spoken to Denver yet. But they probably won't remember him either.'

'Wasn't he photographed at Immigration?'

'We're working on getting the picture.'

Reacher went back to the first fax. The Homeland Security data. The advance passenger information.

'He's British,' he said.

Mauney said, 'Not necessarily. He had at least one British passport, that's all.'

'So what's your play?'

'We start a watch list of our own. Sooner or later Andrew MacBride or Anthony Matthews will show up somewhere. Then at least we'll know where he's going.'

'What do you want from us?'

'You ever heard any of those names?'

'No.'

'No friends anywhere with the initials A and M?'

'Not that I recall.'

'Enemies?'

'Don't think so.'

'Did Orozco know anyone with those initials?'

'I don't know. I haven't spoken to Orozco in ten years.'

'I was wrong,' Mauney said. 'About the rope on his hands and feet. I had a guy take a look at it. It isn't very common after all. It's a sisal product from the Indian subcontinent.'

'Where would someone get it?'

'It's not for sale anywhere in the United States. It would have to come in on whatever gets exported from there.'

'Which is what?'

'Rolled carpets, bales of unfinished cotton fabric, stuff like that.'

'Thanks for sharing.'

'No problem. I'm sorry for your loss.'

Mauney left and they went up to Dixon's room. No real reason. They were still dead-ended. But they had to be somewhere. O'Donnell cleaned blood off his switchblade and checked over the captured Hardballers in his usual meticulous fashion. They had been manufactured by AMT not far away in Irwindale, California. They were fully loaded with jacketed .45s. They were in fine condition and fully operational. Clean, oiled, undamaged, which made it likely that they had been very recently stolen. Dope dealers were not usually careful with weapons. Their only limitations came from being faithful copies of a design that had been around since the year 1911. Magazine capacity was only seven rounds, which must have seemed more than OK in a world full of six-shooters, but which didn't stack up very well against modern capacities of fifteen or more.

'Pieces of shit,' Neagley said.

'Better than throwing stones,' O'Donnell said.

'Too big for my hand,' Dixon said. 'I like the Glock 19, personally.'

'I like anything that works,' Reacher said.

'The Glock holds seventeen rounds.'

'It only takes one per head. I've never had seventeen people after me all at once.'

'Could happen.'

The dark-haired forty-year-old calling himself Andrew MacBride was on the underground train inside the Denver airport. He had time to kill so he was riding it back and forth over and over again between the main terminal and Concourse C, which was the last stop. He was enjoying the jug-band music. He felt lightened, unburdened, and free. His luggage was now minimal. No more heavy suitcase. Just an overnight roll-on and a briefcase. The bill of lading was inside the briefcase, folded into a hardcover book. The padlock key was zipped into a secure pocket.

The man in the blue suit in the blue Chrysler sedan dialled his cell phone.

'They're back in the hotel,' he said. 'All four of them.'

'Are they getting close to us?' his boss asked.

'I have no way of telling.'

'Gut feeling?'

'Yes, I think they're getting close.'

'OK, it's time to take them down. Leave them there and come on in. We'll make our move in a couple of hours.'

FORTY-ONE

O'Donnell stood up and walked to Dixon's window and asked, 'What have we got?'

It was a routine question from the past. It had been a big part of the special unit's standard operating procedure. Like an unbreakable habit. Reacher had always insisted on constant recaps. He had insisted on combing through accumulated information, restating it, testing it, re-examining it, looking at it from new angles in the light of what had come afterwards. But this time nobody answered, except Dixon, who said, 'All we've got is four dead friends.'

The room went quiet.

'Let's get dinner,' Neagley said. 'No point in the rest of us starving ourselves to death.'

Dinner. Reacher recalled the burger barn, twenty-four hours previously. Sunset Boulevard, the noise, the thick beef patties, the cold beer. The round table for four. The conversation. The way the centre of attention had rotated freely between them all. Always one talker and three listeners, a shifting pyramid that had swung first one way and then another.

One talker, three listeners.

'Mistake,' he said.

Neagley said, 'Eating is a mistake?'

'No, eat if you want to. But we're making a mistake. A major conceptual error.'

'Where?'

'My fault entirely. I jumped to a false conclusion.'

'How?'

'Why can't we find Franz's client?'

'I don't know.'

'Because Franz didn't have a client. We made a mistake. His was the first body found, so we just went ahead and assumed this whole thing was about him. Like he had to have been the prime mover here. Like he was the talker and the other three were the listeners. But suppose he wasn't the talker?'

'So who was?'

'We've been saying all along he wouldn't have put himself on the line except for someone special. Someone he was obligated to somehow.'

'But that's back to saying he *was* the prime mover. With a client we can't find.'

'No, we're imagining the hierarchy all wrong. It doesn't necessarily go, first the client, then Franz, then the others helping Franz. I think Franz was actually lower down the pecking order. He wasn't at the top of the tree. See what I mean? Suppose he was actually helping one of the others? Suppose he was a listener, not the talker? Suppose this whole thing is basically Orozco's deal? For one of *his* clients? Or Sanchez's? If *they* needed help, who were they going to call?'

'Franz and Swan.'

'Exactly. We've been wrong from the start. We need to reverse the paradigm. Suppose Franz got a panic call from Orozco or Sanchez? That's certainly someone he regards as special. That's someone he's obligated to somehow. Not a client, but he can't say no. He's got to pitch in and help, no matter what Angela or Charlie think.'

Silence in the room.

Reacher said, 'Orozco contacted Homeland Security. That's difficult to do. And it's the only really proactive thing we've seen so far. It's more than Franz seems to have done.'

O'Donnell said, 'Mauney's people think Orozco was dead before Franz. That might be significant.'

'Yes,' Dixon said. 'If this was Franz's deal, why would he farm out the heavy-duty inquiries to Orozco? I imagine Franz was better equipped to handle them himself. That kind of proves the dynamic was flowing the other way, doesn't it?'

'It's suggestive,' Reacher said. 'But let's not make the same mistake twice. It could have been Swan.'

'Swan wasn't working.'

'Sanchez then, not Orozco.'

'More likely both of them together.'

Neagley said, 'Which would mean this was something based in Vegas, not here in LA. Could those numbers be something to do with casinos?'

'Possibly,' Dixon said. 'They could be house win percentages taking a hit after someone worked out a system.'

'What kind of thing gets played nine or ten or twelve times a day?'

'Practically anything. There's no real minimum or maximum.'

'Cards?'

'Almost certainly, if we're talking about a system.'

O'Donnell nodded. 'Six hundred and fifty unscheduled winning hands at an average of a hundred grand a time would get anyone's attention.'

Dixon said, 'They wouldn't let a guy win six hundred and fifty times for four months solid.'

'So maybe it's more than one guy. Maybe it's a cartel.'

Neagley said, 'We have to go to Vegas.'

Then Dixon's room phone rang. She answered it. Her room, her phone. She listened for a second and handed the receiver to Reacher.

'Curtis Mauney,' she said. 'For you.'

Reacher took the phone and said his name and Mauney said: 'Andrew MacBride just got on a plane in Denver. He's heading for Las Vegas. I'm telling you this purely as a courtesy. So stay exactly where you are. No independent action, remember?'

FORTY-TWO

They decided to drive to Vegas, not fly. Faster to plan and easier to organize and no slower door to door. No way could they take the Hardballers on a plane, anyway. And they had to assume that firepower would be necessary sooner or later. So Reacher waited in the lobby while the others packed. Neagley came down first and checked them out. She didn't even look at the bill. Just signed it. Then she dumped her bag near the door and waited with Reacher. O'Donnell came down next. Then Dixon, with her Hertz key in her hand.

They loaded their bags into the trunk and slid into their seats. Dixon and Neagley up front, Reacher and O'Donnell behind them. They headed east on Sunset and fought through the tangle of clogged freeways until they found the 15. It would run them north through the mountains and then north of east out of state and all the way to Vegas.

It would also run them close to where they knew a helicopter had hovered more than three weeks previously, at least twice, three thousand feet up, dead of night, its doors open. Reacher made up his mind not to look, but he did. After the road brought them out of the hills he found himself looking west toward the flat tan badlands. He saw O'Donnell doing the same thing. And Neagley. And Dixon. She took her eyes off the road for seconds at a time and stared to her left, her face creased against the setting sun and her lips clamped and turned down at the corners.

They stopped for dinner in Barstow, California, at a miserable roadside diner that had no virtues other than it was there and the road ahead was empty. The place was dirty, the service was slow, the food was bad. Reacher was no gourmet, but even he felt cheated. In the past he or Dixon or Neagley or certainly O'Donnell might have complained or heaved a chair through a window, but none of them did that night. They just suffered through three courses and drank weak coffee and got back on the road.

The man in the blue suit called it in from the Chateau Marmont's parking lot: 'They skipped out. They're gone. All four of them.'

His boss asked, 'Where to?'

'The clerk thinks Vegas. That's what she heard.'

'Excellent. We'll do it there. Better all around. Drive, don't fly.'

The dark-haired forty-year-old calling himself Andrew MacBride stepped out of the jetway inside the Las Vegas airport and the first thing he saw was a bank of slot machines. Bulky black and silver and gold boxes, with winking neon fascias. Maybe twenty of them, back to back in lines of ten. Each machine had a vinyl stool in front of it. Each machine had a narrow grey ledge at the bottom with an ashtray on the left and a cup holder on the right. Perhaps twelve of the twenty stools were occupied. The men and women on them were staring forward at the screens with a peculiar kind of fatigued concentration.

Andrew MacBride decided to try his luck. He decided to designate the result as a harbinger of his future success. If he won, everything would be fine.

And if he lost?

He smiled. He knew that if he lost he would rationalize the result away. He wasn't super-stitious.

He sat on a stool and propped his briefcase against his ankle. He carried a change purse in his pocket. It made him faster through airport security, and therefore less noticeable. He took it out and poked around in it and took out all the quarters he had accumulated. There weren't many. They made a short line on the ledge, between the ashtray and the cup holder.

He fed them to the machine, one by one. They made satisfying metallic sounds as they fell through the slot. A red LED showed five credits. There was a large touchpad to start the game. It was worn and greasy from a million fingers.

He pressed it, again and again.

The first four times, he lost.

The fifth time, he won.

A muted bell rang and a quiet *whoop-whoop* siren sounded and the machine rocked back and forth a little as a sturdy mechanism inside counted out a hundred quarters. They rattled down a chute and clattered into a pressed metal dish near his knee.

Barstow, California, to Las Vegas, Nevada, was going to be about two hundred miles. At night on the 15, with due deference to one state's Highway Patrol and the other's State Police, that was going to take a little over three hours. Dixon said she was happy to drive all the way. She lived in New York, and driving was a novelty for her. O'Donnell dozed in the back. Reacher stared out the window. Neagley said, 'Damn, we forgot all about Diana Bond. She's coming down from Edwards. She's going to find us gone.'

'Doesn't matter now,' Dixon said.

'I should call her,' Neagley said. But she couldn't get a signal on her cell phone. They were way out in the Mojave, and coverage was patchy.

They arrived in Las Vegas at midnight, which Reacher figured was exactly when the place looked its absolute best. He had been there before. In daylight, Vegas looked absurd. Inexplicable, trivial, tawdry, revealed, exposed. But at night with the lights full on it looked like a gorgeous fantasy. They approached from the bad end of the Strip and Reacher saw a plain cement bar with peeled paint and no windows and an unpunctuated four-word sign: *Cheap Beer Dirty Girls*. Opposite was a knot of dusty swaybacked motels and a single faded high-rise hotel. That kind of neighbourhood was where he would have started hunting for rooms, but Dixon drove on without a word toward the glittering palaces a half-mile ahead. She pulled in at one with an Italian name and a swarm of valets and bellmen came straight at them and grabbed their bags and drove their car away. The lobby was full of tile and pools and fountains and loud with the chatter of slot machines. Neagley headed to the desk and paid for four rooms. Reacher watched over her shoulder.

'Expensive,' he said, reflexively.

'But a possible shortcut,' Neagley said back. 'Maybe they knew Orozco and Sanchez here. Maybe they even gave them their security contract.'

Reacher nodded. *From the big green machine to this*. In which case *this* had been a huge step up, at least in terms of potential salary. The whole place dripped money, literally. The pools and the fountains were symbolic. So much water in the middle of the desert spoke of breathtaking extravagance. The capital investment must have been gigantic. The cash flow must have been immense. It had been quite something if Sanchez and Orozco had been in the middle of it all, safeguarding this kind of massive enterprise. He realized he was intensely proud of his old buddies. But simultaneously puzzled by them. When he had quit the army he had been fully aware that what faced him was the beginning of the rest of his life, but he had seen ahead no further than one day at a time. He had made no plans and formed no visions.

The others had.

How?

Why?

Neagley handed out the key cards and they arranged to freshen up and meet again in ten minutes to start work. It was after midnight, but Vegas was a true twenty-four-hour town. Time had no relevance. There were famous clichés about the lack of windows and clocks in the casinos, and they were all true, as far as Reacher knew. Nothing was allowed to slow the cash flow down. Certainly nothing as mundane as a player's bedtime. There was nothing better than a tired guy who kept on losing all night long.

Reacher's room was on the seventeenth floor. It was a dark concrete cube tricked out to look like a centuries-old salon in Venice. Altogether it was fairly unconvincing. Reacher had been to Venice, too. He opened his folding toothbrush and stood it upright in a glass in the bathroom. That was the sum total of his unpacking. He splashed water on his face and ran a palm across his bristly head and went back downstairs to take a preliminary look around.

Even in such an upmarket joint most of the ground-level real estate was devoted to slot machines. Patient, tireless, microprocessor-controlled, they skimmed a small but relentless percentage off the torrent of cash fed into them, twenty-four hours a day, seven days a week. Bells were ringing and beepers were sounding. Plenty of people were winning, but slightly more were losing. There was very light security in the room. No real opportunity to steal or cheat either way around, given a slot's mechanistic nature and the Nevada Gaming Board's close scrutiny. Reacher made only two people as staff out of hundreds in the room. A man and a woman, dressed like everyone else, as bored as everyone else, but without the manic gleam of hope in their eyes.

He figured Sanchez and Orozco hadn't spent much energy on slots.

He moved onward, to huge rooms in back where roulette and poker and blackjack were being played. He looked up, and saw cameras. Looked left and right and ahead, and saw high rollers and security guards and hookers in increasing concentrations.

He stopped at a roulette table. The way he understood it, roulette was really no different from a slot. Assuming the wheel was honest. Customers supplied money, the wheel distributed it straight back to other customers, except for an in-built house percentage, as relentless and reliable as a slot machine's microprocessor.

He figured Sanchez and Orozco hadn't spent much energy on roulette.

He moved on to the card tables, which was where he figured the real action was. Card games were the only casino components where human intelligence could be truly engaged. And where human intelligence was engaged, crime came soon after. But major crime would need more than a player's input. A player with self-discipline and a great memory and a rudimentary grasp of statistics could beat the odds. But beating the odds wasn't a crime. And beating the odds didn't earn a guy sixty-five million dollars in four months. The margin just wasn't there. Not unless the original stake was the size of a small country's GDP. Sixty-five million dollars over four months would need a dealer's involvement. But a dealer who lost so heavily would be fired within a week. Within a day or an hour, maybe. So a four-month winning streak would need some kind of a huge scam. Collusion. Conspiracy. Dozens of dealers, dozens of players. Maybe hundreds of each.

Maybe the whole house was playing against its investors.

Maybe the whole town was.

That would be a big enough deal for people to get killed over.

There was plenty of security in the room. There were cameras aimed at the players and the dealers. Some of the cameras were big and obvious, some were small and discreet. Probably there were others that were invisible. There were men and women patrolling in evening wear, with earpieces and wrist microphones, like Secret Service agents. There were others, undercover, in plain clothes. Reacher made five of them within a minute, and assumed there were many more that he was missing.

He threaded his way back to the lobby. Found Karla Dixon waiting by the fountains. She had showered and changed out of her jeans and leather jacket into a black pant suit. Her hair was wet and slicked back. Her suit coat was buttoned and she had no blouse under it. She looked pretty good.

'Vegas was settled by the Mormons,' she said. 'Did you know that?'

'No,' Reacher said.

'Now it's growing so fast they print the phone book twice a year.'

'I didn't know that either.'

'Seven hundred new houses a month.'

'They're going to run out of water.'

'No question about that. But they'll make hay until they do. Gambling revenues alone are close to seven billion dollars a year.'

'Sounds like you've been reading a guide book.'

Dixon nodded. 'There was one in my room. They get thirty million visitors a year. That means each one of them is losing an average of more than two hundred bucks per visit.'

'Two hundred thirty-three dollars and thirty-three cents,' Reacher said, automatically. 'The definition of irrational behaviour.'

'The definition of being human,' Dixon said. 'Everybody thinks they're going to be the one.'

Then O'Donnell showed up. Same suit, different tie, maybe a fresh shirt. His shoes shone in the lights. Maybe he had found a polishing cloth in his bathroom.

'Thirty million visitors a year,' he said.

Reacher said, 'Dixon already told me. She read the same book.'

'That's ten per cent of the whole population. And look at this place.'

'You like it?'

'It's making me see Sanchez and Orozco in a whole new light.'

Reacher nodded. 'Like I said before. You all moved onward and upward.'

Then Neagley stepped out of the elevator. She was dressed the same as Dixon, in a severe black suit. Her hair was wet and combed.

'We're swapping guide book facts,' Reacher said.

'I didn't read mine,' Neagley said. 'I called Diana Bond instead. She got there and waited an hour and went back again.'

'Was she pissed at us?'

'She's worried. She doesn't like Little Wing's name out there. I said I'd get back to her.'

'Why?'

'She's making me curious. I like to know things.'

'Me too,' Reacher said. 'Right now I'd like to know if someone scammed sixty-five million bucks in this town. And how.'

'It would be a big scam,' Dixon said. 'Pro-rated across a whole year it would be close to three per cent of the total revenue stream.'

'Two point seven eight,' Reacher said, automatically.

'Let's make a start,' O'Donnell said.

FORTY-THREE

They started at the concierge desk, where they asked to see the duty security manager. The concierge asked if there was a problem, and Reacher said, 'We think we have mutual friends.'

There was a long wait before the duty security manager showed up. Clearly social visits were low on his agenda. Eventually a medium-sized man in Italian shoes and a thousand-dollar suit walked over. He was about fifty years old, still trim and fit, in command, relaxed, but the lines around his eyes showed he must have done at least twenty years in a previous career. A harder career. He disguised his impatience well and introduced himself and shook hands all around. He said his name was Wright and suggested they talk in a quiet corner. Pure reflex, Reacher thought. His instincts and his training told him to move potential trouble well out of the way. Nothing could be allowed to slow the cash flow down.

They found a quiet corner. No chairs, of course. No Vegas casino would give guests a comfortable place to sit away from the action. For the same reason the lights in the bedrooms had been dim. A guest upstairs reading was no use to anyone. They stood in a neat circle and O'Donnell showed his D.C. PI licence and some kind of an accreditation note from the Metro PD. Dixon matched it with her licence and a card from the NYPD. Neagley had a card from the FBI. Reacher produced nothing. Just tugged his shirts down over the shape of the gun in his pocket.

Wright said to Neagley, 'I was with the FBI, once upon a time.'

Reacher asked him, 'Did you know Manuel Orozco and Jorge Sanchez?'

'Did I?' Wright said. 'Or do I?'

'Did you,' Reacher said. 'Orozco's dead for sure, and we figure Sanchez is, too.'

'Friends of yours?'

'From the army.'

'I'm very sorry.'

'We are, too.'

'Dead when?'

'Three, four weeks ago.'

'Dead how?'

'We don't know. That's why we're here.'

'I knew them,' Wright said. 'I knew them pretty well. Everyone in the business knew them.'

'Did you use them? Professionally?'

'Not here. We don't contract out. We're too big. Same with all the larger places.'

'Everything's in house?'

Wright nodded. 'This is where FBI agents and police lieutenants come to die. We get the pick of the litter. The salaries on offer here, they're lining up out the door. Not a day goes by that I don't interview at least two of them, on their last vacation before retirement.'

'So how did you know Orozco and Sanchez?'

'Because the places they look after are like training camps. Someone gets a new idea, they don't try it out here. That would be crazy. They perfect it someplace else first. So we keep people like Orozco and Sanchez sweet because we need their advance information. We all hook up once in a while, we talk, conferences, dinners, casual drinks.'

'Were they busy? Are you busy?'

'Like one-armed paperhangers.'

'You ever heard the name Azhari Mahmoud?'

'No. Who is he?'

'We don't know. But we think he's here under an alias.'

'Here?'

'Somewhere in Vegas. Can you check hotel registrations?'

'I can check ours, obviously. And I can call around.'

'Try Andrew MacBride and Anthony Matthews.'

'Subtle.'

Dixon asked, 'How do you guys know if a card player is cheating?'

Wright said, 'If he's winning.'

'People have to win.'

'They win as much as we let them. Any more than that, they're cheating. It's a question of statistics. Numbers don't lie. It's about how, not if.'

O'Donnell said, 'Sanchez had a piece of paper with a number written on it. Sixty-five million dollars. A hundred grand, times six hundred and fifty separate occasions, over a four-month period, to be precise.'

'So?'

'Are those the kind of numbers you would recognize?'

'As what?'

'As a rip-off.'

'What's that in a year? Almost two hundred million?'

'Hundred and ninety-five,' Reacher said.

'Conceivable,' Wright said. 'We try to keep wastage below eight per cent. That's like an industry target. So we lose way more than two hundred million in a year. But having said that, two hundred million in one specific scam would be a hell of a large proportion all in one go. Unless it was something new, over and above. In which case our eight per cent target is shot all to hell. In which case you're starting to worry me.'

'It worried them,' Reacher said. 'We think it killed them.'

'It would be a very big deal,' Wright said. 'Sixty-five million in four months? They'd need to recruit dealers and pit bosses and security people. They'd need to jinx cameras and erase tapes. They'd have to keep the cashiers quiet. It would be industrial-scale scamming.'

'It might have happened.'

'So why aren't the cops talking to me?'

'We're a little ways ahead of them.'

'The Vegas PD? The Gaming Board?'

Reacher shook his head. 'Our guys died across

the line in LA County. Couple of sheriffs out there are dealing with it.'

'And you're ahead of them? What does that mean?'

Reacher said nothing. Wright was quiet for a beat. Then he looked at each face in turn. First Neagley, then Dixon, then O'Donnell, then Reacher.

'Wait,' he said. 'Don't tell me. The army? You're the special investigators. Their old unit. They talked about it all the time.'

Reacher said, 'In which case you understand our interest. You worked with people.'

'If you find something, will you cut me in?'

'Earn it,' Reacher said.

'There's a girl,' Wright said. 'She works in some awful place with a fire pit. A bar, near where the Riviera used to be. She's tight with Sanchez.'

'His girlfriend?'

'Not exactly. Maybe once. But they're close. She'll know more than I do.'

FORTY-FOUR

Wright went back to work and Reacher checked with the concierge as to where the Riviera had been. He got directions back to the cheap end of the Strip. They walked. It was a warm dry desert night. The stars were out, on the far horizon, beyond the pall of smog and the wash of the street lights. The sidewalks were matted with discarded full-colour postcards advertising prostitutes. It seemed like the free market had driven the base price down to a penny under fifty bucks. Although Reacher had no doubt that sum would inflate pretty fast once some hapless punter actually got a girl to his room. The women in the pictures were pretty, although Reacher had no doubt they weren't real. They were probably library shots of innocent swimsuit models from Rio or Miami. Vegas was a city of scams. Sanchez and Orozco must have been permanently busy. *Like one-armed paperhangers*, Wright had said, and Reacher was completely ready to believe him.

They got level with the peeling cement bar with the cheap beer and the dirty girls and turned right into a mess of curving streets flanked by one-storey tan stucco buildings. Some were motels, some were grocery stores, some were restaurants, some were bars. All had the same kind of sign, white boards behind glass on tall poles, with horizontal racks for slot-in black letters. All the letters were in the same pinched vertical style, so it required concentration to tell one type of establishment from another. Groceries advertised six-packs of soda for $1.99, motels boasted about air and pools and cable, restaurants had all-you-can-eat breakfast buffets twenty-four hours a day. The bars majored on happy hours and permanent low prices for well shots. They all looked the same. They walked past five or six before they found one with a sign that said: *Fire Pit*.

The sign was outside a plain stucco shoe box short on windows. It didn't look like a bar. It could have been anything at all. It could have been an STD clinic or a fringe church. But not inside. Inside it was definitely a Vegas bar. It was a riot of décor and noise. Five hundred people drinking, shouting, laughing, talking loud, purple walls, dark red banquettes. Nothing was straight or square. The bar itself was crowded and long and curved into an S-shape. The tail of the S curled around a sunken pit. In the centre of the pit was a round fake fireplace. The flames were represented by jagged lengths of orange silk blown upright by a hidden fan. They swayed and moved and danced in beams of bright red light. Away from the fire the room was divided into plush velvet booths. All the booths were full of people. The fire pit was packed. People were standing everywhere. Music played from hidden speakers. Waitresses in abbreviated outfits threaded expertly through the crowds with trays held high.

'Lovely,' O'Donnell said.

'Call the taste police,' Dixon said.

'Let's find the girl and take her outside,' Neagley said. She was uncomfortable in the press of people. But they couldn't find the girl. Reacher asked at the bar for Jorge Sanchez's friend and the woman he was talking to seemed to know exactly who he meant but said she had gone off duty at midnight. She said the girl's name was Milena. For safety's sake Reacher asked two of the waitresses the same question and got the same answers from both of them. Their colleague Milena was tight with a security guy called Sanchez, but she was gone for the night, home, to sleep, to get ready for another hard twelve-hour shift the next day.

Nobody would tell him where home was.

He left his name with all three women. Then he fought his way back to the others and they threaded their way out to the sidewalk. Vegas at one in the morning was still lit up and humming, but after the inside of the bar it felt as quiet and peaceful as the cold grey surface of the moon.

'Plan?' Dixon said.

'We get back here at eleven thirty in the morning,' Reacher said. 'We catch her on her way in to work.'

'Until then?'

'Nothing. We take the rest of the night off.'

They walked back to the Strip and formed up

four abreast on the sidewalk for the slow stroll back to the hotel. Forty yards behind them in the traffic a dark blue Chrysler sedan braked sharply and pulled over and came to a stop by the kerb.

FORTY-FIVE

The man in the dark blue suit called it in immediately: 'I found them. Unbelievable. They just popped up right in front of me.'

His boss asked: 'All four of them?'

'They're right here in front of me.'

'Can you take them?'

'I think so.'

'So get it done. Don't wait for reinforcements. Get it done and get back here.'

The guy in the suit ended the call and moved his car off the kerb and swerved it across four lanes of traffic and stopped again in a side street outside a grocery that offered the cheapest cigarettes in town. He climbed out and locked up and headed down the Strip, on foot, fast, with his right hand in his coat pocket.

Las Vegas had more hotel rooms per square inch than any other place on the planet, but Azhari Mahmoud wasn't in any of them. He was in a rented house in a suburb three miles from the Strip. The house had been leased two years ago for an operation that had been planned but not executed. It had been safe then, and it was safe now.

Mahmoud was in the kitchen, with the Yellow Pages open on the counter. He was leafing through the truck rental section, trying to figure out how big of a U-Haul he was going to need.

The Strip had a permanent redevelopment tide that slopped back and forth like water in a bathtub. Once upon a time the Riviera had anchored the glamour end. It had sparked investment that had raced down the street block by block. By the time the improvements had reached the other extremity the stakes had been raised way high and the Riviera had suddenly looked old and dowdy by comparison with the newer stuff. So the investment had bounced right back again, racing block by block in the reverse direction. The result was a perpetually moving block-long construction site that separated the brand new stuff that had just been built from the slightly older stuff that was just about to be demolished again. The roadway and the sidewalks were being straightened as the work progressed. The new lanes continued uninterrupted. The old route looped through rubble. The city felt briefly quiet and deserted there, like an uninhabited no-man's-land.

That uninhabited no-man's-land was exactly where the man in the blue suit came up behind his targets. They were walking four abreast, slowly, like they had a place to go but all the time in the world to get there. Neagley was on the left, Reacher and then O'Donnell were in the centre, and Dixon was on the right. Close together, but not touching. Like a marching formation, across the whole width of the sidewalk. Collectively, they made a target maybe nine feet wide. It had been Neagley who had chosen the old sidewalk. She had followed it as if by arbitrary choice and the others had simply followed her.

The man in the suit took his gun out of his right-hand pocket. The gun was a Daewoo DP 51, made in South Korea, black, small, illegally obtained, unregistered, and untraceable. Its magazine held thirteen nine-millimetre Parabellums. It was being carried in what its owner's long training had taught him was the only safe-transport mode: chamber empty, safety on.

He held the gun right-handed and dry-fired against the locked trigger and rehearsed the sequence. He decided to prioritize and put the biggest targets down first. In his experience that always worked best. So, centre-mass into Reacher's back, then a small jog to the right into O'Donnell's back, then a radical swing left to Neagley, then all the way back to Dixon. Four shots, maybe three seconds, from twenty feet, which was close enough to be sure of hitting without being so close that the deflections left and right would be extreme. Maximum traverse would be a little more than twenty degrees. Simple geometry. A simple task. No problem.

He glanced all around.

Clear.

He looked behind.

Clear.

He pushed the safety down and gripped the Daewoo's barrel in his left hand and racked the slide with his right. Felt the first fat shell push upward, neatly into the chamber.

The night was not quiet. There was a lot of urban ambient noise. Traffic on the Strip, distant rooftop condensers roaring, extractors humming, the muted rumble of a hundred thousand people playing hard. But Reacher heard the rack of the slide twenty feet behind him. He heard it very clearly. It was exactly the kind of sound he had trained himself never to miss. To his ears it was a complete complex split-second symphony, and every component registered precisely. The scrape of alloy on alloy, its metallic resonance partially damped by a fleshy palm and the ball of a thumb and the side of an index finger, the grateful expansion of a magazine spring, the smack of a brass-cased shell socketing home, the return of the slide. Those sounds took about a thirtieth of a second to reach his ears and he spent maybe another thirtieth of a second processing them.

His life and his history lacked many things. He had never known stability or normality or comfort or convention. He had never counted on anything except surprise and unpredictability and danger. He took things exactly as they came, for exactly what they were. Therefore he heard the slide rack back and felt no disabling shock. No panic. No stab of disbelief. It seemed entirely natural and reasonable to him that he should be walking down a street at night and listening to a man preparing to shoot him in the back. There was no hesitation, no second-guessing, no self-doubt, no inhibition. There was just evidence of a

271

purely mechanical problem laid out behind him like an invisible four-dimensional diagram showing time and space and targets and fast bullets and slow bodies.

And then there was reaction, another thirtieth of a second later.

He knew where the first bullet would be aimed. He knew that any reasonable attacker would want to put the biggest target down first. That was nothing more than common sense. So the first shot would be aimed at him.

Or possibly at O'Donnell.

Better safe than sorry.

He used his right arm and shoved O'Donnell hard in the left shoulder and sent him sprawling into Dixon and then fell away in the opposite direction and crashed into Neagley. They both stumbled and as he was going down to his knees he heard the gun fire behind him and felt the bullet pass through the V-shaped void of empty air where the centre of his back had been just a split second before.

He had his hand on his Hardballer before he hit the sidewalk. He was calculating angles and trajectories before he had it out of his pocket. The Hardballer had two safeties. A conventional lever at the left rear of the frame, and a grip safety released when the butt was correctly held.

Before he had either one set to fire he had decided not to shoot.

Not immediately, anyway.

He had fallen on top of Neagley toward the inside edge of the sidewalk. Their attacker was in the centre of the sidewalk. Any angle vectoring from the inside of the sidewalk through the centre would launch a bullet out toward the roadway. If he missed the guy, he could hit a passing car. Even if he hit the guy, he could still hit a passing car. A jacketed .45 could go right through flesh and bone. Easily. Lots of power. Lots of penetration.

He made a split-second decision to wait for O'Donnell.

O'Donnell's angle was better. Much better. He had fallen on top of Dixon, toward the kerb. Toward the gutter. His line of sight was inward. Toward the construction. A miss or a through and through would do no harm at all. The bullet would spend itself in a pile of sand.

Better to let O'Donnell fire.

Reacher twisted as he hit the ground. He was in that zone where his mind was fast but the physical world was slow. He felt like his body was mired in a vat of molasses. He was screaming at it to *move move move* but it was responding with extreme reluctance. Beyond him Neagley was thumping dustily to earth with slow-motion precision. In the corner of his eye he saw her shoulder hitting the ground and then her momentum moving her head like a rag doll's. He moved his own head with enormous effort, like it was strapped with heavy weights, and he saw Dixon sprawling underneath O'Donnell.

He saw O'Donnell's left arm moving with painful slowness. Saw his hand. Saw his thumb dropping the Hardballer's safety lever.

Their attacker fired again.

And missed again. With a pre-planned shot

into empty air where O'Donnell's back had been. The guy was following a sequence. He had rehearsed. *Fire-move-fire*, Reacher and O'Donnell first. A sound plan, but the guy was unable to react to unexpected contingencies. He was a slow, conventional thinker. His brain had vapourlocked. Good, but not good enough.

Reacher saw O'Donnell's hand tighten around the grip of his gun. Saw his finger squeeze the slack out of the trigger. Saw the gun move up, up, up.

Reacher saw O'Donnell fire.

A snapshot, taken from an untidy uncompleted sprawl on the sidewalk. Taken before his body mass had even settled.

Too low, Reacher thought. *That's a leg wound at best.*

He forced his head around. He was right. It was a leg wound. But a leg wound from a high-velocity jacketed .45 was not a pretty thing. It was like taking a high-torque power drill and fitting it with a foot-long half-inch masonry bit and drilling right through a limb. All in a lot less than a thousandth of a second. The damage was spectacular. The guy took the slug in the lower thigh and his femur exploded from the inside like it had been strapped with a bomb. Immense trauma. Paralysing shock. Instant catastrophic blood loss from shattered arteries.

The guy stayed vertical but his gun hand dropped and O'Donnell was instantly on his feet. He scrambled up and his hand went in and out of his pocket and he covered the twenty feet full tilt and slammed the guy in the face with his knuckles. A straight right, with two hundred pounds of charging body mass behind it. Like hitting a watermelon with a sledgehammer.

The guy went down on his back. O'Donnell kicked his gun away and crouched at his side and jammed the Hardballer into his throat.

Game over, right there.

FORTY-SIX

Reacher helped Dixon up. Neagley got up on her own. O'Donnell was scooting around in a tight circle, trying to keep his feet out of the big welling puddle of blood coming from the guy's leg. Clearly his femoral artery was wide open. A healthy human heart was a pretty powerful pump and this guy's was busy dumping the whole of his blood supply onto the street. A guy his size, there had been probably fifteen pints in there at the beginning. Most of them were already gone.

'Step away, Dave,' Reacher called. 'Let him bleed out. No point ruining a pair of shoes.'

'Who is he?' Dixon asked.

'We may never know,' Neagley said. 'His face is a real mess.'

She was right. O'Donnell's ceramic knuckle-duster had done its work well. The guy looked like he had been attacked with hammers and knives. Reacher walked a wide circle around his head and grabbed his collar and pulled him backward. The lake of blood changed to a teardrop shape. Reacher took advantage of dry pavement and squatted down and checked through his pockets.

Nothing in any of them.

No wallet, no ID, no nothing.

Just car keys and a remote clicker, on a plain steel ring.

The guy was pale and turning blue. Reacher put a finger on the pulse in his neck and felt an irregular thready beat. The blood coming out of his thigh was turning foamy. There was major air in his vascular system. Blood out, air in. Simple physics. Nature abhors a vacuum.

'He's on the way out,' Reacher said.

'Good shooting, Dave,' Dixon said.

'Left-handed, too,' O'Donnell said. 'I hope you noticed that.'

'You're right-handed.'

'I was falling on my right arm.'

'Outstanding,' Reacher said.

'What did you hear?'

'The slide. It's an evolution thing. Like a predator stepping on a twig.'

'So there's an advantage in being closer to the cavemen than the rest of us.'

'You bet there is.'

'But who does that? Attacks without a round in the chamber?'

Reacher stepped away and looked down for a full-length view.

'I think I recognize him,' he said.

'How could you?' Dixon asked. 'His own mother wouldn't know him.'

'The suit,' Reacher said. 'I think I saw it before.'

'Here?'

'I don't know. Somewhere. I can't remember.'

'Think hard.'

O'Donnell said, 'I never saw that suit before.'

'Me either,' Neagley said.

'Nor me,' Dixon said. 'But whatever, it's a good sign, isn't it? Nobody tried to shoot us in LA. We must be getting close.'

Reacher tossed the guy's gun and car keys to Neagley and broke down a section of the construction site's fence. He hauled the guy through the gap as fast as he could, to minimize the blood smear. The guy was still leaking a little. Reacher dragged him across rough ground past tall piles of gravel until he found a wide trench built up with plywood formwork. The trench was about eight feet deep. The bottom was lined with gravel. The formwork was there to mould concrete for a foundation. Reacher rolled the guy into the trench. He fell eight feet and crunched on the stones and settled heavily, half on his side.

'Find shovels,' Reacher said. 'We need to cover him with more gravel.'

Dixon said, 'Is he dead yet?'

'Who cares?'

O'Donnell said, 'We should put him on his back. That way we need less gravel.'

'You volunteering?' Reacher said.

'I've got a good suit on. And I did all the hard work so far.'

So Reacher shrugged and vaulted down into the pit. Kicked the guy onto his back and stamped him flat and got him part way embedded in the gravel that was already there. Then he hauled himself back out and O'Donnell handed him a shovel. Between them they had to make ten trips to the gravel pile before the guy was adequately hidden. Neagley found a standpipe and unrolled a hose and turned on the water. She rinsed the sidewalk and chased watery blood into the gutter. Then she waited and followed the others out backward and hosed away their footprints from the construction site's sand. Reacher pulled the fence back into shape. Turned a full circle and checked the view. *Not perfect, but reasonable.* He knew there would be plenty a competent CSI team could get its teeth into, but there was nothing that would attract anyone's attention in the short term. They had a margin of safety. A few hours, at least. Maybe longer. Maybe concrete would get poured right at the start of the work day and the guy would become just one more missing person. Not the only person missing in a building's foundation, he guessed, in Las Vegas.

He breathed out.

'OK,' he said. '*Now* we take the rest of the night off.'

They dusted themselves down and formed up and resumed their walk down the Strip, slowly, four abreast, ready to relax. But Wright was waiting for them in the hotel lobby. The house security manager. For a Vegas guy he didn't have a great poker face. It was clear that he was uptight about something.

FORTY-SEVEN

Wright hurried over to them when they came in and led them away to the same quiet corner of the lobby that they had used before.

'Azhari Mahmoud isn't in any Las Vegas hotel,' he said. 'That's definitive. Also negative on Andrew MacBride and Anthony Matthews.'

Reacher nodded.

'Thanks for checking,' he said.

Wright said, 'And I made a few panic calls to my opposite numbers. Better that than lying awake all night, worrying. And you know what I found? You guys are completely full of shit. No way is this town down sixty-five million dollars in the last four months. It just isn't happening.'

'Can you be sure?'

Wright nodded. 'We all ran emergency cash flow audits. And there's nothing going on. The usual bits and pieces, that's all. Nothing else. I'm going to send you my Prozac bill. I practically overdosed tonight.'

They found a bar off the lobby and bought each other beers and sat in a line in front of four idle slots. Reacher's was simulating a big jackpot win, over and over again, like a tempting advertisement. Four reels were clicking to a stop on four cherries and lights were flashing and strobing and chasing themselves all over the front. Four reels, eight symbols on each. Astronomical odds, even without the microprocessor's covert intervention. Reacher tried to calculate the tonnage of quarters a player would need to get through before he could expect his first win. But he didn't know exactly how much a quarter weighed. Some small fraction of an ounce, obviously, which would add up fast. Tendon damage would be involved, muscle strain, repetitive stress injury. He wondered if casino owners had stock in orthopaedic clinics. Probably.

Dixon said, 'Wright already figured it would have to be industrial-scale scamming. He came right out and said so. Dealers, pit bosses, security guys, cameras, tapes, cashiers. It's not much more of a leap to imagine that apparent cash flow could be massaged. They could have installed a phony program that makes everything look kosher for as long as they need it to. It's exactly what I would do.'

Reacher asked, 'When would they find out?'

'When they do their books at the end of their financial year. By that point the money is either there or it's not.'

'How would Sanchez and Orozco find out ahead of that?'

'Maybe they tapped in lower down the food chain and extrapolated backward.'

'Who would need to be involved?'

281

'Key people.'

'Like Wright himself?'

'Possibly,' Dixon said.

O'Donnell said, 'We talked to him and a half-hour later someone was trying to shoot us in the back.'

'We need to find Sanchez's friend,' Neagley said. 'Before someone else does.'

'We can't,' Reacher said. 'No bar is going to give out a girl's address to a bunch of complete strangers.'

'We could tell them she's in danger.'

'Like they haven't heard that before.'

'Some other way,' Dixon said. 'The UPS thing.'

'We don't have her second name.'

'So what do we do?'

'We suck it up and wait for morning.'

'Should we move hotels? If Wright could be a bad guy?'

'No point. He'll have buddies all over town. Just lock your door.'

Reacher followed his own advice when he got back to his room. He clicked the security lever and put the chain on. No real defence against a determined opponent, but it would buy a second or two, and a second or two was generally all that Reacher needed.

He put the Hardballer in the bedside drawer. Put his clothes under the mattress to press and took a long hot shower. Then he started thinking about Karla Dixon.

She was alone.

Maybe she didn't like that.

Maybe she would appreciate a little safety in numbers.

He wrapped a towel around his waist and padded over to the phone. But before he got to it there was a knock at his door. He changed course. Ignored the peephole. He didn't like to put his eye to the glass undefended. Easiest thing in the world for an assailant in the corridor to wait for the lens to darken and then fire a large-calibre handgun straight through it. Such a move would make a hell of a mess. The bullet, plus shards and fragments of glass and steel, all of them through the eye and into the brain and out the back of the skull. Peepholes were a very bad idea, in Reacher's opinion.

He took off the chain and undid the extra lock. Opened the door.

Karla Dixon.

She was still fully dressed. She would be, he guessed, for a walk through the corridors and a ride in the elevator. Black suit, no shirt.

'Can I come in?' she said.

'I was just about to call you,' Reacher said.

'Right.'

'I was on my way to the phone.'

'Why?'

'Lonely.'

'You?'

'Me for sure. You, I hoped.'

'So can I come in?'

He held the door wide. She came in. Within a minute he discovered a shirt wasn't the only thing she wasn't wearing under the suit.

* * *

283

Neagley called on the bedside phone at nine thirty in the morning.

'Dixon's not in her room,' she said.

'Maybe she's working out,' Reacher said. 'Jogging or something.'

Dixon smiled and moved at his side, warm and lazy.

Neagley said, 'Dixon doesn't work out.'

'Then maybe she's in the shower.'

'I've tried her twice.'

'Relax. I'll try her. Breakfast in a half-hour, downstairs.'

He hung up with Neagley and gave the phone to Dixon and told her to count to sixty and then call Neagley's room and say she had just gotten out of the bath. Thirty minutes later they were all eating breakfast together in a lounge restaurant full of the noise of slot machines. An hour after that they were back on the Strip, heading for the bar with the fire pit again.

FORTY-EIGHT

Vegas in the morning looked flat and small and exposed under the hard desert sun. The light was pitiless. It showed up every fault and compromise. What by night had looked like inspired impressionism looked like silly fakery by day. The Strip itself could have been any worn-out four-lane in America. This time they walked it in a quadrant of four, two ahead, two behind, a smaller collective target, alert and always aware of who was ahead and who was behind them.

But there was nobody ahead and nobody behind. Traffic on the street was thin and the sidewalks were empty. Vegas in the morning was as close as it ever got to quiet.

The construction zone halfway down the Strip was quiet, too.

Deserted.

No activity.

'Is it Sunday today?' Reacher asked.

'No,' O'Donnell said.

'A holiday?'

'No.'

'So why aren't they working?'

285

There were no cops there. No crime scene tape. No big investigation. Just nothing. Reacher could see where he had bent the fence panel the night before. Beyond it the dirt and the sand was muddied where Neagley had hosed it off. The old sidewalk had a huge dry stain on it. The old roadbed's gutter had the last of a thin damp slick running to a drain. A mess, for sure, but no construction zone was ever tidy. *Not perfect, but reasonable.* There was nothing overt that could have attracted anyone's attention.

'Weird,' Reacher said.

'Maybe they ran out of money,' O'Donnell said.

'Pity. That guy's going to start to smell soon.'

They walked on. This time they knew exactly where they were going and in the daylight they found a shortcut through the mess of curved streets. They came up on the bar with the fire pit from a different direction. It wasn't open yet. They sat on a low wall and waited and squinted in the sun. It was very warm, almost hot.

'Two hundred eleven clear days a year in Vegas,' Dixon said.

'Summer high of a hundred and six degrees,' O'Donnell said.

'Winter low of thirty-six.'

'Four inches of rain a year.'

'One inch of snow, sometimes.'

'I still didn't get to my guide book,' Neagley said.

By the time the clock in Reacher's head hit twenty to twelve people started showing up for work. They came down the street in loose knots, separated out into ones and twos, men and women moving slow without visible enthusiasm. As they passed by, Reacher asked all the women if they were called Milena. They all said no.

Then the sidewalk went quiet again.

At nine minutes to twelve another bunch showed up. Reacher realized he was watching the bus timetable in action. Three women walked past. Young, tired, dressed down, with big white sneakers on their feet.

None of them was called Milena.

The clock in Reacher's head ticked around. One minute to twelve. Neagley checked her watch.

'Worried yet?' she asked.

'No,' Reacher said, because beyond her shoulder he had seen a girl he knew had to be the one. She was fifty yards away, hurrying a little. She was short and slim and dark, dressed in faded low-rider blue jeans and a short white T-shirt. She had a winking jewel lodged in her navel. She was carrying a blue nylon backpack on one shoulder. She had long jet-black hair that fell forward and framed a pretty face that looked about seventeen. But judging by the way she moved she was nearer to thirty. She looked tired and preoccupied.

She looked unhappy.

Reacher got up off the wall when she was ten feet away and said, 'Milena?' She slowed with the kind of sudden wariness any woman should feel when randomly accosted in the street by a giant of a stranger. She glanced ahead at the bar's door and then across at the opposite sidewalk as if assessing her options for a fast escape. She stumbled a little as if caught between the need to stop and the urge to run.

Reacher said, 'We're friends of Jorge's.'

She looked at him, and then at the others, and then back at him. Some kind of slow realization dawned on her face, first puzzlement, then hope, then disbelief, and then acceptance, the same sequence Reacher imagined a poker player must experience when a fourth ace shows up in his hand.

Then there was some kind of muted satisfaction in her eyes, as if contrary to all expectations a comforting myth had proved to be true.

'You're from the army,' she said. 'He told me you'd come.'

'When?'

'All the time. He said if he ever had trouble, you'd show up sooner or later.'

'And here we are. Where can we talk?'

'Just let me tell them I'm going to be late today.' She smiled a little shyly and skirted around them all and headed inside the bar. Came out again two minutes later, moving faster, standing taller, with her shoulders straighter, like a weight had been taken off them. Like she was no longer alone. She looked young but capable. She had clear brown eyes and fine skin and the kind of thin sinewy hands a person gets after working hard for ten years.

'Let me guess,' she said. She turned to Neagley. 'You must be Neagley.' Then she moved on to Dixon and said, 'Which makes you Karla.' She turned to Reacher and O'Donnell and said, 'Reacher and O'Donnell, right? The big one and the handsome one.' O'Donnell smiled at her and she turned back to Reacher and said, 'They told me you were here last night looking for me.'

Reacher said, 'We wanted to talk to you about Jorge.'

Milena took a breath and swallowed and said, 'He's dead, isn't he?'

'Probably,' Reacher said. 'We know for sure Manuel Orozco is.'

Milena said, 'No.'

Reacher said, 'I'm sorry.'

Dixon asked, 'Where can we go to talk?'

'We should go to Jorge's place,' Milena said. 'His home. You should see it.'

'We heard it was wrecked.'

'I cleaned it up a little.'

'Is it far?'

'We can walk.'

They walked back down the Strip, all five of them, side by side. The construction zone was still deserted. No activity. But no commotion, either. No cops. Milena asked twice more whether Sanchez was dead, as if repeating the question might eventually yield the answer she wanted to hear. Both times Reacher answered, 'Probably.'

'But you don't know for sure?'

'His body hasn't been found.'

'But Orozco's has?'

'Yes. We saw it.'

'What about Calvin Franz and Tony Swan? Why aren't they here?'

'Franz is dead. Swan too, probably.'

'For sure?'

'Franz for sure.'

'But not Swan?'

'Not for sure.'

'And not Jorge for sure?'

'Not for sure. But probably.'

'OK.' She walked on, refusing to surrender, refusing to give up hope. They passed the high-end hotels one by one, moving through sketched facsimiles of the world's great cities all in the space of a few hundred yards. Then they saw apartment buildings. Milena led them through a left turn, and then a right, onto a parallel street. She stopped under the shade of an awning that led to the lobby of a building that might have been the best place in town four generations of improvements ago.

'This is it,' she said. 'I have a key.'

She slipped her backpack off her shoulder and rooted through it and came out with a change purse. She unzipped it and took out a door key made of tarnished brass.

'How long did you know him?' Reacher asked.

She paused for a long moment, trapped into contemplating the use of the past tense, and trying to find a way of making it seem less than definitive.

'We met a few years ago,' she said.

She led them into the lobby. There was a door-man behind a desk. He greeted her with a degree of familiarity. She led them to the elevator. They went up to the tenth floor and turned right on a faded corridor. Stopped outside a door painted green.

She used her key.

Inside, the apartment wasn't a breathtaking spread, but it wasn't small, either. Two bedrooms, a living room, a kitchen. Plain décor, mostly white, some bright colours, a little old-fashioned. Generous windows. Once the place must have had a fine view of the desert but now it looked straight at a newer development a block away.

It was a man's place, simple, unadorned, undesigned.

It was a real mess.

It had been through the same kind of trauma as Calvin Franz's office. The walls and the floor and the ceiling were solid concrete, so they hadn't been damaged. But other than that the treatment had been similar. All the furniture was ripped up and torn apart. Chairs, sofas, a desk, a table. Books and papers had been dumped everywhere. A TV set and stereo equipment had been smashed. CDs were littered everywhere. Rugs had been lifted and thrown aside. The kitchen had been almost demolished.

Milena's cleaning up had been limited to piling some of the debris around the perimeter and stuffing some of the feathers back into some of the cushions. She had stacked some of the books and papers near the broken shelves they had come from. Apart from that, there hadn't been much she could do. A hopeless task.

Reacher found the kitchen trash, where Curtis Mauney had said the crumpled napkin had been found. The pail had been torn off its mounting under the sink and booted across the room. Some stuff seemed to have fallen out, and some hadn't.

'This was more about anger than efficiency,' he

said. 'Destruction, almost for its own sake. Like they were just as much mad as worried.'

'I agree,' Neagley said.

Reacher opened a door and moved on to the master bedroom. The bed was wrecked. The mattress had been destroyed. In the closet clothes were dumped everywhere. The rails had been torn down. The shelves had been smashed. Jorge Sanchez had been a neat person to start with, and his neatness had been reinforced by years of living with military restraints and standards. There was nothing left of him in his apartment. No shred, no echo.

Milena was moving around the space, listlessly, putting more stuff in tentative piles, stopping occasionally to leaf through a book or look at a picture. She used her thigh to butt the ruined sofa back to its proper position, even though no one would ever sit on it again.

Reacher asked her, 'Have the cops been here?'

'Yes,' she said.

'Did they have any conclusions?'

'They think whoever came here dressed up as phony contractors. Cable, or phone.'

'OK.'

'But I think they bribed the doorman. That would be easier.'

Reacher nodded. *Vegas, a city of scams.* 'Did the cops have an opinion as to why?'

'No,' she said.

He asked her, 'When did you last see Jorge?'

'We had dinner,' she said. 'Here. Chinese take-out.'

'When?'

'His last night in Vegas.'

'You were here then?'

'It was just the two of us.'

Reacher said, 'He wrote something on a napkin.'

Milena nodded.

'Because someone called him?'

Milena nodded again.

Reacher asked, 'Who called him?'

Milena said, 'Calvin Franz.'

FORTY-NINE

Milena was looking shaky so Reacher used his forearm to clear shards of broken china off the kitchen countertop, to give her a place to sit. She boosted herself up and sat with her elbows turned out and her hands laid flat on the laminate, palms down, trapped under her knees.

Reacher said, 'We need to know what Jorge was working on. We need to know what caused all this trouble.'

'I don't know what it was.'

'But you spent time with him.'

'A lot.'

'And you knew each other well.'

'Very well.'

'For years.'

'On and off.'

'So he must have talked to you about his work.'

'All the time.'

'So what was on his mind?'

Milena said, 'Business was slow. That's what was on his mind.'

'His business here? In Vegas?'

Milena nodded. 'It was great in the beginning.

Years ago, they were always busy. They had a lot of contracts. But the big places dropped them, one by one. They all set up in-house operations. Jorge said it was inevitable. Once they reach a certain size, it makes more sense.'

'We met a guy at our hotel who said Jorge was still busy. Like a one-armed paperhanger.'

Milena smiled. 'The guy was being polite. And Jorge put a brave face on it. Manuel Orozco, too. At first they used to say, we'll fake it until we make it. Then they said, we'll fake it now we're not making it any more. They kept up a front. They were too proud to beg.'

'So what are you saying? They were going down the tubes?'

'Fast. They did a bit of muscle work here and there. Doorman at some of the clubs, running cheats out of town, stuff like that. They did some consulting for the hotels. But not much any more. Those people always think they know better, even when they don't.'

'Did you see what Jorge wrote on the napkin?'

'Of course. I cleared dinner away after he left. He wrote numbers.'

'What did they mean?'

'I don't know. But he was very worried about them.'

'What did he do next? After Franz's call?'

'He called Manuel Orozco. Right away. Orozco was very worried about the numbers too.'

'How did it all start? Who came to them?'

'Came to them?'

Reacher asked, 'Who was their client?'

Milena looked straight at him. Then she turned

and twisted and looked at O'Donnell, and then Dixon, and then Neagley.

'You're not listening to me,' she said. 'They didn't really have clients. Not any more.'

'Something must have happened,' Reacher said.

'I don't know what you mean.'

'I mean someone must have come to them with a problem. On the job somewhere, or at the office.'

'I don't know who came to them.'

'Jorge didn't say?'

'No. One day they were sitting around doing nothing, the next day they were as busy as blue-assed flies. That's what they used to call it. Blue-assed flies, not one-armed paperhangers.'

'But you don't know why?'

Milena shook her head. 'They didn't tell me.'

'Who else might know?'

'Orozco's wife might know.'

FIFTY

The wrecked apartment went very quiet and Reacher stared straight at Milena and said, 'Manuel Orozco was married?'

Milena nodded. 'They have three children.'

Reacher looked at Neagley and asked, 'Why didn't we know that?'

'I don't know everything,' Neagley said.

'We told Mauney the next of kin was the sister.'

Dixon asked, 'Where did Orozco live?'

'Down the street,' Milena said. 'In a building just like this.'

Milena led them another quarter-mile away from the centre of town to an apartment house on the other side of the same street. Orozco's place. It was very similar to Sanchez's. Same age, same style, same construction, same size, a blue side-walk awning where Sanchez's had been green.

Reacher asked, 'What is Mrs Orozco's name?'

'Tammy,' Milena said.

'Will she be home?'

Milena nodded. 'She'll be asleep. She works nights. In the casinos. She gets home and gets the

297

children on the school bus and then she goes right to bed.'

'We're going to have to wake her up.'

It was the building's doorman who woke her up. He called upstairs on the house phone. There was a long wait and then there was a reply. The doorman announced Milena's name, and then Reacher's, and Neagley's, and Dixon's, and O'Donnell's. The guy had picked up on the mood and he used a serious tone of voice. He left no doubt that the visit wasn't good news.

There was another long wait. Reacher guessed Tammy Orozco would be matching the four new names with her husband's nostalgic recollections, and putting two and two together. Then he guessed she would be putting on a housecoat. He had visited widows before. He knew how it went.

'Please go on up,' the doorman said.

They rode the elevator to the eighth floor, packed tight in a small car. Turned left on a corridor and stopped at a blue door. It was already standing open. Milena knocked anyway and then led them inside.

Tammy Orozco was a small hunched figure on a sofa. Wild black hair, pale skin, a patterned housecoat. She was probably forty but right then she could have passed for a hundred. She looked up. She ignored Reacher and O'Donnell and Dixon and Neagley completely. Didn't look at them at all. There was some hostility there. Not just jealousy or vague resentment, like Angela Franz had shown. There was real anger instead.

She looked directly at Milena and said, 'Manuel is dead, isn't he?'

Milena sat down beside her and said, 'These guys say so. I'm very sorry.'

Tammy asked, 'Jorge too?'

Milena said, 'We don't know yet.'

The two women hugged and cried. Reacher waited it out. He knew how it went. The apartment was a larger unit than Sanchez's. Maybe three bedrooms, a different layout, facing a different direction. The air was stale and smelled of fried food. The whole place was battered and untidy. Maybe because it had been tossed three weeks ago, or maybe it was always in a state of chaos with two adults and three children living in it. Reacher didn't know much about children, but he guessed Orozco's three were young, from the kind of books and toys and scattered clothing he saw lying around. There were dolls and bears and video games and complex constructions made from plastic components. Therefore the children were maybe nine, seven, and five. Approximately. But all recent. All post-service. Orozco hadn't been married in the service. Reacher was fairly sure of that, at least.

Eventually Tammy Orozco looked up and asked, 'How did it happen?'

Reacher said, 'The police have all the details.'

'Did he suffer?'

'It was instantaneous,' Reacher said, as he had been trained to long ago. All service KIAs were said to have been killed instantly, unless it could be definitively proved otherwise. It was considered a comfort to the next of kin. And in

299

Orozco's case it was technically true, Reacher thought. After the capture, that was, and the mistreatment and the starvation and the thirst and the helicopter ride and the writhing, screaming, twenty-second free fall.

'Why did it happen?' Tammy asked.

'That's what we're trying to find out.'

'You should. It's the very least you can do.'

'It's why we're here.'

'But there are no answers here.'

'There must be. Starting with the client.'

Tammy glanced at Milena, tear-stained, puzzled.

'Client?' she said. 'Don't you already know who it was?'

'No,' Reacher said. 'Or we wouldn't be here asking.'

'They didn't have clients,' Milena said, as if on Tammy's behalf. 'Not any more. I told you that.'

'Something started this,' Reacher said. 'Someone must have come to them with a problem, at their office, or out in one of the casinos. We need to know who it was.'

'That didn't happen,' Tammy said.

'Then they must have stumbled over the problem on their own. In which case we need to know where and when and how.'

There was a long silence. Then Tammy said, 'You really don't understand, do you? This was nothing to do with them. Nothing at all. It was nothing to do with Vegas.'

'It wasn't?'

'No.'

'So how did it start?'

'They got a call for help,' Tammy said. 'That's how it started. One day, suddenly, out of the blue. From one of you guys in California. From one of their precious old army buddies.'

FIFTY-ONE

Azhari Mahmoud dropped Andrew Macbride's passport in a Dumpster and became Anthony Matthews on his way to the U-Haul depot. He had a wad of active credit cards and a valid driver's licence in that name. The address on the licence would withstand sustained scrutiny, too. It was an actual building, an occupied house, not just a mail drop or a vacant lot. The billing address for the credit cards matched it exactly. Mahmoud had learned a lot over the years.

He had decided to rent a medium-size truck. In general he preferred medium options everywhere. They stood out less obviously. Clerks remembered people who demanded the biggest or the smallest of anything. And a medium truck would do the job. His science education had been meagre, but he could do simple arithmetic. He knew that volume was calculated by multiplying height by width by length. Therefore he knew a pile containing six hundred and fifty boxes could be constructed by stacking them ten wide and thirteen deep and five high. At first he had thought that ten wide would be a greater dimension than any available truck could accommodate, but then he realized he could reduce the required width by stacking the boxes on their edges. It would all work out.

In fact he knew it would all work out, because he was still carrying the hundred quarters he had won in the airport.

They gave their condolences and Curtis Mauney's name to Tammy Orozco and left her alone on her sofa. Then they walked Milena back to the bar with the fire pit. She had a living to earn and she was already three hours down on the day. She said she could get fired if she missed the happy hour crush later in the afternoon. The Strip had gotten a little busier as the day had worn on. But the construction zone was still deserted. No activity at all. The slick in the gutter had finally dried. Apart from that there was no change. The sun was high. Not blazing, but it was warm enough. Reacher started thinking about how shallow the dead guy was buried. And about decomposition, and gases, and smells, and curious animals.

'You get coyotes here?' he asked.

'In town?' Milena said. 'I never saw one.'

'OK.'

'Why?'

'Just wondering.'

They walked on. Took the same shortcut they had used before. Arrived outside the bar a little after three o'clock in the afternoon.

'Tammy's angry,' Milena said. 'I'm sorry about that.'

'It's to be expected,' Reacher said.

'She was there when the bad guys came to search. Asleep. They hit her on the head. She was unconscious for a week. She doesn't remember anything. Now she blames whoever it was who called for all her troubles.'

'Understandable,' Reacher said.

'But I don't blame you,' Milena said. 'It wasn't any of you that called. I guess half of you were involved and half of you weren't.'

She ducked inside the bar without looking back. The door closed behind her. Reacher stepped away and sat down on the wall, where he had waited that morning.

'I'm sorry, people,' he said. 'We just wasted a lot of time. My fault, entirely.'

Nobody answered.

'Neagley should take over,' he said. 'I'm losing my touch.'

'Mahmoud came here,' Dixon said. 'Not LA.'

'He probably made a connection. He's probably in LA right now.'

'Why not fly direct?'

'Why carry four false passports? He's cautious, whoever he is. He lays false trails.'

'We were attacked here,' Dixon said. 'Not in LA. Makes no sense.'

'It was a collective decision to come here,' O'Donnell said. 'Nobody argued.'

Reacher heard a siren on the Strip. Not the bass bark of a fire truck, not the frantic yelp of an ambulance. A cop car, moving fast. He glanced up, toward the construction zone a half-mile away. He stood up and moved right and shaded his eyes and watched the short length of the Strip he could see. One cop was nothing, he thought. If some construction foreman had finally showed up for work and found something, there would be a whole convoy.

He waited.

Nothing happened. No more sirens. No more cops. No convoy. Just a routine traffic stop, maybe. He took one step more, to widen his view, to be certain. Saw a wink of red and blue beyond the corner of a grocery store. A car, parked in the sun. A red plastic lens over the tail light. Dark blue paint on a fender.

A car.

Dark blue paint.

He said, 'I know where I saw that guy before.'

FIFTY-TWO

They stood around the Chrysler at a cautious and respectful distance, like it was a roped-off exhibit in a modern art museum. A 300C, dark blue, California plates. It was parked tight to the kerb, locked up, still and cold, a little travel-stained. Neagley took out the keys that Reacher had found in the dying guy's pocket and held them arm's length like the guy had held the gun and pressed the remote button once.

The blue Chrysler's lights flashed and its doors unlocked with a ragged *thunk*.

'It was behind the Chateau Marmont,' Reacher said. 'Just waiting. That same guy was in it. His suit matched the sheet metal exactly. I took it for a car service with a gimmick.'

'The others told them we would come,' O'Donnell said. 'At first as a threat, I suppose. And then later as a consolation. So they sent the guy to take us out. He spotted us on the sidewalk, I guess, just after he hit town. We were right there in front of him. He got lucky.'

'Real lucky,' Reacher said. 'May all our enemies have the same kind of extreme good fortune.'

He opened the driver's door. The car smelled of new leather and plastic. The interior was unmarked. There were maps in the door pocket, crisp and folded. That was all. Nothing else on show. He slid in and stretched a long arm over to the glove box lid. Opened it up. Came out with a wallet and a cell phone. That was all that was in there. No registration, no insurance. No instruction manuals. Just a wallet and a phone. The wallet was a slim thing designed to be carried in a trouser pocket. It was a stiff rectangle made of black leather with a money clip built in on one side and a credit card pocket built in on the other. There was a wad of folded cash in the clip. More than seven hundred dollars, mostly fifties and twenties. Reacher took it all. Just pulled it out of the clip and stuffed it in his own pants pocket.

'That's two more weeks before I need to find a job,' he said. 'Every cloud has a silver lining.'

He turned the wallet over. The credit card section was jammed. There was a current California driver's licence and four credit cards. Two Visas, an Amex, and a MasterCard. Expiration dates all far in the future. The licence and all four cards were made out to a guy by the name of Saropian. The address on the licence had a five-digit house number and a Los Angeles street name and a zip that meant nothing to Reacher.

He dropped the wallet on the passenger seat.

The cell phone was a small silver folding item with a round LCD window on the front. It was getting great reception but its battery was low. Reacher opened it up and a larger window lit up in colour. There were five voice messages waiting.

He handed the phone to Neagley.

'Can you retrieve those messages?' he asked.

'Not without his code number.'

'Look at the call log.'

Neagley scrolled through menus and selected options.

'All the calls in and out are to and from the same number,' she said. 'A 310 area code. Which is Los Angeles.'

'Land line or cell?'

'Could be either.'

'A grunt calling his boss?'

Neagley nodded. 'And vice versa. A boss issuing orders to a grunt.'

'Could your guy in Chicago get a name and address for the boss?'

'Eventually.'

'Get him started on it. The licence plate on this car, too.'

Neagley used her own cell to call her office. Reacher lifted the centre armrest console and found nothing except a ballpoint pen and a car charger for the phone. He checked the rear compartment. Nothing there. He got out and checked the trunk. Spare tyre, jack, wrench. Apart from that, empty.

'No luggage,' he said. 'This guy didn't plan on a long trip. He thought we were going to be easy meat.'

'We nearly were,' Dixon said.

Neagley closed the dead guy's phone and handed it back to Reacher. Reacher dropped it on the passenger seat next to the wallet.

Then he picked it up again.

308

'This is an ass-backward situation,' he said. 'Isn't it? We don't know who sent this guy, or from where, or for why.'

'But?' Dixon said.

'But whoever it was, we've got his number. We could call him up and say hello, if we wanted to.'

'Do we want to?'

'Yes, I think we do.'

FIFTY-THREE

They got in the parked Chrysler, for quiet. The doors were thick and heavy and closed tight and gave the kind of vacuum hush a luxury sedan was supposed to. Reacher opened the dead guy's phone and scrolled through the call log to the last call made and then pressed the green button to make it all over again. Then he cupped the phone to his ear and waited. And listened. He had never owned a cell phone but he knew how they were used. People felt them vibrate in their pockets or heard them ring and fished them out and looked at the screen to see who was calling and then decided whether or not to answer. Altogether it was a much slower process than picking up a regular phone. It could take five or six rings, at least.

The phone rang once.

Twice.

Three times.

Then it was answered in a real hurry.

A voice said, 'Where the hell have you been?'

The voice was deep. A man, not young. Not small. Behind the exasperation and the urgency there was a civilized West Coast accent, professional, but with a faint remnant of streetwise edge still in it. Reacher didn't reply. He listened hard for background sounds from the phone. But there were none. None at all. Just silence, like a closed room or a quiet office.

The voice said, 'Hello? Where the hell are you? What's happening?'

'Who is this?' Reacher asked, like he had every right to know. Like he had gotten an accidental wrong number.

But the guy didn't bite. He had seen the caller ID.

'No, who are you?' he asked back, slowly.

Reacher paused a beat and said, 'Your boy failed last night. He's dead and buried, literally. Now we're coming for you.'

There was a long moment of silence. Then the voice said, 'Reacher?'

'You know my name?' Reacher said. 'Doesn't seem fair that I don't know yours.'

'Nobody ever said life was fair.'

'True. But fair or not, enjoy what's left of it. Buy yourself a bottle of wine, rent a DVD. But not a box set. You've got about two days, max.'

'You're nowhere.'

'Look out your window.'

Reacher heard sudden movement. The rustle of jacket tails, the oiled grind of a swivel chair. *An office. A guy in a suit.* A desk facing the door.

Only about a million of those in the 310 area code.

'You're nowhere,' the voice said again.

'We'll see you soon,' Reacher said. 'We're going

to take a helicopter ride together. Just like you did before. But with one big difference. My friends were reluctant, presumably. But you won't be. You'll be begging to jump out. You'll be pleading. I can absolutely promise you that.'

Then he closed the phone and dropped it in his lap.

Silence in the car.

'First impressions?' Neagley asked.

Reacher breathed out.

'An executive,' he said. 'A big guy. A boss. Not dumb. An ordinary voice. A solo office with a window and a closed door.'

'Where?'

'Couldn't tell. There were no background sounds. No traffic, no airplanes. And he didn't seem too worried that we have his phone number. The registration is going to come back phony as hell. This car, too, I'm sure.'

'So what now?'

'We head back to LA. We should never have left.'

'This is about Swan,' O'Donnell said. 'Got to be, right? We can't make a case for it being about Franz, it's not about Sanchez or Orozco, so what else is left? He must have gotten into something immediately after he quit New Age. Maybe he had it all lined up and waiting.'

Reacher nodded. 'We need to talk to his old boss. We need to see if he shared any private concerns before he left.' He turned to Neagley. 'So set up the thing with Diana Bond again. The Washington woman. About New Age and Little Wing. We need a bargaining chip. Swan's old boss might talk more if he knows we have something solid to keep quiet about in exchange. Besides, I'm curious.'

'Me too,' Neagley said.

They stole the Chrysler. Didn't even get out. Reacher took the key from Neagley and started it up and drove it around to the hotel. He waited in the drop-off lane while the others went inside to pack. He quite liked the car. It was quiet and powerful. He could see its exterior styling reflected in the hotel's window. It looked good in blue. It was square and bluff and about as subtle as a hammer. His kind of machine. He checked the controls and the toys and plugged the dead guy's phone into its charger and closed the armrest lid on it.

Dixon came out of the lobby first, trailing a bellhop carrying her luggage and a valet sprinting ahead to get her car. Then came Neagley and O'Donnell together. Neagley was stuffing a credit card receipt into her purse and closing her cell phone all at the same time.

'We got a hit on the licence plate,' she said. 'It traces back to a shell corporation called Walter at a commercial mail drop in downtown LA.'

'Cute,' Reacher said. 'Walter for Walter Chrysler. I bet the phone comes back to a corporation called Alexander, for Graham Bell.'

'The Walter Corporation leases a total of seven cars,' Neagley said.

Reacher nodded. 'We need to bear that in mind. They'll have major reinforcements waiting somewhere.'

Dixon said she would drive O'Donnell back in her rental. So Reacher popped the Chrysler's trunk and Neagley heaved her bags in and then slid in beside him in the passenger seat.

'Where are we holing up?' Dixon asked, through the window.

'Somewhere different,' Reacher said. 'So far they've seen us in the Wilshire and the Chateau Marmont. So now we need a change of pace. We need the kind of place they won't think to look. Let's try the Dunes on Sunset.'

'What is that?'

'A motel. My kind of place.'

'How bad is it?'

'It's fine. It has beds and doors that lock.'

Reacher and Neagley took off first. Traffic was slow all the way out of town and then the 15 emptied and Reacher settled in for the cruise across the desert. The car was quiet and swift and civilized. Neagley spent the first thirty minutes playing phone tag around Edwards Air Force Base, trying to get Diana Bond on the line before her cell coverage failed. Reacher tuned her out and concentrated on the road ahead. He was an adequate driver, but not great. He had learned in the army and had never received civilian instruction. Never passed a civilian test, never held a civilian licence. Neagley was a much better driver than he was. And much faster. She finished her calls and fidgeted with impatience. Kept glancing over at the speedometer.

'Drive it like you stole it,' she said. 'Which you did.'

So he accelerated a little. Started passing people, including a medium-sized U-Haul truck lumbering west in the right-hand lane.

Ten miles shy of Barstow Dixon caught up with them and flashed her lights and pulled alongside and O'Donnell made eating motions from the passenger seat. Like helpless masochists they stopped at the same diner they had used before. No alternative for miles, and they were all hungry. They hadn't eaten lunch.

The food was as bad as before and the conversation was desultory. Mostly they talked about Sanchez and Orozco. About how hard it was to keep a viable small business going. Especially about how hard it was for ex-military people. They entered the civilian world with all the wrong assumptions. They expected the same kind of certainties they had known before. The straight-forwardness, the transparency, the honesty, the shared sacrifice. Reacher felt that part of the time Dixon and O'Donnell were actually talking about themselves. He wondered exactly how well they were doing, behind their facades. Exactly how it all looked on paper for them, at tax time. And how it was going to look a year from then. Dixon was in trouble because she had walked out on her last job. O'Donnell had been out for a spell with his sister. Only Neagley seemed to have no worries. She was an unqualified success. But she was one out of nine. A hit rate a fraction better than 11 per cent, for some of the finest graduates the army had ever produced.

Not good.

You're well out of it, Dixon had said.

I feel that way, usually, he had replied.

All that we've got that you don't is suitcases, O'Donnell had said.

But what have I got that you don't? he had replied.

He finished the meal a little closer to an answer than before.

After Barstow came Victorville and Lake Arrowhead. Then the mountains reared in front of them. But first, this time to their right, were the badlands where the helicopter had flown. Once again Reacher told himself he wouldn't look, but once again he did. He took his eyes off the road and glanced north and west for seconds at a time. Sanchez and Swan were out there somewhere, he guessed. He saw no reason to hope otherwise.

They passed through an active cell and Neagley's phone rang. Diana Bond, all set to leave Edwards at a moment's notice. Reacher said, 'Tell her to meet us at that Denny's on Sunset. Where we were before.' Neagley made a face and he said, 'It's going to taste like Maxim's in Paris after that place we just stopped.'

So Neagley arranged the rendezvous and he kicked the transmission down and climbed onto Mount San Antonio's first low slopes. Less than an hour later they were checking in at the Dunes Motel.

The Dunes was the kind of place where no room went even close to three figures for the night and where guests were required to leave a security deposit for the TV remote, which was issued with great ceremony along with the key. Reacher paid cash from his stolen wad for all four rooms, which got around the necessity for real names and ID. They parked the cars out of sight of the street and regrouped in a dark battered lounge next to a laundry room, as anonymous as four people could get in Los Angeles County.

Reacher's kind of place.

Another hour later Diana Bond called Neagley to say she was pulling into the Denny's lot.

FIFTY-FOUR

They walked a short stretch of Sunset and stepped into the Denny's neon lobby and found a tall blonde woman waiting for them. She was alone. She was dressed all in black. Black jacket, black blouse, black skirt, black stockings, black high heeled shoes. Serious East Coast style, a little out of place in California and seriously out of place in a Denny's in California. She was slim, attractive, clearly intelligent, somewhere in her late thirties.

She looked a little irritated and preoccupied.

She looked a little worried.

Neagley introduced her all around. 'This is Diana Bond,' she said. 'From Washington D.C. via Edwards Air Force Base.'

Diana Bond had nothing with her except a small crocodile purse. No briefcase, not that Reacher expected notes or blueprints. They led her through the shabby restaurant and found a round table in back. Five people wouldn't fit in a booth. A waitress came over and they ordered coffee. The waitress came back with five heavy mugs and a flask, and poured. They each took a preliminary sip, in silence. Then Diana Bond spoke. She didn't start with small talk. Instead she said, 'I could have you all arrested.'

Reacher nodded.

'I'm kind of surprised you haven't,' he said. 'I was kind of expecting to find a bunch of agents here with you.'

Bond said, 'One call to the Defense Intelligence Agency would have done it.'

'So why didn't you make that call?'

'I'm trying to be civilized.'

'And loyal,' Reacher said. 'To your boss.'

'And to my country. I really would urge you not to pursue this line of inquiry.'

Reacher said, 'That would give you another wasted journey.'

'I'd be very happy to waste another journey.'

'Our tax dollars at work.'

'I'm pleading with you.'

'Deaf ears.'

'I'm appealing to your patriotism. This is a question of national security.'

Reacher said, 'Between the four of us here we've got sixty years in uniform. How many have you got?'

'None.'

'How many has your boss got?'

'None.'

'Then shut up about patriotism and national security, OK? You're not qualified.'

'Why on earth do you need to know about Little Wing?'

'We had a friend who worked for New Age. We're trying to complete his obituary.'

'He's dead?'

'Probably.'

'I'm very sorry.'

'Thank you.'

'But again, I would appeal to you not to press this.'

'No deal.'

Diana Bond paused a long moment. Then she nodded.

'I'll trade,' she said. 'I'll give you outline details, and in return you swear on those sixty years in uniform that they'll go no further.'

'Deal.'

'And after I talk to you this one time, I never hear from you again.'

'Deal.'

Another long pause. Like Bond was wrestling with her conscience.

'Little Wing is a new type of torpedo,' she said. 'For the navy's Pacific submarine fleet. It's fairly conventional apart from an enhanced control capability because of new electronics.'

Reacher smiled.

'Good try,' he said. 'But we don't believe you.'

'Why not?'

'We were never going to believe your first answer. Obviously you were going to try to blow us off. Plus, most of those sixty years we mentioned were spent listening to liars, so we know one when we see one. Plus, some of those sixty years were spent reading all kinds of Pentagon bullshit, so we know how they use words. A new torpedo would more likely be called Little Fish. Plus, New Age was a clean-sheet start up with a free choice of where to build, and if they were working for the navy they'd have chosen San Diego or Connecticut or Newport News, Virginia. But they didn't. They chose East LA instead. And the closest places to East LA are air force places, including Edwards, where you just came from, and the name is Little Wing, so it's an airborne device.'

Diana Bond shrugged.

'I had to try,' she said.

Reacher said, 'Try again.'

Another pause.

'It's an infantry weapon,' she said. 'Army, not air force. New Age is in East LA to be near Fort Irwin, not Edwards. But you're right, it's airborne.'

'Specifically?'

'It's a man-portable shoulder-launched surface-to-air missile. The next generation.'

'What does it do?'

Diana Bond shook her head. 'I can't tell you that.'

'You'll have to. Or your boss goes down.'

'That's not fair.'

'Compared to what?'

'All I'll say is that it's a revolutionary advance.'

'We've heard that kind of thing before. It means it'll be out of date a year from now, rather than the usual six months.'

'We think two years, actually.'

'What does it do?'

'You're not going to call the newspapers. You'd be selling your country out.'

'Try us.'

'Are you serious?'

'As lung cancer.'

'I don't believe this.'

'Suck it up. Or your boss needs a new job tomorrow. As far as that goes, we'd be doing our country a favour.'

'You don't like him.'

'Does anyone?'

'The newspapers wouldn't publish.'

'Dream on.'

Bond was quiet for a minute more.

'Promise it will go no further,' she said.

'I already have,' Reacher said.

'It's complicated.'

'Like rocket science?'

'You know the Stinger?' Bond asked. 'The current generation?'

Reacher nodded. 'I've seen them in action. We all have.'

'What do they do?'

'They chase the heat signature of jet exhaust.'

'But from below,' Bond said. 'Which is a key weakness. They have to climb and manoeuvre at the same time. Which makes them relatively slow and relatively cumbersome. They show up on downward-looking radar. It's possible for a pilot to out-manoeuvre them. And they're vulnerable to countermeasures, like decoy flares.'

'But?'

'Little Wing is revolutionary. Like most great ideas, it starts with a very simple premise. It completely ignores its target on the way up. It does all its work on the way down.'

'I see,' Reacher said.

Bond nodded. 'Going up, it's just a dumb

rocket. Very, very fast. It reaches about eighty thousand feet and then it slows and stops and topples. Starts to fall back down again. Then the electronics switch on and it starts hunting its target. It has boosters to manoeuvre with, and control surfaces, and because gravity is doing most of the work the manoeuvring can be incredibly precise.'

'It falls on its prey from above,' Reacher said. 'Like a hawk.'

Bond nodded again.

'At unbelievable speed,' she said. 'Way supersonic. It can't miss. And it can't be stopped. Airborne defensive radar always looks downward. Decoy flares always launch downward. The way things have been up until now, planes are very vulnerable from above. They could afford to be. Because very little came at them from above. But it's different now. That's why this is so sensitive. We've got about a two-year window in which our surface-to-air capability will be completely unbeatable. For about two years anyone using Little Wing will be able to shoot down anything that flies. Maybe longer. It depends how fast people are with new countermeasures.'

Reacher said, 'The speed will make countermeasures difficult.'

'Almost impossible,' Bond said. 'Human reaction times will be too slow. So defences will have to be automated. Which means we'll have to trust computers to tell the difference between a bird a hundred yards up and Little Wing a mile up and a satellite fifty miles up. Potentially it will be chaos. Civilian airlines will want protection, obviously, because of terrorism worries. But the skies above civilian airports are thick with stacked planes. False deployment would be the norm, not the exception. So they'd have to turn off their protection for takeoff and landing, which makes them totally vulnerable just when they can't afford to be.'

'A can of worms,' Dixon said.

'But a theoretical can of worms,' O'Donnell said. 'We understand Little Wing isn't working very well.'

'This can go no further,' Bond said.

'We already agreed.'

'Because these are commercial secrets now.'

'Much more important than defence secrets.'

'The prototypes were fine,' Bond said. 'The beta testing was excellent. But they ran into problems with production.'

'Rockets or electronics or both?'

'Electronics,' Bond said. 'The rocket technology is more than forty years old. They can do the rocket production in their sleep. That happens up in Denver, Colorado. It's the electronics packs that are giving them the problems. Down here in LA. They haven't even started mass production yet. They're still doing bench assembly. Now even that is screwed up.'

Reacher nodded and said nothing. He stared out the window for a moment and then took a stack of napkins out of the dispenser and fanned them out and then butted them back together into a neat pile. Weighted them down with the sugar container. The restaurant had pretty much emptied out. There were two guys alone in separate booths at the far end of the room. Landscape workers, tired and hunched. Apart from them, no business. Outside on the street the afternoon light was fading. The red and yellow neon from the restaurant's huge sign was becoming comparatively brighter and brighter. Some passing cars on the boulevard already had their headlights on.

'So Little Wing is the same old same old, really,' O'Donnell said, in the silence. 'A Pentagon pipe dream that does nothing but burn dollars.'

Diana Bond said, 'It wasn't supposed to be like that.'

'It never is.'

'It's not a total failure. Some of the units work.'

'They said the same thing about the M-16 rifle. Which was a real comfort when you were out on patrol with one.'

'But the M-16 was perfected eventually. Little Wing will be, too. And it will be worth waiting for. You know which is the world's best-protected airplane?'

Dixon said, 'Air Force One, probably. Politicians' asses always come first.'

Bond said, 'Little Wing could take it out without breaking a sweat.'

'Bring it on,' O'Donnell said. 'Easier than voting.'

'You should read the Patriot Act. You could be arrested for even thinking that.'

'Jails aren't big enough,' O'Donnell said.

Their waitress came back and hovered. Clearly she was hoping for something more lucrative from such a big table than five bottomless cups of coffee. Dixon and Neagley took the hint and ordered ice cream sundaes. Diana Bond passed. O'Donnell ordered a hamburger. The waitress stood and looked pointedly at Reacher. He wasn't seeing her. He was still playing with his pile of napkins. Weighting it down with the sugar canister, lifting the sugar off, putting it back.

'Sir?' the waitress said.

Reacher looked up.

'Apple pie,' he said. 'With ice cream. And more coffee.'

The waitress went away and Reacher went back to his pile of napkins. Diana Bond retrieved her purse from the floor and made a big show of dusting it off.

'I should get back,' she said.

'OK,' Reacher said. 'Thank you very much for coming.'

FIFTY-FIVE

Diana Bond left for the long drive back to Edwards and Reacher neatened his stack of napkins and placed the sugar container back on top of it, exactly centred. The desserts arrived and more coffee was poured and O'Donnell's burger was served. Reacher got halfway through his pie and then he stopped eating. He sat in silence for a moment, staring out the window again. Then he moved suddenly and pointed at the sugar container and looked straight at Neagley and asked, 'You know what that is?'

'Sugar,' she said.

'No, it's a paperweight,' he said.

'So?'

'Who carries a gun with the chamber empty?'

'Someone trained that way.'

'Like a cop. Or an ex-cop. Ex-LAPD, maybe.'

'So?'

'The dragon lady at New Age lied to us. People take notes. They doodle. They work better with pencil and paper. There are no completely paper-less environments.'

O'Donnell said, 'Things might have changed since you last held a job.'

'The first time we talked she told us that Swan used his piece of the Berlin Wall as a paperweight. It's kind of hard to use a paperweight in a completely paperless environment, isn't it?'

O'Donnell said, 'It could have been a figure of speech. Paperweight, souvenir, desk ornament, is there a difference?'

'First time we were there, we had to wait to get in the lot. Remember?'

Neagley nodded. 'There was a truck coming out the gate.'

'What kind of a truck?'

'A photocopier truck. Repair or delivery.'

'Kind of hard to use a photocopier in a completely paperless environment, right?'

Neagley said nothing.

Reacher said, 'If she lied about that, she could have lied about a whole bunch of stuff.'

Nobody spoke.

Reacher said, 'New Age's director of security is ex-LAPD. I bet most of his foot soldiers are, too. Safeties on, chambers empty. Basic training.'

Nobody spoke.

Reacher said, 'Call Diana Bond again. Get her back here, right now.'

'She only just left,' Neagley said.

'Then she hasn't got far. She can turn around. I'm sure her car has a steering wheel.'

'She won't want to.'

'She'll have to. Tell her if she doesn't there'll

be a whole lot more than her boss's name in the newspaper.'

It took a little more than thirty-five minutes for Diana Bond to get back. Slow traffic, inconvenient highway exits. They saw her car pull into the lot. A minute later she was back at the table. Standing beside it, not sitting at it. Angry.

'We had a deal,' she said. 'I talk to you one time, you leave me alone.'

'Six more questions,' Reacher said. 'Then we leave you alone.'

'Go to hell.'

'This is important.'

'Not to me.'

'You came back. You could have kept on driving. You could have called the DIA. But you didn't. So quit pretending. You're going to answer.'

Silence in the room. No sound, except tyres on the boulevard and a distant hum from the kitchen. A dishwasher, maybe.

'Six questions?' Bond said. 'OK, but I'll be counting carefully.'

'Sit down,' Reacher said. 'Order dessert.'

'I don't want dessert,' she said. 'Not here.' But she sat down, in the same chair she had used before.

'First question,' Reacher said. 'Does New Age have a rival? A competitor somewhere with similar technology?'

Diana Bond said, 'No.'

'Nobody all bitter and frustrated because they were outbid?'

'No,' Bond said again. 'New Age's proposition was unique.'

'OK, second question. Does the government really want Little Wing to work?'

'Why the hell wouldn't it?'

'Because governments can get nervous about developing new attack capabilities without having appropriate defence capabilities already in place.'

'That's a concern I've never heard mentioned.'

'Really? Suppose Little Wing is captured and copied? The Pentagon knows how much damage it can do. Are we happy to face having the thing turned around against us?'

'It's not an issue,' Bond said. 'We would never do anything if we thought like that. The Manhattan Project would have been cancelled, supersonic fighters, everything.'

'OK,' Reacher said. 'Now tell me about New Age's bench assembly.'

'Is this the third question?'

'Yes.'

'What about their bench assembly?'

'Tell me what it is, basically. I never worked in the electronics business.'

'It's assembly by hand,' Bond said. 'Women in sterile rooms at laboratory benches in shower caps using magnifying glasses and soldering irons.'

'Slow,' Reacher said.

'Obviously. A dozen units a day instead of hundreds or thousands.'

'A dozen?'

'That's all they're averaging right now. Nine or ten or twelve or thirteen a day.'

'When did they start bench assembly?'

'Is this the fourth question?'

'Yes, it is.'

'They started bench assembly about seven months ago.'

'How did it go?'

'Is this the fifth question?'

'No, it's a follow-up.'

'It went fine for the first three months. They hit their targets.'

'Six days a week, right?'

'Yes.'

'When did they hit problems?'

'About four months ago.'

'What kind of problems?'

'Is this the last question?'

'No, it's another follow-up.'

'After assembly the units are tested. More and more of them weren't working.'

'Who tests them?'

'They have a quality control director.'

'Independent?'

'No. He was the original development engineer. At this stage he's the only one who can test them because he's the only one who knows how they're supposed to work.'

'What happens to the rejects?'

'They get destroyed.'

Reacher said nothing.

Diana Bond said, 'Now I really have to go.'

'Last question,' Reacher said. 'Did you cut their funding because of their problems? Did they fire people?'

'Of course not,' Bond said. 'Are you nuts?

That's not how it works. We maintained their budget. They maintained their staff. We had to. They had to. We have to make this thing work.'

FIFTY-SIX

Diana Bond left for the second time and Reacher went back to his pie. The apples were cold and the crust was leathery and the ice cream had melted all over the plate. But he didn't care. He wasn't really tasting anything.

O'Donnell said, 'We should celebrate.'

'Should we?' Reacher said.

'Of course we should. We know what happened now.'

'And that means we should celebrate?'

'Well, doesn't it?'

'Lay it out for me and see for yourself.'

'OK, Swan wasn't pursuing some private concern here. He was investigating his own company. He was checking why the success rate fell away so badly after the first three months. He was worried about insider involvement. Therefore he needed clerical help on the outside because of eavesdropping and random data monitoring in his office. Therefore he recruited Franz and Sanchez and Orozco. Who else would he trust?'

'And?'

'First they analysed the production figures.

Which were all those numbers we found. Seven months, six days a week. Then they ruled out sabotage. New Age had no rivals that stood to gain anything and the Pentagon wasn't working against them behind the scenes.'

'So?'

'What else was there? They figured the quality control guy had falsely condemned six hundred and fifty working units and the firm was booking them in as destroyed but actually selling them out the back door for a hundred grand a piece to someone called Azhari Mahmoud, a.k.a. whoever. Hence the list of names and the note on Sanchez's napkin.'

'And?'

'They confronted New Age prematurely and got killed for it. The firm cooked up a story to cover Swan's disappearance and the dragon lady fed it to you.'

'So now we should celebrate?'

'We know what happened, Reacher. We always used to celebrate.'

Reacher said nothing.

'It's a home run,' O'Donnell said. 'Isn't it? And you know what? It's almost funny. You said we should talk to Swan's old boss? Well, I think we already did. Who else could it have been on that cell phone? That was New Age's director of security.'

'Probably.'

'So what's the problem?'

'What did you say way back in that Beverly Hills hotel room?'

'I don't know. Lots of things.'

334

'You said you wanted to piss on their ancestors' graves.'

'And I will.'

'You won't,' Reacher said. 'And neither will I, or any of us. Which isn't going to feel good. That's why we can't celebrate.'

'They're right here in town. They're sitting ducks.'

'They sold six hundred and fifty working electronics packs out the back door. Which has implications. Somebody wants the technology, they buy one pack and copy it. Somebody buys six hundred and fifty, it's because they want the missiles themselves. And they don't buy the electronics down here unless they're also buying the rockets and the launch tubes up there in Colorado. That's what we've got to face here. Some guy called Azhari Mahmoud now owns six hundred and fifty brand-new latest-generation SAMs. Whoever he is, we can guess what he wants them for. It'll be some kind of a big, big deal. So we have to tell someone, folks.'

Nobody spoke.

'And a thin minute after we drop that dime, we're buried up to our armpits in federal agents. We won't be able to cross the street without permission, let alone go get these guys. We'll have to sit back and watch them get lawyers and eat three squares a day for the next ten years while they run through all their appeals.'

Nobody spoke.

'So that's why we can't celebrate,' Reacher said. 'They messed with the special investigators and we can't lay a glove on them.'

335

FIFTY-SEVEN

Reacher didn't sleep a wink that night. not a second, not a minute. *They messed with the special investigators and we can't lay a glove on them.* He tossed and turned and lay awake, hour after hour. His eyes were jammed wide open but images and fevered hallucinations flooded at him. Calvin Franz, walking, talking, laughing, full of drive and energy and sympathy and concern. Jorge Sanchez, the narrowed eyes, the hint of a smile, the gold tooth, the endless cynicism that was ultimately as reassuring as constant good humour. Tony Swan, short, wide, bulky, sincere, a thoroughly decent man. Manuel Orozco, the absurd tattoo, the fake accent, the jokes, the metallic clunk of the ever-present Zippo.

Friends all.

Friends unavenged.

Friends abandoned.

Then others swam into sight, as real as if they were hovering just below the ceiling. Angela Franz, clean, carefully dressed, eyes wide with panic. The boy Charlie, rocking in his little wooden chair. Milena, slipping like a ghost from the harsh Vegas sun into the darkness of the bar. Tammy Orozco on her sofa. Her three children, bewildered, roaming through their wrecked apartment, looking for their father. They appeared to Reacher as two girls and a boy, nine, seven and five, even though he had never met them. Swan's dog was there, a long swishing tail, a deep rumble of a bark. Even Swan's mailbox was there, blinding in the Santa Ana light.

Reacher gave it up at five in the morning and got dressed again and went out for a walk. He turned west on Sunset and stamped his way through a whole angry mile, hoping against hope that someone would bump him or jostle him or get in his way so that he could snap and snarl and yell and ease his frustration. But the sidewalks were deserted. Nobody walked in LA, especially not at five in the morning, and certainly nowhere near a giant stranger in an obvious rage. The boulevard was quiet, too. No traffic, except occasional anonymous third-hand sedans bearing humble employees to work, and a lone farting Harley carrying a fat grey-haired jerk in leathers. Reacher was offended by the noise and gave the guy the finger. The bike slowed and for a delicious moment Reacher thought the guy was going to stop and make an issue out of it. But, no luck. The guy took one look and twisted the throttle and took off again, fast.

Up ahead on the right Reacher saw a vacant corner lot fenced with wire. At a bus bench in the side street was a small crowd of day labourers, waiting for the sun, waiting for work, tiny brown men with tired stoic faces. They were drinking coffee from a mission cart set up outside some kind of a community centre. Reacher headed in that direction and paid a hundred of his stolen dollars for a cup. He said it was a donation. The women behind the cart accepted it without a question. They had seen weirder, he guessed, in Hollywood.

The coffee was good. As good as Denny's. He sipped it slowly and leaned back on the vacant lot's fence. The wire gave slightly and supported his bulk like a trampoline. He floated there, not quite upright, coffee in his mouth, fog in his brain.

Then the fog cleared, and he started thinking.

About Neagley, principally, and her mysterious contact at the Pentagon.

He owes me, she had said. *Bigger than you could imagine.*

By the time he finished the coffee and tossed the empty cup he had a faint glimmer of new hope, and the outline of a new plan. Odds of success, about fifty-fifty. Better than roulette.

He was back at the motel by six in the morning. He couldn't raise the others. No answer from their rooms. So he headed on down Sunset and found them in Denny's, in the same booth Neagley had used at the very beginning. He slid into the remaining unoccupied seat and the waitress dealt him a paper place mat and clattered a knife and a fork and a mug after it. He ordered coffee, pancakes, bacon, sausage, eggs, toast and jelly.

'You're hungry,' Dixon said.

'Starving,' he said.

'Where were you?'

'Walking.'

'Didn't sleep?'

'Not even close.'

The waitress came back and filled his mug. He took a long sip. The others went quiet. They were picking at their food. They looked tired and dispirited. He guessed that none of them had slept well, or at all.

O'Donnell asked, 'When do we drop the dime?'

Reacher said, 'Maybe we don't.'

Nobody spoke.

'Ground rules,' Reacher said. 'We have to agree something from the start. If Mahmoud has got the missiles, then this thing is bigger than we are. We have to suck it up and move on. There's too much at stake. Either he's paramilitary and wants to turn the whole Middle East into a no-fly zone, or he's a terrorist planning a day of action that's going to make the Twin Towers look like a day at the beach. Either way around we're looking at hundreds or thousands of KIA. Maybe tens of thousands. Those kinds of numbers trump any interest of ours. Agreed?'

Dixon and Neagley nodded and looked away.

O'Donnell said, 'There's no if about it. We have to assume Mahmoud has got the missiles.'

'No,' Reacher said. 'We have to assume he's got the electronics. We don't know if he's got the rockets and the launch tubes yet. It's even money. Fifty-fifty. Either he collected the rockets first, or the electronics first. But he's got to have both before we drop the dime.'

'How do we find out?'

'Neagley hits up her Pentagon guy. She calls in whatever markers she's holding. He organizes some kind of audit out in Colorado. If anything is missing up there, then it's game over for us. But if everything is still present and correct and accounted for, then it's game on.'

Neagley checked her watch. Just after six in the west, just after nine in the east. The Pentagon would have been humming for an hour. She took out her phone and dialled.

FIFTY-EIGHT

Neagley's buddy wasn't dumb. He insisted on calling back from outside the building, and not on his own cell phone, either. And he was smart enough to realize that any pay phone within a mile radius of the Pentagon would be continuously monitored. So there was a whole hour's delay while he got himself across the river and halfway across town to a phone on a wall outside a bodega on New York Avenue.

Then the fun began.

Neagley told him what she wanted. He gave her all kinds of reasons why it wasn't possible. She started calling in her markers, one by one. The guy owed her a lot of heavy-duty favours. That was clear. Reacher felt a certain amount of sympathy for him. If your balls were in a vice, better that it wasn't Neagley's hand on the lever. The guy caved and agreed within ten minutes. Then it became a logistical discussion. How should the job be done, by whom, what should be considered proof positive. Neagley suggested Army CID should roll up unannounced and match the books with physical inventory. Her guy agreed, and asked for a week. Neagley gave him four hours.

Reacher spent the four hours asleep. Once the plan was settled and the decision was made he relaxed to the point where he couldn't keep his eyes open. He went back to his room and lay down on the bed. A maid came in after an hour. He sent her away again and went back to sleep. Next thing he knew Dixon was at his door. She told him that Neagley was waiting in the lounge, with news.

Neagley's news was neither good nor bad. It was somewhere in between. New Age had no physical plant in Colorado. Just an office. They contracted out their raw missile production, to one of the established aerospace manufacturers in Denver. That manufacturer had a number of Little Wing assemblies available for inspection. An Army CID officer had seen them all and counted them all, and his final tally was precisely what the books said it should be. Everything was present, correct, and accounted for. No problem. Except that exactly six hundred and fifty of the units were currently stored in a separate secure warehouse, crated up and awaiting transport to a facility in Nevada where they were due to be decommissioned and destroyed.

'Why?' O'Donnell asked.

'Current production is specified as Mark Two,' Neagley said. 'They're junking what's left of the Mark Ones.'

'Which just happens to be exactly six hundred and fifty units.'

'You got it.'

'What's the difference?'

'The Mark Twos have a small fluorescent arrow painted on. To make loading easier in the dark.'

'That's all?'

'You got it.'

'It's a scam.'

'Of course it's a scam. It's a way of making the paperwork look legal when Mahmoud's people drive them through the factory gate.'

Reacher nodded. A gate guard would fight to the death to prevent the unauthorized removal of ordnance. But if he saw paperwork with a reason on it, he would pass the load through with a smile and a cheery wave. Even if the reason was the absence of a small painted arrow on something that cost more than he made in a year. Reacher had seen the Pentagon junk stuff for less.

He asked, 'How do the electronics packs fit on?'

'In,' Neagley said. 'Not on. There's an access port in the side. You unscrew it and plug the pack in. Then there's some testing and calibration.'

'Could I do it?'

'I doubt it. You'd need training. In the field it's going to be a specialist's job.'

'So Mahmoud couldn't do it either. Or his people.'

'We have to assume they've got a guy. They wouldn't spend sixty-five million dollars without being shown how to put the things together.'

'Can we nix that transport order?'

'Not without raising an alarm. Which would be the same thing as dropping the dime.'

'You still got any markers left on your guy?'

'A couple.'

'Tell him to have someone call you the second those units roll out.'

'And until then?'

'Until then Mahmoud doesn't have the missiles. Until then we have complete freedom of action.'

FIFTY-NINE

At that moment it became a race against time. When the warehouse door opened in Colorado, a door of a different kind would slam shut in LA. But there was still a lot to prepare. There was still a lot to discover. Including exact locations. Clearly New Age's glass cube in East LA wasn't the centre of anything. For one thing, there was no helicopter there.

And they needed exact identities.

They needed to know who knew, and who flew.

'I want them all,' Reacher said.

'Including the dragon lady?' Neagley asked.

'Starting with the dragon lady. She lied to me.'

They needed equipment, clothing, communications, and alternative vehicles.

And training, Neagley thought.

'We're old, we're slow, and we're rusty,' she said. 'We're a million miles from what we used to be.'

'We're not too bad,' O'Donnell said.

'Time was when you'd have put a double tap through that guy's eyes,' she said. 'Not a lucky low shot to his leg.'

They sat in the lounge like four out-of-towners discussing how to spend their day. As far as ordnance went, they had two Hardballers and the Daewoo DP 51 from Vegas. Thirteen rounds each for the Hardballers, eleven for the Daewoo. Not nearly good enough. O'Donnell and Dixon and Neagley had personal cell phones registered to their real names and real addresses and Reacher had nothing. Not nearly good enough. They had a Hertz Ford 500 rented in Dixon's real name and the captured Chrysler. Not nearly good enough. O'Donnell was in a thousand-dollar suit from his East Coast tailor and Neagley and Dixon had jeans, jackets, and evening wear. Not nearly good enough.

Neagley swore that budget was not a problem. But that didn't help with the time factor. They needed four untraceable pay-as-you-go cell phones, four anonymous cars, and work clothes. That was a day's shopping right there. Then they needed guns and ammunition. Best case, a free choice for each of them and a lot of spare rounds. Worst case, one more make-do handgun and a lot of spare rounds. That was another day's shopping. Like most cities LA had a thriving black market in untraceable weapons, but it would take time to penetrate.

Two days of material preparation.

Maybe two days of surveillance and research.

'We don't have time to train,' Reacher said.

Azhari Mahmoud had time for a leisurely lunch. He took it in a sidewalk café in Laguna Beach. He was staying in a rented townhouse a short walk away. Safe enough. The lease was legitimate. The development had a large transient population. It wasn't unusual to see U-Haul trucks parked overnight. Mahmoud's was two streets away, in a lot, locked up and empty.

It wouldn't be empty for long.

His contacts at New Age had insisted that Little Wing must not be used inside the United States. He had readily agreed. He had said he planned to use the weapon in Kashmir, on the border, against the Indian Air Force. He had lied, of course. He had been amazed that they had taken him for a Pakistani. He had been amazed that they cared what his intentions were. Maybe they were patriotic. Or maybe they had relatives who flew a lot, domestically.

But it had been politic to go along to get along. Hence the temporary inconvenience of the shipping container and the dockside location. But there was an easy remedy. Southern California was full of day labourers. Mahmoud calculated that loading the U-Haul would take them a little less than thirty minutes.

They figured the clothes and the phones would be easy. Any mall would have what they needed. Guns were guns, either obtainable in time or not. Dixon wanted a Glock 19. Neagley's hands were bigger, so she nominated a Glock 17. O'Donnell was a Beretta guy, by choice. Reacher didn't care. He wasn't planning on shooting anybody. He was planning on using his bare hands. But he said he would take a Glock or a SIG or a Beretta or an H&K, or anything that used 9mm Parabellums.

That way, all four of them would be using the same ammunition. More efficient.

Cars were more difficult still. It was hard to find a truly anonymous car. In the end O'Donnell suggested that the best bet would be rice rockets, small Japanese sedans and coupés tricked out with loud big-bore mufflers and lowered suspensions and cotton-reel tyres and blue headlights. And black windows. Three- or four-year-old examples would be cheap, and they were everywhere on the street. Close to invisible, in Southern California. And O'Donnell figured they were a very effective disguise, psychologically. They were so closely identified in the public mind with Latino gang-bangers that nobody would think a white ex-soldier was inside behind the darkened glass.

They gave the cars and the phones priority over the guns. That way two or three of them could start the surveillance, at least. And if they were going to Radio Shack for the phones, they might as well duck into the Gap or a jeans store for clothes, too. After that, wired and blending in, they could separate and hit used car lots until they found the wheels they needed.

All of which required cash money. Lots of it. Which required a visit to a teller's window by Neagley. Reacher drove her in the captured Chrysler and waited outside a bank in Beverly Hills. Fifteen minutes later she came out with fifty thousand dollars in a brown sandwich bag. Ninety minutes later they had clothes and phones. The phones were straightforward talk-only pay-as-you-go cells, no camera function, no games, no calculators. They bought car chargers and earpieces to go with them. The clothes were soft grey denim shirts and pants and black canvas windbreakers bought from an off-brand store on Santa Monica Boulevard, two sets each for O'Donnell and Dixon and Neagley and one set for Reacher, plus gloves and watch caps and boots from a hiking store on Melrose.

They changed at the motel and spent ten minutes in the lounge storing each other's numbers in their phones and learning how to set up conference calls. Then they headed north and west to Van Nuys Boulevard, looking for cars. All cities had at least one strip full of auto dealers, and LA had more than one. LA had many. But O'Donnell had heard that Van Nuys north of the Ventura Freeway was the best of them all. And he had heard right. It was a cornucopia. Unlimited choice, new or pre-owned, cheap or expensive, no awkward questions. Four hours after they arrived most of Neagley's automotive budget was gone and they owned four used Hondas. Two slammed Civics and two slammed Preludes, two silver and two white. All four were beat up and well on their way to being worn out. But they started and stopped and steered, and no one would give them a second glance.

Including the captured Chrysler they had five cars to ferry back to Sunset, but only four drivers, so they had to make two trips. Then they took a Honda each and battled out to East LA for a swing past New Age's glass cube. But traffic was slow and it was late in the day when they got there. The place was locked up and deserted. Nothing to see.

* * *

They planned via a four-way mobile conference call and went out for dinner in Pasadena. They found a burger bar on a busy street and sat at a table for four, two opposite two, shoulder-to shoulder in their new grey denims. A uniform, of sorts. Nobody admitted it but Reacher knew they all felt good. Focused, energized, in motion, up against high stakes. They talked about the past. Escapades, capers, scandals, outrages. Years fell away and Reacher's mind's eye swapped the grey for green and Pasadena for Heidelberg or Manila or Seoul.

The old unit, back together.

Almost.

Back on Sunset two hours later O'Donnell and Neagley volunteered to take first watch at New Age. They planned to get there before five the next morning. Reacher and Dixon were left with the task of buying guns. Before he went to bed Reacher took the dead guy's phone out of the captured Chrysler and redialled the number he had spoken to from Vegas. There was no answer. Just voice mail. Reacher didn't leave a message.

SIXTY

In Reacher's experience the best way to get hold of a random untraceable gun was to steal it from someone who had already stolen it. Or from someone who owned it illegally. That way there were no official comebacks. Sometimes there could be unofficial comebacks, like with the guys behind the wax museum, but they could be handled with minimal hassle.

But to get hold of four specific weapons was a taller order. Groups were always harder to supply than individuals. Limiting the ammunition requirement made it harder still. Concerns about condition and maintenance made it harder again. During his first cup of coffee of the day he ran an idle calculation. The 9mm Parabellum was certainly a popular load, but there were still plenty of .380s and .45s and .22s and .357s and .40s on the street, in all their many different variations. So if there was, say, a one-in-four chance that any particular robbery would yield a pistol that used 9mm Parabellums, and a one-in-three chance that the prize wasn't already trashed beyond redemption, they would have to stage forty-eight separate thefts to guarantee getting what they wanted. They would be at it all day. It would be a crime wave all its own.

Then he thought about finding a bent army quartermaster. Fort Irwin wasn't far away. Or better still, a bent Marine quartermaster. Camp Pendleton was farther away than Irwin, but the roads were better, and therefore it was closer in a sense. And there was an institutional belief among Marines that the Beretta M9 was an unreliable weapon. Armourers were very ready to condemn them as faulty. Some were, some weren't. The ones that weren't went out the back door for a hundred bucks each. Same principle as New Age's own scam. But setting up a buy could take days. Even weeks. Trust had to be gained. Not easy. Years ago he had done it undercover, several times. A lot of work for not very much of a tangible gain.

Karla Dixon thought she had a better idea. She ran through it over breakfast. Obviously she dismissed the notion of going to a store and buying guns legally. Neither she nor Reacher knew the exact details relevant to California, but they both assumed there would be registration and an ID requirement and maybe some kind of cooling-off period involved. So Dixon proposed driving out of LA County into a neighbouring county heavier with Republican voters, which in practical terms meant south into Orange. Then she proposed finding pawn shops and using generous applications of Neagley's cash to get around whatever lesser regulations might apply down there. She thought enhanced local respect for the Second Amendment plus enhanced profit margins would do the trick. And she figured there would be a big choice of merchandise. They could cherry-pick exactly what they wanted.

Reacher wasn't as confident as she was, but he agreed anyway. He suggested she change out of her denims and into her black suit. He suggested they take the blue Chrysler, not one of the beat-up Hondas. That way she would look like a concerned middle-class citizen. Fewer alarm bells would ring. She would buy one piece at a time. He would pose as her adviser. Her neighbour, maybe, calling on some relevant weapons experience from his past.

'The others got this far, didn't they?' Dixon asked.

'Farther,' Reacher said.

She nodded. 'They knew it all. Who, what, where, why and how. But something brought them down. What was it?'

'I don't know,' Reacher said. He had been asking himself the same question for days.

They left for Orange County right after breakfast. They didn't know what time pawn shops opened for business, but they guessed they would be quieter earlier in the day than later. Reacher drove, the 101 and then the 5, the same way O'Donnell's GPS had led them down to Swan's house. But this time they stayed with the freeway a little longer and exited on the other side, to the east. Dixon wanted to try Tustin first. She had heard bad things about it. Or good things, depending on your point of view.

353

She asked, 'What are you going to do when this is over?'

'Depends if I survive.'

'You think you won't?'

'Like Neagley said, we're not what we used to be. The others weren't, for sure.'

'I think we'll be OK.'

'I hope so.'

'Feel like dropping by New York afterward?'

'I'd like to.'

'But?'

'I don't make plans, Karla.'

'Why not?'

'I already had this conversation with Dave.'

'People make plans.'

'I know. People like Calvin Franz. And Jorge Sanchez and Manuel Orozco. And Tony Swan. He planned to give his dog an aspirin every day for the next fifty-four and a half weeks.'

They nosed around the surface streets that ran parallel with the freeway. Strip malls and gas stations and drive-through banks lay stunned and sleepy under the morning sun. Mattress dealers and tanning salons and furniture outlets were doing no business at all.

Dixon asked, 'Who needs a tanning salon in southern California?'

They found their first pawn shop next to a book store in an upmarket strip mall. But it was all wrong. First, it was closed. Metal lattice shutters were down over the windows. Second, it dealt in the wrong kind of stuff. The displays were full of antique silver and jewellery.

Flatware, fruit bowls, napkin rings, pins, pendants on fine chains, ornate picture frames. Not a Glock to be seen. No SIG-Sauers, no Berettas, no H&Ks.

They moved on.

Two spacious blocks east of the freeway they found the right kind of place. It was open. Its windows were full of electric guitars, and chunky men's rings made of nine-carat gold inset with small diamonds, and cheap watches.

And guns.

Not in the window itself, but clearly visible in a long glass display case that stood in for a counter. Maybe fifty handguns, revolvers and automatics, black and nickel, rubber grips and wooden, all in a neat line. The right kind of place.

But the wrong kind of owner.

He was an honest man. Law-abiding. He was white, somewhere in his thirties, a little over-weight, good genes ruined by too much eating. He had a gun dealer's licence displayed on the wall behind his head. He ran through the obligations it imposed on him like a priest reciting liturgy. First, a purchaser would have to obtain a handgun safety certificate, which was like a licence to buy. Then she would have to submit to three separate background checks, the first of which was to confirm that she wasn't trying to buy more than one weapon in the same thirty-day period, the second of which was to comb through state records for evidence of criminality, and the third of which was to do exactly the same thing at the federal level via the NCIC computer.

Then she would have to wait ten days before collecting her purchase, just in case she was contemplating a crime of passion.

Dixon opened her purse and made sure the guy got a good look at the wad of cash inside. But he wasn't moved. He just glanced at it and glanced away.

They moved on.

Thirty miles away north of west Azhari Mahmoud was standing in the sun, sweating lightly, and watching as his shipping container emptied and his U-Haul filled. The boxes were smaller than he had imagined. Inevitable, he supposed, because the units they contained were no bigger than cigarette packs. To book them down as home theatre components had been foolish, he thought. Unless they could be passed off as personal DVD players. The kind of thing people took on airplanes. Or MP3 players, maybe, with the white wires and the tiny earphones. That would have been more plausible.

Then he smiled to himself. *Airplanes*.

Reacher drove east, navigating in a random zig-zag from one off-brand billboard to the next, searching for the cheapest part of town. He was sure that there was plenty of financial stress all the way from Beverly Hills to Malibu, but it was hidden and discreet up there. Down in parts of Tustin it was on open display. As soon as the tyre franchises started offering four radials for less than a hundred bucks he started paying closer attention. And he was rewarded almost immediately. He spotted a place on the right and Dixon saw a place on the left simultaneously. Dixon's place looked bigger so they headed for the next light to make a U and along the way they saw three more places.

'Plenty of choice,' Reacher said. 'We can afford to experiment.'

'Experiment how?' Dixon asked.

'The direct approach. But you're going to have to stay in the car. You look too much like a cop.'

'You told me to dress like this.'

'Change of plan.'

Reacher parked the Chrysler where it wasn't directly visible from inside the store. He took Neagley's wad from Dixon's bag and jammed it in his pocket. Then he hiked over to take a look. It was a big place for a pawn shop. Reacher was more used to dusty single-wide urban spaces. This was a double-fronted emporium the size of a carpet store. The windows were full of electronics and cameras and musical instruments and jewellery. And rifles. There were a dozen sporting guns racked horizontally behind a forest of vertical guitar necks. Decent weapons, although Reacher didn't think of them as sporting. Nothing very fair about hunting a deer by hiding a hundred yards away behind a tree with a box of high velocity bullets. He figured it would be much more sporting to strap on a set of antlers and go at it head to head. That would give the poor dumb animal an even chance. Or maybe better than an even chance, which he figured was why hunters were too chicken to try it.

He stepped to the pawn shop's door and

glanced inside. And gave it up, immediately. The place was too big. Too many staff. The direct approach only worked with a little one-on-one privacy. He walked back to the car and said, 'My mistake. We need a smaller place.'

'Across the street,' Dixon said.

They pulled out of the lot and headed west a hundred yards and pulled a U at the light. Came back and bumped up into a cracked concrete lot in front of a beer store. Next to it was a no-name vitamin shop and then another pawnbroker. Not urban, but single-wide and dusty, for sure. Its window was full of the usual junk. Watches, drum kits, cymbals, guitars. And visible in the inside gloom, a wired-glass case all across the back wall. It was full of handguns. Maybe three hundred of them. They were all hanging upside down off nails through their trigger guards. There was a lone guy behind the counter, all on his own.

'My kind of place,' Reacher said.

He went in alone. At first glance the proprietor looked very similar to the first guy they had met. White, thirties, solid. They could have been brothers. But this one would have been the black sheep of the family. Where the first one had glowing pink skin, this one had a grey pallor from unwise consumption choices and smudged blue and purple tattoos from reform school or prison. Or the navy. He had reddened eyes that jumped around in his head like he was wired with electricity.

Easy, Reacher thought.

He pulled most of Neagley's wad from his pocket and fanned the bills out and butted them

358

back together and dropped them on the counter from enough of a height to produce a good solid sound. Used money in decent quantities was heavier than most people thought. Paper, ink, dirt, grease. The proprietor held his vision together long enough to take a good slow look at it and then he said, 'Help you?'

'I'm sure you can,' Reacher said. 'I just had a civics lesson down the street. Seems that if a person wants to buy himself four pistols he has to jump through all kinds of hoops.'

'You got that right,' the guy said, and pointed behind him with his thumb. There was a gun dealer's licence on the wall, framed and hung just the same as the first guy's.

'Any way around those hoops?' Reacher asked. 'Or under them, or over them?'

'No,' the guy said. 'Hoops is hoops.' Then he smiled, like he had said something exceptionally profound. For a second Reacher thought about taking him by the neck and using his head to break the glass in the cabinet. Then the guy looked down at the money again and said, 'I got to obey the California statutes.' But he said it in a certain way and his eyes hit a sweet spot of focus and Reacher knew something good was coming.

'You a lawyer?' the guy asked.

'Do I look like a lawyer?' Reacher asked back.

'I talked to one once,' the guy said.

Many times more than once, Reacher thought. *Mostly in locked rooms where the table and chairs are bolted to the floor.*

'There's a provision,' the guy said. 'In the statutes.'

'Is there?' Reacher asked.

'A technicality,' the guy said. It took him a couple of tries before he got the whole word out. He had trouble with the harsh consonants. 'Me or you or anybody can't sell or give a gun to someone else without all the formalities.'

'But?'

'Me or you or anybody is entitled to loan one out. A temporary and infrequent loan lasting less than thirty days is OK.'

'Is that right?' Reacher said.

'It's in the statute.'

'Interesting.'

'Like between family members,' the guy said. 'Husband to wife, father to daughter.'

'I can see that.'

'Or like between friends,' the guy said. 'A friend can loan a gun to a friend, thirty days, temporary.'

'Are we friends?' Reacher asked.

'We could be,' the guy said.

Reacher asked, 'What kind of things do friends do for one another?'

The guy said, 'Maybe they loan each other things. Like one loans out a gun, and the other loans out some money.'

'But only temporarily,' Reacher said. 'Thirty days.'

'Loans can go bad. Sometimes you just have to write them off. It's a risk. People move away, they fall out. You can never tell with friends.'

Reacher left the money where it was. Stepped away to the wired-glass cabinet. There was some junk in there. But some good stuff, too. About fifty-fifty revolvers and automatics. The automatics were about two-thirds cheap and one-third premium brands. The premium brands ran about one in four nine millimetre.

Total choice, thirteen suitable pistols. From a stock of about three hundred. Four and a third per cent. Worse than his breakfast calculation, by a factor of close to two.

Seven of the suitable pistols were Glocks. Clearly they had been fashionable once, but weren't any more. One of them was a 19. The other six were 17s. In terms of visual condition they ranged from good to mint.

'Suppose you loaned me four Glocks,' Reacher said.

'Suppose I didn't,' the guy said.

Reacher turned around. The money was gone from the counter. Reacher had expected that. There was a gun in the guy's hand. Reacher had not expected that.

We're old, we're slow, and we're rusty, Neagley had said. *We're a million miles from what we used to be.*

Roger that, Reacher thought.

The gun was a Colt Python. Blued carbon steel, walnut grips, .357 Magnum, eight-inch barrel. Not the biggest revolver in the world, but not very far from it. Certainly it wasn't the smallest revolver in the world. And it was maybe one of the most accurate.

'That isn't very friendly,' Reacher said.

'We ain't friends,' the guy said.

'It's also kind of dumb,' Reacher said. 'I'm in a very bad mood right now.'

'Suck it up. And keep your hands where I can see them.'

Reacher paused, and then he raised his hands, halfway, palms out, fingers spread, unthreatening. The guy said, 'Don't let the door hit you in the ass on your way out.'

The store was narrow. Reacher was all the way in back. The guy was behind the counter, a third of the way to the door. The aisle was cramped. The sunlight was bright in the window.

The guy said, 'Leave the building, Elvis.'

Reacher stood still for a moment. Listened hard. Glanced left, glanced right, checked behind him. There was a door in the back left corner. Probably just a bathroom. Not an office. There was paperwork piled behind the counter. Nobody piles paperwork behind the counter if they have a separate room for it. Therefore the guy was alone. No partner, no back-up.

No more surprises.

Reacher put the kind of look on his face that he had seen in Vegas. The rueful loser. *It was worth a try. You got to be in it to win it.* Then he kept his hands up at his shoulders and stepped forward. One pace. Two. Three. His fourth pace put him directly level with the guy. Just the width of the counter between them. Reacher was facing the door. The guy was ninety degrees to his left. The counter was maybe thirty inches deep. Two and a half feet.

Reacher's left arm moved, straight out sideways from the shoulder.

The boxer Muhammad Ali's reach was reckoned to be about forty inches and his hands were

362

once timed at an average eighty miles an hour as they moved through it. Reacher was no Ali. Not even close. Especially not on his weaker side. His left hand moved at about sixty miles an hour, maximum. That was all. But sixty miles an hour was the same thing as a mile a minute, which was the same thing as eighty-eight feet per second. Which meant that Reacher's left hand took a little less than thirty-thousandths of a second to cross the counter. And halfway through its travel it bunched into a fist.

And thirty-thousandths of a second was way too brief an interval for the guy to pull the Python's trigger. Any revolver is a complex mechanical system and one as big as the Python is heavier in its action than most. Not very susceptible to accidental discharge. The guy's finger didn't even tighten. He took Reacher's fist in his face before his brain had even registered that it was moving. Reacher was a lot slower than Muhammad Ali but his arms were a lot longer. Which meant that the guy's head accelerated through a whole extra foot and a half before Reacher's arm was fully extended. And then the guy's head kept on accelerating. It kept on accelerating right until it crashed against the wall behind the counter and shattered the glass over the gun dealer's licence.

At that point it stopped accelerating and started a slow downward slide to the floor.

Reacher was over the counter before the guy had even settled. He kicked the Python away and used his heel to break the guy's fingers. Both hands. Necessary in a weapons-rich environment, and faster than tying wrists. Then he reclaimed Neagley's cash from the guy's pocket and found his keys. Vaulted back over the counter and stepped to the back of the store and opened the wired-glass cabinet. Took all seven Glocks and pulled a suitcase out of a display of used luggage and piled the guns inside. Then he wiped his fingerprints off the keys and his palm prints off the counter and headed outside to the sunshine.

They stopped at a legitimate firearms dealer in Tustin and bought ammunition. Plenty of it. There seemed to be no restrictions on that kind of purchase. Then they headed back north. Traffic was slow. About level with Anaheim they took a call from O'Donnell in East LA.

'Nothing's happening here,' he said.

'Nothing?'

'No activity at all. You shouldn't have made that call from Vegas. It was a bad mistake. You threw them into a panic. They've gone into full-on lockdown mode.'

SIXTY-ONE

Reacher and Dixon stayed on the 101 all the way to Hollywood and dumped the Chrysler in the motel lot and took a Honda each for the trek out to East LA. Reacher's was a silver Prelude coupé with a chipped and nervous four-cylinder motor. It had wide tyres that tramlined on bad asphalt and a throaty muffler note that entertained him for the first three blocks and then started to annoy him. The upholstery stank of fabric shampoo and there was a crack in the windshield that lengthened perceptibly every time he hit a bump. But the seat racked back far enough for him to get comfortable and the air conditioning worked. Altogether not a bad surveillance vehicle. He had driven far worse, many times.

They got a four-way conference call going on the cell phones and parked far from each other. Reacher was two blocks from the New Age building and had a partial view of the front entrance, from about sixty yards on a diagonal between a document storage facility and a plain grey warehouse. New Age's gate was shut and the lot looked pretty much empty. The reception area doors were closed. The whole place looked quiet.

'Who's in there?' Reacher asked.

'Maybe nobody,' O'Donnell said. 'We've been here since five and nobody's gone in.'

'Not even the dragon lady?'

'Negative.'

'No receptionist?'

'Negative.'

'Do we have their phone number?'

Neagley said, 'I have their switchboard number.' She recited it and Reacher clicked off and thumbed it into his phone and hit the green button.

Ring tone.

But no reply.

He dialled back into the conference call.

'I was hoping to follow someone over to the manufacturing plant.'

'Not going to happen,' O'Donnell said.

Silence on the phones. No action at the glass cube.

Five minutes. Ten. Twenty.

'Enough,' Reacher said. 'Back to base. Last one there buys lunch.'

Reacher was the last one back. He wasn't a fast driver. The other three Hondas were already in the lot when he got there. He put his Prelude in an inconspicuous corner and took the suitcase of stolen guns out of the Chrysler's trunk and locked it in his room. Then he walked down to Denny's. First thing he saw there was Curtis Mauney's unmarked car in the parking lot. The Crown Vic. The LA County sheriff. Second thing he saw was

366

Mauney himself, through the window, inside the restaurant, sitting at a round table with Neagley and O'Donnell and Dixon. It was the same table they had shared with Diana Bond. Five chairs, one of them empty and waiting. Nothing on the table. Not even ice water or napkins or silverware. They hadn't ordered. They hadn't been there long. Reacher went in and sat down and there was a moment of tense silence and then Mauney said, 'Hello again.'

A gentle tone of voice.

Quiet.

Sympathetic.

Reacher asked, 'Sanchez or Swan?'

Mauney didn't answer.

Reacher said, 'What, both of them?'

'We'll get to that. First tell me why you're hiding.'

'Who says we're hiding?'

'You left Vegas. You're not registered at any LA hotel.'

'Doesn't mean we're hiding.'

'You're in a West Hollywood dive under false names. The clerk gave you up. As a group you're fairly distinctive, physically. It wasn't hard to find you. And it was an easy guess that you'd come in here for lunch. If not, I was prepared to come back at dinnertime. Or breakfast time tomorrow.'

Reacher said, 'Jorge Sanchez or Tony Swan?'

Mauney said, 'Tony Swan.'

SIXTY-TWO

Mauney said, 'We've learned a thing or two, over the last few weeks. We let the buzzards do the work for us now. We're out there like ornithologists, any time we get a spare half-hour. You get up on the roof of your car with your binoculars, you can usually see what you need. Two birds circling, it's probably a snake-bit coyote. More than two, it's probably a bigger deal.'

Reacher asked, 'Where?'

'Same general area.'

'When?'

'Some time ago.'

'Helicopter?'

'No other way.'

'No doubt about the ID?'

'He was on his back. His hands were tied behind him. His fingerprints were preserved. His wallet was in his pocket. I'm very sorry.'

The waitress came over. The same one they had seen before. She paused near the table and sensed the mood and went away again.

Mauney asked, 'Why are you hiding?'

'We're not hiding,' Reacher said. 'We're just waiting for the funerals.'

'So why the false names?'

'You brought us here as bait. Whoever they are, we don't want to make it easy for them.'

'Don't you know who they are yet?'

'Do you?'

'No independent action, OK?'

'We're on Sunset Boulevard here,' Reacher said. 'Which is LAPD turf. Are you speaking for them?'

'Friendly advice,' Mauney said.

'Noted.'

'Andrew MacBride disappeared in Vegas. Arrived, didn't check in anywhere, didn't rent a car, didn't fly out. Dead end.'

Reacher nodded. 'Don't you just hate that?'

'But a guy called Anthony Matthews rented a U-Haul.'

'The last name on Orozco's list.'

Mauney nodded. 'Endgame.'

'Where did he take it?'

'I have no idea.' Mauney slid four business cards out of his top pocket. He fanned them out and placed them carefully on the table. His name and two phone numbers were printed on them. 'Call me. I mean it. You might need help. You're not up against amateurs here. Tony Swan looked like a real tough guy. What was left of him.'

Mauney went back to work and the waitress came over again five minutes later and hovered. Reacher guessed no one was very hungry any more, but they all ordered anyway. Old habits. Eat when you can, don't risk running out of energy later. Swan would have approved. Swan ate anywhere, any time, all the time. Autopsies, exhumations, crime scenes. In fact Reacher was pretty sure that Swan had been eating a roast beef sandwich when they discovered Doug, the decomposed dead guy with the shovel in his head.

Nobody confirmed it.

Nobody talked at all. The sun was bright outside the window. A beautiful day. Blue sky, small white clouds. Cars passed by on the boulevard, customers came and went. Phones rang, land lines in the kitchen and cells in other people's pockets. Reacher ate methodically and mechanically without the slightest idea what was on his plate.

'Should we move?' Dixon asked. 'Now that Mauney knows where we are?'

'I don't like it that the clerk gave us up,' O'Donnell said. 'We should steal his damn TV remotes.'

'We don't need to move,' Reacher said. 'Mauney is no danger to us. And I want to know about it when they find Sanchez.'

'So what next?' Dixon asked.

'We rest up,' Reacher said. 'We go out again after dark. We pay New Age a visit. We're not getting anywhere with surveillance, so it's time to go proactive.'

He left ten bucks on the table for the waitress and paid the check at the register. Then they all stepped outside to the sunshine and stood blinking in the lot for a moment before heading back to the Dunes.

*   *   *

Reacher fetched the suitcase and they gathered in O'Donnell's room and checked over the stolen Glocks. Dixon took the 19 and said she was happy with it. O'Donnell sorted through the remaining six 17s and picked out the best three among them. He paired them with the magazines from the rejects so that he and Neagley and Reacher would have fast reloads the first time around. Dixon would have to reload manually after her first seventeen shots. Not a huge issue. If a handgun engagement wasn't over inside seventeen shots, then someone wasn't paying attention, and Reacher trusted Dixon to pay attention. She always had, in the past.

Reacher asked, 'What kind of security can we expect around their building?'

'State of the art locks,' Neagley said. 'An intruder alarm on the gate. I imagine the door opener at reception will be wired as a proximity sensor at night. Plus another intruder alarm, probably. Plus motion sensors all over the place inside. Plus intruder alarms on some of the individual office doors, maybe. All hard-wired out through the phone lines. Possibly with wireless back up, maybe even a satellite uplink.'

'And who's going to respond?'

'That's a very good question. Not the cops, I think. Too low-rent. My guess is it will all pipe straight through to their own security people.'

'Not the government?'

'That would make sense, for sure. The Pentagon is spending zillions there, so you'd think the government would want to be involved. But I doubt if they are. Not everything makes sense nowadays. They gave airport security to private contractors. And the nearest DIA office is a long way away. So I think New Age's security will be handled in house, however cool Little Wing is.'

'How long will we have after we breach the gate?'

'Who says we're going to? We don't have keys and you can't pick a lock like that with a rusty nail. I don't think we'll be able to beat any of the locks.'

'I'll worry about the locks. How long will we have, after we're inside?'

'Two minutes,' Neagley said. 'A situation like that, the two-minute rule is the only thing we can rely on.'

'OK,' Reacher said. 'We'll go at one in the morning. Dinner at six. Get some rest.'

The others headed for his door. He followed them out, with the keys to the captured Chrysler in his hand. Neagley looked at him, quizzically.

'We don't need it any more,' he said to her. 'I'm going to give it back. But first I'm going to have it washed. We should try to be civilized.'

Reacher drove the Chrysler back to Van Nuys Boulevard, north of the Ventura Freeway. The auto strip, where there were car-related enterprises of every kind lined up side by side, one after the other. Dealers, obviously, new and used, cheap and expensive, gaudy and restrained, but also tyre shops, wheel shops, paintless dent repair, lube franchises, muffler-and-shock shops, and accessory stores.

And car washes.

There was a huge choice. Machine washing, brushless hand washing, underbody steam cleaning, three-stage waxing, full service valeting. He drove a mile up and a mile back and picked out four places that offered everything. He stopped at the first of them and asked for the total treatment. A swarm of guys in coveralls took over and he stood in the sun and watched them work. First the interior was vacuumed out and then the whole car was dragged through a glass tunnel on a moving chain and was sprayed by a sequence of nozzles with water and all kinds of foams and fluids. Guys with sponges washed the sheet metal and guys on plastic steps leathered the roof. Then the car passed under a roaring air dryer and was driven out to the apron where other guys waited to attack the interior with aerosols and rags. They went over every inch and left it gleaming and immaculate and damp with oily residue. Reacher paid and tipped and pulled his gloves out of his pocket and put them on and drove the car away.

He stopped a hundred yards farther on, at the second place he had picked out, and asked for the whole process to be repeated all over again. The receptionist looked puzzled for a second and then shrugged and waved a crew over. Reacher stood in the sun again and watched the show. The vacuum, the shampoo, the interior, the aerosols and the towels. He paid and tipped and put his gloves back on and drove back to the motel.

He left the car in a corner of the lot, in the sun, where it would dry. Then he walked a long block south to Fountain Avenue. Found a place that had started out as a pharmacy and then had become the kind of drugstore that sold all kinds of small household items. He went in and bought four flashlights. Three-cell Maglites, black, powerful enough to be useful, small enough to be manoeuvrable, big enough to be used as clubs. The girl at the register put them in a white bag with *I love LA* on it, three capital letters and a red heart-shaped symbol. Reacher carried the bag back to the motel, swinging it gently, listening to the quiet rustle of plastic.

They couldn't face Denny's again for dinner. They called out to Domino's instead, for pizzas, and ate them in the battered lounge next to the laundry room. They drank soda from a noisy red machine outside the door. A perfect meal, for what they had in mind. Some empty calories, some fats, some complex carbohydrates. Time-release energy, good for about twelve hours. An army doctor had explained it all to them, many years before.

'Objectives for tonight?' O'Donnell asked.

'Three,' Reacher said. 'First, Dixon hits the reception desk for anything useful. Second, Neagley finds the dragon lady's office and hits that. You and I hit the other offices for whatever else they've got. A hundred and twenty seconds, in and out. Then third, we ID the security people when they show up.'

'We're waiting around afterward?'

'I am,' Reacher said. 'You guys are heading back.'

*   *   *

Reacher went up to his room and brushed his teeth and took a long hot shower. Then he stretched out full length on the bed and took a nap. The clock in his head woke him at half past midnight. He stretched and brushed his teeth again and dressed. Grey denim pants, grey shirt, black windbreaker zipped all the way up. Boots, tightly laced. Gloves on. The Chrysler keys in one pants pocket, the spare Glock mag in the other. The captured cell phone from Vegas in one shirt pocket, his own phone in the other. The Maglite in one jacket pocket, the Glock itself in the other. Nothing else.

He walked out to the lot at ten minutes before one o'clock. The others were already there, a shadowy trio standing well away from any pools of light.

'OK,' he said. He turned to O'Donnell and Neagley. 'You guys drive your Hondas.' He turned to Dixon. 'Karla, you drive mine. You park it close, facing west, and you leave the keys in for me. Then you ride back with Dave.'

Dixon said, 'Are you really going to leave the Chrysler there?'

'We don't need it.'

'It's full of our prints and hair and fibre.'

'Not any more. A bunch of guys up on Van Nuys just made sure of that. Now let's go.'

They bumped fists like ballplayers, an old ritual, and then they dispersed and climbed into their cars. Reacher slid into the Chrysler and started it up, the heavy V-8 beat slow and loud in the darkness. He heard the Hondas start, their smaller engines coughing and popping and their big-bore mufflers throbbing. He backed out of his slot and turned and headed for the exit. In his mirror he saw three pairs of bright blue headlights strung out behind him. He swung east on Sunset and south on La Brea and then east again on Wilshire and saw the others following him all the way, a ragged little convoy hanging together in the light night-time traffic.

SIXTY-THREE

The Great City went quiet after they passed Macarthur Park and hit the 110. To their right downtown was silent and deserted. There were lights on in Chinatown, but no visible activity. In the other direction Dodger Stadium was huge and dark and empty. Then they came off the freeway and plunged into the surface streets to the east. Navigation had been difficult by day and was worse by night. But Reacher had made the trip three times before, twice as a passenger and once as a driver, and he figured he could spot the turns.

And he did, without a problem. He slowed three blocks before New Age's building and let the others close up behind him. Then he led them through a wide two-block circle, for caution's sake. Then a closer pass, on a one-block radius. There was mist in the air. The glass cube looked dark and deserted. The ornamental trees in the lot were up-lit with decorative spots and the light spilled a little and reflected off the building's mirror siding, but apart from that there was no specific illumination. The razor wire on the fence looked dull grey in the darkness and the main gate was closed. Reacher slowed next to it and dropped his window and stuck his arm out and made a circular gesture with his gloved finger in the air, like a baseball umpire signalling a home run. *One more go-round*. He led them through three-quarters of a round trip and then pointed at the kerb where he wanted them to park. First Neagley, then O'Donnell behind her, then Dixon in his own silver Prelude. They slowed and stopped and he made throat-cutting gestures and they shut their motors down and climbed out. O'Donnell detoured all the way to the gate and came back and said, 'It's a very big lock.' Reacher was still at the wheel of the idling Chrysler. His window was still open. He said, 'The bigger they are, the harder they fall.'

'We doing this stealthy?'

'Not very,' Reacher said. 'I'll meet you at the gate.'

They walked ahead and he put the Chrysler in gear and followed them, slowly. The roads all around New Age's block were standard twenty-two-feet blacktop ribbons, typical of new business park construction. No sidewalks. This was LA. Twenty-one thousand miles of surface streets, probably less than twenty-one thousand yards of sidewalk. New Age's gate was set in a curved scallop maybe twenty feet deep, so that arriving vehicles could pull off the roadway and wait. Total distance between the gate and the far kerb, forty-two feet. Automatically the manic part of Reacher's mind told him that was the same as fourteen yards or 504 inches or .795% of a mile, or a hair over 1,280 centimetres in European terms. He turned ninety degrees into the scallop and straightened head on and brought the Chrysler's front bumper to within an inch of the gate. Then he reversed straight back all the way until he felt the rear tyres touch the far kerb. He put his foot hard on the brake and slotted the transmission back into drive and dropped all four windows. Night air blew in, sharp and cold. The others looked at him and he pointed to where he wanted them, two on the left of the gate and one on the right.

'Start the clock,' he called. 'Two minutes.'

He kept his foot on the brake and hit the gas until the transmission was wound up tight and the whole car was rocking and bucking and straining. Then he slipped his foot off the brake and stamped down on the accelerator and the car shot forward. It covered the forty-two feet of available distance with the rear tyres smoking and howling and then it smashed head on into the gate. The lock ruptured instantly and the gate smashed open and flung back and about a dozen airbags exploded inside the Chrysler, out of the steering wheel and the passenger fascia and the header rails and the seats. Reacher was ready for them. He was driving one-handed and had his other arm up in front of his face. He stopped the driver's airbag with his elbow. No problem. The four open windows defused the percussion shock and saved his eardrums. But the noise still deafened him. It was like sitting in a car and having someone fire a .44 at him. Ahead of him on the front wall of the building a blue strobe started flashing urgently. If there was an accompanying siren, he couldn't hear it.

He kept his foot hard down. The car stumbled for a split second after the impact with the gate and then it picked up the pace again and laid rubber all the way through the lot. He lined up the steering and risked a glance in the mirror and saw the others running full speed after him. Then he faced front and put both hands on the wheel and aimed for the reception area doors.

He was doing close to fifty miles an hour when he reached them. The front wheels hit the shallow step and the whole car launched and smashed through the doors about a foot off the ground. Glass shattered and the doorframes tore right out of the walls and the car continued on inside more or less uninterrupted. It hit the slate floor with the brakes locked hard and skidded straight on and demolished the reception counter completely and knocked down the wall behind it and ended up buried in rubble to the base of the windshield, with the wreckage of the reception counter strewn all around under its midsection.

Which is going to make Dixon's research difficult, Reacher thought.

Then he shut his mind to that problem and unclipped his belt and forced his door open. Spilled out onto the lobby floor and crawled away. All around him tiny white alarm strobes were flashing. His hearing was coming back. A loud siren was sounding. He got to his feet and saw the others hurdling the wreckage in the doorway and running inside from the lot. Dixon was heading straight for the back of the lobby and

380

O'Donnell and Neagley were heading for the mouth of the corridor where the dragon lady had come out twice before. Their flashlights were already on and bright cones of light were jerking and bouncing in front of them through clouds of swirling white dust. He pulled his own flashlight out and switched it on and followed them.

Twenty-one seconds gone, he thought.

There were two elevators halfway down the corridor. Their indicator panels showed it to be a three-storey building. He didn't press the call button. He figured the alarm would have already shut the elevators down. Instead he flung open an adjacent door and hit the stairs. Ran all the way up to the third floor, two steps at a time. The sound of the siren was unbearable in the stairwell. He burst out into the third-floor corridor. He didn't need his flashlight. The alarm strobes were lighting the place up like the disco from hell. The corridor was lined both sides with maple doors twenty feet apart. Offices. The doors had name plates on them. Long black plastic rectangles, engraved with letters cut through to a white base layer. Directly in front of him Neagley was busy kicking down a door labelled *Margaret Berenson*. The stop-motion effect of the alarm strobes made her movements weird and jerky. The door wouldn't give. She pulled out her Glock and fired three aimed shots into the lock. Three loud explosions. The spent brass kicked out of the pistol's ejection port and rolled away on the carpet, frozen by the strobes into a long golden chain. Neagley kicked the door again and it sagged open. She went inside.

Reacher moved on. *Fifty-two seconds gone*, he thought.

He passed a door labelled *Allen Lamaison*. Twenty carpeted feet farther on he saw another door: *Anthony Swan*. He braced himself against the opposite wall and wound up and delivered a mighty kick with his heel just above the lock. The maple splintered and the door sagged but the catch held. He finished the job with a sharp blow from the flat of his gloved hand and tumbled inside.

Sixty-three seconds gone, he thought.

He stood stock still and played his flashlight beam all around his dead friend's office. It was untouched. It was like Swan had just stepped out to the bathroom or gone out for lunch. There was a coat hanging on a hat stand. It was a khaki windbreaker, old, worn, plaid-lined like a golf jacket, short and wide. There were file cabinets. Phones. A leather chair, crushed in places by the weight of a heavy barrel-shaped man. There was a computer on the desk. And a new blank notepad. And pens, and pencils. A stapler. A clock. A small pile of papers.

And a paperweight, holding the papers down. A lump of Soviet concrete, irregular in shape, the size of a fist, grey and polished to a greasy shine by handling, one flat face with faint traces of blue and red sprayed graffiti still on it.

Reacher stepped to the desk and put the lump of concrete in his pocket. Took the pile of papers from under it and rolled them tight and put them in his other pocket. Suddenly became aware of a softness under his feet. He played the flashlight

382

beam downward. Saw rich red colours reflected back. Ornate patterns. Thick pile. An Oriental rug. Brand new. He recalled the cord on Orozco's wrists and ankles and Curtis Mauney's words: *It's a sisal product from the Indian subcontinent. It would have to come in on whatever gets exported from there.*

Eighty-nine seconds gone, he thought. *Thirty-one to go.*

He stepped to the window. Saw Karla Dixon far below in the darkness, already on her way out of the lot. Her pants and her jacket were scuffed and coated with white dust. She looked like a ghost. From crawling around in the wallboard dust, he guessed. She was carrying papers and some kind of a white three-ring binder. She was lit up in short blue pulses by the strobe on the front of the building.

Twenty-six seconds to go.

He saw O'Donnell run out below like he was escaping from a burning house, taking giant strides, carrying stuff clutched to his chest. And then Neagley a second later, running hard, long dark hair streaming out behind her, arms pumping, with a thick wad of green file folders gripped in each hand.

Nineteen seconds to go.

He crossed the office and touched the jacket on the hat stand, gently, on the shoulder, like Swan was still in it. Then he stepped back behind the desk and sat down in the chair. It creaked once as he settled. He heard the sound quite clearly over the siren.

Twelve seconds to go.

383

He looked out at the manic flashing in the corridor and knew he could just wait. Sooner or later, maybe in less than a minute, the men who had killed his friends would show up. As long as there were fewer than thirty-four of them he could sit right where he was and take them all down, one by one.

Five seconds to go.

Except that he couldn't, of course. Nobody was that dumb. After the first three or four KIAs had piled up in the doorway the rest of them would regroup in the corridor and start thinking about tear gas and reinforcements and body armour. Maybe they would even think about calling the cops or the FBI. And Reacher knew there was no way to be sure of putting the right guys down before he lost a three- or four-day siege against a whole bunch of trained SWAT teams.

One second to go.

He exploded out of the chair and out through the broken door and jinked left into the corridor and right into the stairwell. Neagley had wedged the door open for him. He hit the ground floor about ten seconds over budget. He dodged around the inert Chrysler in the lobby and was out in the lot fifteen seconds late. Through the wrecked gate and out in the street forty seconds late. Then he ran toward the pale gleam of the silver Prelude. It was a hundred yards away, distant and innocent and alone. The other two Hondas were already gone. He covered the hundred yards in twenty seconds and hurled himself inside. He slammed his door after him and struggled upright in his seat. He was breathing hard, mouth wide open. He turned his head and saw a set of headlights in the far distance, moving very fast, coming toward him, swinging around corners, then diving low from braking.

SIXTY-FOUR

Altogether three cars showed up. They came in fast and stopped short all over the road outside the wrecked gate and they stayed there, parked at random angles, engines still running, headlights blazing through the night mist. They were brand new Chrysler 300Cs, dark blue, pretty much identical to the one already parked in New Age's lobby.

Altogether five guys got out of the three cars. Two from the first, one from the second, two from the third. Reacher was a hundred yards away and watching through tinted glass and the corner of New Age's fence and he was dazzled by the six headlights, so he couldn't make out much detail. But the guy who had arrived alone in the second car seemed to be in charge. He was a slight man wearing a short raincoat that looked to be black. Under it he had some kind of a white T-shirt. He was staring at the breached gate and gesturing the others to stay well away from it, as if it was somehow dangerous.

An ex-cop, Reacher thought. *Instinctively reluctant to contaminate a crime scene.*

Then the five guys formed up close together in a tight arrowhead formation, with the man in the raincoat closest to the wreckage. They advanced on it, slow and wary, one step at a time, leaning forward from their waists, heads thrust forward, like they were puzzled by what they were seeing. Then they stopped and backtracked fast and retreated behind their cars. The engines shut down and the headlight beams shut off and the scene went dark.

Not too dumb, Reacher thought. *They figure this could be an ambush. They think we could still be in there.*

He watched them until his night vision came back. Then he took out the cell phone he had brought back from Vegas and beeped his way through all the menus until he was on the last number the phone had dialled. He hit the call button and put the phone to his ear and watched out the window to see which of the five guys would answer.

His money was on the guy in the raincoat.

Wrong.

None of the five guys answered.

None of them reacted. None of them pulled a phone from a pocket to check the caller ID. None of them even moved. The ring tone in Reacher's ear went on and on and then cut to voice mail. He clicked off and redialled and the same thing happened. He watched, and nobody moved a muscle. It was inconceivable that a director of security would be out on an emergency alert without his cell phone switched on. It was inconceivable that a director of security would ignore an incoming call in such circumstances. Therefore none of these five was the director of security. Not the guy in the raincoat. He was third man on the totem pole, at best, allowing for Swan's number-two spot. And he was acting like a guy in third place. He was slow, and ponderous. He had no instinctive grasp of tactics. Anybody with half a brain would have figured out his best course of action long ago. A small square building, potential armed hostiles inside, three solid cars at his disposal, he should have solved his problem already. All three cars go in, high speed, different directions, they circle the building, they draw fire, two guys go in the back, two guys go in the front, game over.

Civilians, Reacher thought.

He waited.

Eventually the guy in the raincoat made the right decision. Painfully slow, but he got there in the end. He ordered everyone back in their cars and they manoeuvred for a spell and then burst into the lot at high speed. Reacher watched them circle the building a couple of times and then he started the Honda and headed west.

Reacher kept on the surface streets and stayed off the freeway. He had noticed that the freeways were thick with cops at night, and he hadn't seen any anyplace else. So he erred on the side of caution. He got lost near Dodger Stadium and ended up driving an aimless circle that took him right past the LA Police Academy. He stopped in Echo Park and checked in with the others by phone. They were nearly home, streaming west at circumspect speeds like bombers returning from a night raid.

They regrouped in O'Donnell's room dead on three o'clock in the morning. The captured paperwork was laid out on the bed in three neat piles. Reacher unrolled Swan's stuff from his pocket and added it to the line. It wasn't very interesting. Most of it was a memorandum about future overtime requirements for his secretarial staff. The rest of it was a justification for the overtime they had already worked.

O'Donnell's collection wasn't very interesting either, but it was instructive in a negative way. It proved that the glass cube was purely an administrative centre. It had been relatively unsecured because it contained very little worth stealing. Some minor design work happened there, and some component sourcing, but most of the square footage was given over to management functions. Personnel stuff, corporate finance stuff, routine transport and maintenance and bureaucracy. Nothing inherently valuable.

Which made it all the more important to find the plant location.

Which was where Dixon's stuff made all the difference. She had dug through the wreckage of the reception area and crawled under the crashed Chrysler and in about fifty seconds flat she had come up with solid gold. In the shattered remains of a locked drawer she had found New Age's internal phone directory. Now it was right there on the bed, a thick wad of loose-leaf pages punched into a white three-ring binder, a little

389

battered and covered in dust. The cover was printed with New Age's corporate logo and most of the pages were printed with names that meant nothing, with matching four-digit telephone extensions. But right at the front of the book was a block diagram detailing the company's various divisions. Names were printed in boxes and lines connected the boxes downward through all the various hierarchies. The security division was headed by a guy called Allen Lamaison. His number two had been Tony Swan. Below Swan two lines led to two other guys, and below them five more lines fanned out to five more guys, one of whom had the name Saropian, and was as dead as Tony Swan, in a Vegas hotel foundation. A total staff of nine, two down, seven survivors.

'Turn to the back,' Dixon said.

The last section had account numbers for FedEx and UPS and DHL. Plus full street addresses and land line phone numbers for two of New Age's operations, which was what courier services needed. The East LA glass cube, the contracting office up in Colorado.

And then, bizarrely, a third address, with a note printed in bold and underlined: *No deliveries to this location*.

The third address was for the electronics manufacturing plant.

It was in Highland Park, halfway between Glendale and South Pasadena. Six and a half miles north and east of downtown, nine miles east of where they were standing.

Close enough to taste.

'Now turn back a few pages,' Dixon said.

Reacher leafed backward. There was a whole section showing remote telephone extensions out there in the manufacturing plant.

'Check under P,' Dixon said.

The P section started with a guy called Pascoe and finished with a guy called Purcell. Halfway through the list was *Pilot's office*.

Dixon said, 'We found the helicopter.'

Reacher nodded. Then he smiled at her. Pictured her running in with her flashlight, running out fifty seconds later covered in dust. His old team. *He could send them to Atlanta and they would come back with the Coke recipe.*

Neagley had personnel files on the whole security division. Nine green file folders. One was Saropian's, one was Tony Swan's. Reacher didn't look at either of those. No point. He started with the top boy, Allen Lamaison. There was a Polaroid photograph clipped to the first sheet inside. Lamaison was a bulky thick-necked man with dark blank eyes and a mouth too small for his jaw. His personal information was on the next sheet and showed he had done twenty years inside the LAPD, the last twelve in Robbery-Homicide. He was forty-nine years old.

Next up were the two guys sharing the third spot in the hierarchy. The first of them was called Lennox. Forty-one years old, ex-LAPD, grey buzz cut, heavy build, meaty red face.

The second was the guy in the raincoat. His name was Parker. Forty-two years old, ex-LAPD, tall, slim, a pale hard face disfigured by a broken nose.

'They're all ex-LAPD,' Neagley said. 'According to the data they all quit around the same time.'

'After a scandal?'

'There are always scandals. It's statistically difficult to quit the LAPD any other way.'

'Could your guy in Chicago get their histories?'

Neagley shrugged. 'We might be able to get into their computer. And we know some people. We might get some word of mouth.'

'What was on Berenson's office floor?'

'A new Oriental rug. Persian style, but almost certainly a copy from Pakistan.'

Reacher nodded. 'Swan's place, too. They must have done the whole executive floor.'

Neagley dialled her cell for the call to her Chicago guy's voice mail and Reacher put Parker's details on one side and checked the photographs of the four remaining foot soldiers. Then he closed their files and butted them together into a neat stack and piled it on top of Parker's jacket, like a category.

'I saw these five tonight,' he said.

'What were they like?' O'Donnell asked.

'Lousy. Really slow and stupid.'

'Where were the other two?'

'Highland Park, presumably. That's where the good stuff is.'

O'Donnell slid the five separated files toward him and asked, 'How did we lose four guys to the Keystone Cops?'

'I don't know,' Reacher said.

SIXTY-FIVE

Eventually, like he knew he would, Reacher opened Tony Swan's New Age personnel file. He didn't get past the Polaroid photograph. It was a year old and not remotely close to studio quality but it was much clearer than Curtis Mauney's video surveillance still. Ten years after the army Swan's hair had been shorter than when he was in. Back then the craze for shaved heads had already started among enlisted men but hadn't spread upward to officers. Swan had worn a regular style, parted and brushed. But over the years it must have thinned and he had changed to an all-over half-inch Caesar. In the army it had been a chestnut brown. Now it was a dusty grey. His eyes were pouched and he had grown balls of fat and muscle at the hinges of his jaw. His neck was wider than ever. Reacher was amazed that anyone made shirts with collars that size. Like automobile tyres.

'What next?' Dixon asked, in the silence. Reacher knew it wasn't a genuine enquiry. She was just trying to stop him reading. Trying to spare his feelings. He closed the file. Dropped it on the bed well away from the other files, in a category all its own. Swan deserved better than to be associated with his recent colleagues, even on paper.

'Who knew, and who flew,' Reacher said. 'That's what we need. Anyone else can live a little longer.'

'When will we know?'

'Later today. You and Dave can go scope out Highland Park. Neagley and I are going back to East LA. In an hour. So take a nap, and make it count.'

Reacher and Neagley left the motel at five in the morning, in separate Hondas, driving one-handed and talking to each other on the phone like commuters everywhere. Reacher said he guessed that when the alarm call came in Lamaison and Lennox had headed straight for Highland Park. Standard emergency protocol, he figured, because Highland Park was the more sensitive location. The attack in East LA might have been nothing more than a decoy. But an uneventful night would allay those fears and they would head to the scene of the real crime around dawn. They would declare the glass cube unusable for normal operations and give everyone the day off. Except for department heads, who would be called in to inventory the damage and list what was missing.

Neagley agreed with his analysis. And she grasped the next part of the plan without having to ask, which was one of the reasons why Reacher liked her so much.

They parked a hundred yards apart on different streets, hiding in plain sight. The sun was over the horizon and the dawn was grey. Reacher was fifty yards from New Age's building and could see his car reflected in the mirror glass, tiny and distant and anonymous, one of hundreds dumped all around. There was a flatbed truck backed up to the wrecked reception area. A steel cable snaked inside into the gloom. The guy called Parker was still there in his raincoat. He was directing operations. He had one foot soldier with him. Reacher guessed the other three had been sent up to Highland Park to relieve Lamaison and Lennox.

The flatbed's cable jerked and tightened and started hauling. The blue Chrysler came out of the lobby backward, a lot slower than it had gone in. It had scars on the paint and some front-end damage. The windshield was starred and a little concave. But overall the car was in excellent shape. As subtle as a hammer, as vulnerable as a hammer. It came to rest on the flatbed and the driver strapped the wheels down and drove it away. As soon as it was out of the lot its undamaged twin drove in. Another blue 300C, fast and confident. It stopped just inside and Allen Lamaison climbed out to inspect the smashed gate.

Reacher recognized him instantly from his file photograph. In the flesh he was about six feet tall and could have been two hundred and forty pounds. Big shoulders, small hips, thin legs. He looked fast and agile. He was dressed in a grey suit with a white shirt and a red necktie. He was holding the necktie flat against his chest with one hand, even though the weather wasn't windy. He took a brief look at the gate and climbed back in his car and drove on through the lot. He got out again just short of the shattered doors and Parker came over in his raincoat and they started talking.

Just to be sure Reacher took out the phone he had brought back from Vegas and redialled. Fifty yards away Lamaison's hand went straight to his pocket and came out with a phone. He glanced at the caller ID on the screen and froze.

Got you, Reacher thought.

He wasn't expecting an answer. But Lamaison picked up. He flicked the phone open and brought it up to his face and said, 'What?'

'How's your day going?' Reacher asked.

'It only just started,' Lamaison said.

'How was your night?'

'I'm going to kill you.'

'Plenty of folks have tried,' Reacher said. 'I'm still here. They aren't.'

'Where are you?'

'We got out of town. Safer that way. But we'll be back. Maybe next week, maybe next month, maybe next year. You better get used to looking over your shoulder. That's something you're going to be doing a lot of.'

'I'm not scared of you.'

'Then you're a fool,' Reacher said, and clicked off. He saw Lamaison stare at his phone, and then dial a number. Not a call back. Reacher waited, but his phone stayed silent, and Lamaison started talking, evidently to someone else.

Ten minutes later Lennox showed up in another blue 300C. Black suit, grey buzz cut, heavy build, meaty red face. The other number three, Swan's junior, Parker's equal. He was carrying a cardboard tray of coffee and disappeared into the building. Fifty minutes after that Margaret Berenson showed up. The dragon lady. Human resources. Seven o'clock in the morning. She was in a mid-size silver Toyota. She made a right off the roadway and drove through the lot and parked neatly in a slot close to the door. Then she picked her way inside through the wreckage. Lamaison came out briefly and despatched the remaining foot soldier to the gate, for sentry duty. Parker made a second line of defence at the door. He was still in his raincoat. Two more managers showed up. Probably financial and the building super, Reacher figured. The sentry waved them through the absent gate and Parker checked them in at the door. Then some kind of a CEO showed up. An old guy, a Jaguar sedan, deference at the gate, a ramrod posture from Parker. The old guy conferred with Parker through the Jaguar's window and went away again. Clearly he had a hands-off management style.

Then the scene went quiet, and it stayed quiet for more than two hours.

Halfway through the wait Dixon called in from Highland Park. She and O'Donnell had been on station since before six in the morning. They had seen the three foot soldiers show up. They had seen Lamaison and Lennox leave. They had seen workers show up. They had driven all around the plant on a two-block radius, for a fuller picture.

'It's the real deal,' Dixon said. 'Multiple buildings, serious fence, excellent security. And it's got a helipad out back. With a helicopter on it. A white Bell 222.'

At half past nine in the morning the dragon lady left. She picked her way through the mess and stood on the shallow step outside the reception area for a moment and then headed back toward her Toyota. Reacher's cell phone rang. The Radio Shack pay-as-you-go, not the Vegas guy's. It was Neagley.

'Both of us go?' she asked.

'Absolutely,' Reacher said. 'You close, me deep. Time to rock and roll.'

He pulled his gloves on and started his Honda at the same time that Berenson started her Toyota. She had made a right coming in, and therefore she would make a left going out. Reacher eased off the kerb and drove twenty yards and U-turned in the mouth of the next side street. He was stiff from sitting still so long. He came back slowly, along New Age's fence. Berenson was hustling through the lot. A block away he could see Neagley's Honda, riding low, trailing a cloud of white vapour. Berenson reached the wrecked gate and swept through without pausing. Made the left. Neagley made a parallel left and fell in twenty yards behind her. Reacher slowed and waited and then made his own turn and tucked in about seventy yards behind Neagley and ninety behind Berenson.

SIXTY-SIX

The Prelude was a low-slung coupé and therefore
Reacher didn't have the best angle in the world,
but most of the time he got a decent view of the
silver Toyota up ahead. Berenson was driving
well under the speed limit. Maybe she had points
on her licence. Or things on her mind. Or maybe
the car-crash scars were more vivid in her
memory than they were on her face. She made a
right onto a road called Huntington Drive, which
Reacher was pretty sure had been a part of the
old Route 66. She headed north and east on it.
Reacher started singing to himself, about getting
his kicks. Then he stopped. Berenson was slowing
and her turn signal was flashing. She was getting
ready to make a left. She was heading for South
Pasadena.

His phone rang. Neagley.

'I've been behind her too long,' she said. 'I'm
taking three sides of the next block. You move up
for a spell.'

He kept the line open and accelerated.
Berenson had turned into a road called Van
Horne Avenue. He turned into it about fifty

yards behind her. He couldn't see her. The road curved too much. He accelerated again and eased off and came around a final curve and spotted her about forty yards ahead. He cruised on and in his mirror he saw Neagley swing back on the road behind him.

Monterey Hills gave way to South Pasadena and at the municipal line the road changed its name to Via Del Rey. A pretty name, and a pretty place. The California dream. Low hills, curving streets, trees, perpetual spring, perpetual blossom. Reacher had grown up on grim military bases in Europe and the Pacific and people had given him picture books to show him what home was all about. Most of the pictures had looked exactly like South Pasadena.

Berenson made a left and then a right and pulled into a quiet residential cul-de-sac. Reacher glimpsed small smug houses basking in the morning sun. He didn't follow. The slammed Honda was pretty anonymous in most of LA, but not in a street like that. He braked and came to a stop thirty yards farther on. Neagley pulled in behind him.

'Now?' she asked, on the phone.

There were two main ways to engineer a visit with someone returning to their home. Either you let them settle and then gave them a compelling reason why they should let you in later, or you followed hard on their heels and rushed them while they still had their keys out or their door open.

'Now,' Reacher said.

They slid out and locked up and ran. Safe

enough. A lone man running could look suspicious. A lone woman rarely did. A man and a woman running together were usually taken as jogging buddies, or a couple just out having fun.

They made it into the cul-de-sac and saw nothing at first. There was a rise, and then a curve. They made it through the curve in time to see a garage door opening next to a house about a third of the way down the street on the right. Berenson's silver Toyota was waiting on a blacktop driveway. The house was small and neat. Faced with brick. Painted trim. The front yard was full of rocks and gravel and all kinds of colourful blooms. There was a basketball hoop over the garage. The rising door was letting in enough light to show a tangle of kid stuff stacked against a wall inside. A bike, a skateboard, a Little League bat, knee pads, helmets, gloves.

The Toyota's brake lights went off and it crept forward. Neagley sprinted. She was much faster than Reacher. She made it inside the garage just as the door started back down. Reacher arrived about ten seconds after her and used his foot to trip the safety mechanism. He waited until the door rose again to waist height and then he ducked under it and stepped inside.

Margaret Berenson was already out of her car. Neagley had one gloved hand in her hair and the other clamped around both of her wrists from behind. Berenson was struggling, but not much. She stopped altogether after Neagley forced her face down and tapped it twice against the Toyota's hood. At that point she went limp and started yelling. She stopped yelling exactly a second later after Neagley straightened her up again and turned her toward Reacher and Reacher popped her in the solar plexus, once, gently, just enough to drive the air out of her lungs.

Then Reacher stepped away and hit the button and the door started down again. There was a weak bulb in the opener on the ceiling and as the sunlight cut off it was replaced by a dim yellow glow. At the right rear of the garage there was a door to the outside, and another on the left that would lead to the interior of the house. There was an alarm pad next to it.

'Is it set?' Reacher asked.

'Yes,' Berenson said, breathlessly.

'No,' Neagley said. She nodded toward the bike and the skateboard. 'The kid is about twelve years old. Mom was out early this morning. The kid made the school bus on his own for once. Probably unusual. Setting the alarm won't be a part of his normal routine.'

'Maybe Dad set it.'

'Dad is long gone. Mom isn't wearing a ring.'

'Boyfriend?'

'You must be kidding.'

Reacher tried the door. It was locked. He pulled the keys out of the Toyota's ignition and thumbed through the ring and found a house key. It fit the lock and turned. The door opened. No warning beeps. Thirty seconds later, no lights, no siren.

'You tell a lot of lies, Ms Berenson,' he said.

Berenson said nothing.

Neagley said, 'She's human resources. It's what they do.'

403

Reacher held the door and Neagley bundled Berenson through a laundry room and into a kitchen. The house had been built before developers started making kitchens as big as aircraft hangars, so it was just a small square room full of cabinets and appliances a few years off the pace. There was a table and two chairs. Neagley forced Berenson down into one and Reacher headed back to the garage and rooted around until he found a half-used roll of duct tape on a shelf. With gloves on he couldn't unpick the end so he stepped back to the kitchen and used a knife from a maple block. He taped Berenson tight to the chair, torso, arms, legs, fast and efficient.

'We were in the army,' he said to her. 'We mentioned that, right? When we needed information, our first port of call was the company clerk. That's you. So start talking.'

'You're crazy,' Berenson said back.

'Tell me about the car wreck.'

'The what?'

'Your scars.'

'It was a long time ago.'

'Was it bad?'

'Awful.'

'This could be much worse.' Reacher put the kitchen knife on the table and followed it with the Glock from one pocket and Tony Swan's lump of concrete from the other. 'Stab wounds, gunshot wounds, blunt trauma. I'll let you choose.'

Berenson started to cry. Hopeless, helpless sobs and wails. Her shoulders shook and her head dropped and tears dripped into her lap.

'Not helping,' Reacher said. 'You're crying at the wrong guy.'

Berenson lifted her head and turned and looked at Neagley. Neagley's face was about as expressive as Swan's lump of concrete.

'Start talking,' Reacher said.

'I can't,' Berenson said. 'He'll hurt my son.'

'Who will?'

'I'm not allowed to say.'

'Lamaison?'

'I can't say.'

'It's time to make your mind up, Margaret. We want to know who knew and who flew. Right now we're including you in. You want us to include you out, you've got some serious talking to do.'

'He'll hurt my son.'

'Lamaison will?'

'I can't say who.'

'Look at it from our side, Margaret. If in doubt, we'll take you out.'

Berenson said nothing.

'Be smart, Margaret,' Reacher said. 'Whoever is threatening your son, you make a good case against him, he'll be dead. He won't be able to hurt anyone.'

'I can't rely on that.'

'Just shoot her,' Neagley said. 'She's wasting our time.'

Reacher stepped to the refrigerator and opened it up. Took out a plastic bottle of Evian water. Still, French, gallon for gallon three times as expensive as gasoline. He unscrewed the top and took a long drink. Offered the bottle to Neagley. She shook her head. He emptied the rest of the water in the sink and stepped back to the table and used the kitchen knife to saw an oval hole in the bottom of the bottle. He fitted it over the Glock's muzzle. Adjusted it neatly so that the screw neck lined up exactly with the barrel.

'A home made silencer,' he said. 'The neighbours won't hear a thing. It only works once, but once is all it has to.'

He held the gun a foot and a half from Berenson's face and aimed it so that she was staring straight into the bottle with her right eye.

Berenson started talking.

SIXTY-SEVEN

In retrospect it was a tale that Reacher could have scripted in advance. The original development engineer up at the Highland Park plant was now the quality control manager and he had started showing signs of severe stress. His name was Edward Dean and he lived way to the north, beyond the mountains. By chance his annual performance review was scheduled three weeks after he started his weird behaviour. Being a trained professional, Margaret Berenson noticed his distress, and she pursued the matter.

At first Dean claimed his move north was the root of his problem. He had wanted a relaxed lifestyle and had bought acres of land out in the desert some ways south of Palmdale. The commute was killing him. Berenson didn't buy that. All Angelinos had the commute from hell. So then Dean said his neighbours were problematical. There were outlaw bikers and meth labs close by. Berenson was readier to believe that. Stories about the badlands were legion. But a pained echo in a chance remark about Dean's daughter led her to believe that the kid was in some way the problem.

She was fourteen years old. Berenson put two and two together and made five. She figured maybe the kid was hanging with the bikers or experimenting with crystal and causing big problems at home.

Then she revised her opinion. The quality problems up at Highland Park became common knowledge inside the company. Berenson knew that Dean had a difficult split responsibility. As a director of the corporation he had a fiduciary duty to see it do well. But he also had a parallel responsibility to the Pentagon to make sure New Age sold it only the good stuff. Berenson figured the conflict in his mind was causing his stress. But overall he was doing the right thing according to the law, so she shelved her concerns.

Then Tony Swan disappeared.

He just vanished. One day he was there, the next day he wasn't. Being a trained professional, Margaret Berenson noticed his absence. She followed up. She had split responsibilities of her own. Swan had classified knowledge. There were national security implications. She got into it like a dog with a bone. She asked all kinds of questions of all kinds of people.

Then one day she got home and found Allen Lamaison on her driveway, playing one-on-one basketball with her son.

Berenson was afraid of Lamaison. Always had been. How much, she hadn't really realized until she saw him tousle her twelve-year-old's hair with a hand big enough to crush the child's skull. He suggested the kid stay outside and practise his foul throws while he went inside for an important chat with Mom.

The chat started with a confession. Lamaison told Berenson exactly what had happened to Swan. Every detail. And he hinted as to the reason. This time Berenson put two and two together and made four. She recalled Dean's stress. By and by Lamaison revealed that Dean was co-operating with a special project, because if he didn't his daughter would disappear and be found weeks later with blood running down to her ankles amid a happy band of bikers.

Or, on the other hand, maybe she would never be found at all.

Then Lamaison said the exact same thing could happen to Berenson's son. He said a lot of outlaw bikers were happy to swing both ways. Most of them had been in prison, and prison distorted a person's tastes.

He issued a warning, and two instructions. The warning was that sooner or later two men and two women would show up and start asking questions. Old friends from Swan's service days. The first instruction was that they were to be deflected, firmly, politely, and definitively. The second instruction was that nothing of this current conversation was ever to be revealed.

Then he made Berenson take him upstairs and perform a certain sexual act on him. To seal their understanding, he said.

Then he went out and sank a few more baskets with her son.

Then he drove away.

Reacher believed her. In his life he had listened to people telling lies, and less often to people telling the truth. He knew how to distinguish between the two. He knew what to trust and what to distrust. He was a supremely cynical man, but his special talent lay in retaining a small corner of openmindedness. He believed the basketball part, and the prison reference, and the sex act. People like Margaret Berenson didn't make that kind of stuff up. They couldn't. Their frames of reference weren't wide enough. He took the kitchen knife and cut the duct tape off her. Helped her to her feet.

'So who knew?' he asked.

'Lamaison,' Berenson said. 'Lennox, Parker, and Saropian.'

'That's all?'

'Yes.'

'What about the other four ex-LAPD?'

'They're different. From a different era and a different place. Lamaison wouldn't really trust them on a thing like this.'

'So why did he hire them?'

'Warm bodies. Numbers. And he trusts them on everything else. They do what he tells them.'

'Why did he hire Tony Swan? Swan was always going to be a rod for his back.'

'Lamaison didn't hire Swan. He didn't want him. But I convinced our CEO we needed some diversity of background. It wasn't healthy to have all of them from the same place.'

'So you hired him?'

'Basically. I'm sorry.'

'Where did all the bad stuff happen?'

'Highland Park. The helicopter is there. And there are outbuildings. It's a big place.'

410

'Is there somewhere you can go?' Reacher asked.

'Go?' Berenson said.

'For a couple of days, until this is over.'

'It won't be over. You don't know Lamaison. You can't beat him.'

Reacher looked at Neagley.

'Can we beat him?' he asked.

'Like a drum,' she said.

Berenson said, 'But there are four of them.'

'Three,' Reacher said. 'Saropian is already down. Three of them, four of us.'

'You're crazy.'

'They're going to think so. That's for damn sure. They're going to think I'm completely psychotic.'

Berenson was quiet for a long moment.

'I could go to a hotel,' she said.

'When does your son get home?'

'I'll go get him out of school.'

Reacher nodded. 'Pack your bags.'

Berenson said, 'I will.'

'Who flew?' Reacher asked.

'Lamaison, Lennox, and Parker. Just the three of them.'

'Plus the pilot,' Reacher said. 'That's four.'

Berenson went upstairs to pack and Reacher put the kitchen knife away. Then he put Swan's rock back in his pocket and pulled the Evian bottle off the Glock.

'Would that really have worked?' Neagley asked. 'As a silencer?'

'I doubt it,' Reacher said. 'I read it in a book

411

once. It worked on the page. But in the real world I imagine it would have exploded and blinded me with shards of flying plastic. But it looked good, didn't it? It added an extra element. Better than just pointing the gun.'

Then his phone rang. His Radio Shack pay-as-you-go, not Saropian's cell from Vegas. It was Dixon. She and O'Donnell had been on station in Highland Park for four and a half hours. They had seen all they were going to see, and they were starting to feel conspicuous.

'Head home,' Reacher said. 'We've got what we need.'

Then Neagley's phone rang. Her personal cell, not her pay-as-you-go. Her Chicago guy. Ten thirty in LA, lunchtime in Illinois. She listened, not moving, not asking questions, just absorbing information. Then she clicked off.

'Preliminary data from the LAPD grapevine,' she said. 'In twenty years Lamaison fought eighteen Internal Affairs investigations and won all of them.'

'Charges?'

'You name it. Excessive force, bribery, corruption, missing dope, missing money. He's a bad guy, but smart.'

'How does a guy like that get a job with a defence contractor?'

'How does he get one with the LAPD in the first place? And then promotions on top? By putting up a front and working hard to keep his record clean, that's how. And by having a partner who knew when and how to keep quiet.'

412

'His partner was probably just as bad. It usually works that way.'

'You should know,' Neagley said.

Forty minutes later Berenson came downstairs with two bags. An expensive black leather carry-on, and a bright green nylon duffel with a sports logo on it. Hers, and the kid's, Reacher guessed. She loaded them into the Toyota's trunk. Reacher and Neagley walked down to get their cars and drove them back and formed up into a close protection convoy. Same basic method as surveillance, different purpose. Neagley stayed tight, and Reacher hung back. After a mile he decided O'Donnell had been wrong about the tricked-out Hondas being the most invisible cars in California. The Toyota fit that bill better. He was staring right at it and could barely see it.

Berenson stopped at a school. It was a big tan spread with the kind of black-hole silence around it that schools get when all the kids are inside working. After twenty minutes she came back out with a brown-haired boy in tow. He was small. He barely reached her shoulder. He looked a little puzzled, but happy enough to be dragged away from class.

Then Berenson drove a little ways on the 110 and came off in Pasadena and headed for an inn on a quiet street. Reacher approved of her choice. The place had a lot in back where the Toyota wouldn't be seen from the road, and a bellman at the door, and two women behind a counter inside. Plenty of vigilant eyes before the elevators and the rooms. Better than a motel.

Reacher and Neagley stayed on site to give Berenson and her kid time to settle in. They figured ten minutes would do it. They used the time getting lunch, in a bar off the lobby. Club sandwiches, coffee for Reacher, soda for Neagley. Reacher liked club sandwiches. He liked the way he could pick his teeth afterwards with the tasselled thing that had held the sandwich together. He didn't want to be talking to people with chicken fibres caught in there.

His phone rang as he was finishing up his coffee. Dixon again. She was back at the motel, with O'Donnell. There was an urgent message waiting at the desk. From Curtis Mauney.

'He wants us up at that place north of Glendale,' Dixon said. 'Right now.'

'Where we went for Orozco?'

'Yes.'

'Because they found Sanchez?'

'He didn't say. But Reacher, he didn't tell us to meet him at the morgue. He said meet him at the hospital across the street. So if it's Sanchez, he's still alive.'

SIXTY-EIGHT

Dixon and O'Donnell were starting from the Dunes motel and Reacher and Neagley were starting from the inn in Pasadena. Both locations were exactly equidistant from the hospital north of Glendale. Ten miles, along different sides of the same shallow triangle.

Reacher expected that he and Neagley would get there first. The way the freeways lined up with the flanks of the San Gabriel mountains gave them a straight shot on the 210. Dixon and O'Donnell would be heading northeast, at right angles to the freeways, a difficult trip battling surface congestion all the way.

But the 210 was jammed. Within a hundred yards of the ramp it was completely static. A river of stalled cars curved ahead into the distance, winking in the sun, burning gas, going nowhere. A classic LA panorama. Reacher checked his mirror and saw Neagley's Honda right behind him. Hers was a Civic, white, about four model-years old. He couldn't see her behind the wheel. The screen was tinted too dark. It had a band of plastic across the top, dark blue with the words *No Fear* written across it in jagged silver script. Very appropriate, he thought, for Neagley.

He called her on the phone.

'Breakdown up ahead,' she said. 'I heard it on the radio.'

'Terrific.'

'If Sanchez made it this far, he can make it a few minutes more.'

Reacher asked, 'Where did they go wrong?'

'I don't know. This wasn't the toughest thing they ever faced.'

'So something tripped them up. Something unpredictable. Where would Swan have started?'

'With Dean,' Neagley said. 'The quality control guy. His behaviour must have been the trigger. Bad numbers on their own don't necessarily mean much. But bad numbers plus a stressed-out quality control guy mean a lot.'

'Did he get the whole story out of Dean?'

'Probably not. But enough to join the dots. Swan was a lot smarter than Berenson.'

'What was his next step?'

'Two steps in parallel,' Neagley said. 'He secured Dean's situation, and he started the search for corroborating evidence.'

'With help from the others.'

'More than help,' Neagley said. 'He was basically subcontracting. He had to, because his office situation was insecure.'

'So he didn't talk to Lamaison at any point?'

'Not a chance. First rule, trust no one.'

'So what tripped them up?'

'I don't know.'

'How would Swan have secured Dean's situation?'

'He'd have talked to the local cops. Asked for protection, or at least asked for a car to swing by on a regular basis.'

'Lamaison is ex-LAPD. Maybe he still has buddies on the job. Maybe they tipped him off.'

'Doesn't work,' Neagley said. 'Swan didn't talk to the LAPD. Dean lived over the hill. Outside of LAPD jurisdiction.'

Reacher paused a beat.

'Which actually means that Swan didn't talk to anyone,' he said. 'Because that's Curtis Mauney's kingdom up there, and he didn't know anything about Dean or New Age. Or even anything about Swan, except through Franz.'

'Swan wouldn't leave Dean unprotected.'

'So maybe Dean wasn't the trigger. Maybe Swan didn't know anything about him. Maybe he found a different way in.'

'Which was?' Neagley asked.

'No idea,' Reacher said. 'Maybe Sanchez will be able to tell us.'

'You think he's alive?'

'Hope for the best.'

'But plan for the worst.'

They clicked off. Their lane moved a little. In a minute and a quarter of conversation they had covered about five car-lengths. In the next five minutes of silence they covered about ten more, six times slower than walking. All around them people were enduring. They were talking on the phone, reading, shaving, applying makeup, smoking, eating, listening to music. Some were tanning. They were hitching up their sleeves and holding their arms out their open windows.

Reacher's pay-as-you-go rang. Neagley again.

'More from Chicago,' she said. 'We're into parts of the LAPD mainframe. Lennox and Parker were about as bad as Lamaison. The two of them were partners together. They resigned rather than face their twelfth IA inquiry in twelve years. They must have been out of work about a week before Lamaison hired them on at New Age.'

'I'm glad I don't hold New Age stock.'

'You do. It's all Pentagon money. Where do you think it comes from?'

'Not from me,' Reacher said.

Two hundred yards later the freeway straightened and rose in front of them and they saw the source of the delay, in the far distance, in the haze. There was a broken-down car in the left lane. A trivial blockage, but the whole road was at a standstill. Reacher clicked off with Neagley and redialled and called Dixon.

'You there yet?' he asked.

'Maybe ten minutes away.'

'We're stuck in traffic. Call us if there's good news. Call us if there's bad news, too, I guess.'

It took another quarter of an hour to reach the stalled car and some bold lane changes to get past it. Then the flow freed up and everyone continued on their way at seventy miles an hour like nothing had happened. Reacher and Neagley were at the county facility ten minutes later. Ten miles in forty minutes. Average speed, fifteen miles an hour. Not great.

They ignored the morgue and parked in the hospital's visitor lot. They walked through the sun to the main entrance. Reacher saw O'Donnell's Honda in the lot, and then Dixon's. The main entrance gave on to a lobby full of red plastic chairs. Some of them were occupied. Most of them weren't. The place was fairly quiet. There was no sign of Dixon or O'Donnell. Or Curtis Mauney. There was a long desk with people behind it. Not nurses. Just clerks. Reacher asked one of them for Mauney and got no response. He asked for Jorge Sanchez and got no response. He asked about emergency John Doe admissions and got redirected to another desk around a corner.

The new desk reported no recent John Doe admissions and knew nothing about a patient named Jorge Sanchez or an LA County sheriff named Curtis Mauney. Reacher pulled out his phone but was asked not to use it inside the building in case its signal upset delicate medical equipment. He stepped out to the lot and called Dixon.

No reply.

He tried O'Donnell's number.

No reply.

Neagley said, 'Maybe they're switched off. Because they're in an ICU or something.'

'Who with? They never heard of Sanchez here.'

'They have to be here somewhere. They just got here.'

'This feels wrong,' Reacher said.

Neagley took Mauney's card out of her pocket. Handed it over. Reacher dialled Mauney's cell number.

No answer.

His land line.

No answer.

Then Neagley's phone rang. Her personal cell, not her pay-as-you-go. She answered. Listened. Her face went pale. Literally bloodless, like wax.

'That was Chicago,' she said. 'Curtis Mauney was Allen Lamaison's partner. They were together twelve years in the LAPD.'

SIXTY-NINE

Something tripped them up. Something un-predictable. Neagley had been right, but only half right. Dean had been a major factor, but not the original trigger. Swan had gotten to him much later in the process, some different way, after the others were already on board. No other way to explain the scale of the disaster. Reacher stood in the hospital lot and closed his eyes and pictured the scene. Saw Swan talking to Dean, the final part of the puzzle, at home, north of the mountains, out in the desert near Palmdale, a city refugee's paradise, a sanctuary, a young girl moving silently past an open doorway, fear on Dean's face, concern on Swan's. Reacher saw Swan extracting the whole story, as always reassuring and solid and confident. Then Reacher saw Swan driving straight to some dusty sheriff's office, talking to Mauney, explaining, asking for help, demanding it. Then he saw Swan leaving, and Mauney picking up a phone. Sealing Swan's fate right there and then. And Franz's, and Orozco's, and Sanchez's.

Something unpredictable.

Reacher opened his eyes and said, 'We're not going to lose another two. Not while I live and breathe.'

They abandoned Neagley's Civic in the hospital lot and used Reacher's Prelude. They had nowhere to go. They were just moving for the sake of moving. And talking for the sake of talking. Neagley said, 'They knew we'd show up sooner or later. The suspense was killing them. So they manipulated the timeline to suit themselves. Mauney pushed Angela Franz into calling me. He spun the bait story to keep Thomas Brant on board. He was tracking us every step of the way and feeding us things we already knew to keep us close and asking us what else we'd found out and waiting to see if we'd give up and get out of their hair. And when we never did, they decided to go ahead and take us out. First Vegas, and then now.'

They swung back onto the 210. It was flowing fast and free.

'Plan?' Neagley asked.

'No plan,' Reacher said.

The phone directory that Dixon had captured was in O'Donnell's room at the motel, but they didn't want to go anywhere near Sunset Boulevard. Not at that point. So they pieced together half-remembered fragments of the manufacturing plant's Highland Park address and headed in that direction.

They found Highland Park easily enough. It was a decent place full of streets and houses and business parks and small clean hi-tech manufacturing enterprises. It was harder to find New Age's specific location. They weren't expecting a billboard and didn't get one. Instead they looked for unmarked buildings and serious fences and helipads. They found several. It was that kind of a neighbourhood.

'Dixon called the helicopter a Bell 222,' Reacher said. 'Could you recognize one of those if you saw one?'

'I've seen three in the last five minutes,' Neagley said.

'She said it was white.'

'Two in the last five minutes.'

'Where?'

'The second one was a mile back. Two lefts and a right. The first one was three places before that.'

'Both places with fences?'

'Check.'

'Outbuildings?'

'Both of them.'

Reacher braked and pulled an illegal U across the full width of the road and headed back the way they had come. He took two lefts and a right and slowed and Neagley pointed at a collection of grey metal buildings squatting behind a fence that would have looked right at home outside a super-max prison. It was at least eight feet tall and close to four feet thick, two faces of tight barbed wire with giant coils of razor wire heaped between them and huge concertinas of the same stuff piled on top. It was one hell of a barrier. There were four buildings behind it. One was a large shed and three were smaller constructions. There was a huge concrete rectangle with a long-nosed helicopter parked on it, white, still and quiet.

'That's a Bell 222?' Reacher asked.

'Unmistakable,' Neagley said.

'So is this the place?'

'Hard to say.'

Next to the helipad was an orange windsock on a tall pole. It was hanging limp in the warm dry air. There was a small parking lot full of thirteen cars. Nothing expensive. No blue Chryslers.

'What would assembly workers drive?' Reacher asked.

'Cars like those,' Neagley said.

Reacher drove on, past one place, past another. The third place in line was very similar to the first. A serious fence, four blank buildings with grey metal siding, a parking lot full of cheap cars, a helipad, a parked Bell 222, white. No names, no markings, no signs.

Reacher said, 'We need the exact address.'

'We don't have time. The Dunes is a long way from here.'

'But Pasadena isn't.'

They made the short hop east on York Boulevard and the 110. Pulled up outside the inn in Pasadena fifteen minutes later. Five minutes after that they were in Margaret Berenson's room. They told her what they needed. They didn't tell her why. They wanted to preserve an illusion of competence, for her sake.

Berenson told them the first place they had seen was the place they wanted.

424

*   *   *

Fifteen minutes later they cruised past the first place again. The fence was appalling. Brutal. A main battle tank might have breached it. A car almost certainly wouldn't. Not a Honda Prelude. Not even a big lump like the Chrysler. Not even a heavy truck. It was a question of the wire's resilience. The outer strands would stretch like guitar strings before they broke, dissipating the force of impact, slowing the vehicle, robbing its momentum. Then the inner coils would compress. Like a sponge. Like a spring. The vehicle would tangle and slow and stall. No way through on wheels. And no way through on foot. An individual with a bolt cutter would bleed to death before he was a quarter of the way in. And there was no way over the top, either. The concertinas were too broad and too loosely coiled to allow scaling by ladder.

Reacher drove all the way around the block. The whole facility occupied a couple of acres. It was roughly square, about a hundred yards on a side. Four buildings, one large, three small. Dried brown grass and cinder footpaths between them. The fence was four hundred yards long in total and had no weak spots. And only one gate. It was a wide steel assembly that slid sideways on wheels. Welded to its top rail was more concertina wire. Flanking it was a guard hut.

'Pentagon requirement,' Neagley said. 'Has to be.'

There was a guard in the hut. An old guy, grey hair. Grey uniform. A belt around his hips, a gun in the belt. A simple job. The right pass and the right paperwork, he would hit a button and the gate would roll back. No pass and no paperwork, he wouldn't and it wouldn't. There was a light bulb above the guy's head. It would be lit after dark. It would throw a soft yellow halo for twenty feet all around.

'No way through,' Reacher said.

'Are they even in there?'

'Must be. It's like a private jail. Safer than stashing them anywhere else. And it's where they put the others.'

'How did it go down?'

'Mauney arrested them in the hospital lot. Maybe he had help from Lamaison's guys. Crowded place, total surprise, what were they going to do?'

Reacher drove on. The Prelude was an unremarkable car, but he didn't want it to be seen too many times in the same place. He turned a corner and parked a quarter of a mile away. Didn't speak. Because he had nothing to say.

Neagley's phone rang again. Her personal cell. She answered. Listened. Clicked off. Closed her eyes.

'My Pentagon guy,' she said. 'The missiles just rolled out the gate in Colorado.'

SEVENTY

If Mahmoud has got the missiles, then this thing is bigger than we are. We have to suck it up and move on. Reacher looked at Neagley. She opened her eyes and stared right back.

'How much do they weigh?' Reacher asked.

'Weigh?'

'As in weight. Pounds and ounces.'

'I don't know. They're new. I never saw one.'

'Guess.'

'Heavier than a Stinger. Because they do more. But still man-portable. Crated, with launch tubes and spare parts and manuals, say fifty pounds each.'

'That's sixteen and a quarter tons.'

'A semi truck,' Neagley said.

'Average speed on the Interstates, fifty miles an hour?'

'Probably.'

'North on I-25 to I-80, then west to Nevada, that's about nine hundred miles. So we've got eighteen hours. Call it twenty-four, because the driver will take a rest period.'

'They're not going to Nevada,' Neagley said.

'Nevada is bullshit, because they're going to use these things, not destroy them.'

'Wherever. Anywhere significant is eighteen hours from Denver.'

Neagley shook her head. 'This is insane. We can't wait twenty-four hours. Or eighteen. You said it yourself, there could be ten thousand KIAs.'

'But not yet.'

'We can't wait,' Neagley said again. 'Easier to stop the truck on the way out of Denver. It could be headed anywhere. It could be headed to New York, JFK, or La Guardia. Or Chicago. You want to think about Little Wing deployed at O'Hare?'

'Not really.'

'Every minute we delay makes that truck harder to find.'

'Moral dilemma,' Reacher said. 'Two people we know, or ten thousand we don't.'

'We have to tell someone.'

Reacher said nothing.

'We have to, Reacher.'

'They might not listen. They didn't listen about September eleventh.'

'You're clutching at straws. They've changed. We have to tell someone.'

'We will,' Reacher said. 'But not yet.'

'Karla and Dave will have a better chance with a couple of SWAT teams on their side.'

'You're kidding. They'll wind up as collateral damage in a heartbeat.'

Neagley said, 'We can't even get through the fence. Dixon will die, O'Donnell will die, ten thousand other people will die, and we'll die.'

'You want to live forever?'

'I don't want to die today. Do you?'

'I really don't care one way or the other.'

'Seriously?'

'I never have. Why would I?'

'You *are* psychotic.'

'Look on the bright side.'

'Which is what?'

'Maybe none of the bad stuff will happen.'

'Why wouldn't it?'

'Maybe we'll win. You and me.'

'Here? Maybe. But later? Dream on. We have no idea where that truck is going.'

'We can find out later.'

'You think?'

'It's what we're good at.'

'Good enough to gamble ten thousand lives against two?'

'I hope so,' Reacher said.

He drove a mile south and parked again on a curving side street outside a custom Harley motorcycle shop. He could see New Age's helicopter in the far distance.

He asked, 'What is their security going to be like?'

'Normally?' Neagley said. 'Motion detectors on the fence and big locks on all the doors and a guy in the sentry hut twenty-four hours a day. That's all they need, normally. But today isn't going to be normal. You can forget about that. They know we're still out here. The whole of New Age security is going to be in there, locked and loaded.'

'Seven men.'

'Seven we know about. Maybe more.'

'Maybe.'

'And they're going to be inside the fence. We're going to be outside the fence.'

'Let me worry about the fence.'

'There's no way through it.'

'Doesn't need to be. There's a gate. What time does it get full dark?'

'Say nine o'clock, to be safe.'

'They won't fly before dark. We've got seven hours. Seven out of our twenty-four.'

'We never had twenty-four.'

'You elected me CO. We've got what I say we've got.'

'They could have shot them both already.'

'They didn't shoot Franz or Orozco or Swan. They're worried about ballistics.'

'This is insane.'

'I'm not going to lose another two,' Reacher said.

They drove around New Age's block one more time, fast and unobtrusive, and fixed the geography in their minds. The gate was in the centre of the front face of the square. The main building was front and centre behind it at the end of a short driveway. In back of that the three outbuildings were scattered. One was close to the helipad. One was a little farther away. The last was standing on its own, maybe thirty yards from anything else. All four buildings were set on concrete pads. They had grey galvanized siding. No signs, no labels. It was a severe, practical establishment. There were no trees. No land-scaping. Just uneven brown grass and hard dirt paths and a parking lot.

'Where are the Chryslers?' Reacher asked.

'Out,' Neagley said. 'Looking for us.'

They headed back to the hospital in Glendale. Neagley collected her car from the lot. They stopped in at a supermarket. Bought a pack of wooden kitchen matches. And two cases of Evian water. Twelve one-litre bottles, nested together in packs of six and shrink-wrapped in plastic. They stopped again down the street at an auto parts store. Bought a red plastic five-gallon gasoline can and a bag of polishing rags.

Then they stopped at a gas station and filled the cars and the can.

They headed southwest out of Glendale and ended up in Silver Lake. Reacher called Neagley on the phone and said, 'We should drop by the motel now.'

Neagley said, 'They might still have surveil-lance going.'

'Which is exactly why we should drop by. If we can take one of them out now, that's one less to worry about later.'

'Might be more than one.'

'Bring it on. The more the merrier.'

Sunset Boulevard ran right through Silver Lake, south of the reservoir. It was a very long road. Reacher found it and headed west. Six miles later he cruised past the motel without slowing. Neagley was twenty yards behind him in her Civic. He led her through a left turn and parked a block away. There were service alleys that gave them a roundabout route into the back of the motel. They walked through the alleys fifteen feet apart. No sense in making two people into a single target. Reacher went first, with his hand wrapped around the Glock in his pocket. He entered the motel lot slowly, from the rear, through a tight passage lined with trash receptacles. The lot looked innocent enough. Eight cars, five out of state plates, no blue Chryslers. Nobody in the shadows. He went to the right. He knew that fifteen feet behind him Neagley would go to the left. It was their default arrangement, established many years before. R for Reacher, L for her middle initial. He made a complete half-circuit of the building. There was nobody out of place. Nobody suspicious. Nobody in the lounge, nobody in the laundry room. Across the width of the lot he could see the clerk all alone in the office.

He stepped out to the sidewalk and checked the street. It was clear. Some activity, but nothing significant. Some cars, but none to worry about. He stepped back into the lot and waited for Neagley to complete her own half-circuit on the other side. She checked the sidewalk and checked the street and stepped back and checked the office. Nothing. She shook her head and they headed for O'Donnell's room, by different routes, still fifteen feet apart, just in case.

O'Donnell's lock was broken.

Or more accurately, O'Donnell's lock was OK, but the door jamb was broken. The wood was splintered. Someone had used a wrecking bar or a tyre iron to lever the door open. Reacher slid the Glock out of his pocket and waited on the hinge side of the door and Neagley joined him on the handle side. She nodded and he slammed the door open with his foot and she dropped to her knees and spun into the doorway with her gun out in front. Another old default arrangement. Whoever was on the hinge side opened the door, whoever was on the handle side entered low to minimize the target. Generally anyone hiding in a room with a gun would aim high, at where he expected centre mass to be.

But there was nobody hiding in the room.

It was completely empty. But it was completely trashed. Searched, and wrecked. All the New Age paperwork was gone, the reject Glock 17s were gone, the spare ammunition was gone, the AMT Hardballers were gone, Saropian's Daewoo DP 51 was gone, the Maglites were gone. O'Donnell's clothes were strewn all around. His thousand-dollar suit had been torn off the closet hanger and trampled. His bathroom stuff was all over the place.

Dixon's room was the same. Empty, but trashed.

And Neagley's.

And Reacher's own. His folding toothbrush was on the floor, stepped on and crushed.

'Bastards,' he said.

They gave the whole place one more go-round, the motel itself, and then a one-block radius outside. Nobody there. Neagley said, 'They're all waiting for us in Highland Park.'

Reacher nodded. Between them they had two

433

Glocks and sixty-eight rounds. Plus their recent purchases in the Prelude's trunk.

Two against seven or more.

No time.

No element of surprise.

A fortified position with no way in.

A hopeless situation.

'We're good to go,' Reacher said.

SEVENTY-ONE

Waiting for dark was always a long and tedious process. Sometimes the earth seemed to spin fast, and sometimes it seemed to spin slow. This was slow. They were parked in a quiet street three blocks from New Age's factory, opposite sides of the street, Neagley's Civic facing west, Reacher's Prelude facing east. They both had a view of the place. Things had changed behind the fence. The assembly workers' cars were gone from the lot. In their place were six blue Chrysler 300Cs. Clearly operations had been abandoned for the day. The decks had been cleared for the coming battle. Beyond the cars they could see the helicopter in the distance, a quarter-mile away. It was nothing more than a small white shape, but they figured they would be able to tell if it started up. And if it started up, all bets were off.

Reacher had both his phones set to vibrate. Neagley buzzed him twice, to pass the time. She was actually close enough to roll down her window and yell, but he guessed she didn't want to attract attention.

435

The first time, she asked, 'Have you been sleeping with Karla?'

'When?' Reacher said, buying time.

'On this trip.'

'Twice,' Reacher said. 'That's all.'

'I'm glad.'

'Thank you.'

'You both always wanted to.'

The second time she called was fifteen minutes later.

'You made a will?' she asked.

'No point,' Reacher said. 'Now they broke my toothbrush I don't own anything.'

'How does that feel?'

'Bad. I liked that toothbrush. It's been with me a long time.'

'No, I mean the rest of it.'

'It feels OK. I don't see that Karla or Dave are really any happier than me.'

'Right now they're not, for sure.'

'They know we're coming.'

'All of us going down together will really cheer them up.'

'Better than going down alone,' Reacher said.

A big white semi truck laboured west on I-70 in Colorado, heading for the state of Utah. It was less than half full, a little over sixteen tons in a rig designed for a forty-ton payload. So it was running light, but it was running slow, because of the mountains. It would stay slow until the turn south on I-15. Then it would run a little easier, all the way down to California. Its driver had budgeted an average fifty miles an hour for the whole trip.

Eighteen hours maximum, door-to-door. He wasn't going to take a rest period. How could he? He was a man on a mission, with no time for frivolities.

Azhari Mahmoud checked his map for the third time. He figured he needed three hours. Or maybe more. He had to cross just about the whole of Los Angeles, south to north. He wasn't expecting it to be easy. The U-Haul was slow and a pig to drive, and he was sure that the traffic was going to be awful. He decided to give himself four hours. If he arrived early, he could wait. No harm in that. He set his alarm and lay down on the bed and tried to will himself to sleep.

Reacher stared straight ahead at the eastern horizon, trying to judge the light. The tint on the windshield didn't help. It was overly optimistic, optically. It made the sky look darker than it really was. He buzzed his window down and leaned out. In reality, not good. There was still at least an hour of daylight left. Then maybe an hour of dusk. Then full dark. He buzzed the window up and settled back and rested. Forced his heartbeat down and slowed his breathing and relaxed.

He stayed relaxed until Allen Lamaison called him.

SEVENTY-TWO

Lamaison called Reacher on his radio shack pay-as-you-go, not on Saropian's cell from Vegas. The caller ID showed he was using Karla Dixon's phone at his end. Openly provocative. There was a lot of smug satisfaction in his voice.

'Reacher?' he said. 'We need to talk.'

'So talk,' Reacher said.

'You're useless.'

'You think?'

'You've lost every round so far.'

'Except Saropian.'

'True,' Lamaison said. 'And I'm very unhappy about that.'

'But you better get used to it. Because you're going to lose another six, and then you and I are going to go around and around.'

'No,' Lamaison said. 'That's not going to happen. We're going to make a deal.'

'Dream on.'

'The terms are excellent. Want to hear them?'

'You better be quick. I'm downtown right now. I've got an appointment with the FBI. I'm going to tell them all about Little Wing.'

'Tell them what?' Lamaison said. 'There's nothing to tell. We had some defective units that were destroyed. It says so, in black and white, on Pentagon-approved paperwork.'

Reacher said nothing.

'Anyway, you're nowhere near the FBI,' Lamaison said. 'You're working out how to rescue your friends.'

'You think?'

'You wouldn't trust their safety to the FBI.'

'You're confusing me with someone who gives a shit.'

'You wouldn't be here at all if you didn't give a shit. Tony Swan and Calvin Franz and Manuel Orozco and Jorge Sanchez told us all about it. Before they died. Apparently we're not supposed to mess with the special investigators.'

'That was just a slogan. It was old then, and it's really old now.'

'They still put a lot of stock in it. So do Ms Dixon and Mr O'Donnell. Their faith in you is quite touching. So let's talk about our deal. You can save your friends a world of hurt.'

'How?'

'You and Ms Neagley come in now, we'll hold you all for a week. Until the heat dies down. Then we'll let you go. All four of you.'

'Or?'

'We'll break O'Donnell's arms and legs and use his switchblade all over Dixon. After having a little guy time with her first. Then we'll put them both in the helicopter.'

Reacher said nothing.

'Don't worry about Little Wing,' Lamaison

439

said. 'That's a done deal. Can't be stopped now. They're going to Kashmir, anyway. You ever been there? It's a dump. A real shit hole. Bunch of towel heads fighting each other. Why should you care?'

Reacher said nothing.

Lamaison said, 'Do we have a deal?'

'No.'

'You should reconsider. Dixon won't enjoy what we've got in mind.'

'Why would I trust you? I'll walk in and you'll shoot me in the head.'

'I agree, it's a risk,' Lamaison said. 'But I think you'll take it. Because you're responsible for your people's situation. You let them down. You're their leader, and you screwed up. I've heard a lot about you. In fact I'm sick of hearing your name. You'll do what it takes to help them.'

'Where are you?' Reacher asked.

'I'm sure you know.'

Reacher glanced ahead through the windshield. Factored in the effect of the window tint and tried to judge the light.

'We're two hours away,' he said, with a little tension in his voice.

'Where are you?'

'We're south of Palmdale.'

'Why?'

'We were going to visit with Dean. To piece it all together, the same way Swan did.'

'Turn around,' Lamaison said. 'Right now. For Ms Dixon's sake. I bet she's a screamer. My guys will be all over her. I'll put her on the phone and let you listen.'

Reacher paused.

'Two hours,' he said. 'We'll talk again.'

He clicked off and dialled Neagley.

'We go in sixty minutes,' he said.

Then he leaned back in his seat and closed his eyes.

Sixty minutes later the sky in the east was a dark navy blue, almost black. Visibility was fading fast. Years before, a pedantic schoolteacher in the Pacific somewhere had explained to Reacher that first comes twilight, and then comes dusk, and then comes night. She had insisted that *twilight* and *dusk* were not the same thing. If he needed a generic word for evening darkness, he was to use *gloaming*.

Gloaming was what he had right then. Plenty of it, but not quite as much as he would have liked.

He dialled Neagley and clicked off after one ring. Her window dropped and she waved. A small pale hand in the darkness. He started his car and eased away from the kerb. No lights. He headed east toward the arriving night and made a right and three blocks later he was skirting New Age's fence, clockwise, along the back line of their property. He made another right and came down the side of their lot and coasted to a stop against the kerb about two-thirds of the way down. If New Age's place was a clock, he was stopped on the four. If it was a compass, he was a little ways south of east.

He got out and stood still and listened. Heard nothing. Saw nothing. Highland Park was a populated area, but New Age's place was part of a commercial zone. The work day was over. People were gone. The streets were dark and quiet.

He opened the Prelude's trunk. Used his fist to smash the courtesy light. Used his thumbnail to slit the plastic around the Evian bottles. He took one out and unscrewed the top and took a long drink. Then he poured the rest of the water away in the gutter. Stood the empty bottle upright in the trunk. He repeated the process eleven more times. Ended up with a neat line of twelve empty one-litre bottles.

Then he took out the gas can.

Five gallons, US liquid measure, which added up to close to nineteen litres. He filled the bottles, very carefully. The benzene fragrance of un-leaded gasoline came up at him. He liked it. It was one of the world's great smells. When the twelfth bottle was full he put the can on the ground. Seven litres still in it. Almost two gallons.

He tore open the bag of polishing rags.

They were foot-square pieces of white cotton jersey. Like undershirts. He rolled them tight, like cigars, and eased them down into the necks of the bottles. Half in, half out. The gasoline soaked upward, pale and colourless.

Molotov cocktails. A crude but effective weapon, invented by Fascists during the Spanish Civil War, named by Finns during their struggle against the Red Army in 1939, as a taunt toward the Soviet foreign minister Vyacheslav Molotov. *I never knew a tank could burn so long*, a Finnish veteran had once recalled.

Tanks, buildings, it was all the same to Reacher.

He rolled a thirteenth rag and laid it on the ground. Dripped gas from the can on it until it was soaked. He found the box of wooden kitchen matches and jammed them in his pocket. Lifted the twelve bottles of gas out of the trunk, one by one, carefully, and stood them upright on the road six feet behind the Prelude's rear bumper. Then he picked up the thirteenth rag and closed the trunk lid and trapped the rag in it, three-quarters out. In the darkness it looked like the car had a tiny white tail. Like a silver lamb.

Showtime, he thought.

He struck a match and held it against the rag trapped in the trunk lid until the rag was burning bright. Then he flicked the match away and picked up the first Molotov cocktail. Lit its wick off the burning rag and stepped back and hurled it high in the air, over the fence. It tumbled through a lazy blazing arc and burst against the base of the main building's end wall. Gas exploded and flared and then settled into a small burning pool.

He threw the second bomb. Same procedure. He lit the wick off the burning rag, stepped back, and threw hard. The bottle sailed through the same arc and hit the same place and burst. There was a brief white-hot flare and then the pool of flames settled and spread wider. They started to lick upward against the siding.

He threw the third bomb directly into the fire. And the fourth. He aimed the fifth a little to the left. It started a brand new fire. He followed it with the sixth and the seventh. His shoulder started to ache from the effort of the giant

443

throws. The grass all around the building's end wall started to burn. Smoke started to drift. He threw the eighth bottle into the gap between the two fires. It fell short and burst and set fire to the grass about eight feet out. Now there was a large irregular patch of flames, maybe ten feet wide, maybe eight feet deep. Maybe four feet high, red and orange and green with chemical acceleration.

He threw the ninth bottle harder, and further to the left. It exploded near the building's door. The tenth bottle followed it. It didn't burst. It rolled and leaked and burning gasoline welled out and flames raced and crackled through the dry grass. He paused and picked his spot and used the eleventh bottle to fill the gap on the building's corner. The twelfth and last bottle followed it. He heaved it hard and it hit the siding high up and burst into flames and burning gas spattered the whole end wall.

He opened the trunk lid and knocked the burning rag out and stamped on it. Then he stepped to the fence and peered through. The grass at the base of the building's end wall and all along the front wall as far as the door was burning fiercely. Flames were leaping high and smoke was pouring upward. The building itself was built of metal and was resisting. But it would be getting warm inside.

Soon be getting warmer, Reacher thought.

He screwed the lid on the gas can and wound up and hurled it like a discus thrower. It soared up over the fence and spun and wobbled through the air and landed dead centre in the flames. Thin red flammable plastic, two gallons of gas inside.

There was a split second's pause and then the can exploded in a huge white fireball. For a time it looked like the whole place was on fire. And when the fireball eventually died the flames left behind were twice as high as before and the paint on the siding was starting to burn.

Reacher got back in the Prelude and started up and pulled a ragged U-turn and headed back the way he had come. The muffler burbled. He hoped Dixon and O'Donnell could hear it, wherever they were. Three blocks later he was back where he started. He pulled in behind Neagley's Civic and killed his motor and sat still and watched out his window. He could see the glow in the distance, far to his left. Clouds of billowing smoke, drifting, up-lit by bright leaping flames below. A decent blaze, getting worse by the minute.

Impressive.

He raised an imaginary glass to Comrade Molotov.

Then he leaned back in his seat and waited for the fire department to show up.

SEVENTY-THREE

The fire department showed up inside four minutes. Clearly New Age had an alarm system hard-wired straight into the precinct house. A Pentagon requirement, Reacher guessed, like the guard shack at the gate. Far to his right in the distance he heard the faint bass bark of sirens and saw blue lights flashing on the horizon. He saw Neagley start her car and put it in gear. He started his own. And then he waited. The sirens grew louder. They changed to a manic continuous shriek, once, then again, at busy intersections. Then they died back to random barking. The blue lights got brighter. The trucks were two blocks away. Headlight beams were bright in the gloom. Neagley eased off the kerb. Reacher followed her. She drove ahead and waited on the stop line. Reacher was right behind her. The fire trucks were a block away, bearing down, coming on fast, honking and flashing. Neagley swooped out and made the left, right in front of the convoy. Reacher followed her, tyres chirping, just yards in front of the leading truck. Its siren blared at him angrily. Neagley drove a couple of hundred yards. One block. Two. Onto New Age's block. She followed the fence along the front of the property. Reacher was behind her all the way. The sirens behind him were yelping furiously. Then Neagley pulled over, like a good citizen. Reacher tucked in behind her. The trucks lurched left and roared past them both. Then more or less immediately they braked hard and turned and headed for New Age's gate. There were three of them. A whole engine company. A priority client.

New Age's gate was rolling back. Because a fire alarm was better than any kind of pass or paperwork.

Then Neagley slammed her car twenty feet into a side street and was out of her seat and running hard through the darkness. Reacher followed her all the way. They crossed the road at maximum speed and caught up with the last truck as it slowed to turn in. They stayed on its left, on the blind side, away from the guard shack, away from the fire. Away from the centre of attention. They ran hard to keep pace. They tracked the truck all the way in through the gate. Its siren was still sounding. Its engine was roaring. It was deafening. Smoke was drifting from the fire, sharp and acrid on the night air. The truck roared straight ahead. Neagley turned a hard left and ran down the inside face of the fence. Reacher headed half left through the grass. He gave it ten long seconds of maximum effort and then flung himself down and rolled and crammed himself flat on his front with his face hard down in the dirt.

A minute later he raised his head.

He was sixty yards from the fire. Between him and it were the three trucks, huge, noisy, blue lights flashing, headlights blazing. Beyond the trucks he could see flames. He could see people moving around. New Age security. They were over by the far fence, trying to see who or what had started the fire. They were darting forward and dropping back, beaten by the heat. Firemen were running everywhere, hauling equipment, unrolling hoses.

Chaos.

Reacher turned his head and strained hard to see through the darkness. Saw a flat humped shape in the grass forty feet away that had to be Neagley.

They were inside the fence.

Undetected.

It took eight minutes for LA's bravest to put out the fire. Then they spent another thirty-one dousing the ashes and taking notes and following up in one way or another. Total duration of their visit, thirty-nine minutes. Reacher spent the first twenty of them surveying the buildings from as close as he dared to get. Then he spent the final nineteen crawling backward as far as he could go. By the time the trucks finished up and rolled out the gate he was jammed up in the far back corner of the property, a hundred and fifty yards from the action.

The closest thing to him was the helicopter. It was still standing on its pad, about halfway along the lot's diagonal, maybe seventy yards away. Beyond it was the closest of the small outbuildings. The pilot's office, Reacher guessed. He had seen a guy in a leather jacket run out the door. Behind him in a blaze of light he had seen charts and maps pinned on a wall.

Equidistant from the helicopter and the pilot's office and thirty yards south of both was the parking lot. It was full of the six blue Chryslers, all of them cold and quiet.

Beyond the pilot's office was the second small outbuilding. A store room of some kind, Reacher guessed. The fire chief had been allowed to take a fast look inside.

Then came the main building. The hub of the operation. The assembly line. Where women in shower caps laboured over laboratory benches. All around it people were still out in the open and moving around. Reacher was pretty sure he recognized Lamaison, by his size and his shape, stamping around in the last of the smoke, yelling orders, directing operations. Lennox and Parker were there, too. Plus others. Hard to say how many. Too much darkness and confusion and milling about. Three at least. Maybe four, or even five.

The third small outbuilding was set far back, away from everything else, toward the corner directly opposite Reacher's. Its door had not opened at any point, and nobody had gone anywhere near it. Not Lamaison or his people, not the firefighters.

That was the prison, Reacher guessed.

The main gate to the street was closed again. It had rolled back into place with a loud shrieking sound after the last fire truck was through and then it had slammed shut with an impact that had sent a shudder through the roll of concertina wire welded to its top rail. The guard was still in his shack. His silhouette was clear behind the glass. The light above his head was spilling out in a soft twenty-foot circle, perfectly round, broken only by four bars of shadow from the window frames.

Beyond the main building the security guys were still looking for something. Lamaison had four of them formed up for a briefing. He split them into two pairs and sent them off to check the fence, one pair clockwise, the other counter-clockwise. Each pair walked slowly, parallel to the boundary, scuffing the grass with their feet, looking down, looking up, looking at the wire. A hundred and fifty yards away Reacher rolled onto his back. Checked the sky. It was close to full dark. The smog that was tan by day was now dull black, like a blanket. There was no moon. No light at all, except the last imperceptible taint of daylight and a little orange scatter from the city's lights.

Reacher rolled onto his front again. The security guys were still in pairs and moving slow. Lamaison was stepping back into the main building. Parker and Lennox were nowhere to be seen. Inside already, Reacher guessed. He watched the searchers. First one pair, then the other. Two different directions. The clockwise guys were Neagley's. The counterclockwise guys were his. They had about a hundred and fifty yards to cover before they got anywhere near him. A little over four minutes, at their current pace. They were concentrating on the fence and a strip maybe fifteen feet wide just inside it. Like the warning track around a baseball field. They had no flashlights. They were searching by feel alone. They would have to fall over something to find it. Reacher crawled twenty yards inward. Found a dip behind a hummock in the grass and pressed himself down into it. No-man's-land. The property covered about two acres, which was 9,680 square yards. Reacher occupied roughly two of them. Neagley, roughly the same. Four square yards out of 9,680. Odds of one in 2,420 against being randomly discovered. If they stayed still and quiet, that was.

Which Reacher couldn't afford to do.

Because the clock in his head had ticked around to the two-hour mark. He got up on his elbows and pulled out his phone and dialled Dixon's cell.

SEVENTY-FOUR

More than a hundred yards away, Lamaison answered the call. Reacher kept his thumb over the phone's bright LCD window. He wanted to preserve his night vision and he didn't want the searchers to look up and see a tiny disembodied face bathed in a distant blue glow. He spoke as normally as he dared.

'We're stuck on the 210,' he said. 'There's a stalled car up ahead.'

'Bullshit,' Lamaison said. 'You're right here in the neighbourhood. You've been throwing gasoline bombs over my fence.' His voice was loud and angry. Over the cellular circuits it came through edgy and penetrating. A little grating and distorted. Reacher slipped the pad of his index finger over the earpiece perforations and glanced up at the searchers. They were a hundred and twenty yards away. They hadn't reacted.

'What bombs?' he said, into the phone.

'You heard me.'

'We're on the freeway. I have no idea what you're talking about.'

'Bullshit, Reacher. You're right here. You

452

started a fire. But it was pathetic. It took them all of five minutes to put it out. I'm sure you saw them do it.'

Eight minutes, actually, Reacher thought. *Give me some damn credit.* But he said nothing. Just watched his pair of searchers. They were a hundred and ten yards away.

'The deal is off,' Lamaison said.

'Wait,' Reacher said. 'I'm still thinking about the deal. But I'm not an idiot. I want a proof of life. You could have shot them already.'

'They're still alive.'

'Prove it.'

'How?'

'I'll call you when we're through this traffic. You can bring them to the gate.'

'No way. They stay where they are.'

'Then we can't do business.'

Lamaison said, 'I'll ask them a question for you.'

The searchers were ninety yards away.

'What question?' Reacher said.

'Think of a question only they can answer. We'll ask them and call you back.'

'I'll call you back,' Reacher said. 'I don't answer the phone when I'm driving.'

'You're not driving. What's the question?'

Reacher said, 'Ask them who they were with before they joined the 110th MP.' Then he clicked the phone off and put it back in his pocket.

The searchers were about seventy yards away. Reacher crawled another twenty yards inward,

453

slow and cautious, parallel with the fence. The searchers managed another ten yards while he was doing it. Now they were forty yards away, coming on slowly, five feet apart, scuffing the grass, peering outward at the fence, checking for breaches.

Reacher saw light at the front of the main building. The door, opening. A tall shape stepped out. Parker, probably. He closed the door behind him and hustled around the near gable wall and headed for the distant shack thirty yards away. He unlocked the door and went in and less than a minute later he came back out and locked up again.

The prison, Reacher thought. *Thank you*.

The searchers were twenty yards away. Eighteen and a quarter metres, sixty feet, 720 inches, 1.13 per cent of a mile. Reacher shuffled ahead a little and closed the gap. The searchers stumbled on. Now they were ten yards ahead, on a diagonal, maybe eight yards to Reacher's left.

His phone vibrated in his pocket.

He hauled it out and cupped it in his hand. The caller ID said Dixon, which meant Lamaison. The answers to his question, recently relayed by Parker.

I said I'd call you, Reacher thought. *Can't talk now*.

He jammed the phone back in his pocket and waited. The searchers were almost dead level with him, eight yards to his left. They moved on. Reacher squirmed around, a silent half-circle on the ground. The searchers walked on. Reacher completed the circle. Now he was behind them.

He got silently to his feet. Took short quiet strides, stepping high to keep his soles from brushing the grass with telltale rustles. He fell in behind the two guys, ten feet back, then eight, then six, centred exactly between them. They were a decent size. Maybe six-two, two-ten, pale and meaty. Blue suits, white shirts, crew cuts. Broad shoulders, thick necks.

He hit the first guy with a massive straight right, dead-centre in the back of the neck, two hundred and fifty pounds and days of rage behind the blow. The guy's neck snapped forward and his skull snapped back and bounced straight off Reacher's fist and smashed forward again until his chin smacked his chest. Whiplash. Like a crash test dummy rear-ended by a speeding truck. The guy went straight down in a heap and his buddy turned toward him in shock and Reacher danced through a short shuffle step and head-butted him full in the face. He knew it was a great one by the sound alone. Bone, gristle, muscle, flesh, the unmistakable crunch of serious damage. The guy stayed vertical but unconscious for a second and then went down flat.

Reacher rolled the first guy on his back and sat on his chest and pinched his nose with one hand and blocked his mouth with his other palm. Then he waited until the guy suffocated. It didn't take long. Less than a minute. Then he did the same thing with the other guy. Another minute.

Then he checked their pockets. The first guy had a cell phone and a gun and a wallet full of cash money and credit cards. Reacher took the gun and the cash money, left the cell phone and the credit cards. The gun was a SIG P226, nine millimetre. The cash money was a little less than two hundred dollars. The second guy had another phone, another SIG, another wallet.

Plus Dave O'Donnell's ceramic knuckleduster.

It was right there in his jacket pocket. Either a reward for good work at the hospital takedown, or a stolen souvenir. Spoils of war. Reacher put it in his own pocket and jammed the SIGs in his waistband and the cash in his back pocket. Then he wiped his hands on the second guy's jacket and crawled away, low and fast, peering into the dark where he imagined Neagley to be. He had heard nothing from that direction. Nothing at all. But he wasn't worried. Neagley against two guys in the dark was about as reliable as the sun setting in the west.

He found another broad dip in the grass and lay down on his elbows and pulled out his phone. Called Dixon's number.

'Where the hell were you?' Lamaison asked him.

'I told you,' Reacher said. 'I don't pick up when I'm driving.'

'You're not driving.'

'So why didn't I pick up?'

'Whatever,' Lamaison said. 'Where are you now?'

'Close by.'

'Before the 110th Dixon says she was with the 53rd MP and O'Donnell says he was with the 131st.'

'OK,' Reacher said. 'I'll call you back in ten. When we arrive.'

He clicked off and sat up cross-legged in the dirt. He had his proof-of-life answers. Only problem was, neither one of them was even remotely true.

SEVENTY-FIVE

Reacher crawled south through the grass, looking for Neagley in the dark. He made it through fifty fast yards and found a corpse instead. He blundered right into it, hands and then knees. It was a man, cooling fast. Blue suit, white shirt. Broken neck.

'Neagley?' he whispered.

'Here,' she whispered back.

She was twenty feet away, lying on her side, propped up on one elbow.

'You OK?' he asked.

'Feeling good.'

'Was there another one?'

'Behind you,' she said. 'To your right.'

Reacher turned. Same kind of guy, same kind of suit, same kind of shirt.

Same kind of injury.

'Any problems?' he asked.

'Easy,' she said. 'And quieter than you. I heard that head butt all the way over here.'

They bumped fists in the dark, the old ritual, about as much physical contact as she liked to permit.

'Lamaison thinks we're on the outside looking in,' Reacher said. 'He's trying to scam us with a deal. If we surrender they'll lock us all up for a week and then let us go when the heat dies down.'

'Like we'd believe that.'

'One of my guys had Dave's knuckleduster.'

'That's not a good sign.'

'They're OK so far. I asked for a proof of life. Personal questions. Dixon says she was with the 53rd MP and O'Donnell says he was with the 131st.'

'That's bullshit. There was no 53rd MP. And Dave was posted to the 110th straight out of officer candidate school.'

'They're talking to us,' Reacher said. 'Fifty-three is a prime number. Karla knew I'd pick up on that.'

'So?'

'Five and three make eight. She's telling us there are eight hostiles.'

'Four left, then. Lennox, Parker, and Lamaison. Plus one. Who's the fourth?'

'That's Dave's message. He's a words guy. One three one. Thirteenth letter of the alphabet, first letter of the alphabet.'

'M and A,' Neagley said.

'Mauney,' Reacher said. 'Curtis Mauney is here.'

'Excellent,' Neagley said. 'Saves hunting him down later.'

They bumped fists again. Then cell phones started to ring. Loud and piercing and insistent. Two of them, different tones, unsynchronized. One each in the dead guys' pockets. Reacher had no doubt at all the same thing was happening fifty yards away. Two more dead guys, two more pockets, two more ringing phones. A conference call. Lamaison was touching base with his foot patrol.

Something unpredictable.

The phones rang six times each and stopped. Silence came back.

'What would you do now?' Reacher asked. 'If you were Lamaison?'

Neagley said, 'I'd get guys in those Chryslers and turn the headlights on bright and fix myself a little motor patrol. I'd run us down in less than a minute.'

Reacher nodded. Against a man on foot, the lot felt big. Against a car, it would feel small. Against more than one car it would feel tiny. In the dark it felt safe. With xenon beams blazing away it would feel like a goldfish bowl. He pictured cars bouncing over the rough ground, pictured himself trapped in their lights, darting left, darting right, shading his eyes, one car chasing, two cars converging.

He glanced at the fence.

'Correct,' Neagley said. 'The fence keeps us in just as well as it kept us out. We're two balls on a pool table and someone's about to turn on the lights and pick up a cue.'

'What are they going to do if they don't find us?'

'How are they not going to find us?'

'Suppose.'

Neagley shrugged and said, 'They're going to assume we got out somehow.'

'And then?'

'They're going to panic.'

'How?'

'They're going to kill Karla and Dave and hunker down.'

Reacher nodded.

'That's my guess too,' he said.

He got up and ran. Neagley followed.

SEVENTY-SIX

Reacher ran straight for the helicopter. It was sixty yards away, large and white and luminous in the city's night-time glow. Neagley jogged at his side, patiently. Reacher was no kind of a sprinter. He was slow and heavy. And he had stuff bouncing around in his pockets. Any college athlete would have done the sixty yards in six or seven seconds. Neagley would have done it in eight. Reacher took closer to fifteen. But he got there in the end. He got there just as the main building's door burst open and light and men spilled out. He dodged left and kept the chopper between him and them. Neagley crowded in at his elbow. Three guys were heading for the parking lot, fast and urgent. Parker and Lennox. And Lamaison. They were all hurrying. For every yard they covered, Reacher and Neagley moved a corresponding inch around the Bell, clockwise, touching its belly lightly with their fingertips, using its bulk as a shield. It was cold and dewed over with night mist, like a car parked on the street. It felt slimy. It smelled of oil and kerosene.

Thirty yards away three Chryslers started up.

Three V-8 engines, suddenly loud in the stillness. Three transmissions slammed into gear. Three pairs of headlights flicked on. They were un-believably bright in the darkness. They were crisp, focused, hard-edged, and super-white. Then they got worse. One by one they switched to high beam. New lenses lit up. Huge cones of dazzling light swayed and bounced as the cars began to move. Reacher and Neagley slid around the Bell's long pointed nose and hugged the other flank. The cars separated like a shell burst and accelerated and headed off in random changing directions.

Within ten seconds they had found all four dead guys.

The cars slewed to a stop at the two sites fifty yards apart. One car where Neagley had been, two where Reacher had been. Their lights went still and threw long grotesque quadruple shadows off the four humped shapes. Three distant figures ran around, flashing instantly from extreme brightness into total darkness as they moved through the beams.

'We can't stay here,' Neagley said. 'They're going to come back this way and light us up like we're on stage at the Hollywood Bowl.'

'How long have we got?'

'They're going to check the fence pretty thoroughly. Four minutes, maybe.'

'Start counting,' Reacher said. He pushed off the helicopter's flank and ran for the main build-ing. Forty yards, ten seconds. The door had been left ajar. Lights had been left on. Reacher paused. Then he walked straight in, very quietly, with his hand on his Glock in his pocket. Saw nobody inside. The place seemed to be deserted. There were small walled-off offices on the right and a big open-plan work area on the left, behind a floor-to-ceiling plate glass screen. The work area had long laboratory benches and bright lights and complex extraction ducts on the ceiling to control dust and a grounded metal grid on the floor to control static electricity. A sliding door in the screen was open. The air coming out smelled of warm silicon boards. Like a brand-new TV.

The offices on the right were little more than eight-by-eight cubicles with head-high walls and doors. One was labeled *Edward Dean*. The development engineer. Now the quality control guy. The next door was labelled *Margaret Berenson*. The dragon lady. A remote facility, Reacher guessed, for when she had to deal with human resources issues without dragging assembly personnel all the way south to the glass cube in East LA. The next door was Tony Swan's. Same principle. Two centres, two offices.

The next door was Allen Lamaison's.

It was standing open.

Reacher took a breath. Took his Glock out of his pocket. Stepped into the doorway. Stood still. Saw an eight-by-eight cube, desk, chair, fabric walls, phones, file cabinets, stacks of papers, memos.

Nothing unusual or out of place.

Except for Curtis Mauney behind the desk.

And a suitcase standing against a wall.

Neagley stepped into the room.

'Sixty seconds gone,' she said.

Mauney just sat there at the desk, immobile. Some kind of blank resignation on his face, like a man with a bad diagnosis waiting for a second opinion he knows will be no better. His hands were empty. They were curled together on the desktop like mating crabs.

'Lamaison was my partner,' he said, like an excuse.

Reacher nodded.

'Loyalty,' he said. 'It's a bitch, ain't it?'

The suitcase was a dark grey hard-shell Samsonite, set neatly against the wall beside the end of the desk. Not the biggest thing Reacher had ever seen. Nothing like the giants some people wrestle through the airport. But it wasn't small, either. It wasn't a carry-on. It had plastic stick-on initials in shallow recesses next to the latches. The initials said: *AM*.

'Seventy seconds gone,' Neagley said.

Mauney asked, 'What are you going to do?'

'With you?' Reacher asked. 'Nothing yet. Relax.'

Neagley aimed her gun at Mauney's face and Reacher stepped up beside the desk and knelt down and laid the suitcase flat on the carpet. Tried the latches. They were locked. He put his Glock on the floor and jammed the tips of his index fingers under the tips of the latches and braced his thumbs and bunched his shoulders and heaved. Reacher, against two thin pressed-metal tongues. No contest. The locks broke instantly.

He lifted the lid.

'Eighty seconds gone,' Neagley said.

'Payday,' Reacher said.

The case was full of fancy engraved paper certificates and letters from foreign banks and small suede drawstring bags that felt heavy in his hand.

'Sixty-five million dollars,' Neagley said, over his shoulder.

'At a guess,' Reacher said.

'Ninety seconds gone,' Neagley said.

Reacher turned his head and looked at Mauney and asked, 'How much of this is yours?'

'Some of it,' Mauney said. 'Not much, I guess.'

Reacher made neat creases and folded the paperwork and handed it to Neagley. He followed it with the drawstring bags. Neagley slid everything into her pockets. Reacher left the suitcase where it was, flat on the floor, empty, the lid up like a clam. He picked up his gun and stood and turned back to Mauney.

'Wrong,' he said. 'None of it is yours.'

'Two minutes gone,' Neagley said.

'Your friends are here,' Mauney said.

'I know,' Reacher said.

'Lamaison was my partner.'

'You told me that already.'

'I'm just saying.'

'So do they know you here?'

'I've been here before,' Mauney said. 'Many times.'

'Pick up the phone.'

'Or?'

'I'll shoot you in the head.'

'You will anyway.'

'I should,' Reacher said. 'You gave up six of my friends.'

466

Mauney nodded.

'I knew how this would end,' he said. 'When we didn't get you at the hospital.'

'LA traffic,' Reacher said. 'It can bite you in the ass.'

'Two minutes fifteen,' Neagley said.

Mauney asked, 'Are we making a deal here?'

'Pick up the phone.'

'And what?'

'Tell the gate guard to open up exactly one minute from now.'

Mauney hesitated. Reacher put the Glock's muzzle against Mauney's temple. Mauney picked up the phone. Dialled. Reacher listened hard and heard ring tone from the earpiece and the Chryslers idling a hundred yards away on the open ground and a muted bell forty yards away in the guard shack.

The call was answered. Mauney said, 'This is Mauney. Open the gate one minute from now.' Then he hung up. Reacher turned to Neagley.

'Am I your CO?' he asked.

'Yes,' she said. 'You are.'

'Then listen up,' he said. 'When the gate opens we head for our cars and we get out of here as fast as we possibly can.'

'And then?' she asked.

'We come back later.'

'In time?'

Reacher nodded. 'We'll make it in time if we're fast right now. They're already in their cars. So we have to really go for it. You're a lot faster than me, so I'll be behind you. But don't wait for me.

Don't even look back. We can't afford to lose a yard, either one of us.'

'Understood,' she said. 'Three minutes gone.'

Reacher grabbed Mauney's collar and hauled him to his feet. Dragged him out from behind the desk, out of the office, down the hallway, into the open area. Over to the main doorway. And then a yard outside, into the night. The smell of wet ash was strong. The three Chryslers were moving again in the distance. They were turning tight circles on the open ground and their headlights were sweeping random patterns against the fence like searchlights in a prison movie.

'Wait for the starting gun,' Reacher said to Neagley.

He watched the gate. Saw the guard move in his booth, saw the concertina wire sway, heard the tortured screech of wheels on a metal rail. Saw the gate start to move. He put the Glock to Mauney's temple and pulled the trigger. Mauney's skull exploded and Neagley and Reacher took off at full speed, like sprinters out of their blocks.

Neagley was ahead after half a step. Reacher stopped dead and watched her go. She flew through the pool of light from the guard hut and dodged like a running buck around the end of the moving gate. She raced out to the street. Then she was lost to sight.

Reacher turned and ran in the opposite direction. Fifteen seconds later he was back where he had started, behind the Bell's long nose.

SEVENTY-SEVEN

Maybe they had seen Neagley go, and assumed Reacher was ahead of her. Or maybe they had just seen the gate move, or heard its sound through their open windows. Certainly they must have heard the gunshot. Possibly they imagined the rest. But they took the bait. They reacted instantly. All three cars braked and manoeuvred and turned and accelerated and headed for the street, fishtailing like crazy and spraying huge rooster tails of dirt high in the air. They went out through the gate like stock cars through a turn. Their headlights lit up the street like day.

Reacher watched them go.

He waited for the night to go dark and quiet again. Then he counted to ten and moved slowly along the Bell's starboard flank. He ignored the cockpit door. He moved right past it and put his hand on the rear door's handle.

He tried it.

It was unlocked.

He glanced over his shoulder at the pilot's hut. No movement there. He eased the handle down. The latch came free. The door opened. It was wide and light and tinny. Like a panel van's. Not at all what he was expecting. Not heavy and pneumatic like an airliner's.

He held the door two feet open and looped around it and climbed inside. Pulled the door after him and paused and then closed it against the latch with one sudden decisive click. He ducked down and peered out the window and watched the pilot's hut.

No reaction.

He turned around in a crouch and knelt on the cabin floor in the darkness. From the inside the Bell looked like a swelled-up version of a minivan. A little wider and a little longer than the kind of things soccer moms drove in television commercials. Less boxy. A little more contoured. Narrower at the front, wider at floor level, pinched in a little more at head height, narrower at the rear. There would have been seven seats, two in the cockpit, three in the centre row, two way in back, except that the centre row was missing. The seats were all bulky high-backed recliners, faced with black leather. They had headrests and arms. Captain's chairs. They had safety harnesses. Below the waistline the bulkheads were lined with black carpet. Above, they were padded with black quilted vinyl. Very corporate. But a little out of date. Leased second-hand, Reacher guessed. The whole interior smelled faintly of jet fuel.

There was a space behind the rearmost seats. For bags, Reacher guessed. A luggage compartment. Just like a minivan. It wasn't a huge space. But it was big enough. He found the levers and flopped the seat backs forward. Climbed over and sat down on the floor, sideways, with his legs out straight and his back jammed against the side bulkhead. He took the captured SIGs out of his waistband and laid them on the floor next to his knees. He leaned forward and hauled the seat backs upright. They clicked and locked in place. Then he slumped down to test whether he could get low enough to keep his head out of sight.

Probably, he thought.

He raised his head again. The cabin windows were misted with dew. Dark and grey and featureless. Like television screens, turned off. Nothing was happening outside. Noises were dulled. Clearly the carpet and the quilting doubled as soundproofing layers.

He waited.

Five minutes.

Ten.

Then the misted windows lit up with bright moving shapes and shadows. The cars, coming back. Three sets of headlight beams, bouncing and turning. They played on the glass for a moment and then they stopped and stabilized. Then they died altogether. The cars, back in the lot. Parked.

Reacher strained to hear.

He heard nothing except slow footsteps and low voices. Agitation, not triumph. The unmistakable sound of failure.

The search was over.

No success.

He waited.

SEVENTY-EIGHT

He waited and grew cold and cramped from sitting still. He pictured the scene forty yards away, Mauney's body in the doorway, the empty Samsonite in the office, discussion, argument, pacing, panic, confusion, apprehension. The side of his face was inches from the seat back in front of him. The leather was close enough to smell. Normally he would have been in severe distress. He hated confinement. Claustrophobia was as close as he ever came to fear. But right then he had other things on his mind.

He waited.

Twenty long minutes.

Then a door opened up front and the helicopter dipped and settled as its undercarriage compressed and recovered. Someone had climbed aboard. The door closed. A seat creaked. A harness buckle clicked. Switches clicked. Faint orange light jumped from dozens of instrument faces and threw sudden shadows on the roof. A fuel pump whirred and chattered. Reacher leaned forward from the waist and moved his head until one eye was lined up with the gap between the seats. He saw the pilot's leather sleeve. Nothing more. The rest of the guy was invisible behind his bulky chair. His hand was dancing over switches and touching the faces of dials one by one as he ran through pre-flight checks. He was talking to himself, quietly, reciting a long list of required technicalities like an incantation.

Reacher pulled his head back.

Then there was an incredibly loud noise.

It was halfway between a gunshot and a split-second blast of compressed air. It came again, and again, and again, faster and faster. The starter mechanism, forcing the rotor around. The floor shook. Then the engines fired up and gears meshed and the rotor caught and settled to a lazy *whop-whop* idle. The torque rocked and twisted the whole craft on its struts, just a little, rhythmically, like it was dancing. The interior was filled with a loud thrumming noise. Driveshafts whirred and spun overhead. Jet exhaust whined outside, high-pitched and piercing. Reacher jammed the muzzles of the captured SIGs under his legs so that they wouldn't bounce and rattle and slide. He took his Glock from his pocket and held it down by his side.

He waited.

A minute later the rear door was wrenched open. A blast of louder noise flooded in. After the noise came the acrid smell of kerosene. After the kerosene came Karla Dixon. Reacher moved his head an inch and saw her dumped on the floor head first like a log. She came to rest on her side, facing away. Her wrists and ankles were tied with rough sisal rope. Her hands were behind her

473

back. The last time he had seen her horizontal had been in his bed in Vegas.

Two minutes later O'Donnell was wrestled in, feet first. He was bigger and heavier and landed harder. He was tied up the same way as Dixon. He rolled face down alongside her, his feet next to her head. They lay there together like cordwood, moving a little, struggling against the ropes.

Then the struts bounced again and Lennox and Parker climbed aboard. They shut their doors and dumped themselves down in the rear seats. The seat back in front of Reacher sagged against a loose mechanism and touched him on the cheek. He jammed his head harder into the corner. His crew cut scraped across the carpet.

The rotor turned slowly, *whop, whop, whop*.

The suspension knelt and rose, knelt and rose, front left corner, right rear corner, less than an inch, like dancing.

Reacher waited.

Then the door up front opposite the pilot wrenched open and Allen Lamaison dumped himself in the seat and said, 'Go.' Reacher heard the turbines spin up and felt the thrill and shiver of vibration fill the cabin and heard the rotor note change to an urgent accelerating *whip-whip-whip* and felt the whole craft go light on its wheels.

Then they were airborne.

Reacher felt the floor come up at him. He heard the wheels pull upward into their wells. He felt rotation and drift and a long steady climb and then the floor tilted forward as the nose went

474

down for speed. He braced himself against spread fingers to stop himself sliding into the seat in front of him. He heard the engine noise settle to a muted whine and then the unique pendulum sensation of helicopter transport came right back at him. He had done his fair share of fast miles in rotary aircraft, a lot of them sitting on the floor.

A familiar experience.

For now.

SEVENTY-NINE

By the clock in Reacher's head the cruise lasted exactly twenty minutes, which was about what he was expecting. He had figured modern corporate machines would be a little faster than the Hueys he had been accustomed to in the service. He figured a military AH-1 might have taken twenty-plus minutes to get itself beyond the mountains, so twenty dead seemed reasonable for something with black leather seats and a carpet.

He spent the twenty minutes with his head well down. Animal instinct, a million years old and still displayed by dogs and children: *If I can't see them, they can't see me.* He kept his arms and legs moving through silent fractions of an inch and kept his muscles tensing and relaxing in a bizarre miniaturized version of a gymnasium workout. He was no longer cold, but he didn't want to get any stiffer. The noise in the cabin was loud but not overwhelming. The engine whine was whipping away in the slipstream. The rotor noise was blending with the rush of air and could be tuned out. There was no conversation going on. No talking. Reacher heard nothing from anyone.

Until the twenty-minute cruise came to an end.

He felt the helicopter slow down. Felt the floor come level and then tip backward a couple of degrees as the nose flared upward. The craft rotated left a little. Like a horse reined in on a movie screen. The cabin got louder. Now they were moving slowly, trapped in a bubble of their own noise.

He bent forward from the waist and put an eye to the gap between the seats and saw Lamaison leaning over with his forehead pressed against his window. Saw him change direction and lean toward the pilot. Heard him speak. Or maybe he only imagined that he heard him speak. He had reconstructed the orders in his head a thousand times since opening Franz's file days before. He felt that he knew them, word for word, in all their cruel inevitability.

'Where are we?' Lamaison asked, in Reacher's mind, and maybe also in reality.

'The badlands,' the pilot said.

'What's below us now?'

'Sand.'

'Height?'

'Three thousand feet.'

'What's the air like up here?'

'Still. A few thermals, but no wind.'

'Safe?'

'Aeronautically.'

'So let's do it.'

Reacher felt the helicopter come to a stationary hover. The engine note dropped down to a deeper key and the rotor thrashed loud.

The floor moved in tiny unstable circles, like a spinning top come to rest. Lamaison turned in his seat and nodded once to Parker and once to Lennox. Reacher heard the click of safety harness catches and then the weight came up off the seats in front of him. Leather cushions inhaled and tired springs recovered and moved the seat backs a precious inch farther from his face. There was no light other than the orange glow from the cockpit. Parker was on the left and Lennox was on the right. They were both in strange half-crouches, knees bent and heads ducked because of limited headroom, feet apart for stability on the moving floor, arms thrust outward for balance. One of them was going to die easy and one of them was going to die hard.

It depended on which one of them was going to open the door.

Lennox was going to open the door.

He half turned and grabbed his trailing safety harness and held on tight with his left hand. Then he crabbed sideways and used his right to grope for the interior door release. He got there and unlatched it and pushed. The door swung half open and wind and noise howled in. The pilot was half turned in his own seat, watching over his shoulder, and he tilted the craft a little so the door fell the rest of the way open under its own weight. Then he brought it level again and put it into a slow clockwise rotation so that motion and inertia and air pressure held the door wide against its hinge.

Lennox turned back. Big, red-faced, meaty, crouched like an ape, his left hand tight on his harness strap, his right pawing the air like a man on ice.

Reacher leaned forward and used his left hand to find the seat release lever. He put his thumb below the pivot and two fingers above it and twisted. The seat back flopped forward. He used his left hand to force it all the way horizontal. He held it there. The cushions exhaled again. He brought the Glock up in his right hand and twisted from the waist and laid his right forearm flat on the seat back. Closed one eye and picked a spot an inch above Lennox's navel.

And pulled the trigger.

The blast was muted in the general roar. Audible, but not as bad as it would have been in a library. The bullet hit Lennox low in the mid-section. Reacher figured it was an instant through and through. Inevitable, with a nine millimetre from a range of about four feet. Which was why he was shooting at Lennox and not at Parker. Reacher was not remotely afraid of flying, but he preferred the aircraft he was in to be undamaged. A shot through Parker's midsection might have hit a hydraulic line or an electrical cable. Through Lennox it went straight out the open door into the night, harmlessly.

Lennox stayed in his awkward half-crouch. A bloom of blood haloed the hole in his shirt. It looked black in the dim orange light. His left hand came off the harness and pawed the air, a perfect mirror image of his right. He crouched there, balanced, symmetrical, a foot from the door sill, nothing behind him except the void, catastrophic physical shock on his face.

Reacher moved the Glock a small fraction and shot him again, this time through the sternum. He figured that on a guy as big and as old as Lennox the sternum would be a well calcified plate maybe three-eighths of an inch thick. The bullet would pass through it for sure, but not before the smashing and splintering of the bone had transferred a little forward momentum into the target. Like the effect of a tiny punch. Maybe enough effect and enough momentum to take the guy with it a little and put him down backward, rather than just dumping him in a vertical heap like a head shot would have. There was too much articulation in the human neck for a head shot to have done what Reacher wanted it to.

But it was his knees that did Lennox in, not his breastbone. He came down just a fraction in back of vertical, like a guy aiming to squat on his heels. But he was big and heavy and he was forty-one years old and his knees had stiffened. They bent a little more than ninety degrees and then they stopped bending. His upper body mass was pitched backward by the sudden obstruction and his ass hit square on the door sill and the weight of his shoulders and his head rolled him over the pivot and took him right out the door into the night. The last Reacher saw of him was the soles of his shoes, still well apart, whipping away into the windy darkness like afterthoughts.

By that point it was much less than two seconds since he had dropped the seat but to Reacher it seemed like two lifetimes. Franz's and Orozco's, maybe. He felt infinitely fluent and languid. He was floating in a state of grace and torment, planning his moves like chess, minutely aware of potentials and drawbacks and threats and opportunities. The others in the cabin had barely reacted at all. O'Donnell was face down, trying to lift his head far enough to turn. Dixon was trying to roll onto her back. The pilot was half turned, immobile in his seat. Parker was frozen in his absurd crouch. Lamaison was gazing at the empty air where Lennox had been, like he was completely unable to understand what had just happened.

Then Reacher stood up.

He dropped the second seat and climbed out over it like a nightmare apparition, a sudden giant figure from nowhere looming silently into the noisy orange glow. Then he stood still, close to fully upright, his head jammed up hard against the roof, his feet a yard apart, perfectly triangulated for maximum stability. His left hand held a SIG, pointing straight at Parker's face. His right held his Glock, pointing straight at Lamaison's. Both guns were motionless. His face was expressionless. The rotor thrashed on. The Bell continued its slow clockwise rotation. The door held wide open, pushed back like a sail. Gales of noise and wind and kerosene stink blew in.

O'Donnell arched his back and got his head high enough to turn. His eyes tracked left to Reacher's boots and closed for a second. Dixon toppled onto her back and rolled over on her bound arms and settled on her other shoulder, facing the rear.

The pilot stared. Parker stared. Lamaison stared.

481

The time of maximum danger.

Reacher could not afford to fire forward. The chance of hitting some essential cockpit avionics was far too great. He couldn't afford to put a gun down and work on freeing O'Donnell or Dixon because Parker was loose in the cabin not more than four feet away. He couldn't take Parker down hand to hand, because he couldn't even move. There was no floor space. O'Donnell and Dixon were occupying it all.

Whereas Lamaison was still strapped in his seat. The pilot was still strapped in his. All the pilot had to do was throw the Bell all over the sky until everyone in the back fell out. They would sacrifice Parker that way, but Reacher couldn't see Lamaison losing sleep over that decision.

Stalemate, if they understood.

Victory, if they seized the moment.

EIGHTY

They didn't understand. They didn't seize the moment. Instead O'Donnell got his head and his feet off the floor and porpoised desperately six inches closer to Reacher and Dixon rolled back the other way and a precious foot of free space opened up between them. Reacher stepped gratefully into it and smashed Parker in the gut with the SIG's muzzle. The breath punched out of Parker's lungs and he folded up at the waist and staggered one instinctive step, straight into the channel that O'Donnell and Dixon had created. Reacher dodged past him like a bullfighter and planted the sole of his boot flat on Parker's ass and shoved him hard from behind and sent him stumbling on stiff legs straight across the cabin and blindly out the door into the night. Before his scream had died Reacher had his left arm hooked around Lamaison's throat with the SIG pointing straight at the pilot and the Glock jammed hard into the back of Lamaison's neck.

After that, it got easier.

The pilot stayed frozen at the controls. The Bell hung there in its noisy hover. The rotor beat loud and the whole craft kept on turning slow. The door stayed open, wide and inviting, pinned back by the airflow. Reacher clamped his elbow and hauled backward on Lamaison's neck and pulled him up out of the seat until his shoulder straps went tight. Then he put the Glock on the floor and fished in his pocket for O'Donnell's knuckleduster. He held it between his fingers like a tool and glanced behind him. He extended his arm and pushed Dixon onto her front and used the knuckleduster's wicked spines to rub at the bonds on her wrists. She tensed her arms and the sisal fibres ruptured slowly, one by one. Reacher felt each success quite clearly through the hard ceramic material, tiny dull harmonic pings, sometimes two at once. Lamaison started to struggle and Reacher tightened his elbow, which had the advantage of choking Lamaison into submission but the disadvantage of aiming the SIG behind the pilot instead of straight at him. But the pilot made no attempt to take advantage. He didn't react at all. He just sat there, hands on the stick, feet on the pedals, keeping the Bell turning slow.

Reacher kept on sawing away, blindly. One minute. Two. Dixon kept on moving her arms, offering new strands, testing progress. Lamaison struggled harder. He was a big guy, strong and powerful, thick neck, broad shoulders. And he was scared. But Reacher was bigger, and Reacher was stronger, and Reacher was angry. More angry than Lamaison was scared. Reacher tightened his arm. Lamaison struggled on. Reacher debated taking time out to hit him, but he wanted him conscious, for later. So he just worried on at the ropes and suddenly a whole skein of sisal fibres unravelled and Dixon's wrists came free and she pushed herself up into a kneeling position. Reacher gave her the knuckleduster and his Glock and swapped the SIG from his left hand to his right.

After that, it got a whole lot easier.

Dixon did the smart thing, which was to ignore the knuckleduster and haul herself across the cabin like a mermaid to Lamaison's pockets, where she found a wallet and another SIG and O'Donnell's switchblade. Two seconds later her feet were free, and five seconds after that O'Donnell was free. Both of them had been tied up for hours, and they were stiff and cramped and their hands were shaking pretty badly. But they didn't have difficult tasks ahead of them. There was only the pilot to subdue. O'Donnell grabbed the guy's collar in one fist and jammed a SIG's muzzle up under his chin. There was no chance of him missing with a contact shot, however badly his hands were shaking. No chance at all. The pilot understood that. He stayed passive. Reacher stuck his SIG in Lamaison's ear and leaned the other way, toward the pilot, and asked, 'Height?'

The pilot swallowed and said, 'Three thousand feet.'

'Let's take it up a little,' Reacher said. 'Let's try five thousand feet.'

EIGHTY-ONE

The climb took the Bell out of its slow rotation and the open door flapped around for a moment and then slammed itself shut. The cabin went quiet. Almost silent, by comparison. O'Donnell still had his gun to the pilot's head. Reacher still had Lamaison arched backward in his seat. Lamaison had his hands on Reacher's forearm, hauling downward, but listlessly. He had gone strangely passive and inert. Like he sensed exactly what was threatened, but couldn't believe it was really going to happen.

Like Swan couldn't, Reacher thought. *Like Orozco couldn't, and Franz couldn't, and Sanchez couldn't.*

He felt the Bell top out and level off. Heard the rotor bite stationary air, felt the turbines settle to a fast urgent whine. The pilot glanced in his direction and nodded.

'More,' Reacher said. 'Let's do another two hundred and eighty feet. Let's make it a whole mile.'

The engine noise changed and the rotor noise changed and the craft moved upward again,

486

slowly, precisely. It turned a little and then came back to a hover.

The pilot said, 'One mile.'

Reacher asked, 'What's below us now?'

'Sand.'

Reacher turned to Dixon and said, 'Open the door.'

Lamaison found some new energy. He bucked and thrashed in his seat and said, 'No, please, please, no.'

Reacher tightened his elbow and asked, 'Did my friends beg?'

Lamaison just shook his head.

'They wouldn't,' Reacher said. 'Too proud.'

Dixon moved back in the cabin and grabbed Lennox's seat harness in her left hand. Held on tight and groped for the door release with her right. She was smaller than Lennox had been and for her it was more of a stretch. But she got there. She clicked the release and pushed off hard with spread fingertips and the door swung open. Reacher turned to the pilot and said, 'Do that spinning thing again.' The pilot set up the slow clockwise rotation and the door opened up all the way and pinned itself back against its hinge straps. Shattering noise and cold night air poured in. The mountains showed black on the horizon. Beyond them the glow of Los Angeles was visible, fifty miles away, a million bright lights trapped under air as thick as soup. Then that view rotated away and was replaced by desert blackness.

Dixon sat down on Parker's folded seat. O'Donnell tightened his hold on the pilot's collar.

Reacher twisted Lamaison's neck up and back with his forearm hard against his throat. Pulled him upward against the limits of the harness. Held him there. Then he reached over and used the SIG's muzzle to hit the harness release. The belts came free. Reacher pulled Lamaison backward all the way over the top of the seat and dumped him on the floor.

Lamaison saw his chance, and he took it. He pushed himself up into a sitting position and scrabbled his heels on the carpet, trying to get his feet under him. But Reacher was ready. Readier than he had ever been. He kicked Lamaison hard in the side and swung an elbow that caught him on the ear. Wrestled him face down on the floor and got a knee between his shoulder blades and jammed the SIG against the top of his spine. Lamaison's head was up and Reacher knew he was staring out into the void. His feet were drumming on the carpet. He was screaming. Reacher could hear him clearly over the noise. He could feel his chest heaving.

Too late, Reacher thought. *You reap what you sow*.

Lamaison flailed weak backhand blows that didn't come close to landing. Then he put his hands flat on the floor and tried to buck Reacher off. *No chance*, Reacher thought. *Not unless you can do a push-up with two hundred and fifty pounds riding on your back*. Some guys could. Reacher had seen it done. But Lamaison couldn't. He was strong, but not strong enough. He strained for a spell and collapsed.

Reacher swapped the SIG into his left hand

and looped his right over Lamaison's neck from behind like a pincer. Lamaison had a big neck, but Reacher had big hands. He jammed his thumb and the tip of his middle finger into the hollows behind Lamaison's ears and squeezed hard. Lamaison's arteries compressed and his brain starved for oxygen and he stopped screaming and his feet stopped drumming. Reacher kept the pressure on for a whole extra minute and then rolled him over and spun him around and sat him up like a drunk.

Grabbed his belt and his collar.

Pushed him across the floor on his ass, feet first.

He got him as far as the door sill and held him there, arms pinned behind him. The helicopter turned, slowly. The engines whined and the rotor beat out discrete bass thumps of sound. Reacher felt every one of them in his chest, like heartbeats. Minutes passed and fresh air blew in and Lamaison came around to find himself sitting upright on the edge with his feet hanging out over the void like a guy on a high wall.

A mile above the desert floor. Five thousand, two hundred and eighty feet.

Reacher had rehearsed a speech. He had started composing it in the Denny's on Sunset, with Franz's file in his hand. He had perfected it over the following days. It was full of fine phrases about loyalty and retribution, and heartfelt eulogies for his four dead friends. But when it came to it he didn't say much. No point. Lamaison wouldn't have heard a word. He was crazy with terror and there was too much noise. A cacophony. In the end Reacher just leaned forward and put his mouth close to Lamaison's ear and said, 'You made a bad mistake. You messed with the wrong people. Now it's time to pay.'

Then he straightened Lamaison's arms behind his back and pushed. Lamaison slid an inch and then lunged forward to try to jack his ass backward on the sill. Reacher pushed again. Lamaison folded up and his chest met his knees. He was staring straight down into the blackness. One mile. A speeding car would take a whole minute to cover it.

Reacher pushed. Lamaison let his shoulders go slack. No leverage.

Reacher put his heel flat against the small of Lamaison's back.

Bent his leg.

Let go of Lamaison's arms.

Straightened his leg, fast and smooth.

Lamaison went over the edge and disappeared into the night.

There was no scream. Or maybe there was. Maybe it was lost in the rotor noise. O'Donnell nudged the pilot and the pilot yawed the craft and reversed the rotation and the door slammed neatly shut. The cabin went quiet. Silent, by comparison. Dixon hugged Reacher hard. O'Donnell said, 'You certainly left it until the last minute, didn't you?'

Reacher said, 'I was trying to decide whether to let them throw you out before I saved Karla. Tough decision. Took some time.'

490

'Where's Neagley?'

'Working, I hope. The missiles rolled out of the gate in Colorado eight hours ago. And we don't know where they're going.'

EIGHTY-TWO

There was nothing the pilot could do to them without killing himself also, so they left him alone in the cockpit. But not before checking the fuel load. It was low. Much less than an hour's flying time. There was no cell reception. Reacher told the pilot to lose height and drift south to find a signal. Dixon and O'Donnell latched the rear seat backs upright and sat down. They didn't strap themselves in. Reacher guessed they were done with confinement. He lay on his back on the floor with his arms and legs flung wide like a snow angel. He was tired and dispirited. Lamaison was gone, but no one had come back.

O'Donnell asked, 'Where would you take six hundred and fifty SAMs?'

'The Middle East,' Dixon said. 'And I'd send them by sea. The electronics through LA and the tubes through Seattle.'

Reacher raised his head. 'Lamaison said they were going to Kashmir.'

'Did you believe him?'

'Yes and no. I think he was choosing to believe a lie to salve his own conscience. Whatever else

492

he was, he was a citizen. He didn't want to know the truth.'

'Which is?'

'Terrorism here in the States. Got to be. It's obvious. Kashmir is a squabble between governments. Governments have purchasing missions. They don't run around with Samsonite suitcases full of bearer bonds and bank access codes and diamonds.'

Dixon asked, 'Is that what you found?'

'Highland Park. Sixty-five million dollars' worth. Neagley's got it all. You're going to have to convert it for us, Karla.'

'If I survive. My plane back to New York might get blown up.'

Reacher nodded. 'If not tomorrow, then the next day, or the next.'

'How do we find them? Eight hours at fifty miles an hour is already a radius of four hundred miles. Which is a half-million-square-mile circle.'

'Five hundred and two thousand seven hundred and twenty,' Reacher said, automatically. 'Assuming you use only three decimal places for *pi*. But that's the bargain we made. We could stop them when the circle was small, or we could come for you guys.'

'Thanks,' O'Donnell said.

'Hey, I voted to stop the truck. Neagley over-ruled me.'

'So how do we do this?'

'You ever seen a really great centrefielder play baseball? He never chases the ball. He runs to where the ball is about to arrive. Like Mickey Mantle.'

'You never saw Mantle play.'

'I saw newsreels.'

'The United States is close to four million square miles. That's bigger than centre field at Yankee Stadium.'

'But not much,' Reacher said.

'So where do we run to?'

'Mahmoud isn't dumb. In fact he strikes me as a very smart and cautious guy. He just spent sixty-five million dollars on what are basically just components. He must have insisted that part of the deal was that someone would show him how to screw the damn things together.'

'Who?'

'What did Neagley's woman friend tell us? The politician? Diana Bond?'

'Lots of things.'

'She told us that New Age's engineer does the quality control tests because so far he's the only guy in the world who knows how Little Wing is supposed to work.'

Dixon said, 'And Lamaison had him on a string somehow.'

'He was threatening the guy's daughter.'

O'Donnell said, 'So Lamaison was going to pimp him out. Lamaison was going to take him somewhere. And you threw Lamaison out of the damn helicopter before you asked him.'

Reacher shook his head. 'Lamaison talked about the whole thing like it was firmly in the past. He said it was a done deal. There was something in his voice. Lamaison wasn't taking anyone anywhere.'

'So who?'

'Not who,' Reacher said. 'The question is, where?'

Dixon said, 'If there's only one guy, and Lamaison wasn't planning to take him somewhere, they'll have to bring the missiles to him.'

'Which is ridiculous,' O'Donnell said. 'You can't bring a semi full of missiles to a garden apartment in Century City or wherever.'

'The guy doesn't live in Century City,' Reacher said. 'He lives way out in the desert. The middle of nowhere. The back of beyond. Where better to bring a semi full of missiles?'

'Cell phones are up,' the pilot called.

Reacher pulled out his Radio Shack pay-as-you-go. Found Neagley's number. Hit the green button. She answered.

'Dean's place?' he asked.

'Dean's place,' she said. 'For sure. I'm twenty minutes away.'

EIGHTY-THREE

The Bell had GPS, but not the kind that drew a road map on a screen. Not like O'Donnell's rental car. The Bell's system produced a pair of always-changing latitude and longitude readings instead, pale green numbers, plain script. Reacher told the pilot to get himself somewhere south of Palmdale and wait. The pilot was nervous about fuel. Reacher told him to lose altitude. Helicopters sometimes survived engine failures at a few hundred feet. They rarely survived at a few thousand.

Then Reacher called Neagley back. She had gotten Dean's address from Margaret Berenson in the Pasadena hotel. But she had no GPS either. She was adrift in the dark, behind two last-generation headlights made weaker by blue paint on the lenses. And cell coverage was patchy. Reacher lost her twice. Before he lost her a third time he told her to find Dean's spread and drive in tight circles with her lights on bright.

Reacher took Lamaison's seat up front and pressed his forehead to the window the same way Lamaison had. Dixon and O'Donnell took side windows in back. Between them they covered a one-eighty panorama. Maybe more. For safety's sake Reacher had the pilot turn wide circles once in a while, in case what they wanted was way behind them.

They saw nothing.

Nothing at all, except vast featureless blackness and occasional pinpoints of orange light. Gas stations, maybe, or tiny parking lots outside small grocery stores. They saw occasional cars on lonely roads, but none of them was Neagley's Civic. Yellow headlight beams, not blue. Reacher tried his phone again. No service.

'Fuel's really low,' the pilot said.

'Highway on the left,' Dixon called.

Reacher looked down. Not much of a highway. There were five cars on it within a linear mile, two heading south and three heading north. He closed his eyes and pictured the maps he had looked at.

'We shouldn't be seeing a north-south highway,' he said. 'We're too far west.'

The Bell tilted and swung away east on a long fast curve and came level again.

The pilot said, 'I'm going to have to set down soon.'

'You'll set down when I tell you,' Reacher said.

North of the mountains the air was better. Some dust, some heat shimmer, but basically it was clear to the horizon. Way far ahead in the distance a tiny grid of lights winked and twinkled. Palmdale, presumably. A nice place, Reacher had heard. Expanding. Desirable. Therefore expensive. Therefore a guy looking for acres and isolation and maximum bang for the buck would stay well away from it.

'Turn south,' he said. 'And climb.'

'Climbing eats fuel,' the pilot said.

'We need a better angle.'

The Bell climbed, slowly, a couple of hundred feet. The pilot dropped the nose and turned a wide circle, like he was hosing the horizon with an imaginary searchlight.

They saw nothing.

There was no cell coverage.

'Higher,' Reacher said.

'Can't do it,' the pilot said. 'Look at the dial.'

Reacher found the fuel gauge. The needle was riding the end stop. Officially the tanks were empty. He closed his eyes again and pictured the map. Berenson had said Dean had complained about the commute from hell. To Highland Park he had only two choices. Either Route 138 on the east flank of Mount San Antonio, or Route 2, to the west, past the Mount Wilson Observatory. Route 2 was probably smaller and twistier. And it joined the 210 at Glendale. Which probably made it more hellish than the eastern approach. No reason to choose it unless it was a total no-brainer. Which meant Dean was starting from somewhere due south of Palmdale, not east of south. Reacher looked straight ahead and waited until the distant grid of lights slid back into view.

'Now pull a one-eighty and head back,' he said.

'We're out of fuel.'

'Just do it.'

The craft turned in its own length. Dipped its nose and clattered onward.

Sixty seconds later they found Neagley.

A mile in front and four hundred feet down they saw a cone of blue light turning and pulsing like a beacon. It looked like Neagley had the Civic on maximum lock and was driving a thirty-foot circle and flashing between dipped and brights as she went. The effect was spectacular. The beams swept and leapt and threw moving shadows and cleared a couple of hundred feet where there were no obstructions. Like a lighthouse on a rocky shore. There were small buttes and mesas and gullies, thrown into dramatic relief. To the north, low buildings. Power lines to the east. To the west the fractured land fell away into a shallow arroyo maybe forty feet wide and twenty deep.

'Land there,' Reacher said. 'In the ditch. And keep the wheels up.'

The pilot said, 'Why?'

'Because that's the way I want it.'

The pilot drifted west a little and dropped a couple of hundred feet and turned to line up with the arroyo. Then he took the Bell down like an elevator. A siren went off to warn that he was landing with the undercarriage up. He ignored it and kept on going. He slowed twenty feet off the ground and eased on down and pancaked gently on the arroyo's rocky bed. Stones crunched and metal grated and the floor tipped a foot from horizontal. Out the windows Reacher could see Neagley's lights coming toward them through a sandstorm kicked up by the rotor wash.

Then the fuel ran out.

The engines died and the rotor shuddered to a stop.

The cabin went quiet.

Reacher was first out the door. He batted his way through clouds of warm dust and sent Dixon and O'Donnell ahead to meet with Neagley and then turned back to the Bell. He opened the cockpit door and looked in at the pilot. The guy was still strapped to his seat. He was flicking the face of the fuel gauge with his fingernail.

'Nice landing,' Reacher said. 'You're a good pilot.'

The guy said, 'Thanks.'

'That thing with the rotation,' Reacher said. 'The way it kept the door open up there. Smart move.'

'Basic aerodynamics.'

'But then, you had plenty of practice.'

The pilot said nothing.

'Four times,' Reacher said. 'That I know about, at least.'

The pilot said nothing.

'Those men were my friends,' Reacher said.

'Lamaison told me I had to do it.'

'Or?'

'I would lose my job.'

'That's all? You let them throw four live human beings out of your helicopter to save your job?'

'I'm paid to follow instructions.'

'You ever heard about a trial at Nuremberg? That excuse really doesn't cut it any more.'

The pilot said, 'It was wrong, I know.'

'But you did it anyway.'

'What choice did I have?'

'Lots of choices,' Reacher said. Then he smiled. The pilot relaxed a little. Reacher shook his head like he was bemused by it all and leaned in and patted the guy on the cheek. Left his hand there, far side of the guy's face, a friendly gesture. He worked his thumb up toward the guy's eye socket, pressed his index finger on the guy's temple, worked his other three fingers behind the guy's ear, into his hair. Then he broke the guy's neck, one-handed, with a single convulsive twist. Then he bounced the guy's head around, front to back, side to side, to make sure the spinal cord was properly severed. He didn't want the guy to wake up a paraplegic. He didn't want the guy to wake up at all.

He walked away and left him there, still strapped in his seat. Turned back after fifty feet and checked. A helicopter in a ditch, slightly tilted, wheels up, tanks empty. A crash. The pilot still on board, impact injuries, an unfortunate accident. *Not perfect, but reasonable.*

Neagley had parked a hundred feet from the arroyo, which was about half the distance to Edward Dean's front door. Her lights were still on bright. When Reacher got to the car he turned and looked back and checked again. The Bell was hidden pretty well. The crown of the rotor was visible, but only just. The blades themselves drooped out of sight under their own weight. The dust was settling. Neagley and Dixon and

O'Donnell were standing together in a tight group of three.

'We OK?' Reacher asked.

Dixon and O'Donnell nodded. Neagley didn't.

'You mad with me?' Reacher asked her.

'Not really,' she said. 'I would have been if you'd screwed up.'

'I needed you to work out where the missiles were headed.'

'You already knew.'

'I wanted a second opinion. And the address.'

'Well, here we are. No missiles.'

'They're still in transit.'

'We hope.'

'Let's go see Mr Dean.'

They piled into the tiny Civic and Neagley drove the hundred feet to Dean's door. Dean opened up on the first knock. Clearly he had been rousted by the helicopter drone and the flashing lights. He didn't look much like a rocket scientist. More like a coach at a third-rate high school. He was tall and loose-limbed and had a shock of sandy hair. He was maybe forty years old. He was barefoot and dressed in sweatpants and a T-shirt. Night attire. It was close to midnight.

'Who are you people?' he asked.

Reacher explained who they were, and why they were there.

Dean had no idea what he was talking about.

EIGHTY-FOUR

Reacher had been expecting some kind of a denial. Lamaison had warned Berenson to stay quiet, and clearly he would have done the same or more with Dean. But Dean's denial seemed genuine. The guy was puzzled, not evasive.

'Let's start at the beginning,' Reacher said. 'We know what you did with the electronics packs, and we know why you had to do it.'

Suddenly there was something in Dean's face. Just like with Margaret Berenson.

Reacher said, 'We know about the threat against your daughter.'

'What threat?'

'Where is she?'

'Away. Her mother, too.'

'School's not out.'

'An urgent family matter.'

Reacher nodded. 'You sent them away. That was smart.'

'I don't know what you're talking about.'

Reacher said, 'Lamaison is dead.'

There was a flash of hope in Dean's eyes, just for a split second, hard to see in the darkness.

'I threw him out of the helicopter,' Reacher said.

Dean said nothing.

'You like bird-watching? Wait a day and drive a mile or two south and get up on the roof of your car. Two buzzards circling, it's probably a snake-bit coyote. More than two, it's Lamaison. Or Parker, or Lennox. They're all out there somewhere.'

'I don't believe you.'

Reacher said, 'Show him, Karla.'

Dixon pulled out the wallet she had taken from Lamaison's pocket. Dean took it from her and turned to the light burning in his hallway. He spilled the contents into his palm and shuffled through them. Lamaison's driver's licence, his credit cards, a New Age photo ID, his Social Security card.

'Lamaison is dead,' Reacher said again.

Dean put the stuff back in the wallet and handed it back to Dixon.

'You got his wallet,' he said. 'Doesn't prove you got him.'

'I can show you the pilot,' Reacher said. 'He's dead, too.'

'He just landed.'

'I just killed him.'

'You're crazy.'

'And you're off the hook.'

Dean said nothing.

'Take your time,' Reacher said. 'Get used to it. But we need to know who's coming, and when.'

'Nobody's coming.'

'Someone has to be.'

'That was never the deal.'

'Wasn't it?'

'Tell me again,' Dean said. 'Lamaison's dead?'

'He killed four of my friends,' Reacher said. 'If he wasn't dead, I sure as hell wouldn't be standing here wasting time with you.'

Dean nodded, slowly. He was getting used to it.

'But I still don't know what you're talking about,' he said. 'OK, I signed off on phony paperwork, I admit that, six hundred and fifty times, which is terrible, but that was all I did. There was never anything about me assembling units or showing anyone else how to do it.'

'Who else knows how?'

'It's not difficult. It's plug and play. It's simple. It has to be. Soldiers are going to do it. No offence. I mean, in the field, at night, under stress.'

'Simple for you.'

'Relatively simple for anyone.'

'Soldiers never do anything until they're shown how.'

'Sure, they'll have training.'

'From who?'

'We'll set up a course at Fort Irwin. I guess I'll teach the first class.'

'Lamaison knew that?'

'It's standard practice.'

'So he pimped you out for a preview.'

Dean just shook his head. 'He didn't. He didn't say anything about a preview. And he could have. It wasn't like I was in a position to refuse him anything.'

'Nine hours,' Neagley said.

'Another hundred and thirty thousand square miles,' Dixon said.

A hundred thirty-three thousand five hundred thirty-five, Reacher thought, automatically. The increase alone was as big as most of California and more than half of Texas. The area of a circle was equal to *pi* times the radius squared, and it was the *squared* part that made it increase so fast.

'They're coming here,' he said. 'They have to be.'

Nobody answered.

Dean led them inside. His house was a long low shack built from concrete and timber. The concrete had been left raw and was fading to a yellowed patina. The timber was stained dark brown. There was a big living room with Navajo rugs and worn furniture and a fireplace heaped with last winter's ash. There were plenty of books in the room. CDs were piled everywhere. There was a stereo with vacuum tube amplifiers and horn speakers. Altogether the place looked exactly like a city refugee's dream.

Dean went to make coffee in the kitchen and Dixon said, 'Nine hours twenty-six minutes.' Neagley and O'Donnell didn't get the point, but Reacher did. Assuming three decimal places for *pi* and a speed of fifty for the truck, then nine hours and twenty-six minutes made the potential search area exactly seven hundred thousand square miles.

'Mahmoud is cautious,' Reacher said. 'He's not going to buy a pig in a poke. Either it's his money and he doesn't want to waste it, or it's someone else's money and he doesn't want to get his head cut off for screwing up. He's coming.'

'Dean says not.'

'Dean says he wasn't told in advance. There's a difference.'

Dean came back and served the coffee and nobody spoke for a quarter of an hour. Then Reacher turned to Dean and asked, 'Did you do your own electrical work here?'

Dean said, 'Some of it.'

'Got any plastic cable ties?'

'Lots of them. Workshop out back.'

'You should drive north,' Reacher said. 'Head for Palmdale, get some breakfast.'

'Now?'

'Now. Stay for lunch. Don't come back until the afternoon.'

'Why? What's going to happen here?'

'I'm not sure yet. But whatever, you shouldn't be around.'

Dean sat still for a moment. Then he got up and found his keys and left. They heard his car start up. Heard the crunch of power steering on gravel. Then the noise faded to nothing and the house went quiet again.

Dixon said, 'Nine hours forty-six minutes.' Reacher nodded. The circle was now three-quarters of a million square miles in size.

'He's coming,' Reacher said.

The circle reached a million square miles at seventeen minutes past one in the morning. Reacher found an atlas in a bookcase and traced a likely route and worked out that Denver was eighteen hours away, which made six in the morning a likely rendezvous time. Ideal, from Mahmoud's point of view. Lamaison would have told him about the threat against the daughter, and he would figure under any circumstances the kid would be home at six in the morning. And therefore a perfect reminder of Dean's vulnerability. Maybe Mahmoud was dropping by unannounced, but there was no doubt he expected to get what he wanted.

Reacher got up and went for a stroll, first outside, and then inside. The property consisted of the house and a garage block and the workshop that Dean had mentioned. Beyond that, there was nothing. It was pitch dark but Reacher could feel vast silent emptiness all around. Inside, the house was simple. Three bedrooms, a den, a kitchen, the living room. One of the bedrooms was the daughter's. There were inkjet prints of photographs pinned up on a board. Groups of teenage girls, three or four at a time. The kid and her friends, presumably. By a process of elimination Reacher worked out which girl appeared in every picture. Dean's daughter, he assumed. Her camera, her room. She was a tall blonde girl, maybe fourteen, still a little awkward, braces on her teeth. But a year or two into the future she was going to be spectacular, and she was going to stay that way for thirty years. A hostage to fortune. Reacher understood Dean's distress, and wished Lamaison had screamed a little more on the way down.

*　　*　　*

People say the darkest hour is just before dawn, but people are wrong. By definition the darkest hour is in the middle of the night. By five in the morning the sky in the east was lightening. By five thirty visibility was pretty good. Reacher took another walk. Dean had no neighbours. He was living in the middle of thousands of empty acres. The view was clear to every horizon. Worthless, sunblasted land. The power lines ran south to north and disappeared in the haze. A stony driveway came in from the southeast. It was at least a mile long, maybe more. Reacher walked a little ways down it and turned around and checked what Mahmoud would see when he arrived. The helicopter was out of sight. By chance a lone mesquite bush blocked the rotor crown from view. Reacher moved Neagley's Civic behind the garage block and checked again. *Perfect.* A somnolent group of three buildings, low and dusty, almost part of the landscape. A hundred yards out he saw a flat broken fragment of rock the size and shape of a coffin. He walked over there and took Tony Swan's lump of concrete out of his pocket and rested it on the slab, like a monument. He walked back and ducked into the workshop. The door was unlocked. The place was laid out neatly and smelled of machine oil heated by the sun. He found a tray of black plastic cable ties and took eight of the biggest. They were about two feet long, thick and stiff. For strapping heavy cable into perforated conduit boxes.

Then he went back inside the house to wait.

Six o'clock arrived, and Mahmoud didn't. Now

the circle measured more than two and a half million square miles. Six fifteen came and went, two point six million square miles. Six thirty, two point seven million.

Then, at exactly six thirty-two, the telephone bell dinged, just once, brief and soft and muted.

'Here we go,' Reacher said. 'Someone just cut the phone line.'

They moved to the windows. They waited. Then five miles south and east they saw a tiny white dot winking in the early sun. A vehicle, closing fast, trailing a cloud of khaki dust that was backlit by the dawn like a halo.

EIGHTY-FIVE

They moved away from the windows and waited in the living room, tense and silent. Five minutes later they heard the crunch of stones under tyres and the wet muffled beat of a worn Detroit V-8. The crunching stopped and the engine died and they heard a parking brake ratchet on. A minute after that they heard a tinny door slam and the sound of random footsteps on gravel. The driver, stumbling around, yawning and stretching.

A minute after that, they heard a knock at the door.

Reacher waited.

The knock came again.

Reacher counted to twenty and walked down the hall. Opened the door. Saw a man standing on the step, framed against the light, with a mid-size panel truck parked behind him. The truck was a rented U-Haul, white and red, top heavy, a little ungainly. Reacher felt like he had seen it before. He had never seen the man before. He was medium height, medium weight, expensively dressed but a little rumpled. He was maybe forty years old. He had thick black hair, shiny, beautifully cut, and the kind of mid-brown skin and regular features that could have made him Indian, or Pakistani, or Iranian, or Syrian, or Lebanese, or Algerian, or even Israeli or Italian.

In turn Azhari Mahmoud saw a dishevelled giant of a white man. Two metres tall, easily, a hundred and ten kilos, maybe a hundred and twenty, shaved head, wrists as wide and hard as two-by-fours, hands like shovels, dressed in dusty grey denims and work boots. *A crazy scientist*, he thought. *Right at home in a desert shack.*

'Edward Dean?' he said.

'Yes,' Reacher said. 'Who are you?'

'No cell coverage here, I notice.'

'So?'

'And I took the precaution of cutting your land line ten miles down the road.'

'Who are you?'

'My name doesn't matter. I'm a friend of Allen Lamaison's. That's all you need to know. You are to extend me the same courtesies that you would extend to him.'

'I don't extend courtesies to Allen Lamaison,' Reacher said. 'So get lost.'

Mahmoud nodded. 'Let me put it another way. The threat that Lamaison made is still operative. And today it will benefit me, not him.'

'Threat?' Reacher said.

'Against your daughter.'

Reacher said nothing.

Mahmoud said, 'You're going to show me how to arm Little Wing.'

Reacher glanced at the U-Haul.

'I can't,' he said. 'All you have are the electronics.'

'The missiles are on their way,' Mahmoud said. 'They'll be here very soon.'

'Where are you going to use them?'

'Here and there.'

'Inside the U.S.?'

'It's a target-rich environment.'

'Lamaison said Kashmir.'

'We might ship some units to select friends.'

'We?'

'We're a big organization.'

'I won't do it.'

'You will. Like you did before. For the same reason.'

Reacher paused a beat and said, 'You better come in.'

He stepped aside. Mahmoud was accustomed to deference, so he squeezed past and walked ahead into the hallway. Reacher hit him hard in the back of the head and sent him stumbling toward the living room door, where Frances Neagley stepped out and dropped him with a neat uppercut. A minute later he was hog-tied on the hallway floor with one figure-eight cable tie binding his left wrist to his right ankle and another binding his right wrist to his left ankle. The ties were zipped hard and the flesh around them was already swelling. Mahmoud was bleeding from the mouth and moaning. Reacher kicked him in the side and told him to shut up. Then he stepped back into the living room and waited for the truck from Denver.

*   *   *

The truck from Denver was a white eighteen-wheeler. Its driver was hog-tied next to Mahmoud a minute after climbing down from the cab. Then Reacher dragged Mahmoud out of the house and left him face-up in the sun next to his U-Haul. Mahmoud's eyes were full of fear. He knew what was heading his way. Reacher figured he would prefer to die, which was why he left him there alive. O'Donnell dragged the driver out and dumped him next to his truck. They all stood for a moment and looked around one last time and then crammed themselves into Neagley's Civic and headed south, fast. As soon as cell coverage kicked in they stopped and Neagley called her Pentagon buddy. Seven o'clock in the west, ten in the morning in the east. She told the guy where to look and what he would find. Then they drove on. Reacher watched out the back window and before they even hit the mountains he saw a whole squadron of choppers heading west on the horizon. Bell AH-1s, from some nearby Homeland Security base, he assumed. The sky was thick with them.

After the mountains they talked about money. Neagley gave Dixon the financial instruments and the diamonds, and they all agreed she should carry them back to New York and convert them to cash. First call would be to repay Neagley's expense budget, second call would be to set up trust funds for Angela and Charlie Franz, and Tammy Orozco and her three children, and Sanchez's friend Milena, and the third call would be to make one last donation to People for the

Ethical Treatment of Animals, in the name of Tony Swan's dog, Maisi.

Then it got awkward. Neagley was OK for salary, but Reacher sensed that Dixon and O'Donnell were hurting. Hurting, and tempted, but sensitive about asking. So he went ahead and admitted he was flat broke and suggested they take whatever little margin was left over and divide it up four ways between themselves, as wages. Everyone agreed.

After that, they didn't talk much at all. Lamaison was gone, Mahmoud was in the system, but no one had come back. And Reacher had gotten around to asking himself the big question: if the stalled car on the 210 had not delayed his arrival at the hospital, would he have performed any better than Dixon or O'Donnell? Than Swan, or Franz, or Sanchez, or Orozco? Maybe the others were asking themselves the same question about him. Truth was, he didn't know the answer, and he hated not knowing.

Two hours later they were at LAX. They abandoned the Civic in a fire lane and walked away from it, heading for different terminals and different airlines. Before they split up they stood on the sidewalk and bumped fists one last time, and said goodbyes they promised would be temporary. Neagley headed inside to American. Dixon went looking for America West. O'Donnell searched for United. Reacher stood in the heat with anxious people swirling all around him and watched them walk away.

*   *   *

Reacher left California with close to two thousand dollars in his pocket, from the dealers behind the wax museum in Hollywood, and from Saropian in Vegas, and from the two guys at New Age's place in Highland Park. As a result he didn't run low on cash for almost four weeks. Finally he stopped by an ATM in the bus depot in Santa Fe, New Mexico. As always he worked out his balance first, and then checked to see if the bank's calculation matched his own.

For the second time in his life, it didn't.

The machine told him that the balance in his account was more than a hundred thousand dollars bigger than he was expecting. Exactly a hundred and eleven thousand, eight hundred and twenty-two dollars and eighteen cents bigger, according to his own blind calculation.

111,822.18.

Dixon, obviously. The spoils of war.

At first he was disappointed. Not with the amount. It was more money than he had seen in a long time. He was disappointed with himself, because he couldn't perceive any message in the number. He was sure Dixon would have adjusted the total by a few dollars or cents one way or the other to give him a wry smile. But he couldn't get it. It wasn't prime. No even number greater than two could be prime. It had hundreds of factors. Its reciprocal was boring. Its square root was a long messy string of digits. Its cube root was worse.

111,822.18.

Then he grew disappointed with Dixon. Because the more he thought about it, the more he analysed it, the more he was sure it really was a boring number.

Dixon's head wasn't in the game.

She had let him down.

Maybe.

Or maybe not.

He pressed the button for the mini-statement. A slip of thin paper came out of a slot. Faint grey printing, the last five transactions against his account. Neagley's original deposit from Chicago was still there, first on the list. Then second, his fifty-dollar withdrawal at the Portland bus depot, up in Oregon. Then third, his airfare from Portland to LAX, way back at the beginning.

Then fourth, a new deposit in the sum of one hundred and one thousand, eight hundred ten dollars and eighteen cents.

Then fifth, on the same day, another deposit, in the sum of ten thousand and twelve dollars exactly.

101,810.18.

10,012.

He smiled. Dixon's head was in the game, after all. Totally, completely in the game. The first deposit was 10-18, repeated for emphasis. Military police radio code for mission accomplished, twice over. 10-18, 10-18. Herself and O'Donnell, rescued. Or Lamaison and Mahmoud, beaten. Or both things.

Nice, Karla, he thought.

The second deposit was her zip code: 10012. Greenwich Village. Where she lived. A geographic reference.

A hint.

She had asked: *Feel like dropping by New York afterward?*

He smiled again and balled up the slip of thin paper and dropped it in the trash. Took a hundred dollars from the machine and headed on inside the depot and bought a ticket for the first bus he saw. He had no idea where it was going.

He had answered: *I don't make plans, Karla.*

Choose your next Jack Reacher novel

The Reacher books can be read in any order, but here they are in the order in which they were written:

KILLING FLOOR

Jack Reacher gets off a bus in a small town in Georgia.
And is thrown into the county jail, for a murder he didn't commit.

DIE TRYING

Reacher is locked in a van with a woman claiming to be FBI.
And ferried right across America into a brand new country.

TRIPWIRE

Reacher is digging swimming pools in Key West when a detective comes round asking questions. Then the detective turns up dead.

THE VISITOR

Two naked women found dead in a bath filled with paint. Both victims of a man just like Reacher.

ECHO BURNING

In the heat of Texas, Reacher meets a young woman whose husband is in jail. When he is released, he will kill her.

WITHOUT FAIL

A Washington woman asks Reacher for help. Her job?
Protecting the Vice-President.

PERSUADER

A kidnapping in Boston. A cop dies.
Has Reacher lost his sense of right and wrong?

THE ENEMY

Back in Reacher's army days, a general is
found dead on his watch.

ONE SHOT

A lone sniper shoots five people dead in a heartland city.
But the accused guy says, 'Get Reacher'.

THE HARD WAY
A coffee on a busy New York street leads to a shoot-out
three thousand miles away in the Norfolk countryside.

BAD LUCK AND TROUBLE
One of Reacher's buddies has shown up dead in the California
desert, and Reacher must put his old army unit back together.

NOTHING TO LOSE
Reacher crosses the line between a town called
Hope and one named Despair.

GONE TOMORROW
On the New York subway, Reacher counts
down the twelve tell-tale signs of a suicide bomber.

61 HOURS
In freezing South Dakota, Reacher hitches
a lift on a bus heading for trouble.

WORTH DYING FOR
Reacher runs into a clan that's terrifying the Nebraska locals,
but it's the unsolved case of a missing child that he can't let go.

THE AFFAIR
Six months before the events in *Killing Floor*,
Major Jack Reacher of the US Military Police goes
undercover in Mississippi, to investigate a murder.

A WANTED MAN
A freshly-busted nose makes it difficult for Reacher to hitch a
ride. When at last he's picked up by two men and a woman, it
soon becomes clear they have something to hide . . .

NEVER GO BACK
When Reacher returns to his old Virginia headquarters he is
accused of a sixteen-year-old homicide and hears these words:
'You're back in the army, Major. And your ass is mine.'

PERSONAL
Someone has taken a shot at the French president.
Only one man could have done it – and Reacher
is the one man who can find him.

MAKE ME

At a remote railroad stop on the prairie called Mother's Rest, Jack Reacher finds a town full of silent, watchful people, and descends into the heart of darkness.

NIGHT SCHOOL

Reacher back in his army days, but not in uniform. In Hamburg he teams up with Frances Neagley to confront a terrifying new enemy.

NO MIDDLE NAME

Published in one volume for the first time, and including a brand-new adventure, here are all the pulse-pounding Jack Reacher short stories.

THE MIDNIGHT LINE

Reacher tracks a female officer's class ring back to its owner in the deserted wilds of Wyoming, on a raw quest for simple justice.

PAST TENSE

Deep in the New England woods, Reacher spots a sign to the town where his father was born, while two young Canadians are stranded at a remote, sinister motel . . .

BLUE MOON

On a Greyhound bus, Reacher rescues an old man from a mugger. Elsewhere in the city, two rival criminal gangs are competing for control – will Reacher be able to stop bad things happening?

THE SENTINEL

Reacher works with a local IT nerd to save a small town being held to ransom by a cyber-ware attack.

BETTER OFF DEAD

In an Arizona border town Reacher teams up with an FBI agent in a desperate search for her missing twin brother, with explosive results.

NO PLAN B

In Colorado, Reacher is the sole witness to a murder. The trail leads him to a private prison in Mississippi. And he knows that getting to the truth is worth doing time for.

Alternatively, you can find a list of the books in the order of events in Reacher's life, at www.deadgoodbooks.co.uk/ReacherBooks

Now read on for an extract from
the new Reacher adventure

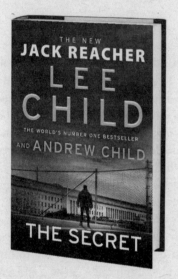

OUT NOW IN HARDBACK,
EBOOK AND AUDIO

ONE

K eith Bridgeman was alone in his room when he closed his eyes. The morning medical rounds were over. Lunch had been delivered and eaten and cleared away. Other people's visitors had clattered along the corridor in search of relatives and friends. A janitor had swept and mopped and hauled off the day's trash. And finally a little peace had descended on the ward.

Bridgeman had been in the hospital for a month. Long enough to grow used to its rhythms and routines. He knew it was time for the afternoon lull. A break from getting poked and prodded and being made to get up and move around and stretch. No one was going to bother him for another three hours, minimum. So he could read. Watch TV. Listen to music. Gaze out of the window at the sliver of lake that was visible between the next pair of skyscrapers.

Or he could take a nap.

Bridgeman was sixty-two years old. He was in rough shape. That was clear. He could debate the cause – the kind of work he had devoted his life to, the stress he had suffered, the cigarettes and alcohol he had consumed – but he couldn't deny the effect. A heart attack so massive that no one had expected him to survive.

Defying odds that great is tiring work. He chose the nap. These days he always chose the nap.

*

Bridgeman woke up after only an hour. He was no longer alone. Two other people were in the room with him. Both were women. Maybe in their late twenties. They were the same height. The same slim build. One was on the left side of his bed, nearer to the door. The other was level with her on the right, nearer to the window. They were standing completely still. In silence. Staring at him. Their hair was pulled back, smooth and dark and tight. Their faces were expressionless like mannequins' and their skin shone in the harsh artificial light as if it was moulded from plastic.

The women were wearing white coats over hospital scrubs. The coats were the correct length. They had all the necessary pockets and badges and tags. The scrubs were the right shade of blue. But the women weren't medics. Bridgeman was sure about that. His sixth sense told him so. It told him they shouldn't be there. That they were trouble. He scanned each of them in turn. Their hands were empty. Their clothes were not bulging. There was no sign of guns or knives. No sign of any hospital equipment they could use as weapons. But Bridgeman still wasn't happy. He was in danger. He knew it. He could feel it as keenly as a gazelle that had been ambushed by a pair of lions.

Bridgeman glanced at his left leg. The call button was where the nurse had left it, lying on the sheet between his thigh and the safety rail. His hand darted toward it. It was a fluid movement. Smooth. Fast. But the woman was faster. She snatched the button then dropped it, leaving it dangling on its wire, almost to the floor, well out of Bridgeman's reach.

Bridgeman felt his heart quiver and tremble in his chest. He heard an electronic *beep*. It came from a piece of equipment on a stand near the head of the bed. It had a screen with a number in the centre of the top half and two jagged lines that zigzagged across the full width of the lower half. The first line showed his pulse. It was spiking wildly. Its peaks were surging closer together like they were chasing one another. The number showed his heart rate. It was climbing. Fast. The *beep*s grew louder. More frequent. Then the sound became continuous. Insistent. Impossible to ignore. The number stopped rising. It began to flash. It changed direction. And it kept going down until it reached 00. The lines flattened out. First at the left of the screen and then all the way across until both were perfectly horizontal. The display was inert. Lifeless. Except for the desperate electronic howl.

It told of total cardiac failure.

But only for a moment.

The second woman had grabbed Bridgeman's right wrist when the alarm began to shriek. She had yanked a square blue clip off the tip of his index finger and attached it to her own. The screen flashed twice. Then the sound cut out. The heart rate started to climb. The two lines began to tick their way from left to right. None of the values were quite the same as Bridgeman's. The woman was younger. Fitter. Healthier. Calmer. But the readings were close enough. Not too high. Not too low. Nothing to trigger another alarm.

Bridgeman clutched his chest with both hands. Sweat was prickling out across his forehead and his scalp. His skin felt clammy. He had to make an effort to breathe.

The woman with the clip on her finger lowered herself into the visitor's chair next to the window. The woman on the left of the bed waited a moment then looked at Bridgeman and said, 'We apologize. We didn't mean to startle you. We're not here to hurt you. We just need to talk.'

Bridgeman said nothing.

The woman said, 'We have two questions. That's all. Answer them honestly and you'll never see us again. I promise.'

Bridgeman didn't respond.

The woman saw him glancing past her, toward the door. She shook her head. 'If you're hoping the cavalry's going to come, you're out of luck. Those clips slip off people's fingers all the time. And what do they do? Stick them right back on. Anyone at the nurses' station who heard the alarm will figure that's what you did. So. First question, OK?'

Bridgeman's mouth was dry. He did his best to moisten his lips then took a deep breath. But not to answer questions. To call for help the old-fashioned way.

The woman read his play. She put a finger to her lips and took something out of her coat pocket. A photograph. She held it out for Bridgeman to take. It showed a gloved hand holding a copy of the *Tribune* next to a window. Bridgeman could read the date on the newspaper. Tuesday, 7 April 1992. It was that day's edition. Then he saw two figures through the glass. A woman and a child. A little girl. Even though they were facing away from the camera Bridgeman had no doubt who they were. Or where they were. It was his daughter and granddaughter. In the home he had bought them in Evanston, after his wife died.

The woman took hold of Bridgeman's arm and felt for his pulse. It was fast and weak. She said, 'Come on now. Calm down. Think of your family. We don't want to hurt them. Or you. We just need you to understand how serious this situation is. We only have two questions, but they're important. The sooner you answer, the sooner we're out of here. Ready?'

Bridgeman nodded and slumped back against his pillow.

'First question. You're meeting with a journalist the day after tomorrow. Where is the information you're planning to give her?'

'How do you know about—'

'Don't waste time. Answer the question.'

'OK. Look. There is no information. We're just going to chat.'

'No credible journalist is going to believe a whistleblower without ironclad proof. Where is it?'

'Whistleblower? That's not what this is. The reporter's from a little weekly rag in Akron, Ohio. Where I was born. The story's about my heart attack. My recovery. It's a miracle, according to the doctors. People back home want to read about it. They say I'm an inspiration.'

'Heart attack? That's what you're going with? When you're sitting on a much bigger story?'

'What bigger story?'

The woman leaned in closer. 'Keith, we know what you did. What you all did. Twenty-three years ago. December 1969.'

'December '69? How do you know . . .? Who are you?'

'We'll come to who we are. Right now you need to tell me what information you're planning to give this reporter from Akron.'

'No information. I'm going to tell her about my recovery. That's all. I will never talk about December '69. Why we were there. What we were doing. What happened. Not to anyone. I swore I wouldn't and I keep my word. My wife never even knew.'

'So you don't have any documents or notes hidden in this room?'

'Of course not.'

'Then you won't mind if I take a look around.'

The woman didn't wait for an answer. She started with the locker next to the bed. She opened the door and rummaged through Bridgeman's spare pyjamas and books and magazines. She moved on to a leather duffel on the floor near the door. It held a set of clothes. Nothing else. Next she checked the bathroom. Nothing significant there, either. So she moved to the centre of the room and put her hands on her hips. 'Only one place left to check. The bed.'

Bridgeman didn't move.

'Do it for your daughter. And your granddaughter. Come on. I'll be quick.'

Bridgeman felt his pulse start to speed up again. He closed his eyes for a moment. Took a breath. Willed himself to relax. Then pushed back the sheet, swung his legs over the side of the mattress, and slid down on to his feet. He looked at the woman in the chair. 'Can I at least sit? I'm older than you. I have one foot in the grave.'

The woman held up her finger with the clip attached.

'Sorry. The cable's too short for me to move. You want to sit, use the windowsill.'

Bridgeman turned and looked at the windowsill. Considered sitting on it. But taking orders from one of the women was bad enough so he settled on leaning against it. He watched as the other woman finished her search of the bed. Again she came up empty.

'Believe me now?' Bridgeman said.

The woman took a piece of paper out of her pocket and handed it to Bridgeman. There was a list of names. Six of them, handwritten in shaky, spidery script. Bridgeman's was one of them. He recognized all the other five. Varinder Singh. Geoffrey Brown. Michael Rymer. Charlie Adam. Neville Pritchard. And beneath the final name there was a symbol. A question mark.

The woman said, 'A name is missing. Who is it?'

Bridgeman's heart was no longer racing. Now it felt like it was full of sludge. Like it didn't have the strength to force his blood into his arteries. He couldn't answer. It would mean breaking his oath. He had sworn to never reveal a single detail. They all had, twenty-three years before, when it became clear what they had done. And the missing name belonged to the flakiest of the group. Better for everyone if it remained off the list.

The woman handed Bridgeman another photograph. Another shot of his daughter and granddaughter, on foot this time, halfway across a crosswalk. The picture had been taken through a car windshield.

Bridgeman was channelling all his energy into trying to breathe. It was only a name that the woman wanted. What harm could come from telling her? Plenty, he knew.

The woman said, 'Bonus question. What happens tomorrow? Or the next day? Is the driver drunk? Do his brakes fail?'

Bridgeman said, 'Buck. The missing name. It's Owen Buck.'

The woman shook her head. 'Buck's dead. He died of cancer a month ago. Right after he wrote that list. So his isn't the name I need. He said there was an eighth name.

He didn't know what it was. But he was certain one of you others do.'

Bridgeman didn't answer. He was struggling to make sense of the information. Buck's conscience must have gotten the better of him. He was always mumbling about doing something stupid. But that didn't explain why he told this woman there was an extra name. Maybe his mind had gone. Maybe whatever cancer drugs they gave him had fried his brain.

The woman said, 'Maybe the driver will be distracted? Maybe he'll be asleep at the wheel?'

'Maybe there is another name.' Bridgeman closed his eyes. 'Maybe someone knows what it is. One of the others might. But not me. I don't think one exists.'

The woman said, 'Maybe there'll be enough of your granddaughter left to bury. Maybe there won't.'

Bridgeman was struggling for air. 'Don't. Please. I don't know. I swear. I gave you Buck's name. I didn't know he's dead. I've been sick. I've been in here. No one told me. So if I knew of some other name I'd tell you it, too. But I don't. So I can't.'

'You can. You don't have to say it. You can do what Owen Buck did. Write it down. He gave me six names. You only need to give me one.'

She pulled a pen from her coat pocket and held it out. Bridgeman stared at it for a moment. Then he took it and added *Owen Buck* to the top of the list.

He said, 'That's the only name I know. I swear.'

The woman said, 'Have you ever seen a child's coffin, Keith? Because if you haven't I don't think anything can really prepare you for how tiny it will seem. Especially when it's next to the full-size one your daughter will be in.'

Bridgeman's knees started to shake. He looked like he was ready to collapse.

The woman's voice softened. 'Come on. One name. Two lives saved. What are you waiting for?'

Bridgeman's body sagged. 'Buck was wrong. There isn't another name. Not that I know of. I was there three years. I never heard of anyone else getting brought on board.'

The woman stared at Bridgeman for ten long seconds, then shrugged. She took the pen and the paper and slid them back into her pocket. 'I guess we're done here.' She stretched out and touched Bridgeman's forehead. 'Wait a minute. You feel awful. Let me open the window. Fresh air will perk you up. I don't want to leave you like this.'

Bridgeman said, 'You can't. The windows don't open in this hospital.'

'This one does.' The woman leaned past Bridgeman, pushed down on the handle, and the window swung out on a broad arc. Then she scrabbled under the collar of her scrubs and pulled a fine chain up and over her head. The key to the window was hanging from it. 'Here.' She dropped the chain into the breast pocket of Bridgeman's pyjama top. 'A present. Something to remember us by, because you're never going to see us again. As promised. There's just one last thing before we go. You asked who we are.' The woman stood a little straighter. 'My name is Roberta Sanson.'

The woman with the finger clip climbed out of her chair. 'And I'm her sister. Veronica Sanson. Our father was Morgan Sanson. It's important you know that.'

Morgan Sanson. The name was an echo from the past. An unwelcome one. Four syllables he had hoped to never hear again. It took a fraction of a second for the significance to hit him then Bridgeman pushed off from the wall. He tried to dodge around Roberta Sanson but he never stood a chance. He was too frail. The space was too cramped. And the sisters were too highly motivated. Roberta shifted sideways and blocked his path. Then she grabbed his shoulders with both hands and drove him back until he was pressed against the sill. She checked that he was lined up with the open window. Veronica bent down and took hold of his legs, just above the ankles. She straightened and Roberta pushed. Bridgeman kicked. He twisted and thrashed. Roberta and Veronica pushed one more time. Two more times, to make sure there was no room for error. Then they let gravity do the rest.

TWO

Jack Reacher had never been to the Rock Island Arsenal in Illinois before, but he was the second Military Police investigator to be sent there within a fortnight. The first visit was in response to a report of missing M16s, which proved to be false. Reacher was the last to join his unit, following his demotion from major to captain, so he had been allocated a less interesting allegation. Inventory tampering.

The sergeant who had filed the complaint met Reacher at the main entrance. There were maybe ten years between them. They were about the same height, six foot five, but where Reacher was heavy and broad the older man was skinny and pinched with pale skin and thin, delicate features. He couldn't have been more than 180 pounds. That would be sixty pounds lighter. His uniform hung off his shoulders a little, causing Reacher to worry about the guy's health.

Once the usual courtesies were taken care of the sergeant led the way to Firing Range E, near the base's western perimeter. He locked the heavy steel door behind them and continued to a loading bench that jutted out from the rear wall. Six M16s were lying on it, neatly lined up, muzzles facing away, grips to the right. The weapons weren't new. They had spent plenty of time in the field. That was clear. But they were well maintained. Recently cleaned. Not neglected or damaged. There were no obvious red flags. No visible indication that anything was wrong with them.

Reacher picked up the second rifle from the left. He checked that the chamber was empty, inspected it for defects, then slid a magazine into place. He stepped across to the mouth of the range. Selected single-fire mode. Took a breath. Held it. Waited for the next beat of his heart to subside and pulled the trigger. A hundred yards down range the red star on the target figure's helmet imploded. Reacher lowered the gun and glanced at the sergeant. The guy's face betrayed nothing. No surprise. No disappointment. Reacher fired five more times. Rapidly. Sharp *crack*s rebounded off the walls. Spent cartridges rattled on to the cement floor. A neat 'T' shape was hammered into the figure's chest. It was textbook shooting. There was no sign of any problem with the gun. And still no response from the sergeant.

Reacher pointed to the magazine. 'How many?'

The sergeant said, 'Sixteen.'

'Vietnam?'

'Three tours. No misfires. If it's not broke . . .'

Reacher slid the fire selector to its lowest position. Full auto. The model was old, from before the switch to three-shot bursts. He aimed at the target's centre mass and increased the pressure on the trigger. The green plastic torso should have been shredded. The ten remaining bullets should have torn through it in less than a second. But nothing happened. Because the trigger wouldn't move. Reacher changed back to single-shot mode and lined up on the target's face. The crude contour representing its nose split in half under the impact. Reacher toggled to full auto. Again, nothing happened. Which left no doubt. The trigger would not move in that position.

He said, 'They all like this?'

The sergeant nodded. 'All of them. The whole case.'

Reacher crossed to the bench and set the gun down. He removed the magazine, cleared the chamber, pushed out the takedown pins, separated the lower receiver, and examined its interior contours. Then he held it out toward the sergeant and said, 'The trigger pocket's the wrong size. It won't accept the auto-sear. And there are only two trigger pinholes. There should be three.'

The sergeant said, 'Correct.'

'This isn't military spec. Someone's switched out the original with a civilian version. It makes the gun semi-auto only.'

'Can't see any other explanation.'

'Where did these come from?'

The sergeant shrugged. 'Admin error. They were supposed to be sent for destruction but two crates got mixed up and these wound up here by mistake.'

Reacher looked down at the guns on the bench. 'These would be considered end-of-life?'

The sergeant shrugged again. 'I wouldn't say so. Ask me, the condition's acceptable for weapons that would generally be held in reserve. Nothing stood out when the crate was opened. Only when a malfunction was reported. Then I stripped the first one down. Saw the problem right away. Just like you did.'

'Who decides which weapons get destroyed?'

'A dedicated team. It's a special procedure. Temporary. Lasted a year, so far. Result of Desert Storm. The war was a great opportunity for units to re-equip. Assets that are designated surplus as a result come back from the Gulf and get sent here for evaluation. Firearms are our responsibility. We test them and give them a category. Green: fully serviceable, to be retained. Amber: marginally serviceable, to be sold or allocated to civilian gun safety programmes. Doesn't apply to fully automatic weapons, obviously. And Red: unserviceable, to be destroyed.'

'You got sent a Red crate when you should have gotten a Green one?'

'Correct.'

Reacher paused for a moment. The account was plausible. There wasn't a kind of equipment the army owned that hadn't been sent to the wrong place, some time or other. Which was usually totally innocent. Like the sergeant said, an admin error. But Reacher was wondering if there could be a broader connection. Something to do with the recent report of stolen M16s. Someone could designate good weapons as unserviceable, fill their crates with the right weight of whatever trash came to hand, send that to the crusher or the furnace, and sell the guns on the black market. Officially the weapons would no longer exist, so no one would be looking for them. It was a feasible method. A loophole someone needed to close. But it wasn't what had happened here. Reacher had read the report. The inspection was unannounced. A full crack-of-dawn shock-and-awe operation. And it had been thorough. All the weapons crates on the entire base had been opened. All had the correct number of weapons inside. Not so much as a pocketknife was missing.

Not so much as a *complete* pocketknife ...

Reacher said, 'When did these guns get delivered to you in error?'

The sergeant looked away while he did the math, then said, 'Fifteen days ago. And I know what you're going to ask me next. You're not going to like the answer.'

'What am I going to ask?'

'How you can trace which unit owned these weapons in the Gulf. Before they were sent back.'

'Why would I want to know that?'

'So you can figure out who's stealing the lower receivers. Someone is stealing them, right? And selling them. So that gangbangers or whoever can make their AR15s fully automatic. The Gulf's the perfect place to swap parts out. Officially every last paperclip is tracked. But in reality? Different units have different systems. A few have switched to computers. Most are still paper based. Paper gets lost. It gets wet. It gets ripped. Digits get transposed. People have handwriting that's impossible to read. Long story short, you'd have a better chance of selling bikinis at a Mormon convention than tracking that crate.'

'You don't think I have a future as a swimwear salesman?'

The sergeant blinked. 'Sir?'

Reacher said, 'No matter. I don't care who had these guns in the Gulf. Because that's not where the parts were stolen.'

Roberta and Veronica Sanson heard the impact all the way from the street outside. They heard the first of the screams over the background grumble of traffic. Then the cardiac monitor at the head of the bed started to howl again. Its lines had slumped back down to the horizontal. Its display read 00. No heart activity. Only this time the machine was correct. At least as far as Keith Bridgeman was concerned.

Roberta turned left into the corridor and made her way to the hospital's central elevator bank. Veronica went right and looped around to the emergency staircase. Roberta reached the first floor before her sister. She strolled through the reception area, past the café and the store that sold balloons and flowers, and continued out of the main exit. She walked a block west then ducked into a phone booth. She pulled on a pair of latex gloves and called American Airlines. She asked for information about their routes and schedules. Next she called United. Then TWA. She weighed up the options. Then she tossed the gloves in a trash can and made her way to the public parking lot in the centre of the next block.

The sergeant led the way to a storeroom that was tacked on to the side of a large, squat building near the centre of the site. The wind had picked up while they were at the range which made it hard for him to heave the metal door all the way open, and after Reacher had gone through the guy struggled to close it again without getting blown over. He finally wrestled it into place then locked it. Inside, the space was square, eighteen feet by eighteen. The floor was bare concrete. So was the ceiling. It was held up by metal girders that were coated with some kind of knobby fire-retardant material and flanked by strip lights in protective cages. There was a phone mounted by the door and a set of shelves against each wall. They were made of heavy-duty steel, painted grey. Each had a stencilled sign attached – Intake, Green, Amber, Red – and a clipboard with a sheaf of papers hanging from its right-hand upright. There were no windows and the air was heavy with the smell of oil and solvents.

The shelves held crates of weapons. Short at the top, long at the bottom. There were fourteen crates on the Red shelves. Reacher pulled one of the long ones out on to the floor and cracked it open. He lifted out an M16. It was in much worse shape than the one he had fired earlier. That was for sure. He field-stripped it, checked its lower receiver, and shook his head.

He said, 'It's original.'

The sergeant opened another crate and examined one of its rifles. It was also pretty scuffed and scraped. He said, 'This one's the same.'

Each crate had a number stencilled on the side. Reacher took the Red clipboard off its hook and turned to the last sheet. It showed that the crate he'd picked had been signed off by someone with the initials UE. The crate the sergeant had chosen had been initialled by DS. Reacher could only see one other set: LH. He picked a crate with a corresponding number, removed the lower receiver from one of the guns inside it, and held the part up for the sergeant to see.

The sergeant said, 'Jackpot.'

Reacher said, 'LH signed off on this. Who's LH?'

'Sergeant Hall. In charge of the inspection team.'

'Sergeant Hall's a woman.'

'Yes. Sergeant Lisa Hall. How—'

'UE and DS are men?'

'Yes. But—'

'There are no other women on the team?'

'No. But I still—'

Reacher held up his hand. 'Fifteen days ago you received a Red crate by mistake. Fourteen days ago we received a report that M16s had been stolen from this facility. We checked. They hadn't.'

'I heard about the raid. I don't see the connection.'

'The report was anonymous, but the voice was female. I read the file.'

'I still don't—'

'Sergeant Hall realized a Red crate was missing the day after it got mishandled. She knew it could be traced back to her so she made a bogus accusation. A serious one. Stolen weapons. The investigators came running, just like she knew they would. They opened all the crates, including hers. They were looking for M16s. Complete ones. That's what they found, so they closed the case. No crime detected. Then if the missing receivers came to light, Hall had just been cleared of theft. She was hoping an investigator would make the same jump you did. That the doctored weapons arrived that way, from the Gulf.'

'No. I know Lisa Hall. She wouldn't do something like that.'

'Let's make sure. Where is she today?'

'Don't know, sir.'

'Then find out.'

'Sir.' The sergeant shuffled across to the phone on the wall. Thin clouds of dust puffed up around his feet. He dialled slowly, made the enquiry, and when he was done he said, 'Not on duty, sir.'

Reacher said, 'OK. So where's her billet?'

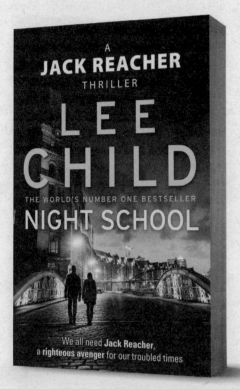

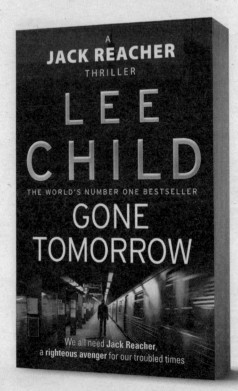

Reacher's body count keeps rising in PERSUADER

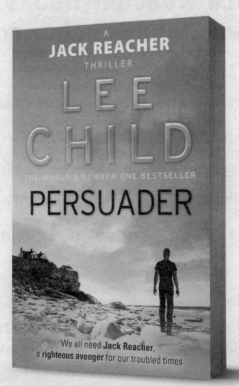

When Reacher witnesses a brutal kidnap attempt,
he takes the law into his own hands. But a cop dies.
Reacher's finger was on the trigger.
Has he lost his sense of right and wrong?

AVAILABLE IN PAPERBACK, EBOOK AND AUDIOBOOK

Find out more about the Jack Reacher books at www.JackReacher.com

- Take the book selector quiz
- Enter competitions
- Read and listen to extracts
- Find out more about the authors
- Discover Reacher coffee, music and more . . .

PLUS sign up for the monthly Jack Reacher newsletter to get all the latest news delivered direct to your inbox.

For up-to-the-minute news about Lee & Andrew Child find us on Facebook

f /JackReacherOfficial

f /LeeChildOfficial

and discover Jack Reacher books on Twitter

🐦 /LeeChildReacher